THE ARYAN AGENDA

THE ARYAN AGENDA

NICK THACKER

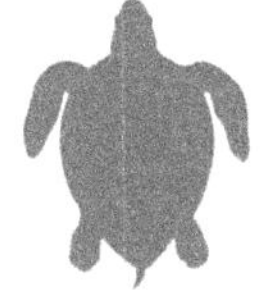

The Aryan Agenda: Harvey Bennett Thrillers, Book #6

Published by Turtleshell Press

PROLOGUE

It is like the Pesach, he thought. *Passover. A symbol, yes, but at the same time a very real reflection of the Lord's power.*

Stephan wheeled the heavy cart through the hallways as he recited the verse in his head.

'For the Lord will pass through to smite the Egyptians; and when he seeth the blood upon the lintel, and on the two side posts, the Lord will pass over the door, and will not suffer the Destroyer to come in unto your houses to smite you.'

Stephan turned left, shifting his weight so he could pull the cart to a stop with his left hand and simultaneously swipe the access door with the card in his right. He heard the beep and the click, then saw the green light appear above the mechanism.

Tonight was like the Pesach, and Stephan himself was going to play the distinguished role of the Destroyer.

He continued reciting, this time from another section of the book of Exodus: *'And it came to pass at midnight that the Lord struck all the firstborn in the land of Egypt, from the firstborn of Pharaoh who sat on his throne to the firstborn of the captive who was in the dungeon, and all the firstborn of livestock. So Pharaoh rose in the night, he, all his servants, and all the Egyptians; and there was a great cry in Egypt, for there was not a house where there was not one dead.'*

He walked through, pushing the cart in front of him once again, now in the main hall. He put the card back into his pocket and pressed his uniform flat with his now-free hand.

He made the sign of the cross with his right hand, taking a moment to appreciate the significance of this event. *This is my Passover,* he said silently to himself. *My Pesach.*

And it *was* only his Pesach — his employer was not as devoutly religious as he; his employer thought of religion the way most secular people thought of it: as an unnecessary distraction to everyday life.

But to Stephan, religion *was* the everyday life — everything *else* was the distraction.

He had been groomed for this work, taken in by the Church long ago and churned through a system of fraternal orders that eventually found him as a student of the Ancient Way. It was a fraternity within the Church, but the belief system the Ancient Way shared could not have been more different from the Church's.

That he had found the Ancient Way *and* his employer was a stroke of luck — or, as he liked to think, of God's hand guiding him along the pathways of his life. He had risen through the ranks of the Ancient Way and discovered that his employer was looking for men just like him — men ready to take their fate into their own hands — and while his employer was not an advocate of his religious beliefs, it was clear their purposes and goals were remarkably aligned.

The cart had a squeaky front wheel, but he managed to get it turned so that the squeak was unnoticeable. There were still people milling about, as the gala hadn't started yet, and he didn't want to earn any unwanted attention. He felt vulnerable enough as it was, wearing the uniform of a guard he'd left dead in the access hallway.

The halls of the Athens National Museum of Archeology were dark, kept that way by design, to corral its visitors through the network of exhibits and rooms in a constant stream. Small ambient fixtures spread warm, yellowish glows down onto paintings, glass cases and the bright LED uplighting inside them held priceless artifacts from Greek history. Amber tracklighting illuminated the path ahead. No other light, natural or otherwise, reached Stephan's eyes.

He liked the dark. It was comfortable to him, a way to hide. He'd never been much for socialization, and the dimly lit museum seemed to be mocking him.

Try to hide, the museum said, *I know you're here. And what you're about to do.*

He swallowed a heavy lump that had risen in the back of his throat.

My Pesach, he reminded himself. *My job to do.*

The cart was heavy, but it was mostly empty. A single jar full of a whitish powder sat beneath a sheet on the top of the cart, but the rest of the weight came from the cart itself and its industrial-strength casters. They rolled smoothly, but he still had the friction gravity provided to contend with.

The path he had chosen was clear: a left turn out of the access hallway into the main museum's atrium, then a right turn into a smaller, central atrium that housed his final destination: The *Antiquities of Thera* exhibit, a brand-new spectacle that Athens and its museum was quite proud of. He'd seen the advertisements for the grand opening: hundreds of artifacts, thought to be from the islands near the coast of Greece, all from thousands of years ago.

Tonight was not the grand opening, but a sort of 'soft opening,' a celebration of the museum's newest attraction, and a way to generate — hopefully — more offerings from the museum's most distinguished donors. The gala was a closed-door affair, an invitation-only event that began as soon as the building closed to the public.

As such, Stephan was in a bit of a hurry. He wouldn't turn any of the guests' heads as long as the museum was open during normal business hours, but once the gala began, security would tighten a bit.

These people were, after all, some of Athens' finest, and that meant they were worth more to the museum than the standard day visitor. These donors and VIPs would begin arriving at any moment, so his window of opportunity would be closing soon.

There were a few minutes between the shift changes when it was safest to move about, without fear that he'd be seen by a regular employee who might not recognize him and grow suspicious.

Relax, he told himself. *Follow the plan. The plan is good, the plan is sound.*

My Pesach.

1

JENNIFER

IN ADDITION TO THE BRAND-NEW *ANTIQUITIES OF THERA* EXHIBIT, THE National Museum had a world-class collection of antiques and sculptures in its numerous divisions, including the well-known Antikythera Mechanism and a massive Epigraphical wing. Built originally in 1829, the museum had moved locations and acquired new curators, exhibits, and names during its nearly 200-year existence.

Now located on a beautiful and grandiose green space in the heart of downtown Athens, the National Museum of Archeology was a glorious throwback of a sight in the midst of a bustling and modern cityscape. Pillared Ionic columns that hearkened back in an upgraded homage to the Parthenon's own Doric architectural design.

As the entrance wound into the first of the grand lobbies where the herd of guests had congealed, Jenny Polanski tugged gently on her husband's arm. *Let's go,* she thought. *We're going to be late.*

She didn't dare say anything.

Her husband, the salt-and-peppered man standing next to her and a full head taller than her, was deep in conversation with another couple in front of them. Both couples were wearing their most elegant outfits — tuxedos for the men and formal dresses for the women. Jenny's own dress was snug, tightly shaped to her lithe, athletic body. Red sequins sparkled out from strategic spots on the dress, calling attention to areas on the outfit she knew would earn admiring looks from the male attendees and a few uneasy glances from their female counterparts.

She hadn't picked out the dress — that had been her husband's work, as he liked everything to be 'perfect,' as long as 'perfect' was defined by him. Jonathan Polanski was a rising star in the political arena in Massachusetts, and his work as a lawyer during the bankruptcy of

Greece had earned him a spot among the Athens elite. They were here tonight to rub elbows with the other VIPs in attendance, including leading economic advisors, political players, and the upper echelon of high-class Grecian celebrities.

She sighed, almost inaudibly, but loud enough that Jonathan would hear. He was a phenom when it came to working a room, and she knew he would have been able to detect her social cues from across the expansive lobby. The fact that he was ignoring her while she was hanging on his arm — again, by his design — meant that he was sending her a nonverbal cue as well.

You're not as important as these two, he was saying.

She made a face, but pointed it toward the marble floor.

The couple her husband was conversing with was one of the high-flying Athens elite — a movie star and his wife, a stunning blonde with a dress that barely covered her thighs and only stretched up far enough to show off an impressive upper body. The dress seemed as though it had been fashioned out of a single, skimpy piece of fabric.

Sheer, nearly see-through fabric.

She knew her husband well enough to know that he was hardly interested in what the other Greek movie star — a man who offered Jonathan Polanski no political value — had to say.

She shook her head.

"We should probably get going," the blond suddenly said, interjecting.

"Right, of course," Jonathan replied. He made a show of looking at his fabulously expensive watch, a gift from President Pavlopoulos of Greece. He looked down at Jenny. "Ready, honey?"

She smiled, but she knew he was reading the fury in her eyes. *Sure, darling,* she thought. *I'm ready.*

He nodded, taking the lead as he dragged Jenny out of the lobby of the museum and down a corridor leading to their destination: the brand-new *Antiquities of Thera* exhibit. The opening was set for a week from tonight, but the museum staff had been working overtime to get this 'soft opening' gala set up for the VIP attendees tonight. It would be another event like all the others, according to Jenny. Plenty of elaborate displays of hors d'oeuvres, shrimp cocktails on massive ice sculptures, bright green inedible flora and fauna that provided a colorful backdrop to the real food, and, of course, live music.

She could hear the strains of one of Haydn's quartets reaching her ears even before they stepped into the lavishly appointed hall. A black-tie staff member greeted them, handing her a program — her VIP husband wasn't deemed lowly enough to carry a piece of paper apparently — and ushered them to their table.

"Will you be dining with Mr. and Mrs. Ellison?" the staffer asked. He motioned to the couple behind them.

The movie star and his trophy wife beamed. “That would be exceptional, if you do not mind,” the movie star said.

Jonathan clenched his jaw once, a tick that Jenny had long ago interpreted as annoyance, and nodded. “Sure,” he said. “That’s fine.”

2

JENNIFER

Always the politician, she thought. Her husband had likely run through the scenarios in his mind in that split-second and decided that it wasn't worth the possible political ramifications of denying the movie star a bit of one-on-one conversation. She knew he had been hoping to get across the table from one of the power players in the room, perhaps a Ralph Friedman, Europe's modern-day John D. Rockefeller, who was bringing solar power to the masses in Western Europe, or Prince Alwalam bin Alam, an oil tycoon and philanthropist who had made his riches the best way possible: by being born into them.

The tables were all-four tops, and the waiter brought them to one near the far corner of the room. It was another slap in the face to her husband, who was now going to be sitting so far out of the limelight he would be lucky to even be noticed by the occupants of the tables right next to them.

I'm sure I'll pay for this later, she mused. He would be craving attention by the end of the night, and if he didn't throw himself on top of her during the limousine ride back to their hotel, it would surely happen as soon as they got into the suite's bedroom.

If Jenny was lucky, her husband might even try to pry the actress-supermodel wife of the movie star off her man's arm and set up a late night 'work meeting' somewhere downtown with her, leaving Jennifer alone to curl up with the latest David Berens novel.

They sat, the waiter pulling Jenny's chair out for her. She placed her clutch on the table beside her and eased down into the seat. The man moved across and performed the same motion for the actor's wife, then stood at the edge of the table and took their drink orders.

Jenny mindlessly ordered 'something with vodka in it, and don't be stingy,' while she watched another black-suited museum staff member hustling through the half-empty room, wheeling a cart in front of him. He seemed nervous, but he kept his gaze straight toward the center of the room.

The waiter left, spinning quickly and heading toward the table nearest theirs. Jenny watched the area just past him, in the center of the large hall, where a beautiful antique bell-shaped object sat, lights from the LED fixtures far above her head shining down on it. It appeared to be some sort of metal — bronze or silver — but it was matte in some places, its sheen worn off from centuries of weather. She took in the scene for a moment, appreciating for the first time since they'd entered the marvelous design of the museum's interior.

The staffer pushing the cart headed straight toward the center of the room. There were two tables flanking the central bell exhibit, one closer to Jenny and one on the opposite side, closer to the man and his cart. Both tables had collections of smaller artifacts on them, each with a tent card in front of it with writing on it. She assumed each one depicted the item in question and where it had been found. The whole display was grand, but it was nothing compared to the stage and food tables set up in the wide nook at one edge of the long hall which could just now be noticed behind the central exhibit display. She had been right about most of it — the ice sculpture, the greenery, the hors d'oeuvres — but one thing was off.

There was no ice sculpture. Or rather, there was no *single* ice sculpture. Arranged around the food, using strategically placed leaves of parsley and other garnishes as tiny pops of color on the otherwise monochromatic sculpture, was a pair of two massive humans, both carved out of ice.

The ice men were embroiled in an intense hand-to-hand duel, their swords still hanging by their sides, both shirtless, wearing a leather cloth around their waist and sandals on their feet.

She caught her breath. It was strikingly beautiful, and the sheen of the slowly melting ice added to the effect, giving her the impression that the two sculptures were actually sweating as they fought one another. The sculptor had somehow even given one of them a ponytail of hair on the back of his head, floating magically in space as the frozen warriors whipped out at one another.

"Impressive, no?"

She turned her head and remembered that there were three other people at the table. "Sorry," she replied, "I just now noticed it. It's — phenomenal."

"It is," the man said. "Henrique Waltham Joaquin," he said, over-enunciating each syllable as if he was simultaneously sucking on a marble. "A French-born sculptor who has made his home in Greece these last few decades. He is sitting right over there, directly next to the piece."

He pointed across the room and Jenny saw the man. Joaquin was hunched over a glass of champagne, both elbows on the table. His hair looked dirty and disheveled, but he wore an impeccable tuxedo, complete with tails. "Interesting," she said.

"Quite interesting," the actor continued. "To gather such a fine assortment of men and women, well — it's really quite remarkable."

Jenny didn't necessarily feel the same way. *With enough money on the table,* anyone *can get some famous people together for a night.*

The man pushing the wheeled cart stopped in front of the giant bell, looking straight at it. He wore a permanent frown, his eyebrows crusty and thick, dark and brooding.

"It's just a fundraiser," she said.

"*Just* a fundraiser — ha!" The movie star was apparently a jovial man, and he let out a few more chuckles before explaining himself. "This event is certainly a fundraiser, my dear," he said. "But it's a fundraiser for more than just a sense of pride."

"Oh?" Jenny looked over at her husband. He had his trademark grin plastered on his face, the one that said to the world *I have no idea what's happening but you'll never be able to tell.* He shrugged.

He'd told her earlier that evening that the fundraiser was simply a way of keeping the museum in the black for the next fiscal year. The country had been thrust into a bit of a depression following the economic collapse that occurred a couple of years ago, so many of the nonprofit institutions like this one had worked toward increasing their donation support.

"Yes, of course," the man said, now addressing Jonathan as well. "The museum will benefit from the support of the fine people here, but it is not intended to be an altruistic effort. There is something quite valuable on the line for the auction."

"The auction?" Jenny looked at the tower of antiquities on the table in the center of the room.

"Not for those piddly objects," he said. "They will live here, like all the other pots and pans from centuries ago. No, some of the museum's silent partners have the distinct privilege of owning some offshore interests it is hoping to sell tonight."

Jonathan was now intrigued, Jenny noticed. He sat up straighter in his chair, leaning slightly inward toward the actor sitting across the table from him.

"For the past five years or so, they have owned a moderately sized parcel of land on the island of Santorini."

Jenny knew of Santorini. Jonathan had been there twice on 'business' while working with the Greek government the past two years, though she suspected that what he meant by 'business' had an entirely different meaning to him than it did to the rest of world.

"They excavated some of these items from that land, but the

pressures of the government as well as a waning interest in the Aegean region for geological history has led them to believe that it is time for a new chapter in their own history. They hope the new owner will take care of the land, even possibly open it to the public as a park or wildlife sanctuary, though they have been quite vague in their descriptions."

It sounded familiar now. She thought she had read something about that in one of the local papers their doorman brought up to the hotel that morning. Something about a museum hoping to cash in a nice piece of land for short-term profit. The paper had taken an anti-capitalism slant, but had ultimately ended with the optimistic statement that Greece would rise again through a focus on the historic past it had come from, not from importing the histories of other nations.

Jenny looked up again at the bell in the center of the room. The staff member who had been pushing the cart toward the bell had stopped directly in front of it, and was now pouring some sort of liquid into a cavity at the bottom of the antique object. He was focusing intently, unaware of the two other museum security guards approaching him from behind.

She frowned. *Odd,* she thought. The guards were in a hurry, one of them taking into a radio while the other had a hand on his side.

Gripping a gun.

3

JENNIFER

She squeezed the edge of the table. The movie star was still yammering on, apparently bored of the philanthropic talk and now onto the subject he was really interested in: himself. Her husband was still wearing the goofy smile, using what little self-control she knew he had to focus on the actor and his story.

The guard with the huge eyebrows finished pouring the vase of liquid into the crevice and tipped the jar back onto his cart. He reached down into the front pocket of his shirt as he knelt down, pushing aside a sheet that had been concealing the lower section of the cart.

Jenny watched closely, but couldn't see what it was the man was fiddling with beneath the sheet. He took a tiny device out of the shirt pocket and set it down next to something larger, but his body was obscuring the view.

The two guards were nearly on him now, approaching silently. Apparently the security lead had ordered them to keep their appraisal of the situation quiet, so as not to disturb the growing number of VIP guests in the room. Jenny imagined their supervisor watching on from a closed-circuit television system in a back room somewhere, communicating with the man holding the walkie-talkie.

She looked at the actor's wife — she was listening intently to her husband's retelling of how they'd met — either doing a great job of pretending as though it were the first time she'd heard the story or it was, in fact, the first time she'd heard it. She looked at the actor himself, suddenly having the strange urge to tell him to shut up, to interrupt him and ask the table to watch what was happening in the center of the room.

She didn't need to look at Jonathan — he hadn't moved since the story had begun, holding his frozen look of interest since they'd sat down. So she glanced around the room to see if anyone else was aware that there was something strange taking place.

The only person she saw watching the scene unfold with her was the artist, Henrique Waltham Joaquin, who was sitting cross-legged across the room from her, his head cocked sideways a bit as the man with the eyebrows knelt in front of his cart.

The first guard was on him at that moment. He grabbed the man's shoulder, urging him upward, and the man obliged. He stood, just as the second guard reached him.

She could see them exchanging words, though she couldn't hear anything over the sound of Mozart and pre-dinner chatter that reached her ears. The thick-browed man shrugged a bit and she could imagine him saying, *I don't know what the problem is. I just came in to check the bell-thingy.*

She looked at the object that had been the subject of the man's focus since entering the room with his cart. It was worn, and shaped like a ceramic cap that had once been covering a tinged metallic bell. It was about six feet tall, four feet in diameter. There were no markings large enough to be visible from where she sat, but the metal structure seemed to have small scratches on it, like writing, around the exterior.

One of the guards inspected the bell while the other continued to question the staffer who had been working on it. She couldn't read lips, but she could tell they weren't speaking English.

The guard inspecting the artifact knelt down and spread the sheet away from the cart and peered in. She watched his back as he studied whatever it was inside.

Jenny waited a few seconds as the man froze, then lifted the radio to his lips and began to speak.

"Jonathan," she whispered, interrupting the actor's story. "We need to go."

"What?" Jonathan asked.

"We need to leave. Now."

"Why?"

She didn't answer. At that moment the man who had brought the cart inside fell to the ground and stabbed through the sheet with his hand. He pulled out the small device that had been sitting on the bottom shelf of the cart and pressed a button on its side.

Jenny heard the guard's radio squawk to life. *"Confirmed,"* a voice said, crackling in English. *"Locating the nearest support."*

The first guard jumped backwards and pulled the pistol from his belt. He shouted something in another language toward the man on the ground, but the man just lay flat on the floor.

Jonathan and the actor were now watching the drama, as well as a few other tables nearby. Jenny started to stand up involuntarily, but Jonathan gripped her wrist.

"Stay down, honey," he said. "We don't know —"

"I don't *need* to know what it is," she hissed. "I don't want to be around it."

He opened his mouth to respond, but Jenny rose before he could speak. She whirled around and started toward the edge of the hall, where she'd seen an exit sign above a doorway that was partially hidden behind an archway.

She heard the guards both shouting now, the tables of guests growing quiet as they turned to watch the action. Glasses stopped clinking and silverware lay silent, but the two guards continued rattling off orders to the man on the ground and into their radios.

Jenny picked up her pace, nearing the archway and door to the exit. She assumed it led outside, but it didn't appear to be a door meant for guests, as it was flanked on both sides by a trash receptacle and a table full of dinnerware.

She was almost at the door when she heard it. A high-pitched hum, throbbing as it rose in pitch and intensity. It sounded like a dog whistle, just a piercing, shrill note, at the stratosphere of her hearing. It continued upward and she found herself trying to pop her ears.

Jenny made it to the door and reached down to the handle. She grabbed it, but her hand slipped as she lost focus.

She stepped back, suddenly unsure of her footing. *Was the floor moving?* She couldn't tell. She felt drunk, as if she'd been drugged or given some sort of sedative.

She struggled back toward the door, finally getting a hand around the knob. She turned it.

Locked.

She screamed as the sound rose even higher, now so high in pitch there was no sound at all — but she could feel it. The pressure level of the sound wave felt like a fork was stabbing at her eyes from inside her head. Her body felt heavy, weighted down by an invisible force, like a thick layer of blankets had been draped over her.

She tried to turn around, to see what might be causing the sound. Her vision grew blurry, but she fought it back. It took all of her focus, and she realized after a few seconds that she was having difficulty breathing.

She fell to one knee.

Through her blurry vision, the peripherals receding into blackness, she saw her table. Jonathan and the actor and his wife. All of them were holding their heads, mouths open wide.

She felt sick to her stomach now, but she couldn't stop watching them. The pain grew to an enormous level, and then she noticed the guards and the man who'd wheeled in the cart. The cart sat idly by the huge bell, but the bell itself seemed to be throbbing. It was moving, pulsating in time with the pressure waves reaching her body, gently pushing the waves out into the room.

What the hell?

She had no idea what to make of that, or if it was just an illusion created by her failing vision. But regardless of what might be happening to the artifact, there was *definitely* something happening to the three men closest to it.

The man laying on the ground was still, looking as though he were asleep, but the two guards next to him were on their knees, their arms hanging at their sides.

Both of them were facing her.

Both of them had a shocked expression on their faces.

And both of them seemed to be made of liquid.

She tried to frown, to improve her vision enough to know if her eyes were playing tricks on her or not. It seemed to help, just a bit.

And that's when she noticed.

The guards' faces were melting. Their cheeks had slid downward, opening their eye sockets wider and wider, their bloodshot eyes now just empty, peering orbs, frozen in an electrified expression. Their chins drooped, their lips curling downward at the sides.

She tried to catch her breath. She tried to scream again, but it was impossible. The weight had increased to twice what it had been, and it was still increasing. The pressure wave throbbed around her, through her. It made her head feel mushy, as if someone had opened her skull and was stirring her brain around with a spoon.

She wanted to lie down, but she no longer had control of her muscles.

Oh God, what is happening?

It was the last thought she had.

With strength she didn't know she had, Jenny reached up to her face, pushing against the great pressure of the bell's pulsing wave, and pointed the fingers of her left hand to the side of her face.

A few more inches and she made contact. It was thick, a pudding-like substance, warm and syrupy.

She pressed on her jaw. Her cheek simply slid through her fingers and dripped onto the floor. It was happening to her, too. She didn't feel it, couldn't feel it, but she knew it was happening.

Her eyes closed then, her peripherals moving in sideways to block her vision completely, and she felt herself falling.

4

SARAH

THE WALL SWELLED UP ABOVE HER, AS IF IT WERE ALIVE. IT HADN'T MOVED, but in the baking sun and the hot, arid air swirling up around her only adding to the effect, she could have sworn the wall itself was the thing moving.

It was hot, and the humidity from the massive lake nearby — Lake Superior — didn't help.

She reached a hand up and placed the back of it onto her forehead. She couldn't tell if it was her hand or her head that felt hotter. She sighed, blinking a few times to fight away the brightness, then looked back down.

This had better be worth it, she thought. *I'm not an archeologist. I'm an anthropologist.*

The two fields were closely related, and ever since her doctoral dissertation and subsequent publications, academia seemed to have a hard time deciding which typecast to fit her to. Her father was an esteemed and well-known archeologist, and while she loved that line of work as much as her own, she'd chosen — or at least tried to choose — many years ago to forge her own path in the world.

It hadn't worked.

Everyone she encountered who recognized her knew her because of her father, Professor Graham Lindgren. She was 'that famous archeologist's daughter,' and her own credentials and degrees were merely an afterthought.

If there's something here, let me find it, she willed. She and her team were digging around in the dirt of Pictured Rocks National Lakeshore in Michigan. The park, a 40-mile tract of land situated on Lake Superior, was a national protected area and one that had taken a bit of maneuvering to access. Natural archways, sandstone cliffs, plenty of hiking trails, and immaculate beaches made the park a destination for outdoorsy types, but it was a bit more difficult to gain access when 'digging up artifacts' was the reason for visiting.

Her father would have been able to simply pick up the phone or send an email and he'd have been granted access.

Sarah, on the other hand, had begged, pleaded, and borrowed favors from her crew and their teams as well as from her own superiors at her university, and even then she was given only a three-day OTG, or on-the-ground. It was hardly enough time to get a decent hole dug, never mind getting some useful data.

Her research hypothesis was fizzling out, and its demise was going to be slow, sad, and potentially dreadful for her career.

She slammed a shovel down into the gritty beach, the sun still bouncing off the cliff and directly onto the front of her body.

"Dr. Lindgren," a voice called to her from behind.

Thank God, she thought. *Anything to justify a break.*

She unfastened the carabiner that held her water bottle from her pack, wondering if it was even worth the energy to trudge back to the tent. *Maybe I can just have them come over here,* she thought. *This is technically* my *expedition.*

But while she was the 'boss' and any of the three undergraduate field assistants she had under her employ would have rushed to her aide, she wasn't about to lose the opportunity to stand inside the tent, in the shade, even for just a few minutes. Maybe she could even come up with some ideas for emails that just had to be written now, giving her a longer break…

"Coming," she called back. She took a swig from the bottle and then screwed the cap back on. Every motion was calculated, measured, as every movement cost something. Energy was a resource now, every calorie of heat burned making her hotter still. She took a few steps forward, away from the towering rock wall where she had been working, eyeing the white canvas tent standing fifty yards away as though it were fifty miles distant.

This is the crap my dad put up with for forty years? she thought. She was happy to be an anthropologist — generally they got to stay inside, working with statistics and maps and other non-field data — but there were occasions, like this one, when the fieldwork could only be performed by her. This was *her* mission, so this was *her* field.

She reached the tent and considered collapsing into one of the four folding camp chairs that had been set up around the interior. She urged herself forward, ignoring the heat exhaustion. The student who had summoned her was standing over the folding table on the opposite of the tent, examining something in front of him.

The boy's name was Alexander Whipple, and he stood nearly a foot taller than her, which was especially striking since she herself was quite tall. He was devilishly handsome, a dark complexion and deep-set features, and it was only by reminding herself that he was nearly a decade her junior — and her employee — that she was able to keep from testing the man's interest in her.

He was Egyptian, born in the United States, but he'd spent many of his summers in Cairo with his extended family, and he had opted to stay on as one of her research assistants until the semester started.

Or until the money ran out.

Sarah had been paying them out of her own pocket for two pay periods now, and she was quickly realizing that there wouldn't be very many more pay periods unless she was able to find and turn in something tangible from this dig.

Alex towered over the tiny camp table, his long, muscled arms extended to their full length in order to reach down to the table. She walked farther inside the tent and stopped, swallowed, then continued forward, trying not to focus too intently on those arms in case he turned around quickly. She'd caught him making a few looks her direction, too, so she knew it wouldn't be a completely fruitless endeavor. He was single, as far as she knew, and he didn't seem at all interested in the other female undergrad in their group.

She watched his shoulder muscles tighten, then relax. She imagined her hand on them, feeling them flex and release, and —

"Dr. Lindgren," Alexander said, turning around. "Thanks for coming. Sorry to bother you." His voice was strong as well, deep and booming, but he spoke with a calm, even tone, like a midwestern farmer who'd studied at Yale.

She sniffed, shook her head quickly, and shifted on her feet. She felt herself blush. *What's wrong with you?* she thought. *Grow up.*

She was nine years older than the young twenty-something, but they were on completely different hemispheres when it came to their professions. Alexander was smart, but he was book-smart. He had none of the drive and boundary-pushing swagger that was needed in a field such as this. Not that it mattered much — Alex was headed toward genetics as a career field, and his work with Sarah in the anthropology department was little more than an elective for him.

He would probably end up in a lab somewhere, taking orders from the edgier, more eccentric scientists who had better funding — nothing but a pharmacist filling geneticists' prescriptions.

Dr. Lindgren wouldn't end up like that — she wasn't afraid to step on toes, but she was also tactful and did it with grace, never admonishing or publicly humiliating a colleague. It had earned her a reputation as a hard-working, easygoing academic who wasn't afraid to get her hands dirty, and it didn't hurt that many, if honest, considered her the most brilliant modern anthropologist in the world.

It certainly didn't hurt that her career was permanently stamped with the words, 'daughter of famous archeologist Graham Lindgren.'

And it *also* didn't hurt that many of those academic types had been swayed at least a bit by her looks. Tall, dark-skinned, and fit, Sarah Lindgren was the daughter of a Jamaican woman and a Swedish man, but had grown up in America. Her petite facial features gave her the look of an innocent young woman, but her overall physical appearance had intimidated more than one of her male counterparts, for better or worse.

She was capable, strong-willed, and intelligent, but there was just something about a *female* anthropologist that the rest of the academic community just couldn't wrap their minds around. Her father, her looks, and her gender had formed an unexpected triumvirate, constantly working against her.

"What's up?" she asked. She stepped up next to Alexander, trying not to notice the size of the young man's bicep as it extended and retracted when he picked up an object from the table.

"This came for you," he said. His voice was deep, older than it should have been, but in a soft, smooth sort of way. It reminded her in some ways of her father. He handed her the envelope, a large, bubble mailer.

"Who's it from?" She asked, turning it over in her hands a few times. She felt a distinct object inside, possibly round, with an enlarged section on one side. She began to open it as she waited for Alex's answer.

"Your father."

Speak of the devil.

If her intelligence, good looks, and charisma was half the reason for her success, having an esteemed archeology professor for a father was the other half. Graham Lindgren taught at Cambridge, had published volumes on modern archeology and how future discoveries in archeology would completely change the understanding of our anthropological history, and had already lived his own version of an Indiana Jones lifestyle.

And he was only in his early sixties — he had a lot of life to live.

Sarah was his only child, and had followed in his footsteps, choosing to study the history of humanity at large rather than focus in on the relative niche of archeology, and he had been delighted to watch her become a successful scientist.

She opened the large envelope and dumped out the object. It fell into her hand, and she was surprised at the weight of it. It seemed to have gained a pound since it had been inside the envelope, though she knew it was just a trick of her imagination. The object was indeed round, circular with a dent on one side of it and a protrusion on the opposite side, as if its creator had pushed the center of the disk outward with their thumb. The object was made of ceramic or some other stone-like material, and it was solid. The brown color told her it had been in the ground for some time. The slight deterioration of the edges around the perimeter told her it had been in the ground a *long* time.

There was also a letter inside, and she placed the object on the table while she retrieved the crisp paper. Typical of her father, the letter was handwritten on expensive faux-parchment and she carefully unfolded it. *Only thing he's missing is a wax seal,* she thought. She smiled and made a mental note to add a 'wax seal kit' to her Christmas gift list.

Her father was an avid historian, and if he hadn't decided to dedicate his life to archeology, he would have made a capable ancient history professor at any college in the world. He had a voracious reading habit, consuming nearly a book a week, and they weren't short, simple reads.

Because of this lifelong habit and his love of history, he had taken up a new ritual when Sarah had attained her doctorate: his fanciful letters always started with an invocation — some intriguing line or sentence, often in another language.

So it wasn't surprising to Sarah that the letter opened with a quote:

'We are twice armed if we fight with faith.'

5

AL JAZEERA

Transcript and translation from *Al Jazeera* JSN (Jazeera Satellite Network):
Breaking: 137 Dead, 4 Wounded in Greek Terror Attack
<TRANSLATED FROM GREEK>

Athens, Greece

Athens National Museum of Archeology

At approximately 8:13 local time, a terrorist attack hit the Athens National Museum of Archeology.

The bomb detonated after the arrival of numerous VIP invitees, all attending the unveiling and celebration of the 'Antiquities of Thera' exhibit scheduled for that evening.

The event was hosted by the museum with private funding provided by undisclosed and anonymous business and personal interests. Initial police reports state that the attack was not carried out by any parties holding a vested interest in the museum.

The bomb, believed to have been some sort of chemical-based weapon, had been placed inside one of the artifacts on display that night, where it was allowed to heat until the chemicals boiled into a vapor-based toxin that spread throughout the room.

"It was unlike anything I have ever seen," said one survivor, Vicard Floros, "It was no bomb, not in the traditional sense. We heard a popping noise, sort of like a gunshot, and then people began to scream.

"I ran inside, only to find many people holding their faces, covering their stomachs. There was a horrible stench, and I believe some guests had vomited."

Floros, a member of the museum's special events catering staff, is currently receiving treatment for third-degree burns and chemical ingestion at Laiko General Hospital of Athens.

Police and state officials have closed the museum indefinitely for analysis, as well as for safety precaution. "We don't understand what we're dealing with here," one officer, who chose to remain nameless, explained. "These people are dead, and we don't know if they infected anyone else, or how this disease spreads. If it's airborne, if it's still alive, we just don't know."

Another survivor, Jennifer Polanski, was attending the event with her husband, Jonathan Polanski, a respected American politician and lawyer. Her husband was found among the dead. Jennifer is also receiving treatment for chemical burns at Laiko and will undergo esophageal surgery early next week.

"It was... like everyone was melting," Polanski says. "The people... everyone... they were just melting. Their faces, their hands. Even mine."

At this time, the local police have asked for the support of the national Hellenic Police's Special Counter-Terrorist Unit, and have asked that citizens and tourists remain clear of the museum while the investigation is underway.

Police Chief Tsouvalas has released a statement: "At this time, we are in no way expecting or anticipating a follow-up attack. We believe this act of terrorism to be anomalous, and while we hope to increase the level of security and protection provided at public institutions such as this, we do not want this event to cause any fear or anxiety to the public at large."

We will continue updating this page as details are released.

6

SARAH

SHE FROWNED, UNSURE OF WHAT IT MEANT.

Odd.

She read the text again, trying to understand what it was all about.

'We are twice armed if we fight with faith.'

Finding nothing useful, and knowing a quick search online would likely turn up the originator of the quote, she continued to read.

'My dearest Sarah: —'

She smiled again. Her father was a modern-day romantic, and he enjoyed nostalgia and elegiac references to a simpler time. His stately openings in his letters were no exception.

'I do hope this letter finds you well. My research has taken me around the globe, and were it not for my fitful health I would be content to stay abroad for the remaining breaths I have been allowed.'

He closed the first paragraph and then lost the nostalgic flair and fell into a more familiar, casual rhythm:

'I've sent you an artifact I discovered while visiting Greenland. I thought it might be helpful in your research.'

Sarah frowned. *Greenland? When did he go to Greenland? And why would this be helpful for studying ancient American history?*

She shook her head, continuing to read as she smiled along.

'It is a most unusual piece, as it does not seem to fit my paradigm of Greenland's history. More importantly, if we are to believe what I am inclined to guess, the piece itself seems to be quite ancient.'

She read past his signature '— *your dearest father* —' and saw the postscript:

'P.S.: consider it an early birthday gift.'

Again, she frowned. *That's odd. My birthday is not for another two months.* It was only August, and the cooler winds from up north apparently hadn't gotten the message that summer in Michigan was supposed to be coming to a close.

In addition, her father hadn't included any ideas as to just *how* ancient the artifact was — that would have been too easy. Her father was a fan of puzzles, and it seemed as though he'd just sent one to Sarah.

She chuckled, wondering what absurd ideas her father had come up with this time. She read the remainder of the letter, finding no more details of the artifact but only updates on his health — good, but not without numerous scoldings from his doctor to slow down a bit, her father's retirement plans — 'there's no such thing as a true retirement' — and a thank-you for the birthday gift she'd sent him.

She folded the letter again and placed it back inside the envelope.

"What did it say?" Alexander asked.

She shook her head. "Not much. The usual fanciful writing, a flair for the dramatic, and a birthday wish."

Alex laughed. "Nothing he couldn't just email over?"

"Nothing at all," Dr. Lindgren said. "It's not like he's a Luddite — he uses email all the time — and he's a gadget geek, too. I think it's just that he thinks I appreciate the extra touch of a *real* letter."

"You *do* appreciate it."

She grinned up at the handsome undergrad. "Can't say I don't. Still, he wants me to check this little thing out," she said as she grabbed the object from the table. "Sending an email would have been quicker. *'Hey, Sarah, check this thing out I'm going to send you,'* would have worked just fine."

"True. And it would have given you time to ask the necessary follow-up questions, like 'where the heck did you find this little circular rock?'"

"Greenland, actually," she said.

She felt the circular rock for a few more seconds, feeling the grooves along the edge and the indentation in the center and protrusion on the opposite side. She could tell it was well-made, even if it had been underground for some time. *But how much time?* she wondered. *And where exactly in Greenland had he found it?*

She had always appreciated her father's romanticism and flair, but in times like this, when he was asking her professional opinion, she wished he would have just cut to the chase.

"Thoughts?" she asked.

Her assistant looked at her, then at the rock, then shrugged. "Beats me, Doc. Seems like it's in good shape, so my guess is that it's been underground, but dry."

She nodded. "Or it's not very old. But he did say he believes it to be 'quite ancient,' whatever that means."

"So, Vikings?" Alex said. "That's most plausible. But it doesn't help us with our research hypothesis, does it?"

"No, not really. The Vikings were pretty prolific, ending up all over the place. But they're not old enough. We need actual, hard proof that Berengia wasn't the only way early settlers got here."

Her hypothesis was that the Americas had been settled long before travelers found the Bering Strait and walked across it during an ice age. She believed that there had been humans settling North, Central, and South America many thousands of years before that.

The problem was that the evidence currently circulating didn't support that conclusion.

She lifted the artifact up and held it up to the line of light that was streaming into the tent. The medallion was worn, but its distinct shape and texture was still intact. She'd seen articles this well-preserved before, and it meant that the item was either a forgery — thus not as old as it purported to be at all — or it had been meticulously stored.

"So it could be a Viking artifact, even though it doesn't help us much. Maybe some sort of idol, a tiny shrine to Odin or something."

She nodded. "Maybe. But then it wouldn't exactly be old enough for him to categorically explain it as 'quite ancient,' would it? The era of Vikings is well within the accepted standards of 'history.' But you're right — I'm not sure what else it could be, if it's real. What's the oldest thing we've found on Greenland?"

He shrugged. "Viking stuff, I believe. Your father wouldn't send over a forgery, would he? What would be the point of that?"

She shook her head. "No, he certainly wouldn't. Which tells me this — whatever it is — was well-preserved, if he's right about how old it is. But what *is* it?"

Again Alexander shrugged. "You're the expert, boss."

She smirked. "Right. I'm supposed to know everything about everything because I'm the *professor.* Alex, I'm an *anthropologist.* I don't study this sort of thing. Didn't you learn that in your Intro to Earth Sciences course?"

Alex laughed, a hearty, genuine chuckle. His long curls of black hair bounced jovially as he crossed his arms in front of him, preparing to get back to whatever it was he'd been doing before Sarah's package came.

He smiled down at her.

She sighed. *In another life, maybe,* she thought.

She barely had enough time to push the thought out of her mind before someone new entered the tent.

7

RACHEL

RACHEL RASCHER PUSHED HER HANDS THROUGH HER HAIR, THEN looked up.

"We need to push forward with the next test," the man in front of her said. "Immediately. If we want to capitalize on the —"

Rachel Rascher raised a hand, silencing the man. The scientist was pacing, thinking out loud, but she'd already made up her mind.

"No," she said, calmly, "we wait. There's not enough of the original mixture left to increase the regularity of the tests. The trial was a success, but it was a limited success. We need to keep as much of the mixture secure as possible, until we are confident we have a synthetic replacement. We'll use a portion of the remaining original compound for the first phase of the trials."

"But we're *close,* Rachel. We can move forward as early as this evening with a second test. If the modifications we've made are anything *close* to what we experienced in Athens —"

"No," she said again. "We are not going to add another test until the scheduled event tomorrow night. Get Frederick Rap down this evening to clean up after the test, and give me the reports he's prepared of the last three events, including this one. As always, make sure he's there only after hours, when everyone else is gone. He's not cleared."

Or rather, he's not one of us, she thought.

"Okay, I can do that," the man said.

"Shaw," she said.

He looked at her. "Yes?"

She smiled. "I know it's getting stressful. The first phase trial forced us to speed things up, but we almost have what we need."

He nodded. "I know."

"And I know where your loyalties lie, Shaw."

He nodded again, even bowing slightly. "Thank you, Rachel."

"When this is over," she said. "We'll all look back and wonder why this took so long. Why we waited so long."

"The world will stop questioning us, that's for sure."

"Agreed," she said.

He stopped pacing, walking over to the small table at the side of the room. Its surface was empty save for an unplugged desk lamp, and all of the drawers — except for one — were empty as well. Besides the wooden bureau and the table Rachel had converted into her workstation and the desk, there was no other furniture in the room. A television stood on a rolling cart, but she rarely turned the thing on. Electricity was a precious commodity down here, and she already had a couple power strips plugged into both outlets that ran the length of the ceiling. The light overhead was a simple bulb, hanging on a chain, that had been mounted directly into the stone ceiling.

She shivered. It was cool down here, but it was the *feeling* it gave her that caused her to shake, not the temperature. *So much history here,* she thought. *So many questions we haven't answered yet. We just need to get inside the Hall...*

Shaw picked up a round, hollow stone object, turning it over in his hands. "This is all that remains?"

"Of the original supply, yes."

She knew he understood. He knew how much of the original mixture was used for each of their tests and trials, and he knew how many of the storage containers they had gone through already.

He twisted the two halves and opened the stone container. "But once we get the synthetic mixture proven and produced, we can ramp up testing once again." Shaw spoke the words as if they were a question, not a statement of fact.

"Yes," she said. "But I am not interested in waiting around for a final solution to be developed."

He frowned, turning to stare at his boss. "Wait, I thought that was..." he paused. "Then how —"

"There is more of the mixture inside the Hall. I'm sure of it."

"How do you know?"

She forced air out of her nose. "It's obvious. This supply — what we've been working through — is all that remains of what we found in the tomb. The Hall itself will not only have more of the mixture, but the original recipe that was used to create it." She grinned. "Assuming the ingredients are *existing* elements, and not some fanciful alien creation, we will be able to produce as much as we want, and the trials can continue. An unlimited supply, in that case."

"The journal says so?"

She nodded, her eyes flicking to the bureau against the wall, where in a locked drawer she kept her journal. The journal belonged to her, but it hadn't been *written* by her. It was a record of the accounts of her great-grandfather and how he had come to find the Hall of Records.

He had never been able to open the Hall, much to his — and his government's — dismay.

The location of the Hall of Records had been kept a tight secret since then, and only a handful of men and women had ever known that it was real, much less its actual location.

The journal was a document written on weathered, brittle pages, bound inside a leather cover, that had barely survived the decades since it had been written. It was a brief account of her great-grandfather's life and career, as well as the firsthand account of his discovery of an ancient document written by Plato himself, and an attempted translation of the remnants of that same document.

Her great-grandfather assumed that Plato had intended the work to be released alongside two of his other dialogues, *Timaeus* and *Critias*, but for whatever reason, no surviving translation of the work existed. Further, no *record* of the work existed.

That was, until her great-grandfather found the original documents, hidden inside a stone box, itself lost among countless familial artifacts. These artifacts had been collected and placed in a chest that had been passed down through his family for ages. The chest was mostly full of his family's own memorabilia, worthless artifacts to most people, but it held lineage documents and family tree information for the Rascher clan, and her great-grandfather had studied and scrutinized each and every one.

The stone box, thought to be some sort of elaborate paperweight, had apparently never been closely examined. When Rachel's great-grandfather came into possession of the chest and the stone box inside, he had pored over every surface of the item until he found a way to twist it open, revealing a decaying and dilapidated scroll, written in Plato's own hand.

It depicted a list of instructions that had been given to Plato by the traveler Solon — the same man whom Plato had mentioned as having traveled to Egypt and back in Plato's *Timaeus*. Plato had reportedly transcribed the words of Solon — which he had called the *Book of Bones* — onto parchment, at which point he had turned over his draft to a scribe to prepare for publication in a more permanent format. Whether the great philosopher himself had changed his mind or the scribe had simply lost the copy was unclear, but the *Book of Bones* had then completely disappeared from history shortly after the publication of Plato's dialogue *Timaeus*.

The knowledge of its existence to the modern world would have remained a secret as well, if not for Rachel's great-grandfather's discovery of it, degraded to time and weather inside its stone tomb. He had tried his best to decipher and translate the entire text, but fragments of the parchment had completely dissolved.

But it was only by a stroke of luck — a serendipitous discovery by a research team working for Rachel's predecessor — that Rachel had reignited the work on Plato's lost *Book of Bones*.

When Rachel took the position at the Egyptian Ministry of Antiquities' Prehistory Division, she and her team inherited the research of her predecessor. Apparently some divers, years ago, had come across a shipwreck off the coast of Greece that had once been bound for Alexandria. The ship had been carrying a collection of sealed urns, one of which had miraculously withstood the pressures and temptations of time.

And inside that urn, the team had found the *Book of Bones*. They didn't know it at the time — it had gone unexamined, stuffed onto a shelf in the stacks of a museum in Florence for years.

But Rachel, upon entering her new position, had decided to establish her headquarters for her new division in Giza, Egypt, and collect all the 'undeclared' possessions of the Egyptian government under one roof. Her team found the urn, and the parchment inside, during one afternoon of examination, and she immediately recognized the words — some of this document was the same as the one her great-grandfather had tried to unravel.

The parchment, written in Plato's own hand, could have netted her millions on the antiquities market, launching her and the team into the archeological spotlight and generating an attractive amount of revenue for the Egyptian government.

But she'd had other plans.

Instead, she'd kept the *Book of Bones* inside its urn, locked away in a vault where no one would find it. Rachel had kept the discovery a secret, only sharing the photocopies of it with those in her close-knit, hand-picked circle of scientists and historians.

Rachel hadn't even shared the book with her major benefactors. The silent partners would have loved to know what she had found, but they would have wrested control of the book from her hands, then flaunted her finding as a groundbreaking discovery. But she wasn't interested in fame for fame's sake — she wanted more.

Specifically, she wanted what she had spent her entire adult life chasing.

She wanted the truth.

She wanted the truth, and she wanted it to be *known*.

8

RACHEL

THE REALITY WAS THAT RACHEL RASCHER WORKED FOR THE EGYPTIAN government, itself a feat few foreign-born citizens had accomplished. She had studied, trained, researched, and published her way into acceptance as a renowned Egyptologist, her knowledge and intuition regarding the history of the ancient world second to none.

And it had been this same intuition that had launched her on the hunt she had embarked upon so many years ago.

Rachel Rascher was German, hailing from a long line of proud German ancestors, from even before Kaiser Wilhelm I's reign of the Kingdom of Prussia began. She grew up hearing the stories and legends of her heritage, of the great kings and rebels who wanted to build a great nation out of the scattered empires of the northern part of the continent.

She had developed an interest in anthropology, specifically the genealogy of her own people, in grade school. That interest carried her through school and into the work force, where she established herself as a politically savvy, brilliant-minded scientist. Ultimately, she had established herself as the newest Head in a short line of Ministry appointees for the Egyptian cabinet, in her case in charge of the Prehistory Division within the Ministry of Antiquities.

Her roles there were varied, but she was given enough freedom to pursue projects that the rest of the Ministry deemed unworthy of significant investment. As her role involved the security for and retrieval of lost antiquities of Egyptian origin, she was given a small allotment of soldiers from the Egyptian Army and Mukhabarat as a personal police force, as well as an impressive number of scientists, researchers, and laboratory specialists. She had autonomy in hiring and firing personnel, and the other cabinet members rarely pried into the Prehistory Division's business. Egyptian History was a hot topic for academic researchers, but it was a dead-end for those with political interest. She had the freedom — and the isolation — to work on her projects on her terms.

It had taken her nearly a decade, but she had finally gotten her team built in a way that her staff was on the same page as her, understanding what their *true* goal was, and what she was asking of them in order to achieve it. It was a noble goal, one her people agreed with and sought to accomplish, and she felt a strong sense of loyalty from every one of her direct reports.

Dr. Ezekiel Shaw was one of those reports, a man whose loyalty and integrity surpassed even his technical abilities. He was a wonderful asset to her team, and he had become her closest ally over the past year. Furthermore, he seemed to be even more passionate about their goal than she was.

"The *Book of Bones* in your journal is a *copy* of a copy, Rachel," he said. "Your great-grandfather could have mistaken some of the wording, or at least the syntax. And our copy from the urn may fare no better under closer scrutiny. Even still — it could be that Plato was given incorrect information."

"It could be," she said. "But we're here, are we not?" She raised a hand, palm-up, and swung it around the cellar-like stone wall, trying to prove her point.

She knew he was a believer, and he wouldn't need to be persuaded. He was playing devil's advocate, but she knew their loyalty to her, and the mission, was strong. None of her employees would need further persuading. It was too late to back out now anyway, as they were so close to achieving everything they had ever dreamed of.

She had established her office in one of many small underground rooms in the Hall of Records' antechambers, each of them connected by a labyrinthine set of hallways that angled and turned back on themselves as they wound around a large, central space. Her government had classified the set of stone chambers and hallways a 'crypt,' although they hadn't found any bodies or remnants of burial ceremonies upon entering. To Rachel, who grew up as an outsider to Egyptian history, it seemed rather typical — the Egyptian government was motivated to present to the world a stable country, one without the social unrest and terroristic undercurrents that she knew plagued the land. They wanted peace, simplicity, and plenty of tourism.

By calling the Hall of Records a 'crypt,' they could ignore its existence and simultaneously repel any requests from outside excavations that wanted more access.

The Hall of Records, therefore, had been kept a secret from the public since its discovery, as the Egyptian government already had trouble with theft and desecration of ancient sites, and it was likely they wanted to further understand what this place was, who had built it, and who it was intended for before revealing any information about it. Typically that sort of research would take decades, as the funding would have to be provided by 'leftover' monies from other, more important government concerns.

So Rachel had made sure the research of this newly discovered 'crypt' fell to her. The journal, and her great-grandfather's translation of Plato's account, as well as the copy of the *Book of Bones* that had been found pointed to this site as the Hall's final resting place, 'beneath the earth' and 'at the end of a set of twisting passageways.'

She knew without a doubt they were inside those passageways now — the antechambers to the great Hall of Records. She also knew, thanks to the Book of Bones, where the Hall was located. Her team had excavated the antechambers, installed lighting, run Ethernet and cat-6e cabling, and set up crude but functional offices and laboratories in the 'crypt's' interior. They had mapped the corridors, rooms, and chambers they so far had access to, even giving each of them a door and a sign depicting the room's number.

And they had, of course, found the entranceway to the Hall. They knew what room served as the final chamber that led to the actual Hall, and they knew that behind one more slab of unmovable stone lay the answers she sought. She knew what was behind the door, inside the temple and the great Hall of Records itself.

The problem now was in figuring out how to *open* it.

9

JOURNAL ENTRY

MARCH 17, 1941

My men have been dispatched to Cairo, to embark upon an auspicious endeavor that could prove fatal to my family's goals. It is crucial to determine the location of the Hall, however, no matter the cost.

Der Fuehrer seems to be growing restless, and his SS officers are feeling more zealous.

My mission remains, however, unchanged. My family has worked toward this goal for centuries, and I will not allow it to die a slow, forgotten death.

Solon tells of a vast fortune to be had; this great 'Hall of Records' he so eloquently describes to the philosopher. 'Only the pure can enter,' he claims, though to my knowledge no one has yet accomplished this feat.

The Hall will no doubt recount the labors of our people, our ancestors' plights as they fled certain destruction. The myth of their existence is but fantasy to most of my colleagues, though the remnants and repercussions of their knowledge and power is alive and well, even to this day.

To find and prove their value to our modern world is to find and prove to my family, once and for all, that our mission has not been in vain.

Plato's original text writes of the original motives of my predecessors. To find what they have hidden means everything. It means more than what my great country is fighting for, even. It means more than any plight of my government's armies.

10

GRAHAM

NESTLED IN THE HEART OF THE STOCKHOLM METROPOLITAN AREA, Långholmen is an island and neighborhood oasis surrounded by thick city development. Originally an island used as a secure location for the city's prison, the neighborhood eventually converted the prison into a hotel and hostel for travelers who want to see and explore the greener side of Stockholm.

Professor Graham Lindgren had loved the island since he was a boy, often remarking to his parents that he would one day settle there. At the time, the island was barren, rocky, and mostly devoid of anything particularly noteworthy. In the mid-seventies, when the prison was closed and renovated, the new, trendy neighborhood grew up around it. Graham, upon looking for an apartment a few years ago, had been delighted to learn that the island was more than habitable — it was one of the most in-demand residential districts in Stockholm.

His apartment was small, but it backed up to a lush garden and sat within sight of water — the Riddarfjarden. The garden was enjoyed for its beauty by visitors and residents alike, and Graham had often spent evenings sitting on the back patio, looking down at the garden and out over the Riddarfjarden, thinking about some problem or another.

Tonight, however, it was a very *specific* problem, and he didn't have the luxury of sitting on the porch to ponder it. He bustled around the small apartment, hardly noticing the beautiful sunset and perfect weather. The breeze coming in from his open windows only served to remind him of the speed with which he needed to move, of the quickly diminishing amount of time he had left.

The apartment was in shambles, boxes and binders of his life's work stacked in haphazard piles in every corner. He ran around the desk in the front office, a converted living room, trying to get his things together. What he was looking for, he wasn't entirely sure. What he needed to find was unclear.

Photographs of Lindgren standing next to university presidents, world-renowned researchers, and other distinguished figures stood propped up on the three massive bookcases lining the wall of the office. Hard, dark oak, the shelves had taken nearly four men a hour to maneuver up the three flights of stairs. They were now filled with all the books of his life: the first tomes he'd read as a young boy that had inspired his career — everything from nonfiction titles like *Lost Trails, Lost Cities,* by Brian Fawcett about the adventures of his father, Percy Fawcett, to the Lester Dent pulp fiction novels — as well as more academic interests, some of which had his own name on the spine.

He was a lifelong fan of learning, whether it was related to his day job or not. He loved reading, and he had amassed quite a collection of hardcover books in his 63 years of life.

But books were the furthest thing from his mind at the moment. He stumbled over a stack of documents, a box of materials he'd borrowed from his last appointment at the university, but caught his balance on the bannister that led upstairs to the two bedrooms.

His girlfriend Bridgette was visiting her parents for the weekend, so he was alone in the house. Still, he felt rushed, as if someone was pulling him along. *Or pushing.*

That's when he glanced at the stacks he'd placed on the couch in the study, across from his desk. He often spent afternoons there, curled up with a book when the summertime sun prohibited him from walking the gardens or watching the boats out front. The books and looseleaf notebooks were scattered about the space, no discernible organization to them. He had thrown them there hours ago, assuming they were of no use to his current quest.

Perhaps there's something there I need, he thought.

He racked his brain. There were no obvious connections or he would already have realized it. These books were philosophical, not practical, treatises on religion and power and politics, not matters of hard science.

He had assumed he'd needed something 'tangible,' an answer that made sense in scientific terms. He knew the answer should be here. He had a veritable library of information in his home, so if the answer they were looking for was not in his stash of hard-copy materials than it would exist somewhere in his online catalog of research papers.

It's just a matter of time, he told himself. *The answer is out there.*

He gave up on the books on the couch — they might lead him the right direction, but he no longer had the luxury of time. He needed to find out *now* what the missing piece to all of this was.

He heard a knock on his door. Nearly inaudible, just a set of raps that made him freeze immediately. He could hear the gentle sounds of the hikers out in the garden, the birds flitting back and forth as they searched for their dusk meal, and the tourists, laughing and conversing in one of the three cafes within walking distance.

But the knock on the door seemed louder than everything else. It pierced his ears, pierced his core. Even though he had been expecting it, it was still somehow the most startling sound he'd ever heard, and in this moment he wasn't sure what to do about it.

The knock came again. No voice to go alongside it, no person on the other side to announce their presence.

But he knew they were there. He knew they would wait. Patiently.

They knew his schedule, and they knew he was alone.

He shuddered, feeling the goosebumps rise on the back of his neck.

I'm out of time.

He walked to the door, still shaking. He considered not opening the door, but he knew that was stupid. There was nowhere to hide, and they surely knew he was home. Besides, there was no other way out of the apartment unless he wanted to risk a multi-story fall from his balcony.

He unlatched the lock and turned the handle. He pulled the door toward him, allowing the cooling evening air to rush inside.

"Good evening, professor," the man on the threshold said. "Ms. Rascher tells me that you have been ignoring her calls. May I come in?"

11

SARAH

JENNIFER ORTIZ. JENNIFER WAS ANOTHER OF HER ASSISTANTS, OLDER THAN the others but still working on her first undergraduate degree. She was a hard worker, earning her place on the team, but Sarah had been a bit cold to her from the beginning of the trip. She felt Jennifer was a bit of a 'teacher's pet,' a know-it-all who liked being the best and the smartest in the class.

Admittedly, Sarah *was* probably a bit harsh on the girl, and she also knew it had nothing to do with the young woman's attitude.

"Hey Jen," Alexander said as Jennifer walked in, his voice warm and friendly.

Instead, it had *everything* to do with the fact that it was clear to the entire four-person crew that Jennifer Ortiz had a *major* crush on Alexander Whipple.

Sarah swallowed, hoping her cheeks hadn't reddened. Her dark skin would mostly hide it if they had, but she didn't want to take the chance.

"Al — Alex. Hi." Jennifer stood there, smiling and swooning over the tall, drop-dead gorgeous undergraduate dominating the scene in the interior of the tent. "I just — I just..." she cleared her throat. "Sorry, I didn't know you were in here, Alex," she muttered.

Bull, Sarah thought. *That's why you came in.*

"What's up, Jen?" Sarah asked, not doing well to hide the fact that she was irritated at the interruption.

"Dr. Lindgren," Jennifer began, "I wanted to ask about, uh, our next..."

Her face fell, and Sarah knew immediately what was happening. Talking about money was awkward, especially for these younger kids who had no idea what it was like to have a rent, a car payment, student loans, medical bills for a parent —

"Will you be cutting our checks on time this month?" Alex asked, interrupting her thoughts. It was an abrupt question, but he asked it in a tactful, respectful way.

She looked at her students. Both intelligent, studious, and valuable to her work.

Both also very expensive.

"Yes, uh, well, I believe we might have to —"

Alex put a hand up. "Dr. Lindgren, I —"

"Sarah."

"Sarah," Alex said. "I don't want to make things awkward. I understand that things are tight, so I wanted to let you know that I would be heading back to Cairo in a week. I've truly enjoyed my time here, but —"

"No," Sarah said, taking a small step forward. "No, don't do that. Both of you —" she looked at them again, taking time to study each of their faces. As irritating as she thought Jen could be, she was a killer student and had a future in whatever field she'd land in. "I value you both too much. We're close here, I can feel it."

Jen and Alex waited.

"I'm going to pay you on time. I promise you that. Stick it out and let's get through the next month. If nothing turns up by then, we'll call it."

You can't afford to pay them both, she thought. *Much less all three.*

The three students she'd brought with her — Alex, Jennifer, and a nerdy graduate student named Russell — were each being paid a reasonable hourly rate plus per diem, but the university's funding of her pet project had run out a month ago. She'd been bootstrapping the operation with her savings account, credit cards, and the petty amount she received from her publisher.

By her rough calculations, she could afford to pay them all once more, but that would mean she'd be eating a bit lighter by the end of the month.

"It's really not a problem, Sarah," Alex said. "I have work lined up there, and if it takes the burden off you here, then —"

Sarah shook her head. "You're both free to leave whenever you want, you know that. But please don't think that I want you to. You're part of this team, and I need you. I'll pay you, and I don't want either of you worrying about it for another second."

She felt her heart begin to beat faster. She'd meant every word, but it was still a tough call — if she finished her work here, successfully, things would work out.

But if she didn't — if there *was* no evidence to suggest that human life in the Americas flourished long before the established date academia had assigned — she was going to spend the next few years of her life grading papers as a teaching assistant for a graduate student.

Or worse, if there is such a thing.

She knew what they were both thinking: *just call your father. He can help us.*

They were right, and that just made it worse. If her old man was anything, it was a decent, compassionate human being, and a wonderful father. He'd drop everything for her and her team without question.

She hated that it was true. She wanted success on her own terms, not with the help of her famous father. Her research needed to be her own, not his. But if she couldn't figure out how to make things work here, there *would* be no research to turn in.

Jen left the tent to resume her dinner preparations for the evening, and Alex went back to reading some of the early research they'd been trying to fit together.

"You really think there's anything here, Sarah?" he asked. "It just doesn't — none of this makes any sense."

"There's evidence, we just have to piece it together the right way."

Alex nodded. "I know, but I'm not sure how. The American Indians who lived here didn't leave much in the way of ancient artifacts. All we've got is their historical record."

"Then that's going to have to be enough."

Sarah had had this argument before, plenty of times. If the American Indians from this region — and plenty of other regions dotting the Americas — had so many similar myths and shared legends, it stood to reason they were all derived from the same common ancestors. Many historians believed this 'common ancestor' was the group of people — or groups of people — who traveled over Berengia when it was an ice bridge, connecting modern-day Alaska with Russia.

The issue she had with this belief was that the myths that were common to the otherwise disparate tribes were all stories that reflected the memory of a cataclysmic event that flooded the world ten thousand or so years ago. The well-known 'flood myth,' as it was called, was a myth Sarah had tracked nearly all around the globe, from the ancestors of the Europeans and North African and Indian peoples to North and South American civilizations.

The flood myth had turned up everywhere on Earth, it seemed, but one place: The vast, wide plateau that made up most of the present-day continent of Asia. As this was the same area the early nomadic peoples that settled the American continent had supposedly descended from, the fact that the early American settlers had the same flood legend meant that they had to have learned of it from someone besides the Berengia nomadic peoples.

Sarah's hypothesis was simple: the Americas were not settled *just* by the Berengia travelers, but by peoples that predated their arrival by millennia: a people who came not from the *East*, but from the *West*.

She wasn't sure how or when it had all happened, but her heart told her that she was on the right track. This research project might not be as fruitful as she'd hoped, but she wouldn't give it up. It may cost her a career, but she'd find her answer.

Jennifer left the tent, and Alex turned to face his team lead. "Are you sure about this, Sarah?"

She looked him over, trying to figure out what he was playing at. "I'm positive. The evidence is there, we just have to find —"

"No, I'm not talking about the prehistoric link," he answered, "I'm talking about the money. Are you sure you can afford it?"

She sighed. He wasn't stupid; none of them were. Her students knew full well that she would be paying them out of her own pocket, and they also knew how shallow those pockets were at the moment.

"I'm sure," she said. "Thank you, Alex. Speaking of, I wanted to give you your bonus." Sarah reached into a pocket of her khakis and pulled out an envelope. "It's not much, but with the usual pay, it'll make for a decent night out on the town."

"Sarah — Dr. Lindgren," he said, falling back into the more formal address. "I can't accept that. You've already done too much, paying us from your own account and all. It's honestly no big deal to head back to Egypt, just for the —"

"Nonsense," she said. "Take it. And don't get any ideas. There's one for each of you."

She made a show of grabbing the other two envelopes from her pocket, one for Jennifer Ortiz and another for Russell Aronson, the graduate student she'd brought on the trip. She set the two envelopes on the camp table next to a pile of small instruments and gear.

"I'll tell Jennifer hers is here," she said. "Any idea where Russell is?"

Alex nodded. He pulled out his phone, opened an app, and showed her on the map. A blinking dot appeared on the screen — the location of Aronson's phone. "He's in town, getting supplies, just like you told him to do. But —" he double-tapped the screen, zooming in a bit, and held it up to her face again as he smiled. "Looks like he stopped for a burger."

Sarah had instructed her field students to download the app and install it on their smartphones. She had done the same, and it allowed the group to know where the other members of the team were at any time. It was a requirement of the university, for liability reasons, but it was also an extremely handy apparatus. Sarah only had to pull it up and let it load to see how spread out her team might be at any given moment.

"Well let him know I've got something for him if you see him before I do," she said.

"You got it, boss."

Alex turned back to the work table and started fiddling with something. Sarah watched the muscles in his triceps bulge a few times, then forced herself to turn around and leave, the envelope with her father's letter and the artifact under her arm.

Just as she reached the front flap of the tent, Jennifer appeared.

"Jenny," she said, "I have something for you. It's over on —"

"There's a call for you," Jennifer said. "On the sat phone. Apparently urgent."

12

RACHEL

"HELLO, MS. POLANSKI," RACHEL SAID. "I HOPE YOU ARE WELL."

It was small talk, something of which Rachel was not a fan, but she was hoping to break the ice with this woman, just a bit.

After all, she thought, *she could be one of us.*

It was unlikely, but the test would tell them.

The trial had been a success. News reports were now calling the event a 'massive terrorist attack,' but to Rachel it was simply a public reveal of what she and her team had been working on for nearly a decade. It was the first of hopefully many trials.

They were getting closer, but they weren't there yet. This woman, Jennifer Polanski, was but the latest in a never-ending stream of evidence to that fact. She had passed the trial at the museum, but she still needed to pass one more test.

This test.

Jennifer looked up at Rachel with puffy, confused eyes. Her face was burned, shining red where the bandages on her neck and cheeks ended. The hospital had done their best with her, but burn scars were going to cover most of her body for the rest of her life.

A life, Rachel knew, that might end right now.

"I want to apologize, Ms. Polanski, for the loss of your husband."

Jennifer sniffed, or did something that seemed to be a sniff, and her eyes welled up. She tried to say something, but her mouth was swollen shut.

"It's okay," Rachel said. "I hear he was a jerk anyway." She snickered. "You're probably not even *upset* about that."

She looked down at the patient on the hospital bed, a questioning look on her face. After a few moments of silence, Rachel began again.

"Shh," she said. "No need to respond. I know you're in pain. I want to end that pain for you, Jennifer."

Jennifer was on a bed that had been cleaned and sterilized, then rolled into one of the many chambers inside the facility. This room, like all of them, was nothing but four walls of stone, with a stone floor and a stone ceiling. It had no natural light, but her team had mounted lighting fixtures — simple bulbs — to provide a bit of workspace illumination.

The rest of the room was empty, save for a cabinet and a coiled hose in the corner.

"It took a bit of persuading, but I was able to convince the hospital to allow my team to bring you back for rehabilitation efforts.

"Jennifer, you've been through a lot," Rachel continued. "You were the *only* survivor who was in the room. The only one who came in direct contact with our trial and yet still made it out alive. That is quite the feat.

"It wasn't easy, but you passed the first of our tests. Your genetics are strong, Jennifer, and they got you this far. I almost didn't believe it when they told me, but seeing you here — right now — it's miraculous."

Jennifer frowned a bit, her face scrunching up in a painful, forced way. Her eyes watched Rachel with interest, curiosity, and not a little bit of terror.

"We need to make sure you're one of us, Jennifer. That your genetics are pure. We've almost perfected the synthetic mixture, the one we used in the museum, but — as you can see — it's not quite ready. It is close, but it leaves... side effects." Rachel waved her hand up and down above Jennifer's body to underline her point. "I wish it wasn't painful for those who are able to make it through, and that is what my team is working on. Once we have a perfect copy of the original compound, our trials can run indefinitely. We'll have an endless supply of the compound, and we won't need to worry about less-than-effective copies, or losing the precious originals any longer.

"Until then, our trials will have to be a bit... *rough*."

She paused, making sure Jennifer was still with her. She was, barely. Her eyes were still puffy, and there was a glassiness to them Rachel hadn't noticed before. "My team is going to bring in the bell, but this time we're going to use a small amount of the *original* compound inside it. This one is the real deal, Jennifer. It's what the Ancients left us, and it is what will tell us, without a doubt, if you are one of us."

Rachel shifted on her feet, then smiled. "We will be able to tell right away if you are actually as pure as our trial originally thought."

She didn't feel it was necessary to tell Ms. Polanski what would happen if she *failed* the test.

She backed away a few steps, then motioned to the door. A staff member wheeled in a cart that had a pedestal balanced on it. On the top of the pedestal sat a small, foot-tall bell-shaped object. It was congruent to the bell that had been on display in the Antiquities of Thera exhibit at the National Museum of Archeology in Athens, but this was a smaller copy. And, unlike the artifact in Athens, this bell had been manufactured here in her laboratory. It had a piped-in power supply, using the lab's power to run the heat source within it.

The technician rolled the pedestal to the center of the room, about five feet away from Jennifer's bed. He plugged in the power source to the back of the bell, then checked his work. Satisfied, he turned back to Rachel and waited for her approval.

She nodded, and the man left the room.

"Jennifer," Rachel said. "We're ready. I hope you are, too. And I truly hope I get to welcome you to the other side."

She smiled again, then backed out the door and closed it behind her.

The man was waiting in the hallway, and she turned to address him. "Get Drs. Shaw and Mikhail. Let them know we're ready when they are."

"You got it," the man said. He immediately swung around and jogged down the hallway.

Rachel stayed for a moment, watching the closed door. She thought about the woman on the other side, wondering if — *hoping* — she would be able to pass the test. *We need more,* Rachel thought. *We need so many more.*

Her battle — *their* battle — would not be fought while hidden in the halls of this ancient site, nor would it take place in the museums and public places they had planned for their next trials.

Their battle was an ancient one, and it would be fought *everywhere.* The civilizations of humanity had been fractured and disconnected for far too long, and their battle — their *war* — was to fix that. Rachel was the one who had been chosen by her ancestors to lead the charge, and she intended to see it through to the end. They were so close.

She stayed for a few more seconds, and then she too turned to leave, heading back to her own office. She would wait there, anxious. It would only take fifteen minutes to hear the test results, but she wouldn't be able to work on anything else until she knew for sure.

The truth was that Rachel felt responsible for Jennifer. Knowing that she might be one of them, of true pure blood, made Rachel feel like her kin. She could be closer to Rachel than a sister, and that meant Rachel was responsible for her.

But the tests don't lie, she thought. *The trials aren't perfect, but the tests with the original compound* never *fail.*

She knew that personally. The majority of her staff had been handpicked and tested, a grueling, decade-long process that had nearly depleted their supply of the original compound. Work on the replacement synthetic compound was under way, but as the trial in Athens had proven, there was still more work to do.

She only hoped she could finish the work before the next test.

They had one final test scheduled to take place the following evening. This was the test she had been putting off for so long. She'd tried to reason her way of it entirely, but she knew it had to be done.

What we will gain is far more important, she told herself as she walked down the narrow corridor. *Far more important than anything we might lose.*

Far more important than anything I *might lose.*

13

SARAH

Sarah frowned. "I have a cell phone. Why would they use the sat phone?"

It was common practice to pack in extra supplies and equipment, even on a short three-day trip like this. The sat phone typically sat in a bag, unused, but it was university policy to keep it on, 'just in case.'

Apparently it had rung, Jennifer had answered, and now Sarah was being summoned. She returned the envelope to the table and smiled at Alex.

"I'll just be a minute," she said.

"That's fine," Alexander said. "I have to help Jennifer with dinner, anyway."

She nodded and walked past Jennifer, trying to remind herself that it wasn't Jennifer's fault that she was no longer alone with Alexander in the tent.

Knock it off. You were just leaving anyway. She felt like a schoolgirl, the memories of petty fights over boys flooding back into her mind. *You have a job to do.*

She walked toward the second of the larger tents they used for cooking and dining. They had each brought a small personal pup tent for sleeping, and the four of them were set up and spread in a half-circle around the two larger tents. Sarah's tent was in immaculate condition, as she had been spending the majority of her nights back at the small apartment she'd rented for three months while she'd set up the dig in preparation for her students' arrival.

The tent was empty — nothing but a folding table, cooking equipment, and a pile of gear inside. She strode to the table where Jennifer had left the sat phone and picked it up.

"This is Dr. Lindgren," she said.

A voice cut into her ear, quiet but clear. It was heavily accented English. *"Dr. Lindgren, my name is Agent Etienne Sharpe of Interpol."*

"Interpol? Like the global police?"

"Yes. I am calling from our Lyon headquarters, in France."

She waited. *Get to the point.*

"Dr. Lindgren, I am calling in regards to your father, professor Graham Lindgren."

"My… father? What about him?"

"Well, Dr. Lindgren, he was declared missing roughly forty-eight hours ago."

She wasn't sure what to say. She gripped the phone tighter. "I — I… I'm not sure I understand. He's 'missing?'"

"Yes. He was last seen leaving his apartment in Stockholm, but he failed to check in with his girlfriend."

She recoiled. *Girlfriend?*

"He… okay. I didn't realize he had a girlfriend," she said.

"Dr. Lindgren, were you not aware that he and Mrs. Lindgren had split up?"

"I *was* aware of that, but I didn't realize he had actually… moved on."

Her parents had split a few months ago, and while on the surface both seemed to be happy Sarah knew that without one another they were hopeless. Now, to hear that her old man had a 'girlfriend…'

"Yes, well," the man on the phone continued. *"I wanted to reach out to you personally as we begin the investigation. Since your father and mother are no longer together, I have not yet attempted to reach her."*

She nodded, not realizing that the man wasn't able to see her.

What's going on? Sarah wondered. "Okay, I don't — I'm not really sure what to do," she said. She felt her heart rising in her throat, the fear and shock of the revelation already starting to take its toll.

"At this point, Dr. Lindgren," the man said, *"there is nothing to do. I have a team handling the investigation, led by me personally, and we will keep you informed of the progress. If you —"*

"So you just called me to tell me not to worry?"

"Ma'am, it's protocol, we just —"

"It's my *father*, Sharpe. He's gone. You think I'm just going to sit here and wait around until you find him? What if he doesn't show up? What if he's…"

She couldn't finish the sentence.

"Ma'am, I would strongly urge you to keep in mind the fact that we are more than capable of handling an investigation such as this. Our staff is already preparing a brief for the local municipalities that need to be informed, and we will have agents in the field by this evening."

"But it's my father," she said again. "I can't just wait around for —"

"You must, Dr. Lindgren. Any involvement on your part could be easily misconstrued as obstruction of justice, and our agency has little tolerance for vigilantism. I am merely contacting you to keep you informed, and —"

She cut the man off. "Well I *appreciate* your obvious concern for my sanity," she said. "But don't worry about contacting me until you've tracked him down. I don't want you wasting any more time just 'keeping me informed.'"

She smashed the 'end' button on the phone's dial pad, wishing there was some sort of seat or charger she could have slammed the receiver down into.

My father's gone missing. Interpol is on it.

She wasn't sure which statement was more unbelievable. She had nothing against Interpol, but it seemed surreal — a worldwide police organization contacting her directly and apparently launching a campaign to find her father.

Dr. Lindgren took a moment to breathe. She calmed herself down, but the questions raced through her head. *Has he really been kidnapped? Who would want to take him? And why?*

She squeezed her eyes shut, focusing on the black nothingness the insides of her eyelids provided. She wanted Alex to walk in, to at least stand next to her and tell her it was going to be alright. Or even Jennifer, to offer her one of the anxiety pills she often saw the young woman taking.

Her mind raced, and inevitably ended up back at the letter. *'My research has taken me around the globe...'*

She knew that since her parents had split, her father had started the beginning of a year-long sabbatical from teaching to travel around the world. Since he was apparently now dating someone, he had no doubt ended up in some exotic locations, but to think that he had been kidnapped while somewhere remote made her shudder.

If that's true, he could be anywhere.

There was no rhyme or reason to her father's exploits, it seemed. He had always had an eccentric flair, wanting to travel around and study the cultures and histories of faraway places, seemingly for no other reason than the place was different from what he was used to.

That said, her father was also a true intellectual. He couldn't help himself; he learned everything there was to learn about every subject he could get his hands on, with a restless desire to compartmentalize it into interrelated connections. Most of it ended up becoming dinner-time trivia, but his passion for learning and knowledge was contagious.

Sarah, their only child, had gotten the bug early, following her father's footsteps into an academic career and a lifelong passion for travel and exploration.

So she had absolutely no idea where her father had been, other than what Agent Sharpe had told her: he had last been seen leaving his apartment in Stockholm. Where had he been heading? What was his plan? How long after he'd been seen in Stockholm had he disappeared?

And, most of all, the biting realization that what she feared most was very likely to be true. It was a truth she didn't want to admit, yet there was something nagging at her, her subconscious unable to let it go.

She replayed the thought over and over again in her head while she picked up her own phone and dialed the number. The one she had memorized, yet hoped she wouldn't have to use. The cellphone began to ring, and once again the thought crossed into her conscious mind.

My father has been kidnapped.

14

RAP

THE INTERIOR OF THE FACILITY WAS STARK. EMPTY, NOISELESS, SAVE FOR the gently swinging bulbs above his head, and bare. The rock walls were cold to the touch, and gave the narrow hallways the feel of being inside a crypt.

Fitting, he thought, *since we* are *in a crypt.*

At least there were no more rats. Hundreds of them had been kept in cages stacked four high in the next corridor over, inside two of the largest rooms. Their squeaks had always been there, diminishing as he walked farther away from their corridor but never completely absent.

He shuddered, fumbling with his latex gloves. It was cold, thanks to the damp, cool stones that made up the underground structure, and the temperature did nothing to help with his trepidation. He wasn't afraid, necessarily, but there still something off-putting about walking the halls of the facility in the middle of the night.

Rap Frederick veered to the left, following the lattice of carved hallways toward the room at the end of the line: *Room 23.* The sign above the door was like all the signs — plastic, mounted on a Velcro strip that had been stuck directly onto the surface of the rock. The doorway was natural, carved from the stone, but the metal door itself was new, sized and shaped to fit perfectly in the rectangular hole, set on two massive hinges that had been pounded into the core of the stone.

Room 23 was a medium-sized, low-ceilinged room that was twice the width of the hallway itself, forming a knobbed end to a long wing of smaller research rooms, and those parts of the crypt had been turned into labs, storage rooms, and a few offices. Most of the rest of the rooms in the crypt were empty, since the organization that had originally repurposed the rooms had no use for more than a couple wings inside of the labyrinthine, maze-like space.

Rap Frederick's employer was a brand-new arm of the Egyptian Ministry of Antiquities called the Prehistory Division, and it was clear to him they were more interested in the privacy the space offered then they were in filling it with researchers and staffers. To date, he had only interacted with a total of three other humans during his employment here: the HR person who had hired him, a boss he only spoke with on the phone and via email, and a technician he sometimes passed on his way in and out.

Tonight was like most nights — he was here to clean up the mess left by the testing in Room 23. A double master's degree in chemistry and applied biology apparently was only good enough to get him a glorified janitorial job at the ends of the earth, sleeping during the day and working while the city slept.

He sighed. At least the salary was good.

He tried not to notice the resonant, empty-sounding clicking of his heels as they smacked against the rock floor and echoed down the hall, and instead focused on the door to 23. It lay in front of him, looming, waiting for him to perform the same duties he'd performed twenty-two other times.

He wondered if there was anything significant about that. *I'm cleaning 23 for the 23rd time tonight,* he thought. He wasn't superstitious, but there was something oddly appealing about ghost stories and myths when working for a department like the Prehistory Division.

The larger organization — the Egyptian Ministry of State of Antiquities — was a typical government structure. Poorly run but admirable in their efforts, the Antiquities Ministry had been established in 2011 with the charter to 'preserve and protect the heritage and history of ancient Egypt.' As such, much of their work was in finding and securing lost Egyptian artifacts, preventing theft, and protecting ancient sites.

The division Rap worked for, however, was all but invisible — he had been offered a job through his LinkedIn profile, but there hadn't been any information online about the sector. The HR person he'd interacted with had told him it was due to 'pressing legal concerns,' and that if he took a few minutes to chat with them he would understand why.

He still didn't understand what, exactly, those pressing legal concerns were, but he'd been impressed enough with the conversation that he'd traveled — on the company's dime, of course — to the facility to take a look around. He wasn't an historian or archeologist, but he had been immediately taken by the crypt which the Prehistory Division called their headquarters. He had been given a map of the facility on his first day, and told how to enter and exit. The folder also contained a list of the duties they required him to complete, and when.

The entire structure, surprisingly, was underground, hidden from view beneath a few hundred feet of sand and rock. The emptiness, he was told, was due to 'just getting started,' and the bare appointment of the research labs was due to the fact that the space had previously been an unused crypt, and the 1,000-year-old space had not been built to modern-day specs. He had also been told the division had not put more resources into the space due to 'not yet reaching a full ramp-up of capabilities.' He was confused, but he'd seen stranger things than half-empty corridors and clean, barren offices.

It was after a week of lonely, late-night cleaning that he began to get suspicious. Perhaps it had been because of the fact he was doing the job of a night janitor rather than a full researcher, or even that he still had yet to meet any of his coworkers — if they existed at all — or perhaps it was simply due to severe loneliness. Either way, he tried to reach out to the HR person who'd brought him in, but the number had been disconnected.

He'd given it another month, just to see if the paychecks kept coming in.

They did, every other week, and they were bigger than any he'd ever received, just as promised. They were bigger than any he'd ever heard of *anyone* in his career field receiving, for that matter.

So he kept his mouth shut. Not that he had anyone to tell — his family and friends were all stateside, and he wasn't much for heading to town and mingling with the Egyptian locals. Besides, he was sleeping when most of them were working, and working when the town went to sleep.

He reached Room 23 and flashed his keycard at the reader mounted on the metal door. It clicked and a green light appeared on it, and the door fell open a crack. He pulled the filtration mask up and over his mouth and nose, then pushed the door open wide.

The stench hit him first. He always tried to prepare for it, but there was no preparation for the completely toxic aroma of fecal matter and vomit, intermixed into a thick paste that covered the area around the drain and in front of the platform in the center of the room. The wave of odorous air hit him hard, and he stumbled backwards.

Smells like more than one day's passed, he thought, trying to remain clinical. *There's a stronger tinge of chlorine in the air, that's why I stumbled.* He didn't need to be a trained chemist to be able to identify the strong, potent smell of chlorine. It stung his eyes and inside his nose, somehow barely stronger than the underlying odor of death.

The foot-tall bell-shaped object stood on its platform near the center of the room, right next to a small drainage ditch that had been hewn into the rock floor by the technicians, and he started toward it. The smell may have been worse tonight, but the mess was smaller. The only spot needing a cleanup was the area around the bell and drain, maybe about five or six feet wide and two across.

Easy, he thought. *One hour, tops.*

He turned to the right and walked over to the wall on the right side of the room. Rap then opened the door of a tall, narrow cabinet that was standing in the corner, revealing the cleaning supplies he would need. He reached for a mop and a bucket, as well as a roll of paper towels and a hose that was coiled up nearby. The hose was fed through a hole that had been cored through the stone, then sealed with caulk around the hose's skin, and the end had a nozzle that allowed him to jet-stream the chunks and detritus down into the sunken section of cut stone that acted as a drain, where it would eventually fall into a hazardous waste-collection container in the next room over.

As he sprayed and cleaned, he thought about the situation. He figured that the only reason the organization had hired a chemist rather than an *actual* janitor to do this job was that they needed his professional opinion of the remains upon entering the room. They didn't just want 23 to be cleaned, polished, and shined back to its rock-walled and crypt-like state, they wanted to know if there was anything 'out of the ordinary' about the space.

And chemically speaking, anything 'out of the ordinary' in this case meant anything besides the mixture of vomit-and-fecal sludge and the hint of a chlorine-like smell, and to date he had not experienced anything besides that. The reports he would write up soon after completing the cleaning and reset tasks said as much, and because of the monotony of it, the isolation of it, he left each cleaning job with the minute feeling that he was wasting his life, his talents underutilized. Every now and then he even wondered if he'd come back the next time he was asked.

But he *did* come back every time. He knew that the job was far better than anything else he could get, and the work each night, while difficult, was short. A few hours a day and he was finished, and most days didn't require a deep-clean of Room 23, but a simple tidying up of the rest of the subterranean facility. The salary was enough to keep him interested in coming back, but as a man with an interest in and a knack for science, he knew deep down that he was coming back every evening for another reason entirely.

He had been recruited to this job because of an affiliation with a particularly controversial religious group back in the States. Most people, at best, thought the organization was a bit *uncouth*. At worst, however, people protested their very existence. Rap was politically aligned with the group, but he'd never been one for public humiliation, so he tended to keep his involvement minimal, sidelined.

Apparently, however, the Prehistory Division of the Ministry of Antiquities in Egypt liked his particular brand of politics, as well as his background and education. They'd offered him far more than any other job he'd be able to find stateside, moving and living expenses, a car, and a retirement package.

And when he'd come aboard and learned a bit about what the organization he now worked for was trying to accomplish — what they were *really* trying to do — he understood the need for all the secrecy, the compartmentalization. He agreed with their premise, with their line of reasoning, and their projected outcome.

He'd drunk the proverbial Kool-Aid.

Sometimes he even thought he would be willing to sacrifice his time and energy for the cause, even without the attractive paycheck.

But that devotion, that loyalty, to the cause meant that there was a longing inside him to *truly* understand what it was they were doing with this little bell-shaped object. He had his theories — he was a scientist, first and foremost.

But he hadn't had the opportunity to actually ask anyone what it was they were working on here. He knew the endgame, the final destination, but he didn't understand this piece — *his* piece — of it all. He didn't understand what, exactly, he was doing.

He wanted to know what the hell was going on in here — in Room 23. He had his theories, but without sufficient testing and time inside a laboratory, there was no way to know for sure.

He started cleaning, holding his breath as he sprayed the space with water and let the remnants and chunks drip and ooze into the drain.

15

REGGIE

"Where are you now?" Reggie asked.

Sarah's voice cut through the cellphone and into his ear. *"Great Lakes. On assignment, but the students can keep it going until I get back."*

Reggie sighed. "That's a hell of a flight, Sarah."

"Well I'm not asking you to cover the airfare," she said. He sensed her bristling on the other end of the line. *"I just need help, and I don't know who else to call."*

Reggie was in Anchorage, sitting in his sparse apartment staring at the television-turned-computer-monitor with the video chat in full-screen mode. The large video playback window made Sarah's face far larger than it should have appeared, and the poor connection caused her face to jump and freeze between sentences.

"I know," he said. "I was just making small talk. Sorry."

He and Sarah Lindgren had a bit of a strained relationship. They'd met on an island off the coast of The Bahamas, working together through an organization called the Civilian Special Operations. Reggie was a member, but Sarah had been considered a consultant on that trip.

They'd barely survived, and Reggie and Sarah had both wanted to take their new professional relationship to a more personal level. Ever since their return from The Bahamas they had tried to make it work, but neither wanted to admit what both knew was true: they weren't meant to be together. Sarah was restless and constantly wanted to move around, to do field research and publish papers, as well as speak at universities around the world.

Reggie was content in Alaska, helping his new organization get off the ground. The CSO was currently working on a massive renovation of his best friend and coworker's private cabin, and it was nearing completion. A second wing and second story, complete with a brand-new communications facility attached to it, the CSO headquarters would be a perfect mix of all the things Reggie loved: high-tech, modern appeal in a reclusive and hard-to-reach location.

"It's okay," Sarah said. *"I'm just scared, I guess. He — he's gone. Why would someone take him?"*

"We don't know that someone did," Reggie replied. "I mean this Interpol grunt didn't really tell you anything, right? Just that they can't find him?"

"He said my father was 'declared missing' roughly forty-eight hours ago.'

"So he just walked to the grocery store and got lost," Reggie said. "It happens. He's old."

There was a pause.

"I'm sorry," he said. "Bad joke. Sarah, I want to help you. But I don't even know where to start. And Mr. E is wanting to get us all together to talk about the future. Some multi-day meeting he's trying to plan."

Mr. E and his wife were their benefactors, the founders of and main investors in the CSO. They had recruited Reggie, his friend Harvey "Ben" Bennett, as well as Ben's fiancée Juliette Richardson after hearing of their success tracking down a criminal organization in the jungles of the Amazon.

"I know," Sarah said. *"Just... there's no one else I can call."*

Reggie sighed again. Dr. Lindgren was not just an acquaintance to him. She was more than a professional contact as well, and if it had been up to Reggie she would have been more than that still.

I'm not getting out of this one, he thought. He wasn't sure Sarah was being rational, but he wasn't about to tell her that. Instead, he took the indirect approach.

"Sarah, how do you know he's been kidnapped? I understand your father's a smart guy, but how can you be *absolutely sure* he isn't just on some self-proclaimed mission or something?"

"My father would have told me he was going into the field, or at least told his new girlfriend where he was going. And he wouldn't have been gone for more than a night. Where would he even sleep?"

"And you hadn't heard from him since before The Bahamas?"

He could sense a hesitation. Her pause wasn't just silence, it was as if he could tell she was considering her next words carefully.

"He — he hadn't called or anything, but he wrote letters. The last one I got was delivered right before I got the call from Interpol."

Something in Reggie changed. A sense, a feeling. He wasn't sure what it was, and it certainly wasn't strong enough to act on just yet, but he knew himself well enough to know that it was worth his attention.

"It was definitely from him. He has a certain style to his writing that I would never mistake. But there was something else in the envelope besides the letter. He wanted me to figure out what it was."

"Something else in the envelope?"

"A rock, or stone. A flat round cylinder with a protrusion on one of the sides and an indentation on the opposite side. Seems to be authentic at first glance, but I have no idea what it is or where it's from, so it's impossible to be certain."

Reggie thought for a moment, chewing on his bottom lip. "We have access to labs here, Sarah. If you could bring it back with you, maybe we —"

"I'm not leaving until I have a lead. My father is probably somewhere in Europe, so there's no way I'm traveling back to Alaska just yet."

"Understood. Maybe you can send the stone over then? Overnight shipping even? I'm sure the CSO will foot the bill."

"No, Reggie. I want to examine it a bit more before I let go of it. It's weird that he sent it to me in an envelope and didn't just snap some pictures and email it over."

"And it's weird that you got the envelope at almost the exact same time as you got the phone call from Interpol."

"You think they're related?"

"I've been in enough sticky situations to know that coincidences are rarely just that — the letter and this item are probably at least a step in the right direction. At the very least, if you can figure out where it's from, you have an idea of where your old man's been."

"That's true. But I'm not an archeologist, and I can't just wait around for a nearby school to get back to me. I need to expedite this, but I don't want a bunch of academics peering over my shoulder."

"You don't have any friends in high places?" Reggie asked.

"Of course I do," she responded. He could tell she was smiling as she spoke the next sentence. *"That's why I called you."*

16

BEN

BEN PACED AROUND THE LIVING ROOM IN HIS TINY, ONE-BEDROOM CABIN while he spoke. "Reggie, it just can't work right now."

Reggie's face was enlarged on the television screen. Harvey 'Ben' Bennett's fiancée, Juliette Richardson, had finagled the connection together and set up a small computer to be able to video chat with the other members of the CSO from the comfort of their living room.

Ben purposefully kept himself far away from anything tech-related, both from a desire to not ignite his already short temper and because Julie was so good at all of it. She was an ex-IT person for the CDC, and she had a background and education in computer science. Setting up a wireless access point and video monitor for communication was Greek to him, while Julie could do it in her sleep.

"It has to work," Reggie said, onscreen. *"She needs us."*

"I get that, and I want to help — I truly do," Ben responded. "But you're the one who wanted to figure out this skull business once and for all. What changed?"

The 'skull business' was a reference to a skull that Reggie had found after one of the CSO's missions in Montana. The skull had been resting in a chest atop a map and a small fortune in Spanish silver. He had been urging the CSO to push the skull to the top of its priorities, citing the organization's mission statement, which directed the CSO to focus only those priorities that were apolitical in nature and outside the realm of what the US military was capable or willing to invest in.

Reggie had been pushing for more and more resources to be thrown toward the skull, as he was very interested in both the skull's history and significance as well as its unknown owner. He was a history buff, interested in the stories and lessons of the past, and ever since digging up the relic he couldn't get it out of his head.

"The skull isn't going anywhere," he finally answered. "Sarah *needs our help."*

"She's not even in Sweden, where her father was taken," Julie said from the couch behind Ben. She made a face at him, and he stopped pacing, plopping down into the armchair next to the couch.

"She's somewhere in the Great Lakes region. Working on a university assignment or something."

"I didn't realize she's still at a university."

"She wasn't clear," Reggie said. *"But she's been trying to publish her opinions and findings about the incident in The Bahamas. Apparently a lot of her colleagues are up in arms about the last couple of papers on it, saying they were made up or at least 'heavily embellished.'"* Reggie made air quotes with his fingers as he said the last words, punctuating his annoyance with the academic establishment.

Ben swallowed. He vividly remembered the saltwater crocodiles swimming around him and the team. The one-on-one standoff with the alpha croc, the narrow misses.

And most of all he remembered the ones who *didn't* make it out of the tank.

The nightmare had been real, and he had a strong urge to have a chat with anyone in the academic or scientific community who thought Dr. Lindgren's assessment was 'heavily embellished.'

"What do we know about her father's disappearance?" Julie asked.

Onscreen, Reggie nodded. *"He was reported missing about two days ago by a neighbor. He has a girlfriend, but it's not apparent yet if she knows about it."*

"I thought he was married?"

"He is — or was, I'm not sure. But they're split up. Interpol called Sarah to let her know the next steps, and they left it up to her whether or not to tell her mom."

"And how far has Interpol gotten with the case?" Julie asked.

"They're being unsurprisingly cloak-and-dagger about it all," Reggie said. *"Besides the initial phone call and email to Sarah, they haven't given her an update. My guess is her father's just a glossy 8x10 on a stack of folders on some jockey's desk."*

Ben nodded in agreement. "Probably. But that doesn't mean we can just rush in and take over the investigation. Besides the obvious overstepping of our *civilian* bounds, the CSO can't be involved *officially*. Besides that, Mr. E wouldn't ever let us take a case like this. We're not private investigators, Reggie."

"I know," Reggie said. *"But we don't need Mr. E's approval."*

That part was true. After their debacle off the coast of The Bahamas, Mr. E and his wife had called a debriefing meeting and the team collectively decided to change how their missions were determined:

voting would take place, and quorum-plus-one would have to be met before launching any trip.

"Still," Julie said. "Ben's right. It's not the sort of thing we need to be involved in, Reggie. I'm sorry. There's nothing of historical importance associated with the mission. It's in Interpol's hands, and that's probably for the best."

Reggie's large smile appeared. *"Actually, that's not entirely true."*

"What else do you know?"

"Sarah believes there is *something significant about this mission."*

"Significant *how?"*

"She thinks her father was kidnapped, and the people who did it are trying to find something of massive *historical significance."*

"Interpol thinks he was kidnapped?"

Reggie nodded. *"That's the working theory anyway. They're still filing it under 'missing persons' until they have more — or any — evidence to the contrary. But Sarah is adamant."*

Ben could see that Reggie had been baiting them, pulling them both into this very moment. He had already decided that he agreed with Sarah. But Reggie's personal feelings for the woman aside, he was an astute observer, and he wouldn't allow their relationship to interfere with good decision-making.

So that meant that Reggie was already on board with this new escapade. Ben and Julie would have the impossible task of trying to talk their friend out of helping Sarah find her missing father.

Maybe we won't have to talk him out of it at all, Ben thought. "What sort of significance? Give it to us straight, buddy."

Reggie's grin grew even larger. "She thinks they sent her their location — where they're keeping her father — by way of ancient artifact."

17

REGGIE

THE CONVERSATION CONTINUED LATER THAT EVENING, WHEN REGGIE finally made it to the cabin. Ben had grilled fish on the back porch, ignoring the two feet of snow piling up outside, and Julie poured them all a new white wine she had found in town. The three of them caught up, shared stories, and ate together before jumping back into the topic du jour.

Ben poured Julie another glass of wine and a glass of whiskey for himself and Reggie, then they found comfortable spots on the couch and armchair in the living room.

"I know Julie's *dying* to know," Ben said. "What's this 'significant thing' that got sent to Sarah?"

Reggie cleared his throat and took a swig of the whiskey. It burned more than it should have. "What is this?" he asked. "More importantly, how much did you *pay* for it?"

Ben looked upset, but Julie laughed.

"There's a homesteader about twenty miles down the road on the way to town," Ben explained. "He's starting to make moonshine. This is a corn whiskey he's had going for a few months."

"Well tell him to *stop* making it. I can feel myself going blind."

"It's perfectly safe, Reggie. Want another ice cube?"

"How about you fill the glass up with ice, add some water, and hold the whiskey next time?"

Julie cracked up, but Ben just pouted. "You don't have to like it. More for me."

"It's all yours, bud." Reggie squinted through the glass and examined the light brown liquid. He could see the wisps of fusel oils from the alcohol stirring up in the drink. Out of generosity, he held the glass up to his lips and tried another sip.

The second sip was even worse.

He coughed, beating his chest with a fist. "God, it burns. I don't think you'll ever have to buy lighter fluid again." He turned to Julie. "Or nail polish remover."

"I don't paint my nails," Julie shot back. "But we can light fires and have a makeup session later. I want to hear about this artifact."

"Right, right." Reggie placed the glass down on the end table and leaned forward in the armchair. "So she got a package from her father, a letter inside. There was also some sort of roundish *thing*. Not sure what it was, but she said it was made out of stone. Circular, with a divot on one side and a bump on the other."

"Okay…" Ben said. "I thought you said the bad guys that apparently kidnapped her father sent it to her?"

He shook his head. "No. Her father sent it to her directly, and she was positive it was from him — his handwriting, his writing style, etcetera. But after she took the call from Interpol, she checked her email and found *another* message. *That* message was from the bad guys."

"How does she know?" Julie asked. "I'm sure the sender wasn't 'bad-guy-at-gmail-dot-com."

Reggie chuckled. "Nope. But there was no subject line and the message was just one sentence long: *'help your father find the answer, we are very interested to know what the object is.'"*

Ben made a *whooshing* sound with his mouth. "Whoa, that's insane. So she got the package and letter, Interpol called, and *then* these guys sent the email?"

Reggie nodded. "Yes, exactly. In that order, and she checked timestamps on the sat phone and email to be sure. It was spooky, obviously."

"Who knew where she was?" Julie asked. "Even taking the unpredictability of a worldwide courier service out of the equation, someone would have to know pretty much her every move in order to time it out like that."

"That's exactly what I told her. She has three assistants in the field with her. Two men and a woman, all from the university."

"She trusts them?" Ben asked.

"As much as she can, I guess. She never questioned them before."

"Maybe they'd never been *paid* as much before."

Reggie shrugged. "Sure, I guess. Everyone's got a price. But it seems unlikely that an undergrad would be working with some clandestine group to kidnap her father."

"So what's her hypothesis?" Julie asked. "Sarah's brilliant. She's obviously been working nonstop to figure this thing out."

"She has," Reggie said. "But she's hit a brick wall. The fatigue, stress, and the fact that she still doesn't have much to go off of has taken its toll.

I tried to call on my way over here, actually — she told me to, no matter the time of day or night. But she didn't answer."

"Are you worried about her?"

Reggie shifted in the chair, looked at the ceiling for a moment, then back at Julie. "No. I want her to be safe, but I don't think she's in any immediate danger. The ransom note — the email — has been delivered. She doesn't know the timeframe, but she knows what they want. They won't do anything to her until they think she can't help them anymore."

"What if they find out she reached out to us?" Ben asked.

"Honestly? I think they already *do* know. Being able to coordinate the timing of the email like that implies at least *some* tech know-how, and my tendency is to assume that they're better than they're letting on."

"That's a good tendency."

"So I think they're counting on her reaching out to us for help. That's part of the reason why I brought it up to you guys — I think Sarah's safe, but only *for now*. If she can't deliver whatever it is they want, her dad gets hurt. Possibly worse."

Ben's face sank, and Reggie understood the same emotions his close friend was feeling. *Fear, regret, confusion, anger.* And not a little bit of exhaustion.

They had, only months ago, returned from The Bahamas. Ben's and Julie's cruise vacation had been cut short for the trip, and Reggie's research and work on the recovered skull had been pushed aside. They'd ended up barely escaping the floating 'theme park' with their lives, and while all of them were hurriedly attempting to get their lives back to normal, the harrowing experience was something none of them would be able to easily forget.

And Reggie knew they'd *never* forget it. He'd spent his early days in the 75th Army Rangers Regiment as a sniper, and later as a mercenary-for-hire on a handful of clandestine missions.

All of the missions had eventually rolled together into one conglomeration of memories, the fighting and injuries and deaths and kills all becoming a single unified mass. He didn't *forget* the missions, as much as he had tried, but time certainly had a way of ironing them out and placing together into a special compartment in his mind.

And even then those weren't the memories he'd wanted to forget most.

"That's why I'm here, guys," he said. "Sarah needs us, and when she explained what her thoughts were on it I knew it was something the CSO was perfect for."

Julie took in a deep breath. "Does Mr. E know?"

Reggie nodded. "I sent him an email. But if we can all vote now, we don't need any further approval."

Ben opened his mouth, closed it again, then turned to Julie. She looked back at him, and Reggie could almost write the dialogue silently passing between them.

What do you think? Ben would be asking.

It's up to you, Julie would respond.

I've made that mistake before, Ben might say.

They stared at each other for a few seconds, then simultaneously turned back to Reggie.

"Yes," Julie said.

Reggie smiled. *Well that was way easier than I'd expected.* He looked at Ben.

Ben shook his head. "You don't need my approval, brother. She says we go, we go."

Julie laughed. "He's not wrong, you know."

The moment felt right, so Reggie steeled himself and grabbed the glass of subpar whiskey on the end table. He lifted it, second-guessed himself, then straightened in the armchair and poured the rest of the ice-cold beverage down his throat.

The burning was intense, and the flavor horrid, and the melted ice had only marginally helped.

His voice was shot, and his throat stung, but he held up the empty glass to the smiling couple across from him.

"Cheers," he croaked.

18

SARAH

Sarah's return to her apartment had been uneventful, but her mind was racing. Munising, Michigan was an easy 30-minute drive from the park, and she had spent many of her nights at the apartment until the team had arrived a few days ago. When she couldn't justify the drive, she spent the night stretched out on the cot in the pup tent. The weather had been nice, and she felt that being part of the group was good for morale.

But she'd decided to head into town after hearing the news of her father. After quickly informing Alexander and Jennifer of her plan, she'd hiked back to the lot where she'd stashed her Corolla. Upon entering the vehicle, her phone dinged with the alert of a new email message.

help your father find the answer, we are very interested to know what the object is.

No capitalization, no subject line, an indiscernible sender.

The email had spooked her, but it only served to confirm what she'd already suspected: her father had indeed been kidnapped. So she'd used the early half of the trip to call Reggie, to inform him and the rest of the CSO team he worked with about the email and the letter, then she spent the rest of it in silence.

Adam's Trail, the narrow, pitch-black road through the park was empty at this hour, but she still didn't speed, allowing herself the extra few minutes of driving to think and plan. When she'd finally made it back to her tiny one-bedroom in Munising, however, she hadn't yet decided what to do.

My father is missing, she thought. *Probably kidnapped. He sent me a package and a note, and then I got a cryptic email.*

Nothing about it felt right, and yet there was nothing she could do. Her financial situation was precariously balanced between 'be careful' and 'flat broke,' and she knew a trip to Sweden wasn't something she could afford.

She'd given her last dime to the students by way of their bonuses, and while she didn't regret it — they deserved it — she did wish she'd saved just a bit for a flight to Europe.

Or at least Alaska, she thought. *Reggie's in Alaska.*

The CSO team could help her, but she didn't know if they would. They would know that getting involved in an international police investigation was not exactly prudent. The agent with Interpol had essentially said the same thing: *'Any involvement on your part could be easily misconstrued as obstruction of justice, and our agency has little tolerance for vigilantism.'*

She left the Corolla on Elm street, parallel parked in one of two spots on this particular block. The street itself looked as though it had been lifted directly out of an old western movie, the multicolored, boxy establishments featuring a small shop or cafe downstairs and an apartment like hers upstairs.

She'd rented hers from a local shopkeeper, a man who owned a few of the buildings on Elm. He'd given her a steal of a price, likely due to the fact that the one-bedroom space had gone empty for about six months. She'd been there three weeks so far, but had only spent the night there three or four times.

She swung open the door leading to the stairs that would take her to the top floor and stepped inside the musty, old stairwell.

Immediately she knew something wasn't right. A shuffle, a faint noise, something she wasn't even fully aware of. Her senses heightened, and she knew she wasn't alone.

"Hello?" Sarah called out to the dark stairs.

She heard more shuffling, louder. *Someone's* definitely *up there.*

She took a step back, nearly tripping over the threshold. The door leading to the street swung shut, but her back caught it before it could close all the way.

"Sarah?"

She frowned. "Alex? Is that you?"

The young man's voice hollered down the stairs. "I — I'm sorry, I must have scared you. I'm sorry," he said again.

Sarah, still shaken, gathered herself together and climbed the stairs. At the top, she fumbled around for her house key and opened the apartment door.

"Come in," she said. She was past caring about how she looked, past caring about how her living quarters might look.

Not that there was much to be worried about. She flicked on the light as the two of them entered, and she could see the stack of three boxes still sitting in the living room. The kitchen was just past that, and it was bare. Her bedroom featured a mattress, lying on the floor and covered with a single sheet. As she used her laptop or tablet for just about everything these days including entertainment, she had no use for a television or stacks of books.

"Sorry for the mess," she said.

Alex chuckled.

"How'd you get here so fast, anyway?" she asked.

"I was parked in the lot closer to our camp, so when I left, you were still hiking to your car."

She nodded. Standing in the center of the living room, realizing for the first time she had nothing to offer this man — no coffee, no alcohol, no chair — she felt awkward. "Sorry, I uh, haven't really had time to move in..."

He waved a hand. "Don't. I'm imposing. And I'm not staying long, I just thought I'd stop by and check on you."

"Check on me?"

"Yeah, you left in a hurry. Seemed like you were a bit out of sorts."

Can he really read me that easily? she thought. *Or am I just that easy to read?*

"No, I'm fine. Thank you, Alex."

He stood there, staring at her. She suddenly felt a bit uncomfortable, so she stepped to the side, hoping he would take the hint as a cue to leave.

"Are you?"

She cocked her head sideways. "Alex... what are you asking?"

He took a step toward her. He seemed even taller in the doorway, his head less than a foot away from the frame. He put his hands into his pockets and looked around at her apartment, as if noticing it for the first time.

"I just want to make sure you're okay. You got the letter today, and that weird object, and then Interpol called you."

"Jennifer told you that?"

He nodded. "Sorry. She said you didn't tell her what they wanted, so we're all still in the dark. But we're worried about you."

"You're worried about me?"

Alex's face softened a bit. "You're... alone. I just thought maybe, if you needed something..."

"Alex, thank you. But I'm good. I promise." She forced a smile, but her eyes betrayed her feelings as she recalled the last few months. "I'm pretty good at being alone."

He offered a casual smile in return, but she could tell he didn't buy it. "Okay, you got it. Like I said, I was on my way to town anyway — picking up some more beer for the group. There's a place at the end of Elm that's still open, apparently."

She nodded. "I've heard of it." She had actually thought about stopping there on the way to her apartment, to maybe grab a glass of wine.

Or something stronger.

Now she wished she had — running the extra errand might have allowed her to miss her awkward encounter with her student.

"I'll be back first thing tomorrow, Alex," she said. "And if I'm not, you guys can close up and finish without me. I might have to make a trip, for family reasons."

"Got it."

"And your paycheck will still come, either way. You have my word."

He nodded again, then turned around and stepped over the threshold. When he'd fully exited, he turned and looked in at her. "Please, Sarah. Let me — us — know if there's anything you might need."

"I will. Thank you."

She closed the door, waited a few seconds, then locked it.

She shuddered. The night had gotten colder than she'd expected. There was no breeze, but the air seemed to hang on her, slowly wearing her down.

Sarah waited until she heard the footsteps on the stairs, then she turned and walked into her bedroom. She collapsed on the mattress, lay there for a few minutes, then reached down and grabbed her laptop from her bag.

Time to find my father.

19

JULIE

THE TROUBLE WASN'T IN DECIDING WHETHER OR NOT THEY SHOULD GO — she knew they should. Julie liked Sarah Lindgren, and she knew Sarah would come to their aid if their roles had been reversed.

The trouble was in deciding *where* to go.

Dr. Lindgren's father was likely somewhere in Europe, as that had been the last place he'd been seen. Sarah was somewhere in the Great Lakes region, which could be anywhere from Minnesota to Pennsylvania. She'd want to get a head start, as whatever trail they might find would already be growing cold, so Julie assumed Sarah would be looking for flights to Sweden right about now.

Interpol was a capable organization, with the resources and manpower to run an intra-European search for the missing person. If CSO was going to get involved, Julie knew they'd need a strong lead for their involvement to be of any use, as well as for plausible deniability — they needed to be able to prove they had gotten involved in the case not for Dr. Lindgren's father, but because there was something of historic value at stake.

Julie wondered what the next move should be. Her hypothesis was that whomever had taken Professor Lindgren had left a cyber footprint somehow, somewhere, but Julie wasn't sure where to begin looking for it.

Thankfully, she wasn't searching alone. Mr. E and his wife controlled the biggest stake in one of the largest communications corporations on the planet, and they had already begun putting feelers out into the worldwide surveillance and intelligence communities.

Nothing had immediately turned up, but that was to be expected. Anything obvious — transactions on the professor's credit card, successive accessing of bank accounts — would be obvious tells, and the criminals would no doubt be smarter than that.

The problem was that while Julie was confident *something* would turn up, she had no idea how long it might take. Any time spent waiting around for a database record to appear onscreen was time lost in the field, chasing down the captors.

But, as she had argued to Ben and Reggie, the computer might be able to tell them *where* to start the chase.

It was the only thing they had to go on at the moment, and it was in this computer system Julie was placing all her trust. Still, she felt nervous: if no leads appeared onscreen, and Mrs. E wasn't able to coax anything else out of the machine, where would that leave them?

"Any luck?" Julie asked.

Mrs. E was on the computer monitor's screen in a picture-in-picture window Julie had resized to fill a quarter of the screen's real estate. They had set up a videoconference to build a search algorithm together, in real-time, to try and make the best use of their collective mind power.

Reggie and her fiancé, Ben, were in the living room enjoying the rest of the bottle of cheap whiskey Ben had opened, and joking about times past. Their voices carried easily to the bedroom desk where Julie was stationed.

"Nothing yet," Mrs. E responded. *"I broadened the search parameters to include his known associates."*

Julie squeezed her brow between two fingers. "He's not a criminal," she said. "He won't *have* any known associates."

"Everyone has known associates, Juliette," Mrs. E said. *"His might be straight-laced colleagues, but they will show up in any searches now. And in a way, that makes the search easier. Anything suspicious should be easy to spot."*

Julie nodded. Of course the woman was correct, but still — that would be too easy. "It's not going to work, E."

"You must have faith. We just need —"

"No, it's too simple. Too *obvious*. The people who took him aren't going to leave a breadcrumb like that — they would make sure anyone at Professor Lindgren's university, any of his friends, any minor associates he's had in the past, were all far away from him at the time of his abduction. It would be too easy for one of them to admit they saw something suspicious. Too easy to call in a police report."

Onscreen, Mrs. E nodded. Then she smiled. *"That is why I have added an additional parameter to our search."*

Julie cocked an eyebrow. "Yeah?"

"I have made sure to pull in any relevant professional associations. Not just people — other universities, appearances, articles, publications, and references."

Julie frowned. "But that's going to give us *everything* there ever was on this guy. It can't all be relevant, and it's going to be a ton of stuff to wade through."

Ben's laugh echoed through the cracks in the doorway. The thick logs and chinking were wonderful sound barriers, but the gaps between doors and doorframes throughout the small cabin allowed plenty of sound in.

She shifted in the office chair and tried to ignore the two mens' racket as Mrs. E responded. She was constantly amazed at mens' ability to compartmentalize. If Reggie was concerned about Sarah, it sure didn't sound like it from in here. The laughing and joking grew to a chaotic level.

And the whiskey probably doesn't help, she thought.

"No, that is the beauty of the algorithm," Mrs. E said. *"It is built to automatically filter out unnecessary details, like anything too old or too far away from him geographically. But any mentions of the man will turn up in the search."*

Julie shrugged. "Anything's worth trying, I guess. Have you gotten any results yet?"

Julie could see Mrs. E's face turn away from the camera as she fiddled with the computer mouse and clicked around the screen. *"There are some results, but I am going to collate the list and have my husband's assistant work through it this evening."*

"Read a couple of the first ones, most recent to older."

Mrs. E nodded. *"A talk Professor Lindgren gave at a university in London, titled, 'A Brief Explanation of Geologic Formations of Early Scotland."* Mrs. E's eyes danced over the screen. *"Next one is another talk, this one called, 'Examples of Prehistoric Weaponry,' given at —"*

"No," Julie said. "That's only slightly more interesting than the first, but there's no way he'd say anything so earth-shattering someone would want to kidnap him because of it."

Mrs. E nodded. *"After that is a paper published in a small periodical, called, '*Timeaus *and* Critias*: An Alternative Interpretation.'"* Mrs. E sighed. *"As I explained, Julie. Most of the data is still compiling, and —"*

"When was that talk?" Julie asked.

"Let me check." Julie heard the sounds of clicking and watched Mrs. E's eyes on the screen in front of her. *"Apparently it was published four weeks ago, though I am not able to see the page. It appears as though the article has been taken down, or the link no longer works.'"*

"Taken down?"

"No information is provided, Juliette. I apologize. The link is dead. I will have our assistant attempt to retrieve an archived copy if it exists anywhere. The publication does not seem to have online copies of all their articles, which means we might have to track down a hard copy."

Julie shook her head, then stood up. "Don't worry about it, E. Thanks. Have her check, but I believe Sarah has access to her father's office — anything he wrote will likely be stored on a computer or hard drive there, if not on the cloud already."

"Yes, of course." She paused, waited for Julie to look at her, then spoke again. *"Do you — do you think there is something in this article that might be helpful?"*

"Hard to say," Julie said. "But the timeline checks out, I guess. Anything earlier than that and I'd wonder what the thieves were waiting around for. But it's the title of the article that strikes me as interesting."

"How so?"

"*Timeaus* and *Critias*," Julie said. "Are you familiar with those?"

"Plato?"

"Yes. I was thinking about the Professor's letter, the one Sarah got just before the call from Interpol. There was a quote on it, one written by Plato: 'We are twice armed if we fight with faith.'"

"Intriguing."

"Maybe," Julie said. "Or maybe it's nothing. There are plenty of good Plato quotes floating around out there."

"Was the quote in Sarah's letter from Timaeus *and* Critias?*"*

"They were two separate dialogues, if I remember correctly. And I'm not sure, but I doubt it."

"So what is the relation?"

"Well," Julie said, "and I'm just thinking out loud here, if Professor Lindgren was *forced* to write a letter to his daughter — a very intelligent historian and anthropologist, so certainly a credible source — but he was told to only ask her for help figuring out what the little object was that came with the letter…"

"Then he would have tried to sneak in some additional information, knowing that he was under pressure, and probably fearful of what might happen to him."

Julie nodded. "It's a bit conspiratorial, I'll admit, but if he was ordered to seek out assistance from someone, and he could convince his captors that the letter was written in his typical 'style' and nothing more, it would have been an ingenious clue."

"But what is *the clue?"* Mrs. E asked.

"No idea," Julie said. "Hang on."

She pulled open a web browser on the computer and typed in a few keywords. *Plato, Timaeus and Critias*. She pressed enter.

She scrolled through the first few results — translations of the two dialogues, an explanation of them and an overview on Plato, and then her eyes stopped on the third result.

She sucked in a breath.

Let's hope it's not that, she thought.

"Find anything?" Mrs. E asked.

Julie had forgotten she was still on a video chat. "M — maybe."

She clicked the search result and waited for the page to load. It was a transcription and summarization of the two famous dialogues in Plato's canon, but the emphasis was on Critias, on a story told through the mouth of a man named Solon.

A story Julie was *very* familiar with.

"What did you find?" Mrs. E asked again.

"Well, if Professor Lindgren is actually trying to leave a clue for us, I think we're going to have a difficult time finding him."

"And why is that? What are the dialogues about?" Mrs. E asked.

Julie sighed, feeling her knuckles gripping the edge of the desk more and more tightly as she read on.

"They're about the legend of Atlantis."

20

RACHEL

Rachel Rascher steeled herself. Her team was counting on her, and she felt like she was about to lose control. The scientists here, the staff, and the handful of investors and supporters she had around the world, the silent partners of their endeavor, were counting on her.

She had built this — her dream — from the ground up, working with fragmented pieces left to her by her grandfather and his predecessors, including her own father. She knew how close they were to a final compound, a solution to the problem that had plagued them for years, but the closer they got the more nervous she became.

She knew the nervousness was based on emotion, not rational thinking, and that by better controlling her emotional state, she could push the thoughts to the back of her mind and continue her work.

Still... nothing has prepared me for this.

Rachel strolled down the dim and narrow hallway, heading toward the room at the end of the hall. *Room 23.*

So many failed trials. So many failed compounds.

They were running low on the original compound, and that meant they were running out of time. Her team had worked for years on this project, and some of them their entire lives.

In her case, she felt like she had worked on this project for *multiple* lives.

Her father had taken over the project in its original form from his grandfather, and it had passed through the family until Rachel was of age and had proven to have enough education, political success, and desire to see it through.

The project had been something Rachel had grown up with. As a young girl, she would often find her father discussing things with members of the team from around the world, speaking softly into the telephone's receiver that sat between his cheek and his shoulder. He would furiously scribble notes, scratch them out, all the while discussing ideas and complex mathematical formulas. She didn't understand the type of work her father was doing in that home office until much later.

When he felt the time was right, immediately after her 30th birthday, her father bequeathed the project to his only child. Rachel was enthused and humbled, but still a bit hesitant. She had spent the time earning her undergraduate and advanced degrees studying history and politics, hoping to break into the political scene somewhere in Europe, as that was where her family was from, and where she'd spent the majority of her studies.

She had just accepted a job working for the Egyptian government, hoping to open the country's research programs to the rest of the world. Her father was supportive of the position, but warned her to not get too involved anywhere before she fully understood the project, and what it meant for her family.

She'd promised to give it some thought. She had also promised to look into it a bit, thinking she could simply shake it off and move on, and her father would forget about his addiction to late-night phone calls and cryptic note-taking.

But when she began to read over her father's and great-grandfather's notes and their conclusions about the project and what it meant, she changed her mind. She accepted the position with the government, but immediately began working on a plan to devote more of her time and resources — both personally and professionally — into furthering the family's research.

The project grew with Rachel's political career. Every step up the totem pole brought her more money, more resources, and more ability to decode the mysterious clues hidden in her past. She cloaked the project behind a curtain of believability, even maneuvering herself into a position with the Ministry of Antiquities' Prehistory Division so that she could continue the research with the full — albeit unknowing — support and resources of the Egyptian government.

And building a team was even easier. After all, the project her family had been working on for decades was one that had unique ties to Egypt's past. It would shake the knowledge of Egypt's history to the core, if only it could be proven. Her recruiting efforts were only slowed by her requirement that each and every one of her employees who worked in direct contact with the project were 'pure.'

She had no need to test herself, of course, as her family line was pure. Besides a single misstep one generation ago, no one had married outside of the great and ancient familial heritage. So many tests had proven the purity of the line.

And that was what brought her here today. The *final* test.

Room 23 sat at the edge of the hallway, its metallic door contrasted against the old, weathered stones into which it had been hung. It was unassuming, but to Rachel the room was everything. It was the project's final proving ground; it was the last step before purity was confirmed and a new member of their growing faction joined their ranks. It was the symbol of everything her family, her employees, and her ancestors had been working on. It was a symbol of what they had been working toward for millennia.

But today, Room 23 was more than just symbolic. Today the room would administer the final test and provide the final outcome for one more member of their faction. The test would consume the remainder of their original compound, the heavy powder they'd found hidden down here in the crypt years ago. This test would be the last one possible without more of the compound, but it was critical to their success.

They were close to having a proper copy of the compound, a synthetic alternative they could create on demand, but they weren't there yet. Her great-grandfather's team had almost finished the compound, but they were sorely misled about a few key components, and therefore those tests and trials had only led them to utter failure and generations of disgrace.

Not today, Rachel thought as she reached for the door. *Not anymore. We're so close. We're ready.*

She looked up, staring at the single bulb hanging from the ceiling. She wasn't religious, as she couldn't effectively place her beliefs into any of the popular segmentations. Still, she knew there was a greater power up there. 'It,' or whatever it was, had given her ancestors the clues, the building blocks, to what her project was now uncovering. It had given her the drive and the determination to prove her family's worth, once and for all, and it had started everything she'd ever known and would ever come to know — for a very specific reason. She didn't believe it was all for naught. She didn't believe there was no *purpose* to her life, or anyone else's. She didn't believe this life was simply the product of advanced evolutionary tactics.

She pushed the door open, took a breath, then stepped inside.

The man lay on the hospital gurney, just as Jennifer Polanski had before when she'd been tested. Polanski, unfortunately, hadn't made it through the final test. The compound and the bell had found her wanting, discarding her as impure and therefore unworthy of the association to and inclusion in their faction.

Rachel had felt responsible for the woman's life, but she knew it was for the greater good. She hadn't shed a tear or lost any sleep over the outcome, as she hadn't done that for any of the failed tests.

But today's test was different.

She thought she could talk herself down, explain to her irrational brain that the test was crucial — it was — and that there was no other way to test this man's purity — there wasn't.

But that didn't change how she felt. She sidled up to the gurney, noticing the bell in the center of the room, watching the scientist she'd hired three years ago mix liquid chlorine into the powdery compound — the last of their stock — and place it into the bell's open top. He poured carefully from the last of the rounded ceramic containers left to them by the Ancients, ensuring that not a drop was spilled unless it was into the bell's hollow chamber, then he placed the round stone container back onto his cart.

She watched as the man then plugged the bell into a battery sitting on the cart. The auxiliary power cable was one of the few liberties they'd taken upon designing and building these miniature copies. The Ancients had somehow found a way to power these objects without electricity, but Rachel wasn't interested in recreating prehistory for fun. She'd wanted results, and she'd wanted them fast.

When the scientist finished, he gave her a nod and left the room.

Rachel turned, finally, to the man laying on the gurney. He, too, had survived the blast at the museum, one of only two people to come into direct contact with the bell's effects. She had lied to Jennifer Polanski, but it didn't matter. The woman was dead, and Rachel had hardly thought it prudent to be truthful with a woman about to meet her death.

The man was scarred, the burn marks covering his exposed flesh. He had some wounds on his cheek that seemed to be leaking some sort of puss. It was hard to look at, but Rachel forced her eyes to remain riveted on the man's face. She forced herself to not look away.

It was clear the man couldn't talk, though she imagined he wanted to. It seemed as though his eyes were widened in surprise, but she couldn't be sure. He could have simply been in pain, unable to control his normally voluntary reactions.

She sniffed. *Hold it together.*

The man stared up at her, wide-eyed. His forehead had deep creases in them, but they were stretched tight against his skull now. He was breathing heavily, the breaths stuttered as they entered and exited his lungs.

She sniffed again, and then felt a tear beginning to stream down her cheek. *Stop it,* she willed herself. *We don't know how the test will go.*

"I'm sorry," she whispered. "But I have to know. I must know for sure. I... had my doubts, but I couldn't bring myself..."

She stopped, composed herself. "I should have done this a long time ago, but... you understand. You told me a year ago that this world was too far gone, that trying to save it would only destroy it."

The man didn't say anything, didn't move.

"But it will be over soon. I promise."

She turned to leave, then stopped herself. She took a final, deep breath, then knelt and kissed the man's forehead.

"I'm so sorry, Daddy."

21

RACHEL

I'M SO SORRY, DADDY.

The words rang in her mind over and over again.

She couldn't shake the feeling that she'd just crossed a line she could never step back over. But there was peace — within minutes she would know the answer to a question she'd long wanted to answer.

There was also pain. The man on the bed in Room 23 was her father, and she loved him.

But he had instilled in her the set of values she now used to justify her actions.

'Never let your emotions get in the way of your truth,' he would say. She hadn't always understood the phrase, but it had been ingrained into her thinking by the time she was a teenager.

Now, she understood. Her emotions were telling her one thing: 'don't worry about it; let your father live.' But her rational, reasonable mind was telling her the exact opposite thing: 'he wanted this more than anything. He wanted the answer, but he never had the opportunity.'

She wanted to finish what he — and his father and his father's father before him — had started.

The Rascher name was one that extended back generations, before Germany was called Germany and even before Europe was considered a continent. The name had meaning to Rachel, but more than that she believed in what the name represented: the lineage of people who had conquered, settled, and expanded the ancient civilizations. Her namesake was one of a handful of names — many of them lost to the generations — that represented exactly what the project her great-grandfather had started so long ago, which itself was just a continuation of the original Ancients' project from thousands of years before.

But the project, when entrusted to Rachel, had taken a slight turn.

The truth she had come to accept as a young woman— that she and the rest of her family was of the pure, Aryan race — had been immediately challenged upon the discovery of a pure, original compound. The compound, left in the crypt by the original builders, was a powder that resisted degradation, heavy enough to remain in place inside each of the roundish cylinders of stone. It, coupled with the technology found in one of the crypt's rooms, allowed the team in Egypt to test the purity of any human subject.

The compound, when rehydrated with water and bleach, then heated into a vaporous gas in one of the bells, would render its subject inert, completely paralyzed as it ran its tests inside the host's body. Rachel's scientists believed the compound was made of something akin to mercury, but its exact properties defied their analyses and laboratory testing. The powdery substance was an enigma, a liquid metal that seemed to be something altogether otherworldly. Rachel knew it wasn't — she knew that the compound was simply an element the modern world hadn't yet discovered. Something the Ancients knew of, in the vastly different world they'd lived in with its different atmospheric and chemical compositions.

Time and effort would give them the solution, but time was running out. Their next event was planned already, and they had already run out of the compound, save for what was inside the bell in Room 23. Her father's was the final test. His father — Rachel's grandfather — had been born into the pure lineage, but in a moment of weakness he had married outside of that line. Their child, Rache's father, corrected that mistake by remarrying into the lineage, allowing Rachel to enjoy the purity of the master race.

But my father cannot enjoy that luxury...

Rachel stepped out of the room and closed the solid metal door behind her. She would watch the test from her own office, from a place she felt safe from her employees in case her emotions began to run wild. She walked the empty hallway in silence, wondering if she'd be able to make it back to her private space before an employee or scientist caught up with her and noticed her emotional state.

Thankfully she made it, swinging into her open office on a heel, then quickly closing and locking the door. She strode to her computer and opened the monitoring program on the machine and began watching the feed.

The test was already underway.

She leaned over the computer chair and watched the screen. She tried to pull her eyes from it, clicking around the small window, but eventually gave up. Still, she felt she needed a distraction. She stood up from the chair and walked over to a plain, cheap side table someone had pushed along one wall of the room. There was a lamp on it, but it wasn't plugged in — each of the offices only had one power line running into them from the large parallel generators they kept upstairs and outside. Her office had a power strip plugged into each of the outlets that broke off from the main line, and she'd filled each of the strip's outlets with her computer, monitor, peripherals, phone charger, and lamp.

There was a television in the room as well, plugged in but mostly sitting dormant in the corner.

The small bureau held nothing besides the old lamp. Each of its drawers were empty, save for one. One drawer near the bottom was locked, and she kept the key in her possession at all times. It was this key she retrieved from her pocket as she reached the bureau. She knelt down, unlocked the door, and pulled out the thick, leather-bound journal from inside.

It was her great-grandfather's journal, passed down to only members of her close family. When she'd expressed interest in her family's history and legacy, it was shown to her.

When she graduated and began her career working toward the same things her father and grandfather had been working toward, it was given to her.

Now it was her most prized possession — a lineage of her family's research, studies, and private accounts, as well as a textbook of scientific discovery and experimentation. It was every question, answer, and thought her great-grandfather — and his son and grandson after him — had found.

And it was the guidebook for the world she was trying to create.

But first, she needed to figure out how to unlock that world's deepest secrets. She needed to find the source of her ancient ancestors' power, the repository of all their knowledge and wisdom. She needed to know how to access it.

More specifically, she needed to know how to *get in*.

She was sitting down the hall from that great repository, the ancient Hall of Records. It was there, hidden beneath the earth, a multi-chambered library of dizzying corridors, rooms, and hallways. Each of those chambers would be filled with the knowledge and source of the Ancients' power. Their secrets, tucked away in a singular, vast archive.

She started to read from the journal, feeling the chill as she remembered the first time she'd encountered her great-grandfather's words in the journal. The hair on the back of her neck rose, goosebumps flooding over the skin on her arms.

It's all real, she thought, the marvel of it still unbelievable, even though she had seen the GPR scans with her own eyes. Even though the Egyptian government had successfully concealed the Great Hall from the outside world, preventing even their own researchers from digging into it, Rachel knew it was there.

She'd had a map drawn up of the hollowed-out spaces under the earth, everything their ground-penetrating radar scans could decipher, including the antechambers their offices were now in. A team of Egyptian government contractors had excavated these first rooms, and she had promptly moved in and established private — and highly classified — offices for her and her closest staff.

She closed her eyes, remembering the rush she'd felt when first stepping down into this ancient antechamber. The feeling of exhilaration, a strength to it she'd never experienced before. She could see her father's and great-grandfather's eyes, the excitement sprawled across each of their faces.

She opened her eyes again and saw the test still streaming on the screen in front of her. Then, with trembling hands, she held the journal up and began to read, her mind automatically translating the German into English.

22

JOURNAL ENTRY

July 8, 1942

Reports have reached me from my men in the field. They have reached the ancient site of the Egyptian structures and have informed me that they have, in fact, found at least one chamber beneath the Great Cat.

Are unsure yet as to the size of this chamber, or if there are others.

Initial excavation has commenced, though completion of the clearing is still a far-off goal.

My main concern at this point is that der Fuehrer will push this side-project into the annals of forgotten history, now that the war has heated. I will, however, do my best to continue to work toward the ultimate end for our race, no matter the outcome.

July 8, 1942

I have finished my translation of Plato's Solon, *working from the original manuscript my men found a decade ago. The tatters have been difficult to parse, though I believe my copy to be a fine rendition. My Attic Greek is strong, but the documents are horribly weathered, as their resting place has allowed them to become quite mangled and challenging.*

It is my dearest hope that this last remaining copy of Plato's work be hidden from sight for as long as time permits — at least until my family completes its journey. Shall it ever be found and examined beneath the light of unworthy scrutiny, it would spell disaster to our mission. My copy, thus, will be sealed and transported, kept merely as an insurance against loss of the original.

The most intriguing passage I have translated tonight, to end the words as written by Plato and told to him by Solon, is thus:

'For there shall forever lie the secrets and powers of this great and mighty host; I have prior explained their capabilities.

'Come the time the Great Hall is found, it shall be opened only by the purest of the pure.'

It seems that der Fuehrer has been correct in his assumption that using Die Glocke as 'The Destroyer,' as a means of seeking out the most pure, was what the Ancients intended. It is written as such in the passages of the Pesach. However, it challenges my scientific mind to know that he is wasting precious energies on the cleansing of those who are clearly not of the purist descent.

We have but little of the Ancients' elixir; to waste it on those not obviously of the Aryan race is to waste it on non-prudent endeavors.

23

GRAHAM

GRAHAM SIGHED. SINCE HE'D BEEN TAKEN FOUR DAYS PRIOR, HE'D BEEN treated reasonably well. *For a prisoner.*

The man who'd come to his door had been an employee of Ms. Rascher's. He was the brute-force grunt-type laborer, the type of man Graham despised. He had always appreciated the use of one's *mind* as a tool over resorting to the use of one's physical prowess.

In his defense, however, the man hadn't laid a hand on Graham. Professor Lindgren had, admittedly, not wanted to let it escalate to physical violence, but he was glad when the man allowed him to step out of his apartment unaided, retaining just a bit of dignity.

The man had driven him to the private airstrip and even opened the door for him, keeping a close eye on his captive but allowing the older gentleman the freedom to board the plane without interference. He was given a seat inside, told to get some rest, then offered food and drink before they'd even taken off.

He'd declined the meal, opting instead to sleep.

Wherever they're taking me, it's not going to be as comfortable as my bed.

He was right about that.

The cell he was in now had been turned into a room, but it was still very much a prison. The rock walls and low ceiling alone were enough to induce claustrophobia in even the most self-confident person, but the lack of adequate lighting and comfortable furniture told him everything he'd needed to know: he was a prisoner. Plain and simple.

Now that he was being interrogated, sitting in a chair in the center of his room, there was no question.

"You sent her the object, did you not?"

Graham Lindgren looked up at the woman, who had previously introduced herself as Rachel Rascher, standing over him. "I did," he said.

There was no hesitation in his voice. No sense of remorse. "You already know that."

The woman nodded. "Of course we know that. But I want to understand *why* you sent it to her. Our labs here could —"

"Your laboratory here is suitable to determine what the object is made of, yes," Graham said. "But it is not a matter of *equipment.* Solving this problem needs something besides technology."

Rascher shook her head, allowing the single lock of graying hair to fall over her eye. She brushed it back over her ear, annoyed, adding it back to the rest of her light brown, straight hair she kept tied up in a large, loose bun.

Graham examined his captor. She was slightly squat, but pretty, in the way a scientist or librarian would be. Simple, nothing striking about her looks, and makeup seemed to be something of an afterthought, if it was there at all.

In another life — and if he were thirty years younger — he might even have been attracted to her.

Now, sitting in a chair in the middle of a cold, dark cellar, the ancient rock walls bleeding its cool condensation that added humidity to the already damp room, all he felt was discomfort.

"Why did you bring me here?" Graham asked. "Why not ask for my help like a normal person?"

The woman smiled. "And you believe that you would have offered to help us willingly?"

"Sure," he said. "It's just theoretical, right? I'm an archeologist, as you know. We deal in hypotheticals. Situations that may or may not have happened. These stories don't *affect* anyone today, at least not directly. We try to put together the pieces of the past, in a way that makes them —"

"That's all we're trying to do here, Mr. Lindgren. That's all we've *ever* been trying to do."

"Yet you had to resort to kidnapping? Why?"

The woman paced in front of him. "We didn't *have* to. We *decided* to. *I* decided to."

Graham raised an eyebrow. "Well, thank you very much. Any chance you'd be willing to let me go?"

"Of course," Rascher said. "After you tell us what you know about the object."

"The *object?"* Graham scoffed. "It's an artifact! Nothing but a piece of rock, something I found in Greenland."

He paused. *Have I said too much? Does she already know where I found it? Of course she does,* he thought. *She's known everything so far. She knows I sent it to Sarah.*

My Sarah. He felt a knot of anxiety growing in his chest. He wondered where she was now. *Has she received the object? Perhaps she doesn't know how to open it.*

His thoughts were once again interrupted by the woman.

"Professor Lindgren," Rascher said impatiently. She paced again. She was thin, with broad shoulders and a small, round face. Her lips and nose were small, but her eyes made up for their size. Graham thought she looked a bit like a character from one of the Disney movies he and Sarah used to watch when she was younger.

Bambi? Maybe that rabbit from that movie? What was her name? Or was it a 'he?'

"*Professor Lindgren,*" she said again, louder this time. "We're running out of time. The first event was a success, even if it was small. The second trial is coming up, and I would hate for you to be a part of that."

"Why?" Professor Lindgren asked. Since he'd been brought here — wherever 'here' was — he'd been trying to piece together what was happening.

After publishing his paper, *Timeaus and Critias: An Alternative Interpretation,* on his personal weblog on the university's server, he'd put his attention toward researching the object that he had mentioned in the research analysis: a round, heavy piece of rock, one face of it protruding outward in a knob-like shape, the opposite face depressed inward.

To most people it was nothing; an odd piece of ancient history that would look nice on a mantle or, if the finder was generous, in a museum display.

To Professor Lindgren, however, it was much more intriguing. The first clue was that the object was hollow, formed out of two separate pieces of rock, molded together with nearly perfect precision so that the two faces came together with an artisanal level of symmetry.

The second thing that seemed remarkable about the object was its final resting place: according to his research, nothing like it had ever been found anywhere in the world, and especially not in Greenland. Only inhabited for the past 4,500 years, the island was considered the least densely populated territory on the planet, and even then a third of its residents lived in a single city, Nuuk.

Graham had been there for a vacation — a trip that Merina, the woman he was dating, liked to refer to as a 'work-cation.' He had never been to the world's largest island, and it had always intrigued him, but as a vacation destination, Greenland was not typically at the top of the list.

They'd spent two weeks there, and Graham had talked her into doing a 'brief' three-day tour of the southwestern areas surrounding Saqqaq, where the earliest known settlers had landed and founded their city. There, he'd been able to talk one of the museum docents into allowing him to explore the caves surrounding Disko Bay, and in one of these he'd found the object.

It had been lying in a pile of broken rock, and without any tools or equipment he hadn't been able to determine whether or not the rock was part of some larger object, but beneath the pile of shards he'd found it. The round, reddish disk. He'd picked it up and immediately knew it was something of value.

Nothing like this should have existed in that corner of the world.

He had been working on his controversial paper about Plato's writings for some time, and this object, while not directly related, seemed to be the perfect addendum.

He turned his attention back to Rachel Rascher. "Why should I be afraid of your 'next event?' What are you planning?"

She frowned.

"You haven't told me anything yet, yet you want my help. What is this all about? The paper I published —"

"The *paper* you published is nothing, Professor Graham. And my team has removed all traces of it from your university's servers. It was controversial, but that's it. A vast overreach on your part."

"Okay, then —"

"The *object* you reference," Rachel continued, "is what we were interested in."

"It's an artifact. Something I found in Greenland, of all places."

"We know. In the paper, you wrote that artifacts '*...such as the one I procured on a recent trip to Greenland prove the validity of assertions made by my predecessors, that our historic genealogy is assumed complete. These pieces of history prove that we know little about where our ancestors called home.*'"

Graham was at first impressed by the woman's ability to recount with perfect accuracy the statement from his paper, but his confusion quickly returned. "Again, it's just an artifact. I haven't even been able to do the proper amount of research into it. I have no idea —"

"It's real, Professor," Rascher said. "It's as old as you suggest in your paper. And it is, as you claimed, *not* from anywhere near Greenland."

"You know where it's from?"

She nodded. "I do. But I *need* that artifact, Professor. That is what this is all about. You could have simply sent it to me, but instead you shipped it — using a courier that could easily have misplaced it — across the world, to your daughter."

He winced. *Sarah*. He'd inadvertently gotten her involved in all of this. He should never have ignored the first email he'd gotten from Rachel.

'Professor Lindgren,' the email began.

'I have been observing your career for some time, and I hope you will grant me the honor of calling myself your fan.

'I have read the paper you published yesterday, and I am intrigued by its premise: that our history is yet to be properly defined. Specifically, I am intrigued by the ideas you put forth regarding the 'messiness of our imperialism,' in that our artifacts have ended up scattered around the world.

'You mention in a footnote an artifact you have recently come across in Greenland. I am vastly taken by the mysterious promise this object seems to imply; would you be open to arranging a time we can meet?'

The email seemed innocent enough. But to Professor Graham it came across like a ransom note: *give us the artifact, or we're coming to get you.* There would have been no reason to suspect that but for three things:

First, the email had no sender. After extracting the email headers — a trick he'd learned long ago from a colleague — he'd found out that the 'sender' had hidden their address behind a wall of server-generated gibberish.

Second, no one had paid any attention at all to the artifact when he'd submitted the paper for peer review. Sure, the 'peer review' had been just the fifteen or so others in his department at the university, as well as a few friends and colleagues he'd come to know and trust, but if anyone should have been keen on discovering more about this 'throwaway' artifact he'd discovered in Greenland, it would have been them.

Finally, whomever had sent the email had done it only a day after he'd published the article, and even then it had only been published online, on one of the university's blogs. It could hardly be considered a worldwide publication, and he knew the web crawlers for the search engines that would spread the content throughout the internet would take at least a week to pick it up.

So he did the only reasonable thing he could think of: he'd sent the artifact to his daughter. She was remarkably brilliant, and if anyone could figure out where, exactly, something like this had originated, without making a fuss about it or trying to publish something in contradiction to his own work, it would be her. He couldn't send it to an estranged colleague in the states, as they might dawdle and take their time with it, and his own laboratory resources were tied up with bigger problems.

Besides that, he felt the pressure of time weighing down on him. Whoever the mysterious emailer was, he got the sense that they weren't interested in negotiating.

At the time of the email, however, he was under no impression that anyone's life was in danger, and certainly not his own. He'd taken his time in sending it to Sarah, only after doing a bit of research on his own.

He'd come to some remarkable, even unbelievable, conclusions, but nothing he'd found seemed to imply that there was anything he needed to worry about.

That was, until, he'd gotten the *second* email from the same encrypted sender:

'Your time is up, Professor. We are coming to get the answer.'

24

BEN

"JULIE, THAT'S NOT A CLUE," REGGIE SAID.

Ben watched his tall, lean friend pacing back and forth in the living room. Julie had explained everything she'd learned, as well as her conversation with Mrs. E.

The cold Alaskan night air whipped around the double-paned windows and in through microscopic cracks, hitting Ben's skin just as the heat from the wood-burning stove met with the air and knocked the frigid out of it.

"It's… all we have."

"It's nothing. Where are we supposed to go? Atlantis?"

Julie shrugged.

"Maybe it's another clue," Ben said. "Maybe wherever Sarah's father is *relates* to Atlantis somehow."

Reggie paced. "Probably so. And it probably relates to that little rock he sent her, too. Still, that's not enough to go on. We can't call up Mr. E and tell him, 'hey boss, we're just going to take the private jet out to Atlantis, look around until we find it.'"

Julie walked farther into the room. "So what do you suggest? You and Ben aren't really doing much to help out."

"That's because of the whiskey," Reggie snapped.

"You mean it's that bad?" Julie asked. "Or you're already drunk?"

"No," Reggie said. "We ran out. Ben and I were using it as 'thinking juice.'"

Ben looked up at his fiancée with a goofy grin on his face. He blinked a few times, trying to make the two Julies standing there turn back into just one. He shrugged, then tried to stand. "I'll — I'll get more."

Julie pushed him back down onto the sofa. "No, I'll do it. You'll just break something."

He laughed but didn't argue. As soon as Julie left the room, Reggie stopped pacing and turned back to Ben. "Okay, buddy. Time to decide."

Ben looked up at him. "Wh — what are you talking about? I thought we'd already decided to go? We just need to figure out *where* —"

"No," Reggie said. "I'm talking about *Julie*. You going to actually marry her, or are you just going to keep bumping it off?"

"Bumping it off?" Ben asked. He tried to focus on Reggie, but his eyes were again failing him.

"Yeah. You were *supposed* to be married a few months ago. Went on a cruise so you could plan it out and everything. Remember? You guys were so excited about it, and —"

"If I *recall*," Ben started, "*you* showed up. You yanked us off the boat and sent us to a floating theme park. And we got shot at, and almost eaten by giant crocodiles. At the *same time*. *That*'s what I remember."

Reggie laughed. "You didn't have to go. Besides, we made it through — so why are you waiting around? Why not just keep the date and get it over with. I keep telling you, buddy, stop waiting around or I'm going to —"

"Shut up, Reggie," Julie called out from the kitchen. "You know I can take you out."

"I've been drinking," he said, still laughing. "That means I'm even stronger. Don't mess with me."

"Wouldn't dream of it, hotshot."

Ben was lost in thought. He had been trying to consider what Julie had told them, about her theory, and now Reggie's comment about getting married, but he felt the alcohol pushing his thoughts around and mashing them together, as if his mind was just a lump of clay. He and Julie had been engaged, and he assumed they still were, but they hadn't talked much about it since the incident in The Bahamas.

He loved her, but he felt like there was a reason they kept drifting apart. Sure, they lived together, but their adventures — and near-death experiences — made things difficult. To them, 'normal' was getting attacked by a killer saltwater crocodile or hanging off a frozen ice cliff in Antarctica, with a Chinese army bearing down on them.

He pushed the thought away and looked back at Reggie. "What did Sarah say her dad was researching, anyway?"

Reggie frowned, thinking. "I don't think she did."

"And she's researching… what?"

Reggie thought for a moment, steadying himself on the edge of the flatscreen television. Ben hoped Reggie hadn't had too much too drink, as the TV wasn't mounted securely onto anything. "Uh, I think she said something about… people? Maybe old people?"

"She's an anthropologist, Reggie."

"Right. So yeah, definitely people."

Ben rolled his eyes. "Why would he send *her* that artifact? It didn't have anything to do with her research, and she's not even an archeologist."

Julie walked back, carrying two glasses of whiskey, an ice cube in each. She handed one to Reggie, then set Ben's on the end table.

"You trying to skimp on me, Jules?" Reggie asked, holding the glass up eye level to his head, noticing that it was less than half full.

"No, just trying to save a little money. You guys drank the cheap stuff already, so we had to start in on the top-shelf stuff."

Reggie flashed Ben a surprised glance. "You have a *top* shelf?"

Ben laughed.

"What were you two just talking about?" Julie asked.

"We were trying to remember what it was that Sarah was studying. Ben was saying that it was weird that Sarah's old man sent *her* the artifact he found."

"Why?"

"Because he's a professional archeologist. He could send it *anywhere* to be examined. Surely there's a big, boring old lab somewhere that just sits around waiting for him to send them stuff to look at under microscopes. So why send it to her?"

"She's his daughter, and she's intelligent. Maybe he —"

"No," Reggie said, "I'm with Ben. It's a little fishy."

"He was trying to alert her, to tell her something. We decided that already, right? That he wrote the letter to try to tell her where he was headed, or at least where he had been?"

Reggie and Ben nodded.

"But he didn't just come out and say it, which tells me someone didn't want him to be broadcasting it around the world."

"Or he didn't *know* where he was going," Reggie said. "Maybe he knew there was a price on his head and he wanted to get a message out, but he wasn't sure exactly where we should start looking for him. So he told her what he knows: there's a weird old rock and some quote that got him thinking about Atlantis. He doesn't know where it is, but maybe he thought that's where they'd take him."

Ben smiled, but Julie was already moving on to another theory. "But what if that quote *was* something more? What if it's code for something else, something he didn't want prying eyes to see? She did say the old man loved that sort of thing."

Reggie lifted off from the corner of the television and started pacing again. "The quote is from Plato, an old dead guy, and he's the one who came up with the myth of Atlantis?"

Ben nodded. "That's what I remember, anyway."

"No," Julie said. "He didn't come up with it. He just wrote it down, and his is the one we quote most often."

"But there are others?" Reggie asked. "I mean, I remember hearing that Plato only wrote down what was told to him, but I didn't realize there were more documents referencing Atlantis."

"Well," Julie began, "from what I just read, there aren't any documented references from *before* Plato's time, but that could simply be because they haven't survived. But there are quite a few people who came *after* Plato who wrote about Atlantis."

Ben squeezed his eyes shut, trying to force back the buzz he was feeling. "But — but that's hardly credible, right? They could have just been rehashing what Plato wrote."

"And I'm sure most of them are," Julie said. "But there are a couple that seem to be reiterating, in their own words, what Plato was saying — but they're not necessarily *based* on Plato's words."

"So they heard the story as well, and wrote it down?" Reggie asked.

"That's what some scholars believe," Julie said. "It's really impossible to tell. But I think Sarah's father was on to something, or at least he thought he was."

"And his captors thought he was, too," Ben added.

"Right. He made a big deal of sending a cryptic letter and an artifact to his daughter, so I think it's worth exploring," she said. "It could end up being nothing, but then again it could —"

Julie's voice died away as Ben felt the cellphone in his pocket vibrate. He pulled it out, noticing that Reggie and Julie were mimicking his movements, each reaching for their own phones.

He lifted the phone up and read the message they'd all just received.

'Pack your bags. We have a destination.'

25

SARAH

NEXT DAY

SARAH HITCHED THE BACKPACK UP OVER HER SHOULDER AND TOOK A DEEP breath. *This is it,* she thought. *Now or never.*

She fumbled with the bundle of papers in her hand and stepped into the security line at the airport, dragging a rolling carryon suitcase behind her. *This airline should have a way to do ticketless boarding,* she thought. She was used to flying with only her phone, using the phone's wallet app to flash the boarding pass code on the screen during TSA security checkpoints and for boarding.

She was also used to having the time to select the perfect flight that allowed her plenty of time on either end of the departure and arrival.

Today, however, she was traveling in a hurry, and she hadn't had the luxury of being able to select her flight. Sawyer International to Chicago O'Hare, then on to Stockholm Arlanda, in order to make a quick check-in at her father's apartment. She'd requested at least that from the CSO team, who'd graciously offered to purchase the flights for her. They'd done it even though it was understood Interpol or the local Stockholm police would likely be at the apartment performing their own investigation.

But she had to try.

She knew her father would have done the same for her. *Start at the beginning of a mystery,* he'd often say, his cryptic phrases underlined by his lopsided grin. *The beginning is the only place.*

For her, the 'beginning' of this mystery was his own apartment. If there was anything there that might clue her in on where he was now, she would find it. She didn't distrust Interpol, but she knew they were merely facilitating the investigation with local, on-the-ground law enforcement. Both parties were performing their duties as established by law, but they weren't personally motivated like she was.

She would only spend a night in Stockholm, then she would be back at the airport and off to the next destination.

That had been the other thing about this trip that was odd — she had no idea where they were ultimately sending her. They'd apparently reached an agreement and told her they needed her input, and then what time to be at the airport. She was grateful for the help, and didn't ask questions. Normally her tickets were purchased by her, funded by her university. Today's travel, however, had been purchased and assigned to her by the CSO, the organization Reggie was working with.

Reggie.

She took another deep breath. *Now or never,* she thought again. *Either see him now or don't see him ever again.*

She wasn't sure where the thought had originated, but she had a feeling it was something her mother would have told her. Her mother was always the pragmatist, constantly reminding her only daughter that time was a luxury no man or woman could afford, and that chasing dreams was something one should spend only free time doing. *'If you want something, get it. Stop daydreaming about it.'*

Sarah had never fully understood her mother's straightforward pragmatism, but she understood the sentiment behind it. Her mom had never been one to waste time doing anything. She was far from lazy, constantly bustling around finishing chores and preparing for the many evenings entertaining her husband's invited dinner guests.

Sarah had grown up with a father who was constantly chasing his dreams, following one whim after another and somehow stringing together one massive success after another until he'd built a career around it. She'd also grown up with a mother who tried her best to make their home — wherever it may have been each season — feel steady, constant. She strove for security and consistency where her husband strove for excitement and satisfaction. They were polar opposites in many ways, but absolutely perfect for each other nonetheless.

The TSA staffer hurriedly pulled her forward with an impatient wave of his hand. She shuffled her ID, boarding pass, shoulder bag, and carryon suitcase, hoping the man would get the point and offer assistance.

He didn't. Instead, he huffed and looked around, clearly annoyed.

"Sorry," she said. "I don't usually go through security, they typically let me use my —"

"Just your ID, please," the man said, interrupting. "Then your boarding pass. One at a time."

He held out a fat, tired hand. She placed the ID in it and he grabbed it. She wasn't able to fully remove her own hand from his closing fist as it withdrew, and she felt the cold, clammy sweat of the overworked and underpaid government employee.

"Boarding pass," he said.

She handed it over, and waited for it to click and light up the green light on the display meter above his station. When it did, she hurried forward and started the agonizing process of waiting in line behind a gaggle of anxious travelers removing shoes and belts and laptops, feeling rushed even though she had a solid ten minutes before she could resume her pace to her gate.

Ten minutes before I get to the gate, and another thirty before we board. Then another ten or so hours before I see him again.

She wasn't sure if she was excited to see the man again or if they would pick up right where they'd left off. *Scared, angry, hurt, pained.*

In love.

26

SARAH

She picked up her pace and reached the departure gate after fifteen minutes of walking and riding in one of the many intra-airport shuttles. After waiting twenty minutes at the gate, she boarded and sat down.

She considered sleeping while the rest of the passengers boarded — she had a window seat, so there wouldn't be any reason for her to get up until they landed again — but decided instead to take a look at the object her father had sent her. It was in her shoulder bag, which she had stowed underneath her seat. She reached for it and withdrew the small, round artifact.

The object was just as she'd remembered. Clay or ceramic, fired to an incredible hardness that had allowed it to stand up to the elements for an untold amount of years. Round, with a protrusion in one side that carried through to the opposite face. She held it up to the light streaming in from the airplane's window, studying it. She hadn't even thought to inspect it since hearing of her father's disappearance, but there wasn't much else to see.

Still, she rolled it back and forth in her hands, impressed at the artistry and craftsmanship. It was a simple circle, but it seemed to be perfectly formed, as if it had been created with a clay wheel. The knob-like protrusion on the top and the indentation on the bottom of the object were also formed with delicate precision.

The only reason she agreed with her father's assessment that the object was ancient was the slight deterioration along the edges. She could see a few areas where the otherwise perfect circle edges had been chipped away, and the weathering discoloration on the faces added more intrigue.

She reached up and flicked on the overhead light, then brought the object closer to her face. She examined the indentation on what she was calling the 'bottom' of the object, rubbing her thumb around the inside of it.

There.

There was something odd about the indentation, and she brought it still closer to her eye. A faint line appeared, a slight score in the ceramic all the way around the inside of the indentation.

She pushed her thumb harder into the indentation, then twisted the object around in her hand. She felt something click, then saw the crack in the ceramic widen slightly.

No way, she thought. *It actually opens.*

Apparently the object wasn't just a solid piece of rock or ceramic. It was some sort of storage container, and she had accidentally discovered how to open it. She held her thumb steady and continued twisting until another crack widened along the center of the outer edge of the circle and she could get her finger inside.

It came apart in her hands. It was a screw mechanism — threads ran along the inside of the two pieces, and pushing the indentation in and twisting the two halves apart did the trick. Something from inside the object fell into her lap, but she hardly noticed. She was staring at the two pieces of rock that had just opened in front of her.

Unbelievable. She was in awe. Whatever the origin of this artifact, it was using technology discovered *centuries* after its time. She didn't know the exact history of the screw and screwdriver, but she was dead certain there had been no screwed-together ceramics from the pre-bronze era.

There was still the consideration that the artifact was a fake, but then what was the point? A fancy, ancient-looking storage container didn't seem to be a useful application of someone's clay-forming artistry. Plus, she doubted her father had somehow stumbled across a fabricated artifact in the sparse backcountry of Greenland.

This is real, she thought, getting more excited. *And it* means *something. Something significant.*

Her father had once again given her a mystery to solve.

Only then did she remember the object that had been hidden inside. She reached to her lap and retrieved it. It was a necklace, a small rock hanging from a thin silver chain. The chain seemed to be a standard sterling silver piece, something easily purchased online or at any big-box store. The stone also seemed to be nothing extraordinary. Off-white color, with hints of glossier specks, and semi-smoothed on one side, as if it had been broken off a larger chunk of rock that had once been exposed on one side to moving water. She recognized it as opal, her birthstone.

She rolled it around in her hand, feeling the cool, smoothed edges that sank into the rougher section. The entire stone was only dime-sized, insignificant. It was an odd gift, but then again there was little about her father and his affinity for eccentricities that she wouldn't describe as 'weird.'

As she held the present, she remembered the postscript of his letter:

'P.S.: consider it an early birthday gift.'

She now knew that the artifact was merely the delivery mechanism for his *actual* gift: the necklace and the tiny stone on it.

Odd, she thought. *This means Dad knew the object could be opened. He put this in here for me to find.*

It was a fun way to deliver a birthday present, but there were still too many unanswered questions. *Why put it in a priceless artifact? Why send me this two months* before *my birthday?* It was August, and her birthday was at the end of October. *What's he trying to tell me?*

And, above all, *where in the world is he?*

She sighed, gently unfolding the silver chain and placing it around her neck, then clasping it together. She slowly slid the stone down to the center of the chain, then tucked it beneath her shirt. Sarah had never been much of a jewelry wearer; she found the trinkets and accessories more of a pain than an asset. But a gift was a gift, and she wasn't about to refuse a missing father his desire to please his daughter.

She returned the artifact to the box she'd packed it in, careful to make sure the two layers of bubble wrap were protecting the object. It was an old habit she'd learned from her father, and she heard his voice echoing in her mind: *'never can be too careful with things you know little about.'* She closed her eyes, imagining his stern reminder to treat his collection of historic artifacts and treasures he kept in his office with respect and courtesy.

The memory pained her. She felt no closer to solving the mystery of her missing father, and to make things worse, she had no idea if the objects he had given her were meant to be harmless fun, from one scientist to another, or something more meaningful:

A clue.

27

RACHEL

SHE SAT DOWN IN HER EXECUTIVE CHAIR, SWIVELING AROUND SO SHE WAS face to face with the main display on her desk. She tapped a few keys, then watched as the small window grew to fill her screen.

She could see her father, lying on the gurney, the flashes of light temporarily blinding the camera as the bell heated up the contents of the mysterious compound it held within. Her father bucked and fought against the straps holding him to the hospital bed, his strength surprising considering the state he was in.

He knew what was happening; he was, after all, one of the original project managers she'd hired. Her father was a die-hard believer in the project, and he had made possible nearly everything she had achieved. He knew exactly what this was.

But that didn't mean he wasn't against it. She and her father had been at odds over the past year; both father and daughter wanting to approach the problem from completely different sides. Her father wanted to take more time, to allow the scientists time to complete their synthesis of the compound and recreate it in a scalable way. He had wanted to move slower, to push their beliefs out to the masses in a controlled way and let the effects of social media and the speed of modern life set the pace.

She, on the other hand, had pushed for a rapid launch of their technology, using fear and terror as a tactical advantage. She argued for the historic truth of their experiments, feeling that since their cause had been given to them millennia ago, their cause was true. She wanted to expand their research, testing more and more of the population every year, and in order to do that she needed to have a copy of the compound that was as reliable as the original.

She wasn't a killer, after all. She wasn't some mad scientist hell-bent on world domination. She wanted the world to know the truth, and she wanted to increase the reach of her tests.

But at the end of the day, she wanted to *save* the world. Population was already increasing at an alarming rate, and most experts believed the growth rate of the human population was already unsustainable.

To Rachel it was obvious — the world was never meant to host so many people. The Ancients and their civilization — *her* civilization — had planned for every contingency, including overpopulation. And to Rachel, that solution was as elegant as it was effective. Her silent partners didn't want the exact same thing, but their interests were aligned enough at these early stages that their support was all but guaranteed.

Plus, she had no interest in *informing* them that their end goals were not the same.

The chemical compound — whatever it was — allowed the Ancients to keep their race pure, to test any hopeful members of their growing cult and deem them worthy of joining or worthy of death. The test was perfect, infallible and trustworthy, and Rachel had the genetic code to back it up. While her team was still hard at work decoding the exact makeup of the hereditary traits that were passed down through the ages from the pure Ancients, she had reason to believe that the 'Code of the Pure,' as she liked to call it, was a DNA match with the Ancients of at least 99.99999% accuracy. 'Five nines accurate,' her geneticists described the material, referring to the five nines found after the decimal place.

Her team was currently working to sequence the rest of the DNA in the pure lineage. Only then would she be able to make an accurate analysis of the exact makeup of the 'pure' genetic material — the material in the human genetic code that defined the purity of the individual.

Her father had come close to finding this answer, but he had credited too much to his own grandfather. He had relied too heavily on the research done by Nazi Germany, by the SS scientists and researchers who worked for Heinrich Himmler and, ultimately, Adolph Hitler. Her father had believed the papers and research produced and subsequently hidden by the Nazis; he had assumed their studies and findings were accurate.

He believed that his own grandfather, Sigmund Rascher, had been close to finding a suitable compound with which to test individuals. His government had used the compound in the gas chambers in the concentration and death camps, and while it had proven to be an effective poison, it hadn't given the Nazis any reliable data as to the purity of the many races tested within those camps.

In short, the project had failed. Nazi propaganda and a worldwide, century-long rebranding of the Nazi's experimentations had led the world to believe that their testing of the purity of the races was merely a misguided effort to eradicate the Jewish and other 'non-Aryan' races from the planet.

But Rachel knew the truth. She had her great-grandfather's private journal, a piece once thought lost to history. She knew what her great-grandfather's struggle had been, what he was worried about, what he had intended to accomplish. Hitler was a monster, but according to Rachel he hadn't been *all* wrong — the world was a place that needed policing, the human effort one that needed leadership. The ancients had established their stronghold amidst many other prosperous civilizations, and had quickly asserted their authority and power. They had held their rightful place as the dominant race for centuries, and only because of a freak accident had their place been usurped.

Rachel pushed the window on her screen to another monitor, this one larger and providing a better view of what was happening in Room 23. She watched as her father bucked and fought against the straps, trying to break free from the terror he was currently experiencing.

The test was odd in that it affected the psychology of the individual as much as it affected the physiology. Subjects experienced hallucinations, some even so strong that they believed the walls, the floor or ceiling, or even other people in the room, were melting. The hallucinogenic drug gave subjects the impression that the entire room was somehow on fire, an inferno so hot everything around them was liquefying. The psychological effect was only strengthened by the *physical* effects — the subject was, after all, being poisoned. The compound, converted from a liquid to a gas by the heat radiating through the bell, penetrated the skin and the heat blistered any available flesh. The effects were horrendous but temporary.

Either the patient lived or died, and if they lived the blistered regions of skin would heal and the wounds would disappear.

And knowing that her pure lineage meant she was already directly linked to the Ancients — and that she didn't need to go through the tests herself — was the just the affirmation she'd needed. It had given her the drive to continue, the stamina to make it through the hell of testing her entire staff.

But it hadn't been quite enough to get her through this.

She started to cry once again, feeling the tears, the searing heat of the saline as it rolled slowly down her cheek. She watched the screen, unable to see but unable to ignore it, as her father fought against the very thing he had sworn his life to. The bell was a cruel and unyielding dictator, unbending. Her father was a true German, a man who looked and acted the part — a man with ambition, drive, steadfastness, and determination. A man who wanted nothing but success, and showed up early for it and refused to settle for less than the best.

But, like the Nazi party and its scientists before him, her grandfather hadn't realized that *German* was in itself nothing but a bastardization of the race the Ancients had designed and perpetuated. To be German meant one was *from Germany,* not necessarily *as pure as the Ancients,* and a person's physical appearance sometimes was more of a coincidence than a determining factor.

For her blond-haired, blue-eyed father, Germany was a homeland, a dream, and a goal. But to Rachel, it was a speed bump. Germany was simply a diversion, a sideshow to the ultimate goal of creating a pure, *ancient*-worthy race of humanity.

A humanity that would eventually prove its worth, and one that she would potentially lead.

Rachel focused on her father's face, already seeing the welting and bruising caused by the serum.

No, she thought. *Please, don't be true.*

She knew what was going to happen, but she hated to admit it, even to herself. She'd had her suspicions, known for many years that her father had been the illegitimate product of a German-born man and a foreign woman. Thanks to his decision to marry within the race, however, the purity in Rachel Rascher's bloodline had been restored. She would have passed the test, but she was afraid her father would not.

He threw his head up and back down upon the gurney's headrest multiple times, each time more forceful, until he lay back down. Still.

No, she thought.

The test was inevitable. The serum was infallible. She told herself this fact, reminded herself of it over and over again.

Still, she couldn't stop watching the screen. Her father lay still, motionless, unmoving on his bed.

Or his deathbed.

No, she thought, before the thought could infect her mind. *He could still be pure enough.*

But she knew the truth. She'd known it all her life, and it was the one thought that haunted her for her entire professional career. She knew what the test results would be, and she wanted to ignore it and just move on.

But her eyes were riveted. She was a researcher, a learner, a scientist. She wanted to know, to *see,* what happened. She was analyzing it, studying it. She knew that the compound the ancients had created was working its magic, forming thousands of heat-induced clots beneath his skin, simultaneously working to test his blood for purity. He would be fully catatonic by now, experiencing a completely different reality than what was actually transpiring. Most likely, from his perspective, the walls were melting, the floor and ceiling turning to liquid and dripping down around him.

But from her perspective, the room was silent, quiet and unmoving.

Her father was sleeping, soundly and immobile. She didn't care about what he might be feeling, or what his subconscious mind was telling him about the external world.

The only thing she cared about was whether or not her father was going to wake up.

28

GRAHAM

Professor Graham Lindgren tried to swallow the fava beans, but it was difficult. In his decades of experience traveling the world, Graham had eaten all sorts of odd and eclectic dishes, from just about every corner of the globe. Things like raw cow spine and guinea pigs on a stick were what he called 'cultural delicacies,' devouring them with the veracity of a proper local.

There were a few things, however, that made him draw the line. Mushrooms, of any sort or shape, were one of them. The other thing was peas.

And fava beans, as far as he was concerned, were the same thing as peas.

The dish that had been served to him was called ful medames, essentially a porridge of mashed fava beans with some accoutrements — in this case onions and peppers — served with hard-boiled eggs. It had a protein-rich, earthy taste to it, which would have been otherwise palatable if not for the consistency.

He forced the bean mash down his throat, trying to appreciate the flavor. The dish had been cooked well, and he was grateful of that. It had been delivered as a side, alongside fois gras, which he had always been a fan of. He'd finished the fois gras and bread first, then turned his sights — and taste buds — to finishing the beans.

Something in him refused to let the food go to waste. It was frustrating, but he couldn't shake it. He was a prisoner here, and yet the people retaining him were doing everything they could to make his stay comfortable.

They'd even given him a better pillow after he'd complained about the tissue-thick sleeve of polyester he'd had to sleep on the first three nights.

Ms. Rascher sat in front of him, across the table from her captive. She had done nothing to her appearance, but her large, bright eyes and single strand of gray hair were as unassumingly attractive as they had been before. They were sitting in his 'room,' the rock-walled cell he'd been thrown into, but a table and chairs had been brought in and placed in the center of the room.

If he wasn't mistaken, it seemed as though his captors were interested in his overall comfort level.

"Seems like a bit much for a lowly prisoner," he said.

Rachel Rascher made a face. "A *prisoner*? You are a distinguished guest of my department, Professor."

"Your department? And if I'm a *guest*, I'm assuming I am free to leave?"

"You are free to leave," she said. "Once we have the object."

He waited.

"And my department is part of the Egyptian government."

"The *Egyptian government* is holding me hostage?" Graham asked.

She shook her head, smiling. "No. As I said, you are not a hostage. And the government has nothing to do with this — experiment."

"Care to elaborate?"

Graham swallowed another bite. He found that talking helped him focus on something other than the dirt-tasting retch of the fava dish in front of him.

"My *department* is the Ministry of Antiquities of Egypt."

"We're in Egypt?"

She nodded.

He looked around. "*Where* in Egypt?"

She ignored the follow-up question. "And I am the head of the department."

"*Minister* Rachel Rascher?"

She nodded.

"A German?"

"Good guess," she said. "Yes, I am German, but only by birth."

He frowned.

"I lived in the United States for five years, then thirteen around Europe, but spent my adult years here in Egypt. My lineage goes through modern Germany and can be traced back to the Grecian region."

"And you want this 'object' that I found. In Greenland."

"Yes, exactly."

"What if I don't have it?"

She grinned. "I *know* you don't have it, Professor. That's why you're still here."

"So you're holding me here, against my will, until I get it for you?"

She shrugged. "Or until it comes to us."

"You think my —" he stopped himself. "You believe that someone's just going to deliver this thing right to you?"

"I believe *your daughter* is looking for you. And since you sent the artifact to her, yes. I believe she will bring it right back."

Graham dropped his head. *If only I'd known.*

"Professor," Rachel said, softly. "There is a way you can help us. A way that might prevent anything... *unfortunate* from happening to you or your daughter."

He felt his body tense. The involuntary response of a father, learning his daughter was in possible danger, was too much to hide. At the same time, he forced his mind to relax. *If there's something I can do,* he thought, *I'll do it. Anything.*

"Tell me what was inside the object."

He shifted his head sideways. "You know more about this mysterious object than you've been letting on."

"Professor," she said, taking another bite, "tell me what was inside."

He sighed. Took a deep breath. "Nothing."

"Nothing?" Rachel asked.

"Nothing," he said. "Sorry. It was empty. Once I figured out how to open it, I was excited, but when I twisted it open I saw there was nothing inside."

He wasn't telling the truth, of course — there *had* been something inside the object when he'd finally gotten it open. It was a rock, nothing but a pebble. A rough-edged, whitish pebble.

He recognized it as opal, his daughter's birthstone, so he'd made a necklace out of it, put it back inside the artifact, and sent the whole thing to Sarah.

But Graham knew the woman wasn't looking for a piece of opal. She had hinted at something else — a substance, or a chemical compound of some sort — hiding inside the artifact. Since there was nothing of the sort inside, Graham was technically telling the truth. What the woman and her team was looking for had most certainly *not* been inside the artifact.

He hoped that by proving to the woman that he knew exactly how to open the ceramic artifact that he could also prove to her he was telling the truth, but his mind raced back to the emails she had sent. *She's not going to accept that,* he thought.

"Not even..." she stopped herself. "Are you sure?"

He frowned. "Pretty damn."

"Well then," she said. "I guess we're done here."

"We — we're done?"

"Forgive me," Rachel said, pushing her chair back and standing up. "I meant *I'm* done here. You, on the other hand, are not done here at all."

29

BEN

*A*NOTHER PLANE, BEN THOUGHT. *I REALLY SHOULD HAVE SETTLED DOWN somewhere closer to civilization.*

Ben hated flying. There was a lack of control he felt whenever he boarded an aircraft, and it didn't matter how large or small the craft was — he was equally intimidated. The larger aircrafts reminded him that he was defying the laws of physics, hurtling through the air in a fuel-filled metal tube. And the smaller vehicles he'd flown on — Cessnas, helicopters, and the like — were just as bad. He could feel every movement, every whip of the wind and churn of the turbulence. He could feel the unsettling force of acceleration, knowing that he was tens of thousands of feet above a hard, unforgiving earth.

So, even though Mr. E had sprung for the best-of-the-best, a commercial-quality Learjet 85, decked out in luxury and high-end tech, Ben hardly felt better. The takeoff and ascent had been smooth, but he had gripped the armrest tightly, wishing Julie had sat in the seat next to him. She'd opted for a lounger toward the back, assuring him that the flight would be more comfortable if he'd just learn to relax.

He'd responded to her unhelpful comment by ordering and slamming two shots of whiskey before they'd even taxied across the tarmac at the Anchorage airport. The 'thinking juice' did little to calm his nerves, and it was only after an hour of flight time that he started to feel a bit more at ease.

The jet was a recent purchase by Mr. E's communications company, and allowing the Civilian Special Operations team to borrow it from the corporate office would be a tax write-off for him. The CSO often enjoyed the perks of Mr. E's vast wealth, as they were somewhat of an experimental organization, and Mr. E was greatly interested in proving its worth. Military representatives made up just under half of the organization's board, with Mr. E and his wife, Ben, Julie, and Reggie making up the rest. The military representatives wanted a way to source the projects that were either too public, too risky, or too specialized for the US military to get involved. If it wasn't something that could be appropriately expensed in a line item for Congress' scrutiny, it would fall under the category of 'black ops' or 'table for later.'

The CSO had been set up to handle the 'table for later' items. Civilians, trained to be researchers who knew their way around a sticky situation, were perfect for the projects the US government didn't want to mess around with.

Mr. E had already invested heavily in the group's success, and the results showed. Ben's cabin had been expanded, the two-level wing nearing completion. There would be room for the entire team to stay on-campus, complete with a conference room, workout facility, and hot tub.

The last had been a request from Ben, and Mr. E had apparently thought it prudent to honor the request of the man who owned the land.

The jet was brand-new, and Mr. E's company hadn't even gotten to use it yet. The jet came with a pilot, copilot, and three flight attendants. The onboard staff doubled the size of the passenger manifest.

Ben, Julie, and Reggie were also joined by Mr. E's wife, who sat sprawled back in a reclined seat across the aisle from Ben. He looked over at the gigantic woman and smiled.

"Been awhile," he said.

"It has," Mrs. E said, nodding. "I believe it was over a month ago."

"You came up to the cabin, but didn't stay long."

"Yes," she said. "My husband has me running around, going to business meetings and shaking hands."

"Sounds like fun," Ben said. If there was anyone he knew was more uncomfortable around executive types than he was, it was Mrs. E. The woman was a strong-willed, physically imposing person, and he had seen her in action more than once and was always glad she was on his team. But she hated public appearances, business dealings, and the forced nature of playing a role.

She laughed. "Yes, about as fun as getting shot at."

"You've been shot at plenty of times, E," Ben said. "I'd bet you'd take getting shot at over handling your husband's affairs any day."

She grinned. "Sure, yes. That is actually true. But he does even worse than I do with public appearances. It is quite the irony that he has been able to build such a successful company without ever stepping foot inside of it."

Ben knew that to be true — Mr. E was a recluse, agoraphobic and unwilling to step foot in a public place. Ben had never shaken the man's hand, and any conversations with him had been by way of video chat or conference call. He conducted business remotely, and anything that had to be done in person was either done at his house or through his proxy — Mrs. E.

"Glad you were able to make it," he said. "I like having you in the field."

"I like being there," she said. "Although I must admit that this operation has me feeling a bit unsteady."

"Unsteady?"

She nodded. "We are going after a person, or persons, who we know nothing about. Further, we are not even sure Sarah's father was kidnapped. He sent a cryptic message to his daughter, then turned up missing, but there is just a severe lack of information."

"That's why *we're* the ones going," Ben said. "It's not a military operation, and Interpol won't get further involved without more information. If anyone's going to help Sarah, it's us."

"I know."

"Are you saying we shouldn't go?" he asked.

She threw her head back and laughed. "Hardly, Harvey. I am *excited* to go. Dr. Lindgren deserves our help. I am just pointing out that this mission may not be as fun as we all hope."

"You mean there won't be anything to shoot at."

"Something like that, yes," she said.

He smiled back at her. "Well, if there's anything I'm sure of, it's that the CSO seems to *always* find trouble. We may not have been able to sneak any guns overseas this time around, but Reggie will be able to find some decent stuff for us once we're on the ground. Whatever we run into out there, I think we'll be ready."

He waved over a flight attendant and ordered another whiskey from the man. When it arrived, he took a long, deep sip. He turned again to Mrs. E, who was drinking her own beverage — diet tonic water with a squirt of lemon.

"So," he said. "You finally going to explain to all of us where we're going?"

30

JULIE

THE LAST DAY HAD BEEN A WHIRLWIND FOR JULIE. MRS. E HAD SENT THEM all a message — *'Pack your bags. We have a destination.'* — and had informed them that there would be a company jet waiting in Anchorage for them by the next morning.

Mrs. E herself would join them on the mission, and while en route to their destination she would fill them in on the details. Apparently she had discovered something of interest while researching the work of Professor Graham Lindgren, and it was actionable enough to get them all a first-class ticket to wherever they were heading now.

Julie stretched. She had no way of knowing how long the flight would be, but she was hoping there would be time to sleep a bit after Mrs. E's briefing. She wondered how Ben was doing. He had always been a horrible flier, but he'd gotten better in the two years she'd known him.

Flying was part of life, she'd told him. In the modern age, air travel was usually the best way to get somewhere, especially when you lived in the Alaskan backcountry.

He'd just shrugged, trying to be stubborn but not having anything valuable to say.

When they'd boarded the plane, she'd made a beeline for a seat at the back, as she knew it was capable of reclining all the way back. Ben chose one near the wing so that his peripheral view of the shrinking ground would be blocked, but she knew he would be struggling until they reached cruising altitude.

And unless he gets alcohol into his system, he'll probably be struggling until we land.

Now that they were at their cruising altitude and the team had gotten an hour of sleep, she stood up and turned around to see what Ben was up to. He was laughing and joking with Mrs. E, and Julie walked up and sat in the seat behind her.

"You finally going to explain to all of us where we're going?" Julie heard him ask.

Mrs. E nodded, standing up. "Where is Reggie?" she asked.

Ben and Julie looked around, only now noticing that their teammate was nowhere to be found. A few seconds passed, then Julie heard the click of a lock and the restroom door swinging open.

Reggie had a pained expression on his face, but he walked over to the group and plopped down across from Julie. "Good God, Ben," he said. "That swill you forced me to drink last night is *not* agreeing with me."

Ben laughed. "You sure it was the whiskey, or was it how *much* you drank of it?"

He made a face at Ben, but didn't respond.

"Mrs. E was just going to tell us where it is we're flying," Ben said. "I personally hope it's nowhere near Wyoming, Montana, Brazil, or The Bahamas."

Julie smiled, but she felt the terror of what had happened in each of those locations coming back to haunt her. That she had survived until now was something remarkable.

"Don't forget Philadelphia," Reggie said.

"And Antarctica," Mrs. E added.

"Okay," Ben said, "so the list of possible vacation destinations for us is quickly diminishing. What does that leave?"

Mrs. E opened up her tablet and swiped around until she landed on a note she'd typed. She was quiet for a moment, then she clicked on an image, enlarging it to fit across her screen.

"Our destination is well away from our prior destinations, I can assure you," Mrs. E said. "Anyone recognize this place?"

Julie leaned over the seat back and stared down at the tablet Mrs. E was holding. On the screen there was a satellite image, zoomed in and crisply focused on an island that sat alone in the middle of a deep blue ocean. The island was circular, rounded at the edges, but it wasn't a solid mass of land. It looked like a bowl that had been pushed down into the water until only part of its rim was showing.

Mrs. E spread two fingers over the image, making it even larger still, and Julie could then see the faint outline of another, smaller circular island submerged just beneath the surface of the water.

"Beats me," Ben said.

"An island somewhere," Reggie said. "In the ocean."

Julie shook her head. "Wow, Reggie. *Quite* the observation."

"It *is* an island," Mrs. E said. "And it is our destination."

Ben groaned. "I'm not a fan of islands."

Julie nodded. "I have to agree with him," she said. "After Paradisum, I think I'll stay away from Caribbean destinations for a bit."

Paradisum had been a floating theme park off the coast of The Bahamas, and Julie and Ben had been on vacation in the Caribbean when Reggie had dragged them out to the island. There they had dodged saltwater crocodiles, jellyfish, and plenty of bullets, and the entire time had been a blur of fear and terror.

"Well, this island is not in the tropics at all," Mrs. E said.

"And I'm assuming it's not off the coast of Alaska, either," Ben said. "Meaning we're in for a long flight."

Mrs. E nodded. "Total travel time, including layovers, refueling, and rest stops, is over forty-eight hours."

Julie's jaw dropped. "*Forty-eight hours?* That's *two days*."

"This place is on the other side of the world," Reggie said. "Where are we going, E?"

Mrs. E pinched the image closed and swiped over to the next picture in the series. Another satellite image, this one of a city, many of the buildings white, scattered across wide, steep cliffs.

"Anyone?" she asked.

"Somewhere in the Mediterranean?" Ben asked.

Mrs. E snapped a finger. "Exactly! Greece, actually. Or rather, an island off the coast of Greece."

"That's where we're going?" Julie asked. "It looks beautiful."

"It is a huge tourist destination," Mrs. E said. "But we believe Dr. Lindgren's father is there somewhere."

"What's it called?" Reggie asked.

"This, my friends," Mrs. E said, "is the famous island of Santorini."

31

GRAHAM

Graham paced around the interior of the room, trying to learn everything he could about his surroundings. He had examined every square inch before, finding nothing useful. There were no telltale artifacts of modern human innovation, like drill filings, screws, or leftover building materials. Besides the furniture and the lighting, there was nothing modern about the space.

The walls, as he'd noticed before, were hewn from rock, three of the four sides carved out of what appeared to be a singular block of granite. The other wall was bricked together using smaller, but still substantial, stones. They fit with a precision that excited his inner archeologist, as they told him just a bit about his prison.

I'm in an ancient tomb, he thought. *Or at least a temple or important structure of some sort.*

All ancient peoples, whether they were from the Eastern or Western Hemisphere, north or south, no matter which out-of-the-way space they called home, all shared one important characteristic:

They were all human.

And to Professor Lindgren, who had spent his life and career studying the remains of human ingenuity, had come to understand that to be human meant to be efficient.

And efficiency meant taking care to spend effort where it would be best used, not where it wouldn't matter in the long run.

The pyramids, both at Giza and in Central and South America, were a perfect example of this efficiency. So were the ruins of Ancient Rome, Greece, and Angkor Wat. The ancient wonders of the world were just that for a reason — they had stood against the evil stresses of mother nature and prevailed. They had proven that human drive and motivation were strong enough characteristics to hold up to the greatest oppressor the world had ever known: time.

Graham Lindgren had spent every waking moment of his life exploring these fascinations, and he knew that for the vast majority of human history, societies used whatever resources they could to better their lives, but they cared little for the long-term functionality of the structures they built. Dwellings and communal gathering places, whether the longhouses of the American Indians or the great halls of the Vikings, these buildings were well-crafted structures that utilized sound materials, but were otherwise temporary. They needed constant repair, and even a few years of ignorance could render them utterly useless.

More important places, on the other hand, were given a bit more care. Churches and other religious landmarks, cemeteries, castles, and guideposts were formed from stone and other sturdy materials, meant to last centuries or longer.

But the holiest of places, the most important of all, like the grand cathedrals and colosseums, the temples dedicated to gods and saints, and statues and shrines erected for purposes only now beginning to be understood, were built to last. These formations were meant to not only be impressive. They were meant to live forever.

Graham had stood inside the inner chambers of the Great Pyramid of Giza, atop the temple at Chichen Itza in the Yucatán, and walked the ruins of countless other archeological sites. He'd felt the weight of the presence of thousands of souls who had come before him, each equally in reverent awe of what their fellow man had created.

Now, standing in a dimly lit cellar-type space, Graham felt a similar weight. This weight was, admittedly, probably due to the fact his life was in the hands of a strange, unknown woman and her whims, but he sensed that there was more to the space than that.

For instance, he'd noticed the walls immediately upon entering. Even in the dim light he could tell that three of the walls were solid, single-stone behemoths. That was rare anywhere in the world. Bedrock tended to be porous, and therefore a conglomeration of many different pieces of rock. But it was expensive and difficult to haul in huge, thick stone slabs, as they had to be quarried and cut to size, then sanded and smoothed, as well as dragged a certain distance to their final location. Even then, they had to be placed with precision, as moving a multi-ton piece of rock wasn't an easy task.

In addition, the fourth wall, made up of smaller bricks of the same material, was equally intriguing to Graham. The bricks seemed to have been cut to purpose, as if the builders had known all along what the use for them was going to be. And they fit together better than any modern-day building materials. He guessed that he couldn't even have slid a piece of paper between them. From what he could tell there was no mortar holding the bricks together, either.

Fascinating, he thought for the hundredth time. It was certainly fascinating, but it didn't give him any answers. Although it was uncommon, the style of building was nothing unique. Ancient, but not unique. He could be anywhere in the world. There were plenty of civilizations he knew of that had perfected the art of masonry.

The Inca and Maya of South and Central America. The Egyptians, of course. And the Minoans, Sumerians, Indians, and Chinese — they even had a 1500-mile-long wall to prove it.

Just looking around gave him no clues, so he broadened his search parameters: *My captors.*

The man who'd brought him here had dark features: black hair, dark caramel-colored skin, and deep-set eyes, with bushy eyebrows that seemed to haunt the man's face. Graham would have guessed he was middle eastern, perhaps Israeli, but he could have been from anywhere around the Mediterranean. He could have been convinced the man was Basque, which would have opened up Graham's interpretation to include other Spanish-influenced regions — the Americas, Indonesia, the Caribbean.

He could be from anywhere.

But the woman, Rachel Rascher, was a polar opposite. She had lighter brown hair. Long and straight, where the man's had been slightly curled, and her eyes seemed to be bright and poised. She'd told him she was German, and she looked it. Germanic features, possibly even Scandinavian, with possibly a bit of Italian somewhere in her ancestry.

She'd told him she worked for the Egyptian government, but she didn't look Egyptian, or even remotely middle-Eastern.

Again, Professor Lindgren was at a loss. These days it was nearly impossible to tell a person's heritage from just their looks.

Her name was German — Rascher, from ancient Saxony — but that only told him that her parents or grandparents somewhere along her lineage had married into a German name.

There was a table in the corner of the room. He'd pushed it there after he and Rachel had eaten dinner together earlier, but it was now empty. The bed and chair next to it were the only other things in the room.

He took a deep breath. He'd spent many hours inside of small spaces such as this — he'd built a career around it. But he'd never been held inside of one as a prisoner. He wasn't sure how he felt about it; he wasn't sure if his senses were on high alert, ready to try to build a narrative from only the smallest threads, or if his analytical mind had somehow been compromised because of it.

He shivered. *It's chilly in here.*

He suddenly realized something. Perhaps it was more data, more information he could use to build a narrative of where, exactly, he was. Or perhaps it was nothing.

It's cold in here.

He hadn't noticed it before, but it was definitely chilly. It hadn't changed, either, and he hadn't heard or felt any sort of change in the pressure inside the space, which meant there probably wasn't any climate control system running.

Which means...

He stood straighter. It wasn't much — it still didn't tell him anything useful, but it was a piece of the puzzle. It was better than nothing. He looked again at the walls, the three that were fashioned from single stones, and the fourth that was crafted from perfectly sized bricks. It was obvious this was a man-made structure, and it was obvious this place had been made long ago, and that it had been built to last for a long time.

And now his experience and education were putting the pieces together for him in his subconscious, sending their message up through his brain into consciousness.

He thought about what he knew, what he was hiding from Rascher. What he had tried to convey to Sarah.

They would eventually figure it out — whoever this woman was, she was not going to give up easily. But he hoped he had at least bought Sarah enough time.

Time to figure out my puzzle, he thought. He was frustrated, scared. He wondered if it would have been better to simply give her the solution instead of the clues, but at the time he had no way of knowing that he was sending his daughter a puzzle. The artifact had been an intriguing way of reconnecting with his daughter; that was all there was to it. Now she would be worried about him, wondering if he was alive or dead.

He turned in a slow circle, putting everything together in his mind. What he'd discovered, what he'd *predicted,* was true. He knew it — he could feel it. He could stake his entire career on it.

Looking around at his quarters only confirmed it. Wherever he was in the world, it was all part of his prediction. It wasn't much of a clue, but it wasn't nothing, either. He nodded, knowing that he was right. He looked around one final time and silently moved his mouth to form the words.

I'm underground.

32

REGGIE

"SANTORINI. INTERESTING."

Ben and Julie looked at him. Reggie looked back down at the image.

"Santorini is a *huge* tourist destination. One of the most popular in Europe. Also called Thera, right?"

"Correct," Mrs. E said.

"And why do we think Professor Lindgren is there?" Ben asked.

"Juliette," Mrs. E said, "do you remember that article we were discussing? The one that had been unpublished?"

"'Timeaus and Critias — An Alternative Explanation,'" Julie said. "That one? Did you find an archived copy of it?"

"No, unfortunately. We are still looking. But it was his most recently published work, and I was able to find out what the paper was about."

"How'd you do that?" Reggie asked.

"Easy — I called his university," she explained. "He is not a spy, Reggie. They were happy to discuss his work with me, especially since I told them I was trying to help locate him."

"I see."

"And they told me that the paper was not well-received. The community at large seemed to think it lacked creativity, although it was well-researched."

Reggie sighed, shaking his head. "Academics. Seriously. So what was the paper about?"

"Well, it was a short treatise on Plato's dialogues *Timaeus* and *Critias*, obviously, but it was written from a particularly *geologic* slant."

"That's what they told you?" Reggie asked. "I'm not even sure what that means."

"He is an archeologist, so it is no surprise that he looks at the problem from a physical perspective rather than a historical one.

"They are still trying to retrieve the rough copy of his paper, as it seems it was published directly from his computer and there is no backup of it on their cloud drives. They have been trying to access the professor's files since he went missing, hoping that something on his machine would help track him down."

"But they told you a bit about what the paper was about? About this 'alternative explanation' of Plato's work?" Julie asked.

Mrs. E shook her head. "That is what I thought as well, but no. The paper is not an interpretation of *Plato's* work, the dialogue itself, but an alternative proposal of the *content* of his dialogue."

Reggie frowned, frustrated. "They tell you anything else?"

"They left a lot to be interpreted," Mrs. E said. "I got the sense that they were a bit hesitant. They want to find their colleague, but they certainly did not sound like they approved of his paper."

"So the stodgy old guys are holding back?" Reggie asked. "Hoping this takes care of some of their competition or something?"

"Perhaps," Mrs. E said. "Or they just want to keep their name clear. A scandal like this, if true, would no doubt bring down scrutiny and unwanted press on their institution..."

"But their colleague was *kidnapped*!" Julie said. "Don't they care about that?"

"...and they each have their own theory on Plato's work, and working with us could appear as though they are in agreement with his assessment."

"You can't be serious," Ben said.

"I guess the competition in the academic archeology world is fierce," Mrs. E said. "Still, I was able to press them a bit. The paper was not well-received because it was not peer-reviewed through the same channels as usual. He hardly reached out to any known historians for their opinion.

"He claimed that was due to the sensitive nature of the material he was apparently working with, but his colleagues scoffed at that excuse, saying that he should not have published the paper in the first place if he did not want the information out there."

"E," Reggie said. "*What* information?"

"Right — so I asked them why this was so sensitive that they felt the need to pull the paper back down and remove it from their servers."

"What did they say to that?" Julie asked.

"That is where it got weird," Mrs. E answered. "They said they did no such thing. That he published the paper under his own name, and not that of the university, so there would have been no need to retract it."

"So they didn't do it..."

"No," she said. "Either he pulled it back himself or someone hacked in and did it for him. But the college has no idea who that might be."

"Interesting," Ben said. "So this paper *has* to be related."

"That is what Mr. E and I believe," Mrs. E said. "I still need to confirm it with Sarah herself, but she is flying to Stockholm now, but she'll be on the ground for fewer than three hours. She will then join us in Thera. She did mention when we spoke last that her father could have been researching something that related to Plato's dialogues of *Timaeus* and *Critias,* leading to his excitement, the publication, and subsequent kidnapping. And, of course, we were turned on to the lead in the first place because of his quote in his letter to Sarah."

"But Santorini?" Julie asked. "He could be anywhere."

"He could be, and he might be. But we have to act quickly, and it's unlikely he is outside of Europe, or that they would feel the need to move him off the continent. So if we are on the island of Thera we will be closer to him at least than we are in Alaska. We can move in if we get updated information.

"But, as you know, my husband is never one to act merely upon a hunch. If he did not believe, truly, that Professor Lindgren was in Santorini, we would not be heading there now."

"Explain," Reggie said.

"We have both been doing some research, and we intend to forward it on to Sarah for her input as well. We believe we have a working theory of where Dr. Lindgren was taken after he was abducted.

"As you all know, he was reportedly last seen over two days ago leaving his apartment in the city. Never came home, and his girlfriend never heard from him, either. But his abductors would not just bring him to some warehouse somewhere — they want something. Something Professor Lindgren himself was working hard to find. We believe he found it, or at least *thinks* he found it. His captors, therefore, also believe he has found it, but they need him to help them get to it. Dr. Lindgren is going to Stockholm to check in at his apartment and see if there are any clues the police might have missed."

Reggie cleared his throat. "But you think his paper on Plato's *Timaeus* and *Critias* explains what he found?"

"I do. Unlike all the other academic research papers on Plato's writings, I believe Professor Lindgren's paper studies the *physical* geographic similarities between this island —" she pointed down at the image of Santorini — "and the island from Plato's record. I think Professor Lindgren believes he has found the lost city of Atlantis."

33

SARAH

STOCKHOLM WAS A BUST.

The local police were crawling all over his apartment in Långholmen. The island neighborhood in the heart of Stockholm was apparently a high-end destination for retirees and the wealthy, and therefore a kidnapping was not a common occurrence for its residents. The Stockholm police force had barricaded the entrance and exit to the building, manning the posts day and night, allowing only residents to come and go.

Sarah had considered her options, wondering if it might work to claim she lived there. She did have a key, after all. But trying to explain who she was to the police, then trying to convince them to just let her in for an hour while she looked around — after they'd clearly already deemed the flat a crime scene — was not the sort of thing she felt confident doing.

If anything, she figured, it would only get her a date in the back room of a station, two officers playing good-cop, bad-cop with her, wasting her time.

So she'd made her decision: Stockholm was a waste of time. She headed back to the same block she'd had the Uber driver drop her off, hailed another driver to pick her up, and paid them to take her back to the airport.

That had been over five hours ago.

Now, she was waiting in the airport in Santorini after catching another four-hour flight from Stockholm to the Greek island of Thera. She'd thought the destination was strange, but she'd remembered Mrs. E's comment from two days prior. *'We will fill you in when we arrive. Rest assured, we have good reason to suspect we know where your father is.'*

She remembered feeling a bit concerned that she was putting her fate

— and potentially her father's — in the hands of a woman she'd barely met, and an organization she was only remotely affiliated with.

But it was Reggie who'd talked her into it. He'd assured her that he fully trusted Mr. and Mrs. E's recommendation, and that the only reason for not bringing everyone up to speed before they left was due to a lack of time. They needed to handle the logistics of sending a handful of civilians across the world in a hurry.

She took a deep breath, sat down in one of the old, thin chairs along the wall, then stood back up again.

It had been months since she'd last seen him, and she wasn't sure how she felt about that.

She started pacing back and forth outside the baggage claim area. Reggie was going to be walking through the doors that led in from the tarmac after what would have been a forty-eight hour transcontinental flight, looking for her.

How do I look? she wondered. It was involuntary, a thought she had no control over. Had she felt in control of her thoughts in this moment, she would have reminded herself that she *didn't* care how she looked, because caring about that meant that she *also* cared about what that man thought.

She didn't care. She *couldn't* care. She hadn't allowed herself to care, ever since…

What? What happened between us? Sarah found herself wondering. They had had their little fling, both enjoying it thoroughly, then they'd split up, Sarah heading back to the field, back to the academics and publications and everything else she ran into in her line of work, and Reggie ran back to whatever it was an ex-Army sniper who now worked for a brand-new civilian organization did.

She touched her hair, feeling a few strands that weren't sitting correctly and running through them with two fingers. She hated that she'd spent an extra ten minutes in her bathroom getting ready. Mrs. E had told her to pack for warm weather, but Sarah hated that she'd worn a skirt, one that had been doing nothing but gathering dust in the tiny closet in her Michigan apartment for months, because she knew it made her legs look awesome.

She hated that she'd done it all for *him*.

She didn't hate Reggie, of course — he had done nothing wrong. Or at least she kept reminding herself of that. *Neither of us thought it would work*, she told herself. *Neither of us* wanted *to make it work.*

They had dated a bit, mostly just spending time together to help them cope with and come down off the high of surviving a nightmarish situation. It was guilt, grieving, and camaraderie, all wrapped into one shared emotion. It didn't hurt that they were wildly attracted to each other, but Sarah had known right from the start — from the first time she'd spent the night in his hotel room — that they were going to be a fling. Nothing more, nothing less.

Five minutes. The clock on the wall had declared the jet's arrival time five minutes ago, and it usually took ten minutes total to get off the plane and into the desolate airport. Much quicker than a typical commercial flight, but to Sarah it felt like an excruciatingly long time.

She poked her hair once again, then pressed her palms down and over her skirt, flattening it around her legs. Her shirt was a buttoned blue long-sleeved thing, but she'd rolled the sleeves way up and around her upper arms and left it untucked, so it looked sort of like the way she'd dress if she had been invited to dinner at a restaurant she wasn't sure was very casual or semi-formal.

She checked her phone. No messages, no texts. It seemed like the entire world had come to a stop, yet her heart was quickening with every pulse. *Get yourself together*, she thought. *This is ridiculous.*

She thought of Alexander, the attractive, if not a bit too clingy, student assistant she'd left back in Michigan and wondered why it was always the men in close proximity to her that made her feel this way. It was always the taboo ones — the ones that would only lead to trouble — that she had a thing for. She could look at a chiseled superhero on the big screen and feel nothing, yet a reasonably attractive specimen of the opposite sex working alongside her made her lose her mind.

Perhaps she was attracted to the work? That some men shared an interest in the things she was most passionate about? But no, she'd worked alongside plenty of guys in her time and there were quite a few she couldn't stand.

She sighed. She wished she could just shut her brain off. Standing there, waiting for the door to open and reveal the tall, darkly silhouetted figure of Gareth Red, she felt like a girl on prom night.

Not that she'd gone to prom — she'd spent most of the last year of high school traveling the world with her semi-famous father, running the speaking circuit with him and getting some experience in the field. She'd been begging to go with him for years, and he and her mother had decided that by her senior year of high school she was old enough.

She was certainly intelligent enough, able to pass many of her classes in spite of her poor attendance, and test out of the rest. Thanks to her field experience and grades, she was able to land a full-time scholarship to the University of Pennsylvania, where she'd completed her undergraduate degree summa cum laude.

She saw a crack of daylight stream up onto the ceiling across the room from her, brighter even than the fluorescents above her. The door opened and she was momentarily blinded. A shadow appeared, blocking the entrance, and then it stepped forward into the room.

Ben.

Harvey Bennett stood over six feet tall, wide-shouldered and broad, in a muscular way. His brownish hair fell over his forehead, thick and almost long enough to cover his eyebrow. It wasn't styled but held a sort of purposeful appearance, as if he'd swiped his hand sideways over his bangs and it just stuck that way, and it made him look like a member of The Beatles that had gone too long without a haircut.

A Beatle that had gained an additional hundred pounds.

He was large, bearlike. To her knowledge he'd never set foot inside a gym, yet he held himself like a professional bodybuilder would, turning at the hips, his neck unmoving as he walked toward her.

He grinned and waved. She smiled back, but silently willed him to step sideways a bit so she could see the doorway behind him.

Juliette Richardson walked in next, followed immediately by Mrs. E. Sarah had never met the woman in person, but she had been on conference calls and video chats a few times with her and her husband over the past month. In person, Mrs. E was even more intimidating than Ben. Her short-cropped, military-style hair was blond, juxtaposed against Julie's dark, long hair that fell gracefully over her shoulders. Julie came maybe up to Mrs. E's shoulder, and the larger woman walked with authority, as if she always had somewhere to go and was late getting there.

Reggie had told her that Mrs. E had accompanied them to Antarctica during their excursion there, and she had been an extremely valuable member of the team, knowledgable in intelligence, communications, and trained in hand-to-hand combat.

They both waved, and she smiled and waved back.

Reggie walked in.

She felt her breath catch for a moment, then a blush started to appear just beneath the surface. She fought it off just as Ben reached her, wrapping her up in a bear hug.

"H — hi, Ben," she muttered, her feet lifting completely off the ground. "Great to see you again."

He laughed. "I'm *telling* you, you need to get in on this CSO thing. It's a pretty sweet life, minus the flying everywhere."

She grinned up at him. "I happen to like flying, you know."

They'd been talking about the Civilian Special Operations with her ever since they'd met in The Bahamas, telling her that she'd be a perfect fit for the group. They'd already worked together, and she'd already proven her worth.

The CSO needed people trained in specific areas of expertise that would be beneficial to the CSO's charge: solving mysteries that were either unimportant to the United States military or didn't offer them enough plausible deniability.

She was hesitant, and not just because she enjoyed her career as it was. Joining the CSO would imply that she had taken someone else's spot on the roster, someone the group had lost half a year ago. They were big shoes to fill, and she wasn't about to put herself in a position where she might start comparing herself to the legacy of a dead man.

"Like I said, it's a sweet gig."

"I'm happy here, Ben," she said. "Academia's nice too, you know. We have Keurigs in all the break rooms now, and they even let us pay a discounted rate in the student dining halls."

Ben chuckled, and Julie and Mrs. E stepped forward. Julie gave her a quick hug while Mrs. E extended her hand, continuing the 'admiral on a mission' impression, and Sarah's eyes flipped back to the doorway.

Reggie was nearly caught up to the rest of them now, and he was grinning in that stupid, too-large-for-his-face sort of way she'd grown to love. He was carrying a rucksack over his shoulder, holding his phone in his free hand. He came up behind Mrs. E, the only one in the group tall enough to look him in the eye, and he stopped. The smile stayed the same, but the one in his eyes shifted, grew more serious.

"Hey, Sarah," he said.

She felt that fluttering thing in her chest, that thing she'd told herself she wouldn't do, and she tried to ignore it.

"Hey Reggie," she said back. "Great to see you again."

34

GRAHAM

GRAHAM'S FACE HURT. HE HADN'T EXPECTED THE LARGE, BRUTISH MAN TO *actually* hit him. He sniffed, shifted his jaw left and right, and used his tongue to feel around the inside of his mouth.

Everything's still in place. For now.

"You done?" Graham asked the man. The man was not the same man who had come to Graham's apartment in Stockholm, but the two looked like they could be brothers. Whereas the man at his apartment — the one who had accompanied him to the airport and then to wherever they were now — was tall and thin, this man was tall and *huge*. Muscular, hardly any neck to speak of, and a permanent scowl on his face. He was younger than Graham by about twenty years, by the looks of it, and Graham wondered if his sole purpose in life so far was to beat up on helpless old guys like him.

Sure seems to have a knack for it, he thought. He winced. Apparently there was going to be a bruise.

The man glared down at him. "Where's the powder?"

The what?

Graham filed the information away for later. *They're looking for a powder...*

"That's enough, Igor," Rachel Rascher said from over the man's shoulder. She had been standing in the back of Graham's cell, questioning Graham while the man intimidated him. "No need for that."

"Trying to get on my good side, Rascher?" Graham asked.

She shook her head. "No," she said. "I'm trying to get an answer."

"I already told you —"

"Graham, I know what you *told* me. You said the object was empty. Just a hollowed-out piece of ceramic. But I don't *believe* you."

It wasn't empty, he thought, *but there was certainly no* powder *in it.*

He shrugged. "That's on you, lady. What's the point, anyway? Why do you want this 'object?' Or whatever you think should have been inside of it?"

She ignored him. "Tell me again where you found it."

He took a deep breath. *Yeah, definitely a bruise.* He could feel the early warning signs of a deep bruise forming around his eye. *He hits me like that again and I'll be ready,* he thought.

There wasn't much he could do, but Graham had never been one to sit around and let the world happen to him. He was a dreamer, an imaginative romantic, always wanting to explore and learn. His ex-wife even accused him of being a 'novelty chaser.'

So he wasn't one to sit in a chair and take a beating. Especially when they hadn't even bothered to bind his arms or legs. *Am I really that little of a threat?* he wondered.

He told her again.

"I was just taking a brief break. Walking down by the water, trying to get a look at the boats coming in to port. I saw the museum there, right next to the caves, and I just asked if I could take a look inside."

"You just asked."

"That's what I said."

"And they just let you in?"

He shook his head. "She, not they. An older woman, working the front desk. And she didn't just 'let me in' like I'm some sort of vagabond, Rascher. I told her my name — that gets me into places like that, you know."

Rascher smiled. "Skip ahead. You got inside, you were alone, you walked down to the end of the cavern?"

"Yes — well, a different cavern that was closed to the public. Very unsafe, really, but it was hardly my first time wriggling through a tiny cave. And right at the end of the narrow shaft, half-buried in the clay and mud, I found it. A stream had probably run through there for thousands of years, on and off when the rains came in or the glaciers had a little melt to shed. Anyway, it was right there where the stream should have been. Just the edge of it, sticking out."

"And you decided it was something worth investigating because you're... *you.*"

"You know, I *am* trained in this sort of thing. Is that so hard to believe?"

She chuckled. "But it was empty?"

"When I finally got it out — again, I'm trained, so I wasn't about to just rip it up out of the ground — I could tell it was hollow. The weight was wrong. But there didn't seem to be anything inside, even when I gave it a bit of a shake."

A lie. But again, he knew Rachel wasn't looking for a souvenir.

"But?"

"But *nothing.* There *wasn't* anything inside. It took me a few minutes to figure out how to open the damned thing, but it was empty. Bone-dry. Impressive, considering where it had been buried for all these years."

Rachel rubbed her nose, making a face at the brute. He stepped forward, tightening his fists.

"No, come on," Graham said. "There's no need to —"

Wham! The blow came from the right this time — a left hook. Right to the *opposite* side of his jaw.

This time he felt like he was going to faint. His vision blurred, he felt his upper body rotating around loosely, as if barely affixed to his hips. He tried to breathe, but found the involuntary motion impossibly difficult.

"Wh — why?" Graham stuttered. He was angry now, but the pain was more intense than he imagined it could be. He wanted to get up and fight, to at least assert himself, but his throbbing jaw seemed to have him riveted to the chair.

"Professor Lindgren," Rachel said, stepping forward. "I'm going to leave Igor here with you for half an hour. He may need more time, but I'm hoping he doesn't."

"I — I don't... I can't —"

"I know it's difficult to talk, Professor," she said. "But it is *absolutely imperative* that you tell me what was inside that object."

"There — there was nothing —"

"Please," she said. "For your own good."

She took a few long, steady strides to the small door at the edge of his room and stopped at the threshold.

"Professor Lindgren," she said, her voice dropping. "If you are not able to give me what I want, I am still going to move forward with my plan. I hope you don't think I'm above making sacrifices, Professor. My own *father* died for this cause, so you'd better know that I'm willing to go to *any* length to complete this project, no matter the cost."

He frowned. Or at least he *tried* to frown. *What is she talking about?*

"But in the meantime, I am going to move on to another *source* of information. I do hope you will find it within yourself to comply. For your sake, and for your daughter's."

35

REGGIE

My God, she's beautiful, Reggie thought. *She hasn't changed a bit.*

He tried not to notice her long, skinny legs. She'd worn a skirt, even though he'd come to assume that her de facto uniform was a safari-style shirt and shorts, rolled up over her thighs. The skirt fell around her legs playfully, implying and inviting and —

Knock it off, man. You're an adult. He felt like a teenager all over again, fighting against feelings of inadequacy while simultaneously feeling the swells of confidence whenever a female would look his direction.

He and Sarah had been an item only briefly, but Reggie had been more than a little distraught when it ended. Though it ended amicably enough, he felt that their connection was of the sort that wouldn't ever really end. They had so much in common — a love for history, for learning in general, and for all things in-between. They even shared a similar taste in food: they both loved to eat *anything*. Their dates had been either taking turns whipping up something in the kitchen using nothing but ingredients one of them had on hand or finding the most out-of-the-way local restaurant neither of them had ever visited.

Their relationship had been born out of attraction, forged by trial, and proven through character. They had both needed each other, and they had both agreed on that fact. And it had ended for pragmatic reasons — neither was interested in watching the relationship struggle through the growing pains and inevitable failure of long-distance stresses. They'd decided to give it up, to avoid the awkward phone calls and texts apologizing for not reaching out sooner, the guilt of feeling loneliness and responsibility at the same time, and to avoid the obvious question: what happens after dating turns into something more?

"Hey Reggie. Great to see you again."

She sounds so confident. So nonchalant. It's like she's not even excited to see me.

He wasn't sure what to do with his hands, or his face — or his feet or anything else for that matter — so he just stood there, one hand holding the strap of his rucksack and the other holding his cellphone, and he let the smile on his face sit there unmoving.

After a few more awkward seconds, Ben spoke. "All right lovebirds. Let's get on with it. We've got a lot of planning to do, and I don't plan anything on an empty stomach."

Reggie shot him a dirty look, but Julie stepped in. "You just ate an hour ago, Ben."

"Yeah, but I fell asleep after that. My body thinks it's morning, and technically it is. I get hungry in the sky."

Even though their journey had lasted almost two days, they'd landed around 11am local time while their minds told them it was late evening. Reggie turned back to Sarah. "Know any good places to eat around here?"

She shrugged. "I landed yesterday, and all I grabbed was a doughnut and a cup of coffee."

"You haven't eaten since *yesterday*?" Ben asked. "What's wrong with —"

Julie shoved him out of the way, and they all started toward the parking lot. Sarah had rented an SUV, large enough to fit the five of them and their luggage, and they would be staying in a hotel she'd booked the day before.

"There were about three-hundred Greek places on the way to the airport," she said as they reached the sliding glass doors that led to the lot. "You guys like Greek?"

Reggie felt his mouth water. He liked to tell people that he *loved* Greek food, but in fairness the only Greek meal he'd ever had was a lamb gyro, wrapped in a thick pita roll with some sort of delicious sauce drizzled over it. It was a chain he'd discovered way back in boot camp, and there was usually one in all of the major cities he'd been stationed at over the years.

He wasn't sure if *real* Greek food tasted like that, but his saying was that 'if there was meat involved, he was interested.'

"Sounds awesome," Julie said. Reggie fell in next to Ben and Mrs. E, allowing Julie and Sarah to walk up ahead, both women immediately falling into routine banter, as if they had been friends for life and were now simply catching up on lost time while they'd been apart.

The SUV was huge — clean and still smelling new, and Reggie took up a station at the rear end piling everyone's bags and suitcases inside. Besides Reggie's rucksack, all of it had been couriered over from the jet directly to the waiting vehicle by an airport staffer, apparently a perk of flying on private jets. Reggie had opted to carry his for a simple reason:

he had been trained to pack nothing more than what he could carry over his shoulder, and the Army had set a lifelong habit that was difficult to shed.

He closed the hatch and stepped around to the front of the vehicle. Sarah had rented the vehicle in her name, so she was the listed driver on the account, though they were all legally able to drive if need be. The rest of the group had left the front passenger seat for him, probably assuming that he and Sarah would want to catch up a bit.

He wasn't sure if they were right about that or not — he certainly wanted to talk to her, to just be around her once again, but he wasn't sure if he could pull off the 'small talk' that would be required without jumping headfirst into the deeper conversation he sensed they both wanted to have.

And I'm not sure I want to have that conversation in front of everyone else, he thought.

"So," Sarah said as she fired up the engine and began backing out of the parking spot. "Greek food, then hotel? I checked out the hotel while I was waiting for you all to land. There's a small bar and restaurant in the lobby, where I figured we could chat for a bit about the plan."

Reggie saw her eyebrows raise. She was interested in hearing more about this 'plan' from Mrs. E. He was, too, now that he thought about it. While he trusted the husband-wife pair that served as the governing leadership of the CSO, he was still intrigued by Mrs. E's earlier statements. He wanted to know more.

Sarah maneuvered the large SUV out of the airport parking lot and onto the highway. Reggie noticed that they were the biggest vehicle around, by far. There weren't even any vans, and the vast majority of the cars speeding by were electric vehicles and compact sedans.

"That is wonderful. Thank you for arranging it all, Sarah," Mrs. E said from the third-row seat.

Sarah smiled as she looked in the rearview mirror. "You're the one to thank, E," she said. "You guys footed the bill for everything. In the email you sent, you told me we even have a per diem for the bar, if I recall correctly."

Reggie's eyes widened as Sarah spoke.

"Man, I love this job," Ben said.

"Calm down, bud," Reggie said. "You still owe me a round of drinks, remember? Your per diem's spent already."

"For what?" Ben asked.

Reggie turned in his chair and winked back as his friend. "I recruited you. You wouldn't be here if it wasn't for me."

36

BEN

If Reggie had been serious about using Ben's per diem on drinks for himself, he didn't make mention of it. Ben sat in the hotel bar across the rounded booth from his best friend. Julie was at his side, Mrs. E and Sarah between her and Reggie. Nine glasses sat empty on the large table in front of them.

They had shared a few rounds of appetizers as well, all Greek. Feta psiti, spanakopita, and some sort of small, pie-shaped garlic bread Ben had never heard of before.

All of it was delicious, and all of it was enough to feed twice the amount of people that were sitting around the table. And if they hadn't already stopped for drive-through Greek food on the way to the hotel, all of it would have been gone. For the CSO group, who had been traveling for nearly two days, it felt like the middle of the night.

Ben watched the newest member of the group. If Sarah Lindgren was feeling strange eating and drinking in the late-afternoon as if it were midnight, she didn't let on. In fact, she had kept up with Reggie and Ben so far, already having downed two of the magical local Santorini cocktails that tasted a bit like Long Island iced tea and had nearly as much booze inside.

Reggie and Ben had now moved on to straight whiskey, Reggie opting for a Russian import and Ben choosing a tried-and-true label of bourbon he'd often kept stocked at the cabin. So far, Santorini felt like everything he thought it would be: a destination vacation spot for tourists with enough local flair to give the impression that one was in a faraway land but with enough of the comforts of home to not feel isolated.

He put his hand down on Julie's leg under the table, giving it a light squeeze. She found his fingers and held them while the conversation continued, each of them sharing stories of their harrowing experiences, how they'd all met, and then, finally, listening to Sarah as she explained a bit more about her father's work.

"He's a bit eccentric, admittedly," she said. "I'm sure that's part of the reason why his colleagues were a bit hesitant on the phone with you, Mrs. E. I believe they're both intimidated by him as well as not quite sure where to put him."

"He doesn't fit into the 'academic box,' I take it," Reggie said.

She shook her head. "Not even a little bit. Everything he's ever done he's done his own way. It's only through sheer brilliance that he's been successful in university life. He's hardheaded about it, too, not wanting to change."

Ben took a sip of the bourbon. "But he publishes papers, works on research, does talks and field work. How is he that different from all the rest of you guys?"

Julie released his hand and shot him a glance.

"Sorry," he said. "No offense."

"None taken," Sarah said. "You're right — most of us academic types are pretty standardized. Pretty boring, even. It's not our fault, though. It's part of the system that we've been trained into. You work on research, publishing when you can, and you try to get tenured as fast as possible. From there, it's talks, bigger publications, more attention. More attention, more money. More money, the more opportunity you have to research what you want."

"Right."

"But my father succeeded *in spite* of his intelligence, not because of it. He's a master of just about everything he does, and so spending his life dedicated to digging up old relics has led to a spectacular career."

"Academic circles could not ignore him forever, you mean," Mrs. E said.

"Yes. He's a modern-day Indiana Jones, at least in that world. He was always willing to go the extra mile, literally, to find something that would prove his point. Most of the time he succeeded. He has a scary knack for figuring that stuff out." Sarah smiled, looking up at at the ceiling. "I'm not even sure he's human."

Julie nodded along. "Any idea what this Atlantis stuff is all about?"

"No," Sarah said. "Other than just that — Mrs. E thinks he's found Atlantis."

"The *actual* city," Julie said. "Atlantis. Come on, Sarah, we all know it sounds ridiculous. Do you think we're on to something with this?"

"Of course it sounds ridiculous," she said. "He probably thinks that's why most 'credible' archeologists and historians discount its viability altogether. They don't bother with new theories because the original theory itself lacks a reasonable amount of trustworthy data."

"It does?" Ben asked.

"In a way, yes. Most professionals agree that Plato's works are at least trustworthy for *contextual* purposes, if not altogether allegorical. But most historians are going to want much more than just Plato's reference to Atlantis. And the vast majority of stuff that came *after* Plato doesn't count, since an argument can be made that they were probably just referencing Plato's own reference in the first place.

"So they want substantiated evidence of Atlantis' existence, from more than a singular source. But Plato doesn't tell us much, and what he does tell us is that he heard the legend from Critias, who heard it from a man named Solon, who visited Egypt sometime before that, and heard it from someone *there*."

"Wow," Ben said. "So a lot of 'telephone game' going on."

"Exactly. Not really the sort of thing that can encourage a large pool of grant money or academic papers. And the fact that we *haven't* found an entire lost continent and legendary city since Plato wrote about it only makes it that much more unbelievable. The more time that goes on, the more ridiculous the entire thing seems."

Across from Ben, Reggie shifted in his seat. He was obviously uncomfortable, sitting next to the woman he had recently had a pretty serious relationship with. Reggie would want some time alone with her to talk about that, but Ben knew he was also excited to get started on this new mission. The man's conflicted interests were apparent on his face, and while Ben felt for him, the humor of the awkward moment didn't escape him.

"So, uh, why does your father think it's real?" Reggie asked.

At this, Sarah looked over at Mrs. E. Ben knew Sarah had been just as much in the dark about this trip as the rest of them. Mrs. E took a quick sip of her drink. "We are not entirely certain he does think it's real," she answered. "But whatever he wrote in that paper seemed to convince *someone* that he believed it, or at least that he had a good idea about it."

"So why Santorini?" Sarah asked. "What's special about this place?"

Mrs. E cleared her throat. "One of the companies our corporation has been providing runway investment for has created an artificial-intelligence-aided search function that Juliette and I had been discussing."

She turned to Julie, who was nodding along. "For example, in this case, we had it search through map data and compile potentialities."

"Potentialities? How does that even work?" Reggie asked.

"It is image-based," Julie said, growing more animated as she explained. "By overlaying images of maps — anything that might be tagged as a 'geographic pictograph,' actually — that are scraped from other web searches, and then comparing and contrasting their unique features, the algorithm can interpret drawn, illustrated, and imaged results."

Ben nodded, then put his elbows out in front of him on the table. "So… how does it work?"

Mrs. E grinned, showing a huge set of brilliant white teeth. "Basically we can search keywords — 'mountainous,' 'oceanic,' 'peninsula,' etcetera — as well as filter by those results — size in area, delineated by feet, miles, kilometers. Or by region, biome characteristics, human habitation over time, or more. Think of a 'smart' search engine that only exists to cross-reference history with its geographic and anthropologic details, all superimposed on a modern Mercator projection."

Ben shrugged. "So… magic. Got it."

The others laughed. "What I discovered, after Julie helped me compile the algorithm, was nothing short of a breakthrough," Mrs. E finished. Normally the woman sitting diagonally from Ben was straightforward, all business, but he thought he could sense a bit of a flourishing excitement from her. She was a soldier, a woman who could have been easily written off as a 'grunt' based on her massive, muscular frame and short hair, but he knew better. Mrs. E was almost as brilliant as her husband. The husband-wife pair had grown their communications company into a worldwide conglomerate. They'd remained in complete control until a few years ago when they had begun to hand off the reins to others to manage the day-to-day operations, and instead had begun using their wealth to invest in fledgling tech companies, promising science and research, and, of course, the CSO.

Mrs. E shifted in her seat and leaned toward Ben, scanning left and right across the faces of the group. Her voice lowered to nearly a whisper, heightening the effect. "We believe the island of Santorini is the *exact* island described by Plato in *Timaeus* and *Critias.*"

Ben saw Sarah lean forward in the booth. "Explain," she said, her voice shaky.

Mrs. E pulled out her phone, swiping around the screen for a few seconds.

Julie looked at Mrs. E, her own phone ready in her hand. "First, should we hear the original text? In Plato's own words?"

Ben nodded, sensing that the tension he'd felt in the past ten or so hours was finally going to be resolved.

"I'll pull it up," Julie said.

Ben smiled. "Well I think it's probably helpful to get another drink, in that case. Hold that thought?"

37

BEN

REFRESHED AND TOPPED OFF AFTER A TRIP TO THE RESTROOM AND HOTEL bar, Ben sat back down at the round booth and looked around. "Did you wait for me?" he asked.

Mrs. E nodded. "We did. I was just sharing a bit more with the group about the algorithm we used."

"Well, sorry I missed that."

"Anyway, I will get back to it. Plato's words describing Atlantis: '*For it is related in our records how once upon a time your State stayed the course of a mighty host... and it was possible for travelers of that time to cross from it to the other islands and from the islands to the whole of the continent over against them which encompasses the veritable ocean...*'"

She looked up to see that everyone was still tracking with her, just as Sarah spoke. "So Plato is referencing a great nation, right?"

Ben nodded. "Sounds like it. Who is he referring to when he says 'your state?'"

"I know this one," Sarah answered. "And it's a great question. Since there was a lot of 'he said, she said' stuff going on about Plato's words since his time, it's hard to know for sure. But we're almost positive the 'State' we're seeing here is Athens. Essentially Plato used this dialogue, or at least this section of the dialogue, as a way to brag on Ancient Greece, so it's likely he's paying homage to his ancestors."

Mrs. E nodded and continued. "Right. But the *real* question is: what is this 'great nation' Plato is talking about? Not Athens, but the *other* one in the story."

Again, Ben jumped in. "Atlantis?"

Reggie smiled. "That's the obvious answer, isn't it?" He paused and Ben saw the sly grin on the woman's face as Reggie continued. "Which tells me that the right answer is *not* the obvious one."

"Well," Mrs. E said, "Plato is writing down a story that was told to him by a man who heard it from a man who'd visited Egypt many years prior. Egypt is relevant in the story, but we still believe the 'state' referenced is Athens. And the story, ultimately, *is* about Atlantis, but the syntax of the language — and this is based on linguists' research, not mine, as I can't speak Greek — doesn't line up. It's a weird conundrum."

"I can attest to that," Sarah said. Everyone looked her direction. "I don't speak Greek either, but my father studied it years ago. He always had a fascination with the syntax of the language. How it was sometimes impossible to accurately translate Greek to any modern language. And he definitely said that was true about the way the great Greek philosophers wrote, especially Plato."

"You have heard this before?" Mrs. E asked.

"Yes," Sarah rolled her eyes. "It was one of my dad's favorite topics."

Julie was laughing now, sipping her drink. "Come on, spill it. You've got me in suspense."

Sarah nodded. "Sorry. I can't resist a good mystery, though. Got that from my old man. And part of me still thinks this is his way of giving me yet another mystery to solve. All of this cryptic Plato stuff, Atlantis — I'm not sure if he's playing around or not."

Ben understood what she really meant. *I hope this is all just a game.*

He had a feeling it was *not* a game.

Sarah continued. "Basically, it's extremely difficult to parse the ancient Greek in a way that translates to anything substantive in any modern language, so there's a bit of guesswork at this point. Where do we put commas, periods, semicolons, for example? We all know how crucial punctuation can be in understanding written language." She paused, then laughed. "My dad had a way of explaining that, too. He used to show me an old drawing. The title of it was *Commas Save Lives,* and there were two short sentences beneath the title: 'Let's eat, Grandpa,' and, 'Let's eat Grandpa.'"

The group chuckled while Mrs. E continued the retelling and explanation of Plato's manuscript. "The part that *does* seem quite explicit and easy to understand comes next. In *Critias,* Plato gives us actual measurements of this island:

"'*an island comprising mostly of mountains in the northern portions and along the shore, and encompassing a great plain of an oblong shape in the south extending in one direction three-thousand stadia, but across the center, it was only two-thousand stadia. Fifty stadia from the coast was a mountain that was low on all sides...'*

"He then mentions a 'central island' that was five stades in diameter."

"So Plato actually tells us *exactly* what this island looks like?" Reggie asked.

"He does."

Ben frowned. "What are we missing, then? Those are pretty specific measurements, right? Why can't we just look around the world for an island that matches the descriptions he gave us?"

Ben realized he knew the answer to the question as soon as he'd asked it. If it had truly been that simple, researchers and geographers would have been able to pinpoint the 'continent' of Atlantis long ago. He was about to protest when Reggie shifted in his seat.

"I'm going to guess that's *exactly* why we're here," he said, looking at Mrs. E. "I'd bet good money you think Santorini is one of islands that didn't get flooded."

"Yes," Mrs. E said. "I have read the passage over and over again until it was memorized. We were just trying to find something *tangible* we could extract from Plato's otherwise 'untrustworthy' work. Something that might point us in the right direction. When I thought of Sarah's letter from her father, something clicked. He opened the letter with a quote from Plato, remember? *'We are twice armed if we fight with faith.'* I kept trying to understand why he referenced Plato."

"He's the one who wrote about Atlantis," Julie offered. "That's why we started researching all of this in the first place."

"Right," Mrs. E said. "But I wondered if there was anything *else* to it. Why he'd invoke the words of an old, ancient philosopher in just a letter to his daughter. How antiquated, right?"

"Because he's old?"

Mrs. E smiled, but shook her head. "He was not just giving us a clue as to *what* he was studying, he was giving us a clue as to *where* it might be."

Sarah frowned. "How's that?"

"It is not about the fact that Plato is *old*. It is *how* old he is. Give or take a few hundred years, Plato wrote those words *two-thousand* years ago."

"Yeah, that's old," Ben said. "What's the point?"

"Because Plato himself was invoking a much older writer. He was writing about a time, during Atlantis' reign, approximately 9,000 years before *him*. That's *11,000* years, give or take, before *now*."

Reggie's eyes widened. "I get it. Geography."

Sarah nodded along. "Right. It's my father's life's work — archeology, geology, and history, all coming together. Who's to say the islands that we have today are the *same* islands that were around back then?"

"Precisely," Mrs. E said. "The Earth is constantly changing, going through cataclysmic events. Scholars generally agree that these events happen every ten thousand years or so, and they can even completely reshape the landscape in a certain area."

Julie and Ben smiled, and Ben began to understand. "Right," he said. "Atlantis supposedly sunk beneath the sea, right? In 'one day and one night,' or something like that? Which begs the question — why should we be looking for an island in the first place?"

"Exactly," Sarah said. "Based on all this, we *shouldn't* be looking for an island. We should be scouring the depths of the Atlantic Ocean. And that's where most of the professionals and amateur sleuths have been focusing their attention: finding raised areas of the Atlantic Ocean that could be shaped like Atlantis, searching for underwater cities, and the like."

Mrs. E jumped in. "So we decided to program the search algorithm to search records that were historically appropriate — anything that referenced prehistoric time. Things like ancient Egypt, Greece, Macedonia, etcetera. We told it to look for shapes that matched Plato's description, with a twenty percent margin of error, based on what we knew of the globe at least 9,000 years before Plato's time.

"And to make things interesting, we added in whatever geologic records we could gather that studied that time period and fed that to the program."

"So you were able to search images of the entire world, as it existed 11,000 years ago?" Reggie asked.

"Yes."

"And that's why we're here?" Ben asked. "Because Plato gave us everything but the exact coordinates of Atlantis, and they pointed to this location?"

Mrs. E nodded, a flash of color coming to her face as her obvious excitement grew.

Mrs. E straightened, taking a final sip of her lime and seltzer water. "Yes, Ben. That's correct. And the program only took an hour to figure it out, with less than a three-percent margin of error. Plato was describing, without a doubt, the island of Santorini."

38

JULIE

JULIE UNDERSTOOD THE CONCEPT: USE ARTIFICIAL INTELLIGENCE TO AID IN creating an algorithm that could search any existing maps of the ancient world for an island. An island that would have existed many millennia before Plato's time but matched his description.

She'd helped Mrs. E build the algorithm, then the woman had gone silent as she'd analyzed the results and collected the data.

But to her, it still didn't completely add up. "You're telling me that Plato described the *exact* geology of Santorini, and that's why we're here? Why has no one else considered it yet? And more importantly — there are *people* here. In Santorini. How could they not have noticed that they *live in Atlantis?*"

"Well," Mrs. E said, holding up a hand. "Santorini isn't *exactly* Atlantis. It's just the closest thing to it."

Julie pressed her fingers against the bridge of her nose. *I hope this isn't all a waste of time.* The technology Mrs. E had used to deduce their location was fascinating, but if it didn't actually help them find Sarah's father, it was all for naught.

Mrs. E continued, unfazed. "Remember, Plato's words were describing a place that existed 9,000 years *before* his time. He was describing an island that, by the time Plato had even heard of it, had been underwater for thousands of years.

"So Santorini is only one *portion* of this larger island," Mrs. E said, still smiling. "We are here because our journey — your father's journey, Sarah — begins here."

Sarah nodded. "You sure about that?"

"It *has* to be here," Mrs. E said. "Whether or not Plato was describing the mythical 'Lost Continent of Atlantis,' he was *absolutely,* without a doubt, describing the island that used to exist in this area."

"Can you show us?" Reggie asked.

Julie was intrigued, and glad Reggie asked. Seeing it on a map would be a much better way of visualizing what Mrs. E and her husband had discovered. She waited in anticipation as Mrs. E grabbed one of the napkins from the center of the booth. She looked around awkwardly for a moment.

"I do not carry a purse," she said. "Does anyone have a —"

Before she could finish, Sarah had handed her a pen. Mrs. E thanked her and began to draw. First, she sketched the island they had landed on.

"This is Santorini, or Thira, as it's called in Greece," she said. "It's a set of a few islands — one larger, circular one split into two sections that we're on now, and one smaller one in the middle. It's easy to spot the volcanic ring here, and how the island itself was formed over time."

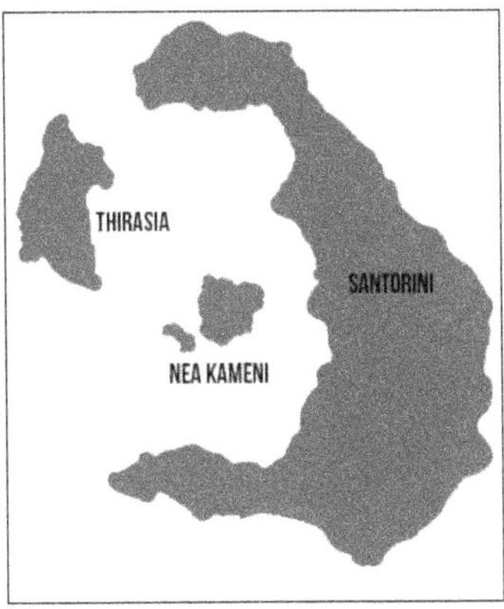

She pointed out the major cities that currently existed, dotting the areas on the coastline around the island.

"There's an old volcano in the middle, called Nea Kameni, and this smaller island," she said as she sketched in the smaller island that existed in the open waters next to the curved archipelago, "used to be a part of the archipelago itself."

"That's Thirasia," Sarah said, jumping in. "There are about three-hundred people currently living there. It's small, out of the way, and pretty much the epitome of Greek countryside living."

"Sounds like you've been there," Reggie said.

"I have, when I was just a kid," Sarah said. "We stopped in Santorini and took a boat out to the island, just to visit. My father had some talk to give or some other work somewhere on the islands, so it was just a quick layover."

Mrs. E was about to continue drawing, but then looked up at the others around the table. "You know what? This is probably easier. Let me just pull it up on my phone." She fumbled around a bit on her phone, then laid it flat on the table. Julie could see on the screen an image of a map, zoomed in to the area northwest of the tiny island of Santorini.

Julie leaned closer and saw at top-left corner of the screen the very edge of Greece, its capital city of Athens barely visible.

"This whole region is the area known as the Cyclades, a group of small Greek islands in the Aegean Sea, off the coast of Athens."

Julie looked at the map, seeing the tiny blobs of white and green, surrounded by endless blue. She silently read the names: Mikonos, Tinos, Andros, Siros. There were countless more, each smaller than the last, forming a huge array of dots set atop the Mediterranean.

"11,000 years ago, however," Mrs. E said, "the region didn't look *anything* like this."

She copied the map onto her napkin, roughly sketching the islands and outlines of the individual Greek states. When she finished, she looked up.

"It turns out that 11,000 years ago, the area of the Cyclades had a much different geography."

She sketched in some of the surrounding area that collected a handful of the islands into a single, unified group:

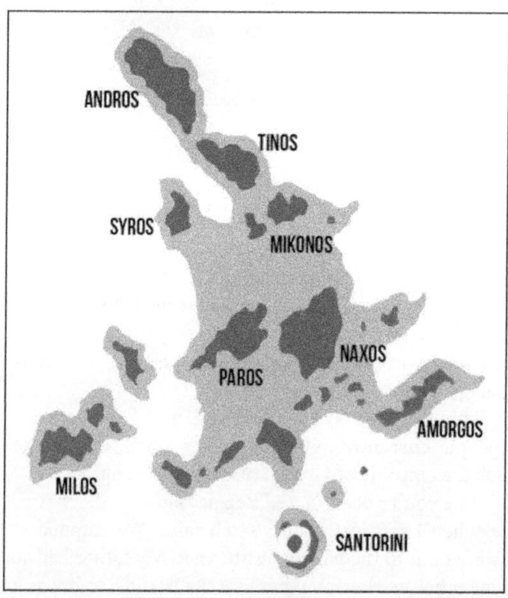

Julie stared down at the drawing. Mrs. E had drawn, very roughly, a triangle. There was a curved, skinny section that stretched up from the top of the triangle toward Athens, and the outermost islands in the group formed the two bottom points at the base of the triangle. The island of Santorini sat apart from the rest, southeast a bit. Santorini looked like the detached head of a larger, two-dimensional creature.

"This is what the Cyclades area looked like approximately nine millennia before Plato."

Mrs. E began circling areas on the map she'd just drawn. "It was called the Cyclades Plateau because this area in the center —" she pointed to the narrow, long section between two islands — "was exactly that. Before the waters rose, it was a large, flat plateau. Plato even references it directly: *'an island comprising mostly of mountains in the northern portions and along the shore, and encompassing a great plain of an oblong shape in the south extending in one direction.'*

"The plateau flooded sometime around 10,000 years ago, for some reason," Mrs. E said. "Some scientists believe it was due to the end of the last ice age. Whatever the reason, the oceans rose about 400 feet, completely altering the geography of the entire planet.

The plateau on the napkin is approximated," Mrs. E continued, "but my husband said the company we have been working with has been able to recreate a very accurate computer model of the larger landmass. It takes into account what we know about the Mediterranean and Aegean region during that time, as well as the volcanic activity that would have led to the creation of this landmass.

"And just before we landed, the lab sent over some even better information: if you translate Plato's writing into modern-day measurements, everything lines up."

Reggie frowned. "Wait, really? He really *was* accurate?"

"It seems so," Mrs. E said. "Look."

She poked around on her phone once again, referencing some note she'd taken earlier, and started writing numbers next to each section of the napkin map.

"Plato writes that the 'oblong shape in the south, extending in one direction' is about 'three-thousand stadia wide,' which, when translated to modern-day measurements, is about 555 kilometers across."

She drew an arrow and line segment across the center of the island and wrote the numbers in just below the line.

"Then he writes, 'but across the center of the island it was two-thousand stadia,' or about 370 kilometers. So there was a smaller valley south of the larger, 555 kilometer-long valley. We believe that was right here."

Mrs. E drew another arrow and line segment across an area just south of the main valley, across one of the modern-day islands of the Cyclades.

"Fifty stadia, or about nine kilometers *from the coast* of this landmass, was a mountain that was low on all sides...' so there was an entirely different — yet much smaller — island, situated just off the coast of the larger landmass of Atlantis. Plato says this smaller island was actually two tiny islands, that one was 'all round about, and that the central island itself was five stades in diameter,' or just under one kilometer in diameter. So there was an island within an island."

She circled the island of Santorini on the napkin map.

"It matches up *perfectly*," Reggie said.

Julie couldn't help but feel excited. She couldn't argue with Mrs. E's assessment, and seeing it unfold in front of her, even just on a napkin, was nothing short of remarkable.

"Later, Plato says that there were two springs, one cold and one hot, that provided water to the island."

"Wait a minute," Ben said. "They had *hot water?* So they had showers?"

Mrs. E smiled. "Perhaps. But yes, Plato says they did indeed have 'two springs,' so we assume he's referring to these two geologic features."

She circled the island of Santorini, which was clearly the collapsed cone of a volcano, and the smaller island inside of it, also now an extinct volcano. "These could have been the sources of the cold freshwater aquifers — the inactive volcano situated southeast of the main island with loads of cool water under pressure stuck inside — and the hot — the active volcano near it."

"Mrs. E," Reggie said, his adulation clear in his voice, "this is amazing. You — you figured this out?"

"No," she replied quickly. "The company and their artificial intelligence program, as well as their tireless staff, provided most of the computing power, and Julie even helped program some of the early search queries. And there are quite a few blog posts and articles written by amateur historians that helped point us in the right direction."

Mrs. E made a dismissive motion with her hand. "My husband and I merely invested in the right companies — and the right people."

"Either way," Ben said. "Reggie's right. This is phenomenal. I can't — there's no way I can argue with it."

Mrs. E beamed, then tried to hide it. "Well, it gets even better," she said. "Plato goes on. He gives us a bottom-line examination of the repercussions of this little island's growing ego: '*the consequence is, that in comparison of what then was, there are remaining in small islets only the bones of the wasted body, as they may be called, all the richer and softer parts of the soil having fallen away, and the mere skeleton of the country being left.*'"

"The islands that still exist today," Julie said. "That's what he's talking about. The 'bones of the wasted body' of the original island are all that exist. Now it's just the smaller, disconnected islands."

"Right," Mrs. E said. "And Santorini is one of those islands, and it's one of the only ones that was almost completely unaffected by the flooding that destroyed the larger island. From what we gather, Plato is describing — literally — this island and the surrounding area to the north of it over the Cyclades Plateau, as it existed 11,000 years ago. At that time, the island of Atlantis was a very literal, very evident reality to the ancient Greeks."

"Fascinating," Julie said. "So where does that lead us? It sounds like this island, Santorini, is only one of many possible locations to search."

Sarah's face fell. "That's true," she said, her voice low and soft. "That's the unfortunate truth. There's not much left of any of the other small islands to search — at least nothing obvious. I know that from my father's studies and some of my own. Santorini is the most populated, up-to-date island, so it makes sense to start here, but I'm not sure what we'll be able to find, and I'm not sure where we're supposed to go next."

Julie sensed Sarah was upset about something besides just the potential lack of leads toward finding Atlantis. She reached out and placed her hand on Sarah's. "We'll find him, Sarah," Julie said. "I promise you that."

"Thank you," Sarah whispered.

No one else spoke for a moment. Mrs. E finally broke the silence. "Well, you youngsters can keep partying, but my body doesn't care if it is only six o'clock here. It feels like the middle of the night, and I could use some shut-eye.

"Besides," she continued, "I need to make sure everything is ready for our excursion tomorrow."

"Excursion?" Reggie asked.

Mrs. E nodded. "We are chartering a boat — a small yacht used for fishing trips. The owner is going to tour us around the interior of the island. He told my husband that he would be ready as soon as we landed on the island, but I knew we would be tired and it would be getting dark soon. I thought we could start by getting an idea of the geography of the place, to see if it lines up with our theory. From there we can determine what our next steps are. But we will need daylight, so tomorrow morning it is. And we will likely need a professional opinion on what we are looking at. For that, I am hoping Dr. Lindgren will help us out."

Sarah nodded. "Of course. Anything that helps."

Around the table, Julie saw the question in everyone else's eyes. She had no doubt the people she was with, the friends she'd committed to, were the best in the world for the task at hand. Each of them had their specialties and strengths, as well as flaws, but they had proven that grit and sheer determination, as well as teamwork, were far better assets to problem-solving than just about anything else.

They *would* find her father, that was not the question.

No, the question she was wrestling with — the one she knew Sarah was wrestling with as well — was far more unsettling:

Will we find him in time?

39

SARAH

Sarah and Reggie sat across from one another, facing each other at the large booth. It was awkward, and it wasn't just because of the massive table, making her feel small.

It was awkward because they were the only two people at the table. The rest of the group had disbanded, citing exhaustion after a nearly two-day travel itinerary. Although they had each gotten a bit of shuteye on the plane, the constant stops and typical impossibility of getting restful sleep on a flight had fatigued them all.

She figured Ben and Julie would want some alone time, and she guessed that Mrs. E probably had to check in with her reclusive husband and give him an update on their safe arrival and progress in addition to working through the itinerary for tomorrow. Still, she couldn't help but think that everyone had purposefully left them alone in the hotel bar.

"So…" Reggie began. "How — how are you?"

She wasn't sure what to say. She took a deep breath, letting the air fill her lungs, deeply in and then out again. *Tell him the truth?*

"You mean, 'how are you after I ditched you and never called?'"

Okay, Sarah, that was a bit harsh. How about the actual *truth next time?*

To his credit, Reggie didn't appear to be angry. He smiled, a pained grin spreading across the lower half of his face. "I called a few times, Sarah."

That was true. But she hadn't *returned* those calls, and besides a few emails here and there, their communication had been mostly through the other members of Reggie's crew.

"Sorry," she said. "I know. It's just…"

"I know."

Reggie took a long sip of his whiskey and waved the waiter over for another. He waited the full six minutes it took for the whiskey to arrive before he spoke again.

"Listen, Sarah," he began. "I like you. Hell, it may even be more than that. I think you know that, but I want you to know that hasn't changed."

"Then why —"

"Because I *had* to, Sarah. I can't really explain it right now — not very well, at least, but I had to cut it off. Between work and training, and the long distance, it was just..."

"Too hard?" Sarah asked.

He didn't answer.

She knew it was too hard, she had admitted that to him before he'd even brought it up. It was half her fault — maybe even more than half. But she couldn't bring herself to apologize, no matter how hard she tried. In her mind, apologizing to him would be admitting defeat.

And something in there is trying to make this work, she realized.

She couldn't admit defeat because she didn't truly want it to be *over*.

"Reggie," she said. "I know it was hard. It will *always* be hard. I'm no stay-at-home housewife, and God knows you're no 9-to-5 office worker who'll be home just in time for dinner every night."

Reggie smiled again, and this time the smile reached his eyes. "You don't seriously think of us like that, do you?"

"Of course not," she said, suddenly feeling herself going on the defensive. "It's just —"

"We're *not* that couple, Sarah," he said. "We were never going to be. What I'm asking is, do you think *that's* why it didn't work?"

Good question.

She shrugged.

"I can tell you why I didn't want to try to make it work, Sarah. I didn't *want* it to work."

"You... what?"

"I didn't want to. It would have been the hardest thing either of us have ever done. Neither of us is going to give up our lives for anything, and that includes each other."

"Reggie, that's not —"

"It *is* true, Sarah. It's harsh, but it's true. You're just as stubborn as I am, and you're a hell of a lot smarter than I am, so I know it would be stupid for you to give up your career for someone else."

She wanted to interject, but she also was interested to hear where he was going with his monologue. She shifted a bit in the soft seat, moving the hand she had been sitting on to the tabletop and uncrossing her legs, then crossing them again the other way. She naturally felt her body closing in on itself, like she was a clam in a shell, slowly feeling the pressure welling up around her.

"Say we tried to make it work," Reggie continued. "What does that even look like? We see each other every few months?"

Sarah couldn't help herself. "More like once a year."

"Right — so once a year? That's ridiculous. And then what? We spend the weekend or week we have together, once a year, catching up? Sarah, that's not a life. That's stasis."

"Maybe stasis is better than nothing."

"Maybe it is," Reggie said.

She knew they were both on the same page. *It's not better. Staying the same is no way to live.*

She took another long, deep breath. "What are we talking about right now, Reggie?"

It was his turn to shrug. "I don't know, honestly. I guess I just want you to know I'm sorry. If it were any different…"

"If it were different you and I wouldn't have ever met."

"Maybe not. But still, this isn't about how I feel about you. It's about who we are, and I just don't think we can be compatible."

"I agree. But that doesn't mean it couldn't work in the meantime."

Reggie grinned. "I'm all for a little fun every now and then, Sarah, but you're worth more than that. You and I both know that wouldn't end well."

She looked down into the top of her drink. *Where are the others?* She felt like she could use a backup right about now. She grabbed her cellphone from her pocket and placed it face-up on the table, looking at the blank screen as if it were about to conjure some sort of remedy for the awkward moment.

"Let's talk about it later," Reggie said, his voice dropping again to scarcely above a whisper. "We can chat about something else for now."

There were a few other patrons in the bar, chatting quietly, and the piped-in music was faint, but she could still barely hear him.

She nodded. "My father, then?"

"Sure, if that's what you'd like to talk about," he said.

Before they could start in on that conversation, Sarah's phone buzzed on the table, then dinged. She looked down at the lockscreen, where the text message that had just come in was displayed.

It was from Alexander. *Can you talk?*

She swiped across the text to remove it from the screen, but she noticed Reggie had already seen it.

"Who's that?" Reggie asked.

She mumbled a response, but focused on the reply. *Not now,* she wrote.

She looked up at her ex-boyfriend. "Sorry — that was, uh, a student. One of my field assistants."

Reggie lifted an eyebrow. "Alexander?"

"You read my phone?"

"It was right there. I wasn't trying to snoop."

"He's my assistant."

"Yeah," Reggie said. "I saw that in the picture."

Sarah looked at Reggie's face, reading it, just as another text message came in. She struggled, trying not to look down, but she couldn't help it.

Understood. Haplogroup X, ever heard of it?

She shook her head slightly, then clicked the screen off.

"*Just* an assistant?" Reggie asked.

"What's that supposed to mean?"

She inhaled a deep breath. When they had been dating, she'd mentioned to Reggie that one of her students seemed to 'have a thing' for her, but she had made it clear to him that she wasn't at all interested. Neither of them were the jealous type anyway, but she knew that long-distance, sporadic relationships were difficult at best.

She also knew that Reggie had seen a picture of Sarah and her team — she'd sent him a few when her research project had kicked off. Alex's tall, dark body and curling black hair were quite prominent in one of the pictures, and he'd even had his arm around her shoulder in one of them.

Sarah saw the door to the saloon-like hotel bar swing open and a man step in. His eyes were beady, tiny little peas that were already scanning the area. He was dressed semi-formally, wearing a suit coat over slacks and a deep-hued shirt, as if he'd carefully chosen his wardrobe earlier that day, but then had gently shed a few layers of formality when afternoon rolled around. He walked farther into the room, putting on a smile and nodding at the bartender.

A second man followed the first. This one was larger, taller and thick, and wearing a long-sleeved gray shirt buttoned to his neck that covered just about all of his upper body. They looked like brothers, both having a slight dimple on their left cheek. They even walked the same, their strides short and steady, not in a hurry but not lazy either.

She watched them enter while Reggie fiddled with his own phone, then she turned back to her ex-boyfriend. "It doesn't mean anything, Reggie. He's — there's nothing between us."

He nodded. "It's fine. I know," he said. "It's just — hard."

She returned the nod, then decided to change the subject. "Thanks for talking them into it," she said.

Reggie smiled and looked up at her. "Sarah — please," he said. "Even if they weren't able to come, they would have sent some sort of support. And they couldn't stop *me* from coming."

She laughed. "Well, I'm hoping this is all just a big misunderstanding, and that my old man is just stuck somewhere without a cell signal. Hopefully it'll blow over in a few days."

Reggie's grin faltered, but he seemed to be doing his best to keep it alive. "Yeah, me too. But listen — Sarah. Sometimes these things... well, sometimes they don't go according to plan. If your father *did* get himself into some sort of trouble..."

She stopped him. "I get it. You don't have to give me the details. I just want to know, you know? I can't live with myself, not knowing what happened to him."

Suddenly the shorter man that had walked into the bar was there, right next to Reggie. "Your father is fine," the man said. His dark, scratchy voice matched his eyes in some strange way. They fit together well.

"Who the hell — "

The man leaned in toward Reggie, forcing him sideways into the booth. Sarah watched Reggie push back against the man, bringing his arms up and toward him. Reggie, however, was in the worse position, his legs stuck beneath the table and his long torso crammed between the upright seat back and the edge of the table itself.

He wasn't in a position to fight back.

"Get the hell off me, man," Reggie said. "I'm not going to ask you —"

He stopped, abruptly. Sarah saw the larger man leaning in over Reggie from behind him, standing behind the booth.

He was holding a gun to the back of Reggie's head.

40

SARAH

"Do not talk," the first man said. "Or I will have Ivan blow a hole through your head."

Reggie swallowed, his bulging eyes staring straight ahead.

Staring at *her*.

Sarah felt tears welling in her eyes. Everything she had been worried about, everything she had feared, was real.

It was real, and it was even *worse* than she could have imagined.

"Your father is fine," the man said again, this time addressing Sarah directly. "Here is a picture."

He tossed down a Polaroid image, the faint smack as it landed on the tabletop hitting Sarah's ears at the same time the image came into focus.

Daddy.

It was her father, the same slightly bent, scrappy old guy that she'd known her entire life, sitting in a chair.

But his arms were slack, his hands sitting on his lap, and he was staring up and over the camera, toward something she couldn't see.

"You see?" the man said. "He is not dead, or harmed."

"What — who are you?" Sarah stammered.

"We are interested in uncovering what your father has been searching for," the man said. "Do you have the artifact?"

Sarah started to respond, but Reggie spoke first. "Listen, asshole," Reggie began, "you didn't answer her —"

The guy with the gun smacked the butt of it against Reggie's head. He shook, faltering, but then recovered and held a hand to his temple.

"We are not murderers," the first man said. "We only wish to expedite matters. It is in everyone's best interest if you would simply allow us to continue our work without interference. Please, we need the artifact."

"I'm not helping you," Sarah said. She could feel the bulge in her pocket where the stone object waited. She wasn't sure what she should do. *Give it to them? It's obviously more important than I understand. Perhaps it will help my father —*

"Give us the artifact and your father doesn't get hurt."

She glared up at them. "No."

"Your father warned us of that," the man said. He kept his voice smooth, calm, as if they were two long-lost friends that had somehow found each other among the hustle and bustle inside the Santorini tourist trap and were catching up on old business. "He told us you would not cooperate. But I assured him that while we are hesitant — though prepared — to actually *kill* either one of you, we are more than happy to do whatever it takes to get the job done."

Sarah looked around. There was a bartender behind the bar, a tall Greek man with curly black hair, dressed in an all-black suit and tie, helping two patrons at the far end of the bar. Two more, a couple on a date, sat near the entrance.

None of them so much as looked their direction.

"I am going to ask that you stand up slowly, follow me outside, and then get into our vehicle. It is not a difficult task, Ms. Lindgren. If your friend here gets in our way, we will shoot him. If he continues to interfere, we will kill you and just continue with only your father to help us.

"And then, when we finish our job, my employer will have your father killed anyway. So I suggest you cooperate."

Sarah clenched her jaw. She fidgeted, staring back at Reggie.

His face was calm, but his eyes were in torment.

She wondered what he might be thinking. *Was he armed? Had he been thinking about a situation like this, and had he prepared for it? What will he do after —*

"Get up, Ms. Lindgren."

Sarah felt the first tear roll slowly down her cheek as she rose from the booth. She noticed her leg swinging outward, onto the floor of the main bar area, and her arm reaching out to push herself up. She felt the cold, hard table, the unforgiving strength of it.

Strength she had no way to use.

She started walking, pulling herself forward with some sort of deep, hidden well of courage, her brain screaming the entire time. The man felt her sides, then reached into her pocket and withdrew the object. He smiled, then handed it to his partner. He then took her phone from her other pocket and slid it into his own.

At least he left it on, she thought. *For now.*

The first man spun and began walking toward the exit, smiling at the bartender and the patrons as he passed. Sarah couldn't look at them. She was afraid to speak, to call out, and therefore afraid to even make eye contact, for fear that they would know what was happening and try to intervene and then cause Reggie to get —

The second man was behind her now, pushing her out the door. She felt the cool air of the lobby, then five steps later to the right and they were out in the humid, chilly Mediterranean air.

The second, larger man — Ivan — stopped. "We wait here for a moment," he growled. "Maybe your friend will run after you?"

Sarah swallowed.

Please, Reggie, she willed, *do not leave the bar. Please.*

The man waited, standing just to the side of the door, holding Sarah's arm in his left hand and hiding the gun behind her body with his right, pointing it toward the hotel's entrance.

To the casual observer or passerby, they looked like two lovers enjoying a brief respite from the bright lights of the hotel interior, or a couple on a smoke break.

The first man was at the vehicle, a low, long boat-like Cadillac or something. She wasn't positive what color it was, but it looked black. There was no front license plate for her to memorize.

The man in the car flicked on the brights, illuminating Sarah and her guard and the front doors, and Sarah knew anyone trying to leave would be immediately blinded as they exited.

Again, she prayed.

Please, Reggie. Stay inside.

"You go to the car," the tall man said. "Now."

She wasn't about to argue, and she didn't need to wonder about the consequences of her trying to run away, so she walked slowly to the passenger side of the vehicle and opened the door.

"Get in," the first man said.

The second man waited by the door for a few more minutes, then turned and jogged to the vehicle and got in the back.

Sarah looked at the driver and saw a small, compact pistol in the man's left hand, just beneath the window. He was watching the front doors, but Sarah felt his peripheral gaze directly on her.

"Okay," the Ivan said from the back seat. "We're good."

The driver — the smaller man — nodded. "Looks like your friend made the right call, Ms. Lindgren. Please buckle your seatbelt. I do not want any accidents to ruin our night."

She clicked her buckle and nodded.

"Where are we going?" she asked.

The man seemed to soften a bit as they hit the edge of the parking lot and sped up onto the main road. It was a small, two-way street that mirrored the coastline down below them, and Sarah's side had a perfect view of the jagged cliff face next to her.

"To the office," he said.

"Your office?"

"Mmhmm."

"Why?"

"Because that is where your father is staying," he said. "And we thought you might like to see him."

41

REGGIE

THINK, REGGIE.

He thought.

He thought harder, and still there was nothing he could to change the situation.

His mind raced, his adrenaline pumping. He felt fresh, ready, as if he hadn't had any alcohol in the past month.

That, of course, was far from the truth, and he wasted a moment wondering if his senses were somehow dampened by the booze he'd been consuming.

Of course not, he thought.

Alcohol certainly slowed his reaction time, but it didn't slow his thinking. His mind was clear, ready to take action, but the problem was that he had no idea what he should be doing.

He'd waited until the trio — including Sarah — moved out into the lobby and rounded the corner. When he was safe from being spotted by the pair of kidnappers, he bolted up and out of his seat and toward the door.

The bartender had yelled something at him as he left, but he waved it off. He'd go back and pay the tab later. Besides, he'd figured, it would be on the CSO anyway, and they were all staying in the hotel.

He'd reached the lobby just in time to see the smaller man hustling to a car parked right in front of the hotel lobby. It was set up like a typical hotel building, with a covered dropoff area cordoned off directly in the front of the building, and the man's car sat parked right between the two columns that held up the overhang, pointing over the shrubs and plants and directly into the lobby.

It'll be a perfect way to blind anyone coming out, he realized. *That means they're going to be waiting for me.* He didn't need to see the second man and Sarah to know they would be waiting somewhere nearby, the larger man holding a gun out and waiting for Reggie to walk right into it.

Without even thinking twice about the situation he spun around and sprinted to the nearest exit sign he could find. It had been off the opposite side of the lobby, and he hurdled a couch and end table that stood in his way.

Upon reaching the hallway that led to the exit, he increased his speed and hit the door with his hip. It flew open, and for a moment he had been worried the glass might shatter, or that another hotel guest could have been on the opposite side of it.

But he didn't slow down. He ran, now unimpeded by couches, end tables, guests, and glass doors. The parking lot wrapped around the hotel on two sides — this side and the front of the building, and he let his legs unravel all the way and sped on.

He'd reached the front of the hotel just in time to see the taller of the two men duck into the back seat and the car back away from the curb. He raced toward it, but it began crawling forward and toward the parking lot exit.

There was a license plate on the back of it that swung suddenly into view, visible only for a split second, but it was all he needed. He committed it to memory as the car pulled onto the small road and sped away.

He was fast, but no one was fast enough to chase down a car that didn't want to be caught.

He grabbed his phone and typed in the license plate number to ensure he wouldn't forget it, only then realizing how strange it seemed that a getaway vehicle even *had* a license plate in the first place.

Was it stolen? Reggie wondered. Perhaps the kidnappers had hotwired a vehicle before coming into the tavern? He saved the note on his phone, turned off the screen, and placed it back into his pocket.

The others would obviously want to know that Sarah had been taken, and he would tell them as soon as he could. But if there was any chance he could call in the stolen vehicle and get it on the record that it was carrying an American kidnapping victim, they might just have a chance at getting the jump on the criminals.

He pulled the phone back out and looked up the number for the local police. Finding it quickly, he pressed the link and the call connected.

He was breathing heavily, only now feeling the alcohol, exhaustion, and travel catching up with him.

Not to mention the fear.

He was terrified, even though he was running through scenarios in his mind, planning out contingencies and working through the options. He had been in this situation before, and he had come out every time the victor. There was no reason for Reggie to expect any different this time, except that this time the *situation* involved someone much closer to home.

The operator on the other end of the line picked up and answered in Greek. He paused, trying to collect his thoughts.

We're not supposed to be here, and they don't know — or care — who the CSO is.

The CSO had been involved in numerous exploits over the past year and had received international attention for its victories — and losses — but Reggie wasn't naive. He knew that any PR love they'd received over the time the CSO had been operating would not translate into any favors from local law enforcement. The impression most people had of them was likely the equivalent of that of a well-known television personality. Reggie and the others were heroes, but the kind of heroes that get book deals and get interviewed on morning shows.

Not the kind of heroes that get to call in to the Santorini police department and order people around.

"I — I need a license plate lookup," Reggie said.

There was a pause, then another few words in Greek.

I didn't even think to get a Greek-English dictionary, he thought.

He tried again, but the woman on the other end was clearly not able to understand him.

He growled, frustrated, then shoved the phone in his pocket once again.

I'll try the front desk, he thought. *They should be able to translate.*

He tried to think ahead to the next steps, the possible outcomes of every situation he could think up, but none seemed logical or plausible. He was a civilian in another country, trying to report a kidnapping without inviting too much scrutiny, as he knew that every local police force around the world all shared a common trait: they asked too many questions.

He wanted Sarah found, but he *also* wanted to find her kidnappers himself.

He had unfinished business with them.

As he walked into the hotel lobby, immediately bombarded by the brilliant white lights from the two fake chandeliers dangling from the ceiling, he saw Ben walking over.

"Hey buddy," Ben said. "You okay? What were you doing outside?"

Reggie didn't need a mirror to see what his face looked like — he could feel it, and he could see it reflected on Ben's own face. "I — I was... Ben, Sarah's gone."

"She's *what?*" Ben said. "I just came down to see if you were still here, thinking you might want a nightcap or something. Sarah's gone? Where'd she go?"

"She was taken, Ben," Reggie said, still struggling with the truth himself. He looked at his best friend, his eyes bloodshot, and he could almost see Ben's understanding. Ben was morphing in front of his eyes, reading Reggie's expression and nonverbal cues, taking it on, making it his own. Ben straightened up, growing a few inches, and his eyes narrowed, waiting for Reggie to explain so Ben could take off in the right direction and destroy whomever it was that was behind this.

Reggie continued, this time his emotions all hitting his lips at the same time. He didn't care who heard; he didn't care what he sounded like. The words fell out, one after another. "Two guys, armed, came into the bar, forced her to follow them, threatened me. I'm not carrying right now, but even if I was — they had a gun to my head, and they just came out of nowhere. One of them was named Ivan, I think. I tried to call the — I don't know Greek, Ben, and I couldn't understand what they — the guys didn't look like military dudes, if you know what I mean, and they almost seemed *nice* about — or at least *calm*, you know — and I ran, but they were already —"

Ben reached out and squeezed Reggie's shoulder. "Hey, hey. It's okay, man. Settle down. You're rattled. You're not the kind of guy who gets rattled, okay? So just take a few breaths and look at me."

Reggie nodded, listening to his friend. "Yeah, okay." Ben was right. Reggie was *not* the sort of guy to get rattled easily, especially in a situation like this one. He usually *thrived* in situations like this.

Except that most situations like this didn't involve *people* like this.

Sarah wasn't just anyone — and she had been taken right out from in front of him.

He was rattled.

"Sorry man," he said. "I'm just — it's a little nerve-wracking. I was *right there,* sitting in front of her. They just came in, and I wasn't even able to move fast enough to do anything about it."

"Let's get upstairs, get the others, and see about following her. We'll track her down."

Reggie nodded. He felt strange, like he was off-balance. Not something he felt often, and it wasn't because of the alcohol.

Alcohol might actually help, he thought as he followed Ben upstairs.

42

SARAH

SARAH'S WRISTS SCREAMED IN PAIN, BUT SHE WAS TOO CAUGHT UP WITH her situation to notice. She'd been bound — a quick wrap of contractor-strength zip ties, cinched tight against her skin — and then thrown into the backseat of the dark SUV. She'd not been able to discern the exact color, but she had seen the make and model of the vehicle just before the larger man had shoved her inside. A Volkswagon *Atlas,* the newest in the VW line of mid-size sport-utility vehicles.

There had been a lot of thoughts going through her mind when she noticed the name of the car. One of those thoughts was regarding the irony of the situation. Atlas was a titan from Greek mythology, one of the titans of Mount Othrys who fought against the gods of Mount Olympus in the *Titanomachy,* the ten-year battle between the older titans and the younger, newer gods of Greek lore.

Atlas, on the losing side, was forever condemned to hold the weight of the heavens, immortalized in sculptures depicting a man, head cocked to one side, a massive globe balanced precariously upon his shoulders.

The titan Atlas also had some well-known landmarks to his name: the Atlantic Ocean and, of course, the mythological continent of Atlantis.

The other thing that crossed her mind was the fact that an SUV like this was an odd vehicle to be licensed to an owner on the island. There were SUVs around, but most of those were owned by rental companies that specialized in making the American tourists feel more at home by renting them the large, gas-guzzling vehicles they were used to.

But this vehicle wasn't a rental — it had a license plate registered to someone on the island and no stickers from a rental agency adorning its back window. *Whoever kidnapped me owns this vehicle,* she thought, *or borrowed it from someone who does.*

It wasn't much help, knowing that, but she filed it away anyway.

Besides that, any information she had about her situation was useless — her phone had been taken hostage even before she had been, and now her hands were bound behind her back. Even if she had her phone and could access it, there would be no way to get it out and send a message to the others before her captors took it.

From what she gathered, these captors weren't fly-by-night amateurs, either. They seemed professional, cool and collected as they'd grabbed her and even had a contingency plan in case Reggie had decided to barrel out of the hotel lobby in pursuit.

As she was joined in the Atlas by the second of the men who'd kidnapped her, she noticed the driver poking at a large in-dash screen. He navigated around the built-in apps until he found the one he was looking for — guidance and navigation — then pressed a pre-programmed location.

She wasn't able to read what the destination was, but when he pulled his hand back and began to drive out of the parking lot, she saw a quick 3D image of the map, including their current GPS-qualified location and their target destination. She saw the curvature of the main highway they were about to join as well as the curvature of the long, skinny island itself.

If she had been from the area the view may have been helpful. As it was, she felt even more frustrated, scared, and lonely. She'd had an opportunity to see where they were headed and come up short.

Reggie, please, she thought, *find me.*

She wanted to find her father, but at the moment she couldn't shake the feeling that there was something far larger going on than just a double kidnapping. She wanted to keep her father front of mind, to remember that she had come here solely to find him, and she couldn't help but feel the anxiety building in her chest. The warmth of panic began to take over her ability to think straight, to supersede the feeling of pain from her bound wrists and the adrenaline rush fighting against it.

She felt like the damsel in distress — her fate no longer in her own hands. She hated the fairy tales and movies, the helpless maidens who relied on big, strong princes and warriors to save them. Now, in the back of an SUV preparing to speed away from the only contact to the rest of the world she had, she couldn't help but feel like one of those princesses, trapped in a castle awaiting her doom.

Or, if she was lucky, her rescue.

As soon as it had appeared, she pushed the thought out of her mind. *Enough of that,* she reasoned. *You're more than capable of handling yourself. Get a grip, take a breath, and start figuring this out.*

And then, as if a second voice was now silently urging her on, she heard, *it's not like they want to kill you or they would have done it by now.*

She nodded. *I agree*.

She leaned forward. "Where are we going?" Sarah asked, leaning forward as the driver turned into oncoming traffic.

The larger man, Ivan, simply stared out the window. The driver's eyes flashed into the rearview mirror. "It does not concern —"

"It bloody well *does* concern me, asshole," she said, suddenly surprised by her confidence. "I'm being *kidnapped*. If it didn't *concern* me, drop me off right here. Now. I'll take care of the zip ties myself."

At that, Ivan chuckled. "Again, it does not concern you. You are merely a stepping stone."

"To what?" she asked. "What the hell are you looking for?"

"You already know what we are looking for, Ms. Lindgren."

"To guys like you, I prefer *Dr.* Lindgren."

"My apologies. Now, if you don't mind —"

"You're looking for Atlantis?" Sarah blurted out.

The driver frowned, and Ivan looked over at him, apparently waiting for some instructions. Finding nothing in his comrade's face, he turned slowly in his chair and looked at Sarah.

"We are not looking for Atlantis," he started.

"Bullshit," she said. "That's why we're here. That's why you kidnapped my father. We're *all* looking for that stupid old —"

"We are not looking for Atlantis because we've already *found* it."

"You've... already *found* it?"

Ivan shrugged. "Of course. Where do you think we've been all this time? This island, the volcano in the center, all of it — what do you think it is?"

"This... place — is Atlantis?"

"Of course. Plato literally describes *this* island in his essays. He tells of an island that matches this island exactly, down to the exact unit of measure. The Cyclades Plateau, you have heard of it?"

Sarah thought about their earlier conversation in the hotel bar. "Well, yes, but —"

"Then you know the entire area is nothing but a sunken island. An ancient *continent*. Everything Plato describes is here — this island, Thira, or Santorini, is but the smallest of the two that made up the continent. You know this, Dr. Lindgren."

"I don't — I don't understand, then... why is there..."

"No sign of the great civilization?"

She nodded.

He smiled. "Atlantis, while advanced, was not what it seems. Many philosophers and scientists have tried to understand what Plato was talking about. Through the years the legend has grown, as all legends do, to a fantastical account of an unbelievably advanced civilization that is, well, unbelievable."

"So this place... the island we're on... it's part of *Atlantis*?"

"It is. Or it was," Ivan said. "It's a relic, only a remnant of what once was. The people here have moved on, forgetting their own history, their own ancestry, until the legend grew larger than the truth. They built new lives, forgetting that their entire lineage was tied to a much larger, much more powerful nation just to the north. One that now lies beneath the sea."

Sarah looked out the window as they passed through the suburbs and entered a winding, dark country road that bordered the ocean. She could see the vast blackness of the ocean, dotted with a few sparkling lights of evening life. *This is Atlantis,* she thought. She tried the words in her mind, playing with them to see if they fit. *This is Atlantis*.

Still, something bothered her. Even if this place *was* the remains of the great lost civilization, she still didn't understand what all the fuss was. These men had *kidnapped* her — kidnapped her father — and were going to demand something from her. They wanted 'an answer,' as they had written. Whatever the answer was, they were willing to go to any lengths to retrieve it.

And that begged the question:

"You're not looking for Atlantis, then?" Sarah asked.

Ivan shook his head, grinning. "No. As I said, we already know where Atlantis is. We're looking for something else entirely."

43

JULIE

THE PAST HOUR HAD DONE NOTHING TO LIFT REGGIE'S SPIRITS, AND JULIE was growing more and more depressed by the minute. When Reggie and Ben had rushed up to the hotel room Julie and Ben were staying in, they'd shared what had happened with Sarah, summoning Mrs. E from her room across the hall.

Reggie had no information besides the general color and style of the getaway vehicle and the license plate number, as well as the appearance of the captors. He was quiet, reserved, and — in Julie's opinion — very different from the man she knew. He was anxious, rocking gently back and forth on the couch against the wall. He hadn't moved from that spot since they'd entered the room.

And he hadn't been the last person to enter the room, either. Etienne Sharpe of Interpol had joined them about ten minutes ago, hoping to visit with Sarah Lindgren. He had narrowly missed the kidnapping incident, but informed them that he was already working to bring the local police up to speed.

"How were you already here, again?" Julie asked him. "You're not based in Santorini. Or Greece, for that matter."

Sharpe stood near the door, his back to the wall. His thick French accent was apparent but his English was otherwise impeccable. He shook his head. "No, I am not. I was trying to meet up with Dr. Lindgren, and I knew from her flight that she would be here. I would have called ahead, but these matters… well, they tend to be a bit delicate."

Julie saw Ben frown, then she turned to address Sharpe. "What do you mean by 'delicate?'"

"More importantly," Ben asked, "you knew about her *flight*? Are you tracking her somehow?"

Sharpe cleared his throat. He was tall, thin, and handsome. His longish brown hair was not styled, but it fell naturally to one side, similar to Ben's. His eyes were deep, brooding, and Julie could tell he wasn't just a desk jockey. His physique, even if hidden under a government-issue gray suit, was well-kept. If she wasn't mistaken, she'd have guessed that he had spent some time as a soldier in his recent past.

He first addressed Ben. "Yes," he said. "We are. Whenever an incident like this goes without resolution for more than 24 hours we begin to track the movements of close friends and family. Her ticket was purchased by your organization, but she needed to be cleared by your government's travel security."

He turned his gaze to Julie. "I apologize for not alerting you all sooner," he said. "But Professor Graham Lindgren has been under close observation for some time now, in both his home country and at our field offices. That is part of the reason we were aware of his abduction so early in the process."

"Why were you watching *him*?" Ben asked.

"He has done nothing wrong, rest assured," Sharpe said. "At least, we have no reason to believe that he has. But over the course of the past six months, there have been an increased amount of pings to his online presence from suspect IP addresses. We've been watching it for about a month, to gain more information and to formulate a plausible explanation. These types of pings, individually, are typically of no concern, as it is usually impossible to tell where the origin point of a server request is."

"Right," Julie said. "Just because you got a hit from an IP address from somewhere in Iran doesn't mean that the *person* doing the search was in Iran."

Sharpe nodded. "Precisely. The public internet is a vast, ever-changing algorithm, and even with purposeful DNS rerouting and IP masking, client requests are sent through quite a few nodes on the way to the server, and different ones on the way back.

"But even *without* such a specialized relocation protocol in place, there are ways to see, on average, the number of requests jumping through a known node that is a bit less-than-reputable. For example, many of the black-market arms dealers we know of use a handful of the same services for encrypting their connections through their devices. It makes it impossible to tell *where* they are, but we know, at the very least, *when* they made the connection and what data centers they were routed through."

"Wait a minute," Ben said. "So you guys are watching this stuff all the time? Like the NSA or something?"

Sharpe smiled. "Not really. This is not 'snooping' as much as it is just a computer program that filters out anomalous hits to a given online resource and generates a report of 'likely points of interest.' The truth is that even the bad people out there also use the web for completely normal, legal, day-to-day transactions, like online shopping and entertainment. Normally that fact makes it difficult to wade through the data, but when there are numerous hits on a resource that all seem to be coming from known criminal sources, we take a closer look at the resource."

Reggie nodded once. "Professor Lindgren's paper," he said.

"Yes," Sharpe said. "You have seen it?"

"No, but we saw a reference to it. *Timeaus and Critias – An Alternative Interpretation.* It's been taken down."

"By Graham himself," Sharpe said. "It seems he retracted the article and deleted what references to it he could find."

"What did it say?" Mrs. E asked.

"We don't know," Sharpe said. "Our database flagged it as a candidate for human follow-up. By the time we saw it two weeks ago it had been taken offline for whatever reason. But our working theory is that someone made a threat to Professor Lindgren, something that scared him enough that he tried to hide any association with them. Anything that might lead them to the professor."

Julie took in a deep breath. "How did you get involved, Agent Sharpe? I was under the impression that Interpol didn't have regular 'field agents?'"

"That is almost correct," Sharpe said. "We don't have many, and those we do have are usually just for liaison purposes between international governments. Information in our databases was requested by the local authorities at the university, who were alerted by the IT staff there. It only escalated to our attention due to a clause in the nation's education policy that suspect matters such as this be immediately and unquestionably brought to the attention of an international policing agency. We had the records available, and things quickly began to look suspicious, so here we are."

"Lucky you were able to help, then," Ben said.

"I only wish I was lucky enough to get here in time," Sharpe said. "And for that matter, I wish we were more equipped to provide on-the-ground support. As it is, Interpol is merely a *resourcing* service for local, regional, and international law enforcement. We can push local law enforcement to help us out, but we do not have the resources in-house to run investigations such as this."

His eyes shifted as he looked at each of them in turn, and in that moment Julie understood why he was here. She also looked around the room, at the others gathered there, her friends and teammates she'd been through hell and back with.

They're not going to like this part, she thought.

She stood up and walked a few paces to the other side of the room, putting physical distance between herself and agent Sharpe. She looked out the small window of the mid-range hotel room, out at the streets and city of Santorini. In the distance she could see the vast expanse of the Mediterranean, still illuminated by the waning cerulean of the evening sun. "You're not here to ask us for our help, are you?"

Sharpe smiled again, but this time it hung a bit on one side. He seemed genuinely concerned, as if delivering this news was his sole purpose for being here and yet it still pained him to do so. "No, Juliette. I am not."

She nodded.

"I have been following your group's success, believe it or not," he continued. "To me you are the epitome of what citizens should be, regardless of their country of origin — capable, informed, aware, and able to take matters into your own hands, should the situation force that. You are patriots, to your country as well as countries like the ones I represent that need everyday heroes.

"But at the end of the day, you are still *citizens*. Civilians. You have no governmental authority, at least not in any way recognizable by Interpol or any European Union or United Nations treaty."

He was correct, of course. The beauty of the Civilian Special Operations was also its curse. To the United States — and any other government — they didn't officially exist. The leaders of all nations had complete plausible deniability when it came to the ragtag group of privately funded self-declared police officers. The branches of the US military had seats on the board, and had a small say in their operations, but they all knew that the CSO had no real stake in the international espionage game.

Sharpe's statement didn't surprise her in the least, but it still stung.

You are not recognized, he was saying. It was a professional truth but it stung personally.

"You're telling us to stand down," Ben said. It wasn't a question. Julie heard the heightened tension in his voice.

"I am," Sharpe said. "I was here on a goodwill mission to help Dr. Lindgren wade through the legal battle concerning her father's abduction, should it come to that... but I am also here to inform you that your presence in an ongoing international investigation is not going to be acknowledged."

"What's that *really* mean, boss?" Reggie said, suddenly snapping to attention. He sniffed, then wiggled his nose a bit, as if trying to force it not to run. Julie may have been briefly worried about Ben's temper, but she was now concerned more for Reggie's. She'd seen what happened when he got too worked up about something, and these guys kidnapping Sarah was just the sort of thing...

"It means we are politely requesting your assistance in the matters of finding Dr. and Professor Lindgren, by —"

"By having us on the sidelines?"

"...by allowing our offices and law enforcement to work unimpeded."

"We wouldn't dare *impede,*" Reggie said, the tinge of sarcasm in his voice barely masking the anger Julie knew was welling up inside him.

"Your reputation suggests otherwise," Sharpe said, just as quick to the draw.

"Our *reputation* is actually impeccable, I believe," Ben said. "In fact, we —"

"Not now, Ben," Julie said.

Ben glared at her, defiantly, but he didn't speak.

She felt actual heat in the room now. Sharpe stood against his wall, on his side, her people stood scattered around their side. Reggie was emotionally compromised, and if his words weren't indicative of that his reddish nose and bloodshot, tear-filled eyes were.

Ben was seething, and she felt like taking a step away from him. He would never do harm to her, but he was also a bit like a bull in a china shop when he was upset. He was *prone to rash behavior,* according to the initial CSO dossier.

"Agent Sharpe," she said, keeping her voice calm and even. "Thank you for coming personally. I know that was a heck of a trip. You must understand that we are *also* tired, having just disembarked from a forty-eight hour trip. We're exhausted, we're angry about Professor Lindgren, and now we're *reeling* from hearing about his daughter. She's our friend."

Sharpe nodded, then coughed into his fist. "Yes, I know," he said. "Again, I apologize. If there was any way I could change this, I would. Truly. But my superiors are not at all interested in help from your group at this point. Please believe me when I tell you: if that changes, I will be there to deliver the news to you personally."

Julie was upset, but she understood. Interpol was trying to keep things clean, simple. There were many organizations it worked with worldwide, and that automatically implied there were plenty of lines of communication and chains of command that would overcomplicate issues. Adding in a crack team of NGO freedom fighters, from their perspective, would drastically muddy the waters. The paperwork alone would be a nightmare.

Still, it hurt to be cast aside so succinctly and effortlessly. Sharpe was a good agent, she could tell, and he seemed like a good man. He didn't want to hurt their feelings, but he also didn't want to upset tried-and-true hierarchies.

She looked at the rest of the members of her team. Mrs. E was silent, taking it all in. Reggie and Ben were quiet, but she knew they were probably both screaming on the inside. She herself felt it. Sarah was gone, they had no good leads, and the information they *did* have they'd effectively just turned over to an organization that didn't want their help.

She thanked Sharpe and showed him out, asking him where he was staying while on the island. He responded with a dismissive, vague answer about another hotel somewhere nearby, then departed. As soon as she closed the door, Ben and Reggie were standing behind her, arms crossed.

She sensed they were upset with her, as if she had been the one to deliver the bad news.

"So we're just supposed to lay low, ignore all of this?" Reggie asked.

"No," Julie said, shaking her head. "That's the last thing we're supposed to do."

44

JULIE

"We're going to make this a matter of national security," Julie said.

"How's that now?" Reggie asked. She could see a visual shift in the man's demeanor. He'd been expecting more disappointment, more anger, more grief. What she'd just given him was hope.

"It's not *just* a kidnapping," she replied. "And it's not just some quack theory about Atlantis."

"It's not?" Ben asked.

The four of them were all standing in the narrow hallway near the door, where Sharpe had just exited. Julie waved them to follow and navigated between them to the more spacious hotel room. *How many times have we planned out some scheme from inside a hotel room like this?* she wondered.

"It's not," she said, continuing. "There's something else going on here. Something bigger — deeper — than just the kidnapping of a couple academics. And certainly bigger than just an unprovable — and improbable — theory about Plato's lost continent. Sharpe said so himself."

"He did?"

Julie nodded. Before she'd worked for the Biological Threat Resistance department of the CDC she'd been a sought-after IT consultant. Her education was in computer science and information systems, and after the incidents at Yellowstone, she'd accepted a job doing part-time consulting and support for the national park her boyfriend Ben worked for.

Her role in the CSO was still one of support, and her knowledge and experience was often put to work to help solve computer-related problems. She wouldn't have called herself a hacker, necessarily, but she understood how systems worked, interfaced, and connected with the outside world. Most importantly, and the piece many 'real' hackers were missing, she knew how *people* worked. She could understand the motives behind why people did what they did, and then translate that to how they may have done it using a computer system.

Sharpe had explained something she knew intuitively — a government or police force can only monitor so much at once. They were limited, like anyone else, with their resources and manpower to determine actionable items. That meant that even with fancy computers and well-scripted algorithms, organizations still couldn't see, hear, and watch *everything.*

So if Interpol had found something worth investigating in person, acting on a tip from a university's IT department and campus police, and then sending someone across the continent to investigate further and provide eyes-on support, it meant that it — whatever it was — was likely a big deal.

As far as she could recall, there hadn't been any international investigations launched for similar kidnappings, even when the person kidnapped claimed to have found Atlantis — a certain famous archeologist named Dan Kotler came to mind. He had stolen the hearts and minds of the public on his own successful archeological excursions, and his kidnappings hadn't raised the hackles of anyone but his closest allies.

So there was something else going on. It was large enough that at least *two* professionals had been kidnapped in the name of 'finding' this version of Atlantis, and Interpol was following a thread of evidence based on a paper published, and subsequently *un*published — by one of the kidnapping victims.

Julie had been lost in her own thoughts, formulating a plan, but she stopped and looked up at the rest of the group. "Yes," she said. "He wouldn't be here if they didn't think it was an international concern."

She noticed Ben eyeing him suspiciously.

"Problem?" Julie asked.

"You're not telling us something," he said.

She exhaled. "Fine," she said. "You're right. But it's probably nothing. I just — I just don't trust him."

"Who, Sharpe?" Reggie asked.

"Something… about him. I don't know. It just seems like he's not telling *us* something, I guess. About this whole mess. And the fact that he's *been* there, everywhere we've gone? Seems strange."

"I agree," Reggie said. "But I'm not sure it's anything actionable."

"The *actionable* thing to do is to take action," Julie said.

"So what's our move, then?" Ben asked.

"Well, Interpol's involved, we think. That means it's an international concern."

"So…"

"So we make it an even *bigger* international concern," she said.

"And… how do we do that?"

"Simple. We get someone involved who believes us, *and* who can pull the right strings."

"You've got someone in mind?" Reggie asked.

Julie looked at Mrs. E, who simply smiled. Ben followed suit, but Reggie sat in the chair across from Julie, silently fuming. Apparently he hadn't followed the breadcrumbs she'd been dropping.

She waited.

Finally, after a few more seconds, he looked up. "I see," he said. "Yeah, that might work. If he's not busy. But we'll need something more concrete. We can't just tell him 'my girlfriend got kidnapped,' then hope that the FBI issues a warrant and sends out a squad."

Julie laughed.

"Is that… wrong?" Reggie asked.

"No, you're right," Julie said. "The FBI's not an international force. I'm just laughing because you just called Sarah your girlfriend."

45

GRAHAM

PROFESSOR GRAHAM LINDGREN STOOD AND STRETCHED. HE HAD EATEN well that evening — a surprisingly positive attribute of his otherwise miserable captivity. He was still a prisoner, of course, but it was apparent that his jailers were truly more interested in finding whatever it was they thought he had than in harming him.

Though after their last threat against his daughter, he wasn't sure what they were capable of or planning. *If I don't give them something...*

He ran through ideas for anything they might be looking for. He'd been working on a unified theory of human civilization based on a question his daughter had posed in one of her papers: '*Where did we all come from?*'

It was an innocent question, one not burdened down by the rigors of religious and cultural overtones. She told him that since they'd last spoken she had been working on a paper trying to show the migration patterns of early American settlers, with the working hypothesis that the first people to arrive in the Americas had *not,* against what popular opinion depicted, arrived via a land bridge that connected present-day Alaska to Siberia over the now-thawed Bering Strait. Her goal was not to prove that the accepted theory was flat-out *wrong,* but to prove that there was another route taken entirely, and earlier — a route on the opposite side of the continent.

Settling the Eastern side of the Americas was something that most scholars believed had been many thousands of years after the migration over Beringia, when civilizations were capable of boatbuilding, sailing, and navigation.

It was already common knowledge that Christopher Columbus hadn't 'discovered' America as much as *re*discovered it for the Europeans, and that Viking explorers had reached the shores of North

America almost half a millennium before. In fact, recent evidence suggested that the Vikings had settled the area of Newfoundland around 1000 AD, suggesting that Europeans were stomping around the Americas long before Columbus was even born.

So for Graham's daughter to suggest that the Vikings *hadn't* been the first Atlantic-born connection to the Americas was not something that should have ruffled a feather, but he knew better than most how academics treated 'new' information — suspicion was their *modus operandi,* no matter how strong the evidence. It usually took mounting evidence, millions of dollars of research grants, and years of healthy-yet-skeptical discourse before a well-established belief was overturned and made mainstream.

Sarah hadn't exactly been shunned for her hypothesis, but it had not been well-received. She had received funding from her school, but he suspected that the money was the sort that came with strings attached. In other words, the money had been the proverbial rope: just long enough to hang herself with. And, he guessed, there might be a bit of familial favor involved: he was an accomplished archeologist with a near-celebrity status, and a refusal of his daughter's funding could generate backlash for her university.

He stretched again, then walked a couple circles through the room. There was nothing to do here — even reading, had he had a book to read — was impossible, as the only light filtering in was from a distant fluorescent bulb hanging in the hallway around the corner. He had no way to legitimately exercise, which caused him to feel lethargic and slow. He worried that his mind, normally sharp and quicker than the rest of his body, would eventually waste away as well.

How long will they keep me here? he thought. *What's their endgame?*

He knew that was the real question. They didn't care about him, or his daughter — they cared about results. They wanted to find whatever it was they were looking for, no matter the cost.

And if they didn't find it, they would make him pay dearly for it.

But how long did they have? What was their timeframe?

These were questions he had no answer for, as he had no idea what in the world they could *possibly* be searching for. He paced, wanting nothing more at the moment than to find out some more answers to his questions.

As if someone had read his mind, he heard the door to his room click open. He whirled around, seeing Rachel Rascher there again. She hadn't joined him for dinner this time around, but she was smiling, holding a bottle of wine.

"A peace offering?" Graham asked. "You *threatened* my daughter. You think I'm going to —"

"We already have your daughter, Professor Lindgren. It took a bit of *coercion,* but she is inbound as we speak."

He seethed, turning to face her fully. He raised a finger, preparing to launch into a tirade.

"Save it, Professor," Rachel said, her kind facade failing. "I am not here for an *offering* of any kind, unless you happen to be a wine drinker. In that case, here. It's a vintage from my own collection. Merlot."

He sucked his teeth. He *was* a wine drinker. Both his current girlfriend and Sarah's mother — his ex-wife — were interested in wine and had been collectors, filling Graham's apartment with both vintage and modern selections of the 'noble reds:' Cabernet Sauvignon, Merlot, Pinot Noir, Chardonnay, Riesling, and Sauvignon Blanc.

But it didn't change the fact that the woman offering him this gift was the same woman who had kidnapped him, his daughter, and was asking for something he didn't have.

"I still don't understand what it is you think I have," he said.

She handed him the bottle. "No matter. You probably need a drink anyway."

He accepted it, popped the cork, and took a swig directly from the bottle. "Where's Sarah?"

"She is fine, if that's what you mean," Rachel said. "As I said, she is on her way here as we speak."

"What do you want with her?"

"The same thing we want from you, professor. We want to know what was *inside* the object — the one you sent her."

The powder.

He shook his head, smiling in an unbelieving way. "There was *nothing* inside. I found it in Greenland, but it was *empty*. Unless you want to know what was in the *air* inside, in which case I would say it it's a combination of mostly oxygen and nitrogen, in a ratio that resembles that of the air found in the rest of the —"

She rocked on her heels. "Fine," she said. "Your daughter will be here in a matter of hours. At that point —"

Graham lost his temper. "At *that point* you can take whatever it is you're looking for and shove it up your —"

"Enough, Professor." She held up a hand. "I believe you, actually. When I mentioned your daughter, you were in pain. Real, actual, pain. I recognized that, because I've felt it. If that wasn't real, you're either the best damned actor I've ever seen or I'm hallucinating. The fact that I'm bringing her here doesn't change anything, however. If you don't know anything, perhaps she will. If she does not, then we will move to more *direct* tactics.

"The contents of the object you retrieved from Greenland are paramount to this investigation. And we need get the compound that was inside that artifact, before the event."

Rachel looked up toward the corner of the dingy cell, as if she'd said too much.

"What event? What are you talking about? As I said, there was nothing inside —"

"I know," she said. "I mean, I believe you. But we are running out of time."

"What *event* are you talking about? And what the hell are you *really* looking for?"

"We are trying to find the solution to an ancient problem."

46

BEN

"COME ON, MAN, THERE'S GOT TO BE *SOMETHING*," BEN SAID. HE WAS stressed, feeling the physical exertion of two days of travel, poor sleep, and a kidnapping of their friend beginning to weigh him down. He rolled his neck back and forth on tight, tense shoulders.

Reggie shook his head, his eyes dropping to the floor. "There's nothing, Ben. I'm sorry. I tried…"

"Nonsense," Julie said, suddenly at Ben's side in the hotel room. "You're good at this, Reggie. The *best*. Your training, experience — "

"My training got me through some situations, but it didn't prepare me for *this*."

Ben knew a bit about his friend's past, that Reggie — Gareth Red — had been an Army sniper, headhunted for a mission to Russia that had ended poorly and with Reggie's dismissal from the United States military. He hadn't rested on his heels, however, beginning a years-long excursion around the world, living wherever he pleased and working wherever he could.

Ben didn't know the details, but he knew that sometimes the man's 'work' was the sort of work that had gotten him kicked out of the military in the first place. He'd eventually settled down in Brazil with a young wife, building a compound on some land he'd purchased and opening up a survival training school and shooting range. He and his wife got a divorce, Reggie met Ben and Julie, and eventually joined up with the CSO.

"It did, Reggie," Ben said. "You got the license plate already. That's a start. Isn't there *anything* else you can remember? What did the guys look like, what was the car like?"

"I already told you all of that. And I told Derrick that, too."

Roger Derrick was an acquaintance of theirs who had helped them out in Philadelphia and Montana not long ago. He was an FBI agent, currently working on an assignment that was keeping him stateside for the time being. Julie had called him up, asked if he could help them with their predicament, and Roger Derrick had given them the best answer he could: 'give me the license plate number and any details you have, and I'll run them through our system.'

Ben, however, knew that Roger's hands were tied. There wasn't much he would be able to do if the car's owner was not a criminal, and he'd be even more helpless if the person wasn't American. The FBI wasn't an international organization, and though they were capable of plenty of surveillance and international intelligence-gathering, Derrick couldn't just hop on a plane and fly to Santorini to help his friends find a kidnapping victim.

Julie's idea to call Derrick was a good one, but it hadn't helped them much. They were still in the hotel, fumbling around for ideas without any solid leads.

Ben's phone vibrated in his pocket. He reached for it when he noticed that Julie's and Reggie's were already in their hands as well.

"Mrs. E texted all of us," Julie said. "Looks like Derrick got back to her."

Ben read the message on his phone as Julie read it aloud. *Derrick says car registered to owner in Santorini. Catholic priest. Likely stolen.*

"A priest?" Julie asked.

"That's why he thinks it was probably stolen," Ben said, shrugging. "I don't know of a lot of priests who are kidnapping people."

"You don't know a lot of priests," Julie said.

He looked up at Reggie. "Any of those grunts look like a priest?"

"No," Reggie said. "But why would they? It's not like they'd give themselves away by wearing a collar and black clothes. Besides, even if a priest was behind all of it, how does that help us?"

Julie frowned, thinking. Ben loved this woman — she was sharp, her mind as quick as anyone he'd ever met. "Maybe," she started, "maybe they were heading to a church? It's a long shot, but —"

Reggie snapped his fingers. "That's it!"

"A church?"

He shook his head. "No. Well, I don't know. But I saw where they were *heading*."

"Yeah, they were going up the highway. Toward the north side of the —"

"No," he said. "I caught a glimpse of their GPS screen inside the car. They didn't know the location of their destination, so they were using the car's built-in dash display screen to find it. I saw the map, recognized the circular shape of the island, the smaller island at the center of the bay."

Ben paced. He knew Reggie was tapping into his subconscious, working hard to recall every detail of the scene as it had played out. He had been trained to take these sorts of things in as a sniper, but he had shared with Ben and Julie in confidence that he had learned most of these 'tricks' from a far different source than the military.

Reggie had visited a counselor — a trained cognitive behavioral therapist who specialized in post-traumatic stress disorder — every week for about a year, many years ago. He had visited the man to help get a handle on the recurring memories that haunted and tormented him.

Memories, he'd shared with them, of the woman he had nearly married, long before he'd met Ben and Julie and the rest of the CSO, and long before he'd met the woman he'd eventually marry and then divorce.

Specifically, they were memories of the *child* — a baby girl — the woman had been carrying. *His* child. She had never been born, thanks to a decision the woman had made. The torture of it had gripped him with fear, panic, and a long-standing case of chronic anxiety. He'd wanted the child, but his girlfriend did not.

The therapist had taught him many tricks to help with the anxiety and panic attacks, including rapid eye movement techniques and the ability to 'see' memories as if they were playing out in real time, on command. By watching these 'movies' the mind created, Reggie's counselor had explained, one can begin to work through traumatic experiences with a sense of detachment, leading to an objective and emotionless analysis of the memory, which could eventually help overcome the anxiety-inducing emotions that came with it.

In this way, and by practicing the methods for years, Reggie was able to recall events that had happened in almost the same way a person with an eidetic memory could. He could 'see' a scene in his mind as if he were a writer, detailing every nuance and feature of the set and its characters as it unfolded. It wasn't always reliable, and it wasn't always completely accurate, but — like the therapist had promised — it had proven to be a useful strategy to stave off the debilitating effects of trauma and anxiety.

Almost immediately after he'd run outside and seen the man pushing Sarah into the back of the vehicle, he'd made up his mind. He wanted to chase down the vehicle — whether or not he'd be able to *do* anything about it if he reached it was another thing altogether — so he'd started running.

He watched the replay in his mind, like a football coach playing game tapes back to the team. He studied the surroundings, most of them faint or hazy, unclear depictions of what they were supposed to represent. Street signs, businesses, other cars — these were all just a blur to his memory.

He'd had a singular focus, and the elements of his subconscious' focus were brilliantly clear in his mind. He saw the car, how the light bounced off its sides, the curves of the vehicle's frame and body. He saw the license plate, locking it into his memory, knowing that he would want to be able to recall that detail later.

He had sped up, almost able to reach the side of the vehicle until it too accelerated and drove away. There was nothing he could do, as the doors would have been locked anyway, but he continued running until he was pacing next to the car as it turned to leave the parking lot.

The rear windows were tinted, the deep black preventing him from seeing Sarah. The front window had a darker shade on them as well, but he could see the screen of the dashboard-mounted display shining out at him.

That's it.

It suddenly came back to him, washing into his head like a surge of water hitting a lagoon. He felt it, *knew* it was real. He knew he could trust his mind's eye to recreate an accurate image. The trouble was this was real life — not some police television show. He couldn't manipulate the image in his mind. There was no zooming in or 'enhancing' it. He had whatever his mind had decided to store, and then whatever it decided to allow him to access.

He closed his eyes, trying as hard as possible to see it all over again. "I don't know any of the geography of the island, but I saw the line on their GPS unit. I can probably get pretty close with a map.

"We started at the airport, then came down to the hotel." He named the iconic highway that traveled around the interior of the main island, butchering the Greek name. "Drove down the... *Eparchiaki Odos Firon-ormou Perissis* and then headed inland a bit to the south."

Julie was already ready. She had retrieved a tablet from one of their backpacks, connected it to the hotel's wifi, and held it up to Reggie, the maps application open on the screen.

Reggie grabbed it, turning his head and tablet as he tried to make it the same size as the map he'd seen on the car's screen. He shifted it, pinched the map to zoom in and out, then frowned and repeated the process. Finally satisfied, he put it down on the bed.

"There," he said, tracing the map with an index finger. Ben saw the highway, *Eparchiaki Odos Firon-ormou Perissis,* labeled on the screen and watched Reggie trace the switchback, the hard-right turn on the highway, then the long straightaway that went through town. The route the highway — and Sarah, apparently — took.

"And then their route was going north, but it split off from the main highway, heading hard to the left, out over this little peninsula up here."

"West," Ben said.

"Yeah, exactly. It ended right at the water..." he paused, zooming in a bit. "Right around here."

"They're heading for a boat?"

"Probably," he nodded. "It was too far away to see with any degree of accuracy, but it seemed like it was just past this church, the *Ekklisia Theoskepasti.*"

Sure enough, there was a winding, twisting road that continued past the church labeled on the map, running nearly all the way to the water.

Julie frowned. "Those are cliffs, I think. That's why the road ends there." She dragged her hand across the north-south border of the island. "This whole section is steep, if not straight down, but enough so that it'd be an impossible climb, especially without gear."

"Well," Ben said, "they're doing it."

Reggie nodded. "He's right. That's where they're headed, I think. Maybe it's to a boat, maybe there's a building or something at the end of the road. But we need to go, *now.*"

Ben smiled, knowing Reggie wouldn't take no for an answer. He, like Ben, never did. "I'll call Mrs. E," he said.

"Do it in the car," Julie said, already moving. "She can join us after. If they're still on the road, we know the license plate. Even if not, the trail just got hot again. She's working on our transportation for tomorrow, but I've got the keys to the rental car here."

Ben and Reggie nodded. "Works for me," Reggie said.

The three of them headed to the door. There was nothing to take, nothing to prepare. They had a lead, and they intended to follow it, no matter where it led.

With any luck, Ben thought, it would lead them to at least another clue.

47

BEN

They reached the SUV in the parking lot and Ben got behind the wheel. There had been no communicating or decision-making. Ben had happened to be the one closest to the door, so he'd gotten in and started the engine. Julie and Reggie tumbled in as well, and before their seatbelts were fastened Reggie told him to move.

"Let's go," he said.

Ben grunted a response, throwing the large vehicle into reverse.

Julie pulled up her phone and found the church, Ekklesia Theoskepasti, on the map. She pressed the button to begin navigating toward it as Ben squealed the tires and sped up, heading out of the hotel's parking lot.

He didn't want to bring unnecessary attention to them, but he had also felt the urgency of the situation. The church was a good distance away, which meant the vehicle they were chasing could still be on the road.

It also meant they needed to be in a *huge* hurry. They would be driving along the coast, up a highway none of them were familiar with, through towns and farms and even a small city.

He gritted his teeth and slammed his foot down on the gas pedal. *Let's hope the cops aren't out tonight,* he thought.

"We're being tailed," Reggie said from the backseat.

"What?" Ben asked. "Already?"

"Not police," he said steadily, his head turned around, facing out the back windshield. "Looks like our Interpol friend."

"You've got to be kidding me," Julie said. "He's following us?"

"He did warn us not to do anything rash," Ben said. "But he's not really law enforcement here. Is there *really* anything he can do?"

Reggie met his eyes in the rearview mirror. "Sure," he said. "He can tail us. And then he can call in the *real* law enforcement, let them know we're driving erratically, speeding on the highway. In a hurry to get somewhere."

"Well let's hope he's just hungry, heading into town for dinner."

"Yeah," Julie said. "Let's hope."

"Julie," Ben said. "Send Mrs. E a text, let her know we took the car. And let her know what's going on."

"Already did," she replied, smiling.

Good, Ben thought. *Hopefully she's able to come up with something.* She wouldn't have a vehicle, he knew, but the woman was resourceful. Uber was a popular ride-sharing and personal taxi service on the island, so if she really needed to get somewhere she'd be able to.

Ben steeled himself and checked the rearview mirror again, gritting his teeth. He wasn't a professional driver, but he doubted the Interpol guy was, either. Still, the man's vehicle was lower to the ground but still heavy, and would likely be a better fit for taking the winding, hairpin turns on their route at a fast pace.

His SUV would have been great if they were somewhere off-road. Even then, the clearance on the suburban gas-guzzler was nowhere near high enough for a *real* off-roading experience. At the parks, Ben's team typically drove around a Subaru or a Jeep, or, if they were hauling something or needed the space, a lifted truck that could push through the mountainous passes that filled with snow in the winter and runoff debris in the spring and summer.

He gripped the steering wheel, continuing to accelerate. The speed limit sign on the side of the highway told him the island-wide limit: 60 kilometers per hour. Ben felt it was a bit slow, but he knew the limit had been imposed due to the narrow, winding roads that cut across the island.

His speedometer told him he was about to hit 85 km/hr.

Ben couldn't see the man driving, but he knew it was the Interpol agent, Sharpe. The car had matched their accelerations and lane changes. The man was clearly not worried about remaining invisible. He didn't care if Ben knew he was following them.

Ben passed a block of cars in the right lane just as the first real turn came up. It was a hard right, and he sped up, hoping he wasn't as bad a judge of the vehicle's center of gravity as he thought he was. "Hold on," he said, pushing the speed up to 95.

He didn't need to warn them. Reggie was holding the handle above his window, Julie grabbing at the door on her right and center console on her left.

Thank God this place has normal roads, Ben thought, preparing for the turn. He couldn't imagine what he'd do if he'd had to try to make the chase while learning to drive on the left side of the road, in the left side of the car.

The turn came quick — *much* quicker than he'd calculated. A few cars swerved out of his way, honking at him as he blew past. He tensed his jaw, leaning to the right. *Come on.* He felt the centripetal force and the inertia as the car door pushed against his left side, but he held fast on the wheel. His tricep was burning against the perceived weight of the vehicle as it struggled to change course.

Come on, he thought again. *Hold on.*

Then the turn was over, and he was faced with a nice, long straightaway. He let out a deep breath and turned to Julie. "You okay?" Ben asked.

She shook her head.

"Well you'd better get used to it," Reggie said from the back seat. There's going to be a few more of those —"

"I'm not concerned with the turns," Julie said. "And that one was pretty tame, when you think about it."

Ben nodded.

"I'm worried about the fact that Sharpe's still on our tail," she said, flicking her eyes to the side mirror next to her. "And now he's got company."

Ben felt his heart race as he looked out the mirror, through the back windshield. Two police cruisers had joined the Interpol sedan, their lights flashing brightly. They'd all made the turn easily and were now even closer to the SUV.

"Crap," he said. "That's not good."

"Nope," Reggie said.

Ben sped up, allowing the large vehicle to use its massive engine. They were traveling light, with only three passengers and no cargo, so Ben hoped they'd be able to outpace the three cars behind him, but it seemed as though the police cruisers were catching up.

He drove on like this for another few minutes, the cars behind him seemingly satisfied with a steady, nonstop chase.

And why shouldn't they? he thought. *They know there's nowhere I can go.*

It wasn't like the chases he'd seen on television. The towns they were zipping through were sleepy, quiet places, with few cars on the roads and plenty of space for drivers to get out of the way. Further, there wasn't a never-ending stretch of countryside to travel through, nor was there a separate jurisdiction those pursuing would have to worry about.

Here on the island the only thing they had to consider was running out of gas.

And he guessed that their cars were *far* better suited for gas mileage than his.

He was about to comment about that fact, asking Reggie for his opinion of their situation, when he noticed a two-car roadblock up ahead. The police behind him had apparently gotten in touch with the rest of their team, who had then scrambled and set up two of their patrol cars just outside the little town, completely blocking the road. Their cars were angled with their fronts toward oncoming traffic, likely an additional security mechanism. By pointing their cars *at* the getaway vehicle and then applying the emergency brake, a head-on impact with the two cars would be less likely to work.

There were two officers standing in front of their vehicles, playing the deadly game of *I bet you'll stop before you hit me.*

"Reggie…" his voice trailed off.

"I see it," Reggie said quietly.

"Ideas?" Ben asked.

"Those cars aren't going anywhere. They've got their brakes on. If we try to push through, those cars will just slide backwards a bit. Even if we get through, it's not going to be on the first try. By then the guys behind us will be on us."

"And if we *do* hit them, we're risking those police officers' lives," Julie said. "Not to mention ours."

Ben sucked in a quick breath, scanning the area. The road was in a desolate area, a good choice for the police. There would be no chance of collateral damage out here, and no one else would be in danger.

To the right side of the road, all the way to the edge of the pavement, was a pile of murderous boulders, piled up and spread over the acre or so of land. *That's a death wish,* he thought.

But to the left of the road…

No, he thought. *No way.*

He flashed a quick glance at Julie. There was no time to talk it out. No time to discuss their options and decide on their best strategy. Reggie and Julie were at his mercy, trusting that he'd make the right call.

To the left of the road, about three feet from the edge, was nothing. A cliff fell hundreds of feet straight down, right into the rocky shallows that abutted the island. The gentle dark sea was just beyond that.

Here goes, he thought.

He turned the wheel, sliding the car off the side of the road. The gravel and rocky earth next to the road immediately shot up behind them as they bounced over it, creating a haze of white in his mirrors. They drifted closer, *closer,* to the cliff. *Hold it together,* he willed himself. He wasn't necessarily afraid of heights, but his peripheral vision was sending out the alarm to the rest of his mind that they were *way* too close to death by driving here.

He turned the wheel back again to straighten it out, aiming the SUV right at the *back* end of the police car on the left.

"Ben," Julie whispered. Her voice was soft, but frantic. "What are you —"

She didn't have time to finish the question. He slammed down on the gas pedal, giving the last bit of juice to the heavy SUV. It screamed in reply, sending them flying forward, directly at the police car. He noticed one of the officers gaping at them as they launched past their position, the other one already dodging the SUV-sized missile.

He held the wheel, his rock-hard grip refusing to give. *Hold it.*

The SUV smacked into the much smaller, much lighter car and kept going forward. The car spun sideways, a sickening crunching and scraping sound reaching his ears as it simply disappeared from his vision. He was thrown forward in his seat, the tight seatbelt cutting into his shoulder, but the airbags didn't deploy.

The SUV barreled through the back of the car as if it weren't even there, and then just like that they were through.

There was nothing but open road behind them.

"Ben!" Reggie shouted. "That... was..."

He smiled, then felt dizzy, feeling the rush of adrenaline pouring into him. Julie laughed, and Reggie continued opening and closing his mouth, but no words were coming out.

He straightened the car out and lined it up in the right lane once again. There was a bit of a pull to the left, and he assumed the undercarriage had received some sort of damaging blow, either to the alignment or the tie rod, but he wasn't about to stop and check.

We're alive, and we're still moving, he thought. *That's good enough for now.*

48

BEN

THE SUV CONTINUED ON AT ITS BREAKNECK PACE. REGGIE KEPT AN EYE out for the police and their Interpol friend, but they were nearly at their destination and there was — so far — no police or Interpol in sight.

There were more switchbacks, but Ben took these slower, not wanting to risk the integrity of the truck frame any more than necessary.

They passed through the city near the end of the route, but they were still clear of any pursuers. At their exit, Ben pulled the SUV off the highway and then down toward the water in the distance. Julie had been right about the area — it seemed to be just a desolate road in the middle of nowhere, a church and its steeple the only structure in sight.

They passed a large behemoth of rock jutting upwards, blocking their view of the tiny church next to the ocean.

"Skaros Rock," Julie said. "A popular tourist attraction." Ben watched her zoom in on the map a bit more, waiting for connection to load and fill in the details. "And it looks like the road ends up there."

Ben saw it. There was a sign, but he couldn't make out any of the writing. It would be in Greek, anyway, but he assumed it was describing the area — Skaros Rock, the Theoskepasti, the hiking trails that led down to both. He slowed down, letting the bright headlights illuminate the area, including the sign.

And, next to the sign, a car.

"Is that —"

"That's it," Reggie said. "It's got to be. Ben, we found it."

The car they had been chasing was parked at the base of a small hill, right next to a large trailhead that seemed to wind around and up the backside of Skaros Rock, which loomed close by.

No lights were on in the lot or the car, and it was only by the light of their headlights they were able to see the two objects at all.

"That's it," Julie said," but there's no one there. I don't see any people anywhere."

She was right. Ben couldn't see anything outside the beam of light from their brights, but he knew there wouldn't be anyone hanging around anyway. Whomever had kidnapped Sarah wouldn't be waiting around by their vehicle.

"They're either up on the rock, down by the church, or they found another path that leads down to the water."

"Pull up," Reggie said. "Let's get out and look around."

"Sounds like it's a bit of a hike down to the church. No roads or anything, and it's about a 20-minute walk. Rocky and difficult to traverse at night."

Ben saw she was reading a review of the site. *Thank God for modern technology,* he thought.

"What's the call, then?" he asked. "They're probably not taking a leisurely sightseeing excursion with Sarah, so I think Skaros Rock is out."

"Right," said Reggie. "And the church seems to be just that — a tiny chapel, used for services maybe, but mostly a tourist attraction now. I don't even think there are any houses around."

"So maybe they took her down to the shoreline?" Julie asked.

"Could be," Reggie said. "Let's at least head toward the church. Any trails that head to the water will probably start there, or at least we'll pass them on the way."

Ben nodded, guiding their vehicle into the lot over the bumpy, dirt-packed road. After their near-death car chase, the 15 km/hr speed they were traveling now felt downright slow, but Ben knew they were traveling about as fast as the car's suspension on the dirt road would allow.

They reached the parking lot — two spaces next to each other that had been carved out of the flat dirt, one of which was occupied by the black sedan that had taken Sarah — and Ben parked. Julie and Reggie fell out of the vehicle before it had even stopped, and Reggie ran toward the path that headed downhill. Ben and Julie followed.

The path was indeed rocky, and Ben nearly lost his balance a few times as they navigated the dark, narrow trail. It turned and buckled back on itself a few times as it descended, and every now and then they could see the church's steeple and dome roof poking out above the horizon.

Ben was no expert hiker, but he'd had more experience than most, thanks to his years spent at national parks. He'd spent most of his career before meeting Julie at Yellowstone National Park, with a brief stint at Rocky Mountain National Park, and then in Alaska at Denali, where he and Julie served together for a short spell before the CSO got off the ground.

In addition, all three were in great shape, thanks to Reggie's constant harping on them to maintain their fitness and good eating habits. Ben even had an unspoken competition with Reggie, both men stubborn and competitive and wanting to outdo the other in just about everything.

Julie, for her part, was simply the type of person for which fitness came naturally. She was a born athlete, with a physique to match, and though she hadn't pursued sports during school and college, her body was as sharp as her mind.

The hike took them all of ten minutes, as they jogged down most of the hills, slowing only to take stock of the winding blind turns and to ensure they wouldn't trip over anything.

As they neared the church at the bottom and slowed their pace a bit, Ben voiced the concern that had been growing in his mind. "We got down here all right, but it'll take twice as long to get back up if we have to. If they didn't come this way..."

He didn't need to finish the thought.

"I'm with you," Reggie said. "But I know we're on the right track. That was their car, for sure. And there's nothing out here but the rock, the church, and —"

He paused, staring down at something.

"Look," he said. "Over here."

Ben stared at where Reggie was pointing. There was a patch of grass that had grown up over a stretch of flat land. The grass ended at the edge of a cliff, but Ben could see a section in the center of the patch that had been trampled by human feet. Even better, he could tell it had been trampled *recently*.

"That's fresh, right?" Julie asked.

Ben and Reggie nodded, but Ben spoke. "Absolutely." He walked closer to the patch of grass, taking out his phone and turning on the flashlight. He held it up and pointed it at the ground, in the spot where the grassy area met the rocky dirt path that led the rest of the way to the church. He moved the light around a bit, then knelt down to examine the ground. "There's even the back of a boot print right here, where the grass starts."

It was unmistakable. He wasn't a trained tracker, but he'd spent a lot of time in the woods. Humans were unbelievably harsh on the natural world, especially when they were in a hurry and not necessarily worried about not leaving a trail. The boot print was the only one he found, but it was clear that whoever had moved through the grass toward the edge of the cliff was in enough of a hurry that they had stomped around on the long strands of grasses, creating a visible path as obvious as a crop circle in a field of corn.

Best of all, it didn't look like a path made by only one person.

"That's it," Reggie said. "You guys check it out, and I'll just run around the church real quick to make sure it's empty."

Ben nodded and looked up at him as he jogged away, toward the church. Only then did he take a real look at the place he was in, lit subtly in the dying light of the evening. It was everything he'd imagined a Mediterranean seaside chapel to be — whitewashed stone walls, blue-domed roofs. The chapel itself was made up of a few small buildings, built to connect to one another. The tallest of these was the one closest to the cliff's edge, and it featured a domed top sitting on an octagonal base. Next to it, set a bit lower, were three bells. The chapel and church compound surrounding these two prominent features was small, and Ben imagined a service inside its walls could host 30, possibly 40, people at most.

He noticed a few embers of light spilling off the rising moon gently cascading toward the church on the hill. This point of land, jutting out and reaching toward the small, shadowy island in the middle of the Santorini ocean, was a secluded spot, devoid of nearly all life. The rocky, tough terrain Ben was walking over would be difficult to work, so the area would have gone mostly unused for farming or ranching ever since the land sprung up millions of years ago from the mouth of the great volcano.

He saw Reggie disappear around the side of the church complex and decided to take a look at the path leading through the grass, to get a better view of the waterline down below. It was only a few hundred feet through the trampled line to the edge, but Ben stopped short when he got there and caught his breath. Julie was suddenly next to him, holding his arm.

The route down wasn't a cliff, but it was close. The slope was dangerous and the trail went straight down, and it would be difficult to navigate even in daylight. Now, without flashlights or sunlight to help, he knew they'd be better off sliding down on their rear end. The straight part of the slope ended about thirty feet away, and twice as many feet down, before cutting a hard right angle to the left and disappearing out of view. Ben could only see water beyond that point, but he assumed the trail continued like that, turning back in on itself and dropping dozens of feet with each pass, the sections all parallel to the shoreline hundreds of feet below.

No way we'll get all the way down there in time, he thought. He knew Sarah and her captors probably hadn't gotten through the Skaros Rock trail as fast as he, Reggie, and Julie had, but he also knew that they had a serious head start. On top of that, they knew where they were going.

"That's... quite the trail," Julie said. "Looks like it's not even a public trail, but like a natural way down the side of the mountain."

"No joke," he replied. *Please be in the church. Please, Reggie, find them hiding in the church so I don't have to stumble down this mess.*

At the same moment, he heard a faint engine noise. A gurgling and sputtering sound, followed by a gentle humming. He looked down at the water, squinting to help make out the details. A tiny outboard motor pushed a white boat, accented against the otherwise black depths of the dark ocean. The boat accelerated out into the bay, launched from some dock or boat slip he couldn't see from this angle.

Crap, he thought. He didn't need sunlight to know that a boat in this area meant only one thing. *We're going to have to go down there and check it out.*

"Did you happen to notice any boat slips or public parks down on the waterline?"

Julie was already shaking her head. "Unfortunately not. That means the only reason there's a boat hidden there is so that Sarah's captors could get away without being spotted."

"That's what I was afraid of," Ben said. "At least we know what we're after, and where they're headed now. That boat's *got* to have Sarah on it, and the only thing in that direction is the island in the center of the bay."

He focused on the boat and thought he could see three shapes — two larger men and a smaller woman — sitting in the boat. It was impossible to tell for sure, he knew, but he had a feeling the motorboat driver wasn't just some hermit who lived in a cave beneath a cliff, out for a nighttime fishing trip with his two buddies.

He took a deep breath, turning around just as Reggie ran up to him. "No one's inside," he said. "Single room, empty."

Ben nodded, pointing down at the boat, then at the path.

"Really?" Reggie said. "I was hoping it'd be a *little* easier than this."

"At least we've got a little time to make a plan," he said, pulling out his phone to call Mrs. E. "Maybe we can head back to town, get Mrs. E, and then see about getting that —"

"Wrong," Julie said from behind them. He whirled around, noticing her beautiful petite figure standing a few feet away, outlined in the darkness by a bright blue-white pair of LED lights.

Headlights.

Their Interpol pursuant, followed by three police cars, pulled onto the dirt road and started down it toward the church.

"*Crap* again," Ben said. "This is ridiculous."

49

JULIE

JULIE'S EYES WATERED FROM THE CRISP, SALTY BREEZE THAT ROSE FROM THE sea and into her face. She had turned back to the bay to try to spot the boat, noticing that it was, in fact, headed right toward the small mound in the center of the round island of Santorini.

She hadn't had a chance to read about the tiny island, but she knew it was called Nea Kameni, and was a volcano that had most recently erupted in the 1950s. It was uninhabited and save for a park and a few tourist spots, nothing of note was on the rock.

In other words, if Sarah's captors were trying to take Sarah somewhere out of the way, secluded, or away from prying eyes, the volcanic mound would be a perfect choice.

And, she saw now, the boat had launched from a point off the coast of Santorini that would make the trip across the stretch of sea much shorter.

She turned back around and saw silhouettes of people — at least six of them — running toward them. It would take them at least ten minutes to get down, as it had her group, but they would be on them shortly after that.

And there's nowhere else to go, she thought.

"Do we head down?" Julie asked.

Ben was on his phone, working hard on a text message, but Reggie responded immediately. "We have to," Reggie said. "Ten minutes and they're here. And I'd bet with that stunt Ben pulled back on the road they're not going to be willing to hang out for a nice chat."

"The stunt *I* pulled?" Ben asked.

"You were driving," Reggie said.

"You didn't offer any better ideas!"

"Boys, I suggest we figure out who's at fault for hitting a police car and breaking through an obvious law enforcement roadblock later."

"Don't forget speeding and reckless driving," Reggie said.

"Right," Julie answered. "Point is, what do we do now?"

"We go get Sarah," Reggie said.

"But there's no way there's *another* boat down there," Ben said. "It's not a dock or a park — there's nothing down there but caves and deep water."

"And unless you can swim faster than a speedboat, I don't think it's a good choice right now."

Reggie's face started to flush, and Julie could tell he was starting to get panicky again. She'd never seen him like this — the man was usually the epitome of cool. Collected, calm, and always smiling. Now, on the edge of a cliff, feeling Sarah's safe retrieval slipping away from him, she could tell he was not himself.

He looked both of them in the eye. "I'm *not* going to sit here and let myself get arrested in a foreign country."

Ben held up a hand. "We're not saying that, buddy. We're just suggesting that maybe they —"

"What do you think they're going to do?" Reggie asked, nearly yelling. "Ask us nicely to stop running away? We're *implicated* now, man! For all we know, they think *we're* behind it all."

"Stop, Reggie," Ben said. "It's going to be —"

"It's *not* going to be fine, Ben! They're coming for *us*, and Sarah's *gone*! They may not shoot at us, but they sure as hell aren't going to let us get back to the hotel and regroup."

"I know they're not going to shoot at us, Reggie. We didn't do anything —"

A gunshot, followed by two more, sounded in the air in front of them, fighting against the crashing waves reaching their ears from far below.

"They're shooting at us?" Julie's voice was high-pitched, frantic, not believing. *They're shooting at us.*

"Get down!" Reggie shouted. Julie ducked one way while Ben and Reggie ran the opposite direction. Julie pushed against Ben, getting him moving, and the pair headed toward a boulder near the edge of the grass, close to the start of the downward slope that led to the cliff.

Two more gunshots rang out, one of the rounds buzzing over their heads.

Is that the police or the Interpol guy? she wondered. *Or both?*

Soon after the shots, Julie heard a man's voice call out in English. "Hold your fire," he yelled.

She turned to her fiancé. "What now?" Julie asked. "Seriously, Ben? Why are they shooting at us?"

"I don't know," he snapped. "We didn't *do* anything. I get that they're pissed about their car, but I didn't think it was a crime worth killing over. You think this the typical MO of Greek law enforcement? Shoot first, ask questions later?"

Julie tried to calm herself down. "Okay, okay. Let's think about this. Maybe they were warning shots or something, something to scare us into not doing anything stupid."

"I'd say shooting *at innocent civilians* is already pretty stupid, Jules. We're well past the 'line of stupidity.'"

"They're probably just on edge," she said. "The terrorist attack in Athens, the economic crisis they're all suffering from. Still, we don't know for sure. I think we should —"

Ben's phone dinged, and his screen lit up. She saw that a text message had come in, and Ben was silently reading it. She sat up straighter to look over his shoulder, risking her head coming into plain view over the top of the boulder.

It was from Mrs. E. At first, she couldn't see what it said, and then when she could she couldn't understand what the context was.

What's she talking about?

Ben looked up at her, just as two more shots smacked against the ground. They sounded much louder — much *closer* — than Julie cared to admit.

Maybe they are *shooting at us,* she thought.

"Jules," he said, looking straight at her. His eyes were steady, fixed onto hers.

"Ben," she replied.

"I need you to trust me."

"I do trust —"

"*No,* Julie. I need you to just follow my lead. And Reggie."

"Okay..." She tried to read his expression, to understand what it was that had him so shaken. "Why not just tell me what you're planning?"

"Because you're not going to like it."

A voice shouted from the other side of the boulder. "Juliette Richardson! Harvey Bennett, Gareth Red!"

Agent Sharpe.

"Now that we have your attention, come out from behind the rocks, we are not going to shoot. You are under arrest for aiding and abetting in the kidnapping of Dr. Sarah Lindgren," he continued.

"What?" Julie whispered. "'Aiding and abetting?"

"As well as charges against you all for reckless driving. I have spoken with the local police, and they will not use force if you agree to come in for questioning *right now*. Otherwise they are prepared to approach you as criminals, using whatever force necessary."

Like shooting us, Julie thought.

"Ben, what are you doing?"

"Julie, listen to me. This is our *only chance*. If Sarah gets to that island, she's *gone*. Understand?"

"Yeah, of course, but —"

"But if we go with Sharpe and the police right now, there's no way we prove our case and we're off the hook in time to get her back. Not to mention her father."

"Ben, I get that. But there's no other option here. Right? What am I missing?"

He smiled, then kissed her. "Like I said, follow my lead."

He checked his phone one last time and then slid it into his pocket. He rolled over onto his knees, then into a squat.

He crawled to the edge of the boulder and whispered over to Reggie. "You ready, brother?"

Reggie didn't say a word, he just nodded.

"Attaboy," Ben said. He turned to Julie. "All right, Jules. I'm sorry in advance."

Without looking back, Julie watched him stand up and start running — sprinting — down the steep path that led to the water. She watched him, horrified.

He can't run all the way down, she thought. *And besides, what's he going to do when he gets —*

Before she could finish the thought, she screamed. Ben wasn't slowing down as he neared the first turn in the trail.

He was actually speeding up, using gravity and momentum to get a good running start.

Oh God, Ben. No, please. Don't —

Again, she couldn't finish the thought. Ben planted his left foot right at the end of the short path, kneeling low and then popping back up and out.

And then he sailed off the edge of the cliff, into the night air, and out of sight.

50

BEN

He had expected fear, terror, maybe a little regret. Instead he felt freedom.

He'd never experienced a sensation like this before. He'd never gone skydiving, BASE jumping, or done any other stupid high-intensity sport like it.

Sure, there was the time he fell off a cliff in Antarctica, but he'd landed on a snow bank not too far below. Besides, that hadn't been *his* choice, but the choice of the Chinese soldiers far above him who'd cut the rope.

This time, however, it had been *his* choice. He'd read enough about this sort of thing to know that the more one thought about it the more difficult it became to pull off.

So when the thought crept into his mind, he decided immediately it was the right call.

He stretched his arms wide, feeling the rush of air and speed and adrenaline as he flew. He was falling, but the first hundred feet felt like hovering — the ocean was dark, the mound in the center of it still so far away, bobbing slightly but not really moving.

Then the ocean started getting bigger — *faster*. He was now feeling the terror of what he'd done. Feeling the stupidity of the mad decision.

Julie's going to kill me, he thought. *If I don't kill myself first.*

He hit the water much harder than he thought he should have, probably because he couldn't see it coming. A fall like this was nearly impossible to prepare for, since he couldn't get an accurate idea of how far he had to go.

The water was cold — *very* cold — and most of it soared straight up his nose. He felt like he'd just had a lobotomy, the water causing his eyes to sear and his nose to sting. He sneezed, forcing the saltwater out of the inside of his face, and then he felt the rest of the pain.

The cool water and the shock of it all had momentarily paused his pain receptors, but they were working again and in high gear, screaming at his brain. His arms were raw, the smacking as he hit the surface causing a bellyflop-like reaction on their undersides.

And his ears were tight, the pressure building. *I'm underwater,* he realized. *I'm going deeper.*

He had no bearings, but he knew that the pressure increasing in his ears wasn't a good thing. He forced through the pain in his arms and kicked with his legs, trying to go the direction he thought was up.

He opened his eyes. Everything was dark. Quiet now. He was still underwater, and he could feel the bubbles tickling the outside of his face even as the water itself tickled the *inside* of it. He surged upward, pushing, fighting.

And then he broke through and was floating. He sucked in a huge breath, laughing. He was still in pain, his nose and eyes and ears still stinging, but he laughed.

The sea was calm here, as he'd jumped far enough out to miss the crashing waves pushing and breaking against the jagged rocks. He whooped, screaming into the night. *What a rush,* he thought.

Not that I'll ever do that again.

And then, as if he suddenly remembered where he was, he looked up.

"Come on, Jules," he whispered. "You got this."

He saw a body launching itself off the edge of the cliff. His heart caught in his throat. *It's so* high, he realized. *Must be at least two-hundred feet.*

The person flying down toward him was Reggie — he could tell by the size of the silhouette as it sailed down, the pencil-thin figure falling in a feet-first dive, hands at his side, as if he had been a cliff diver every day of his life.

He splashed, but it seemed nowhere near as intense as Ben's epic cannonball. He swam over to lend a hand. Reggie, however, was up and treading water in less than three seconds. He had a smile on his face, and he swam over to Ben.

"Have to make me look bad, don't you?" Ben said.

"You didn't *have* to flail your arms around like an idiot," Reggie said. "That was your choice."

"Thanks." Ben looked up at the edge of the cliff, waiting.

Come on, Julie.

He hoped there was enough time. The police and Sharpe would be nearly to their hiding spot by now, or they had already reached it. He hoped Julie hadn't been detained, grabbed by one of the police before she was able to jump.

He watched, still waiting. He felt anxious, feeling again like his decision to jump off a cliff and hope the others followed suit may have been a bit too rash.

No going back now.

Just as the thought crossed his mind he saw another silhouette, this one smaller, launch themselves from the cliff.

"That's Julie," Reggie said.

She was screaming, yelling something Ben couldn't quite understand, and then she was in the water. She'd landed a few feet from Reggie, and he immediately stuck his head underwater to retrieve Ben's fiancée.

She gasped and spit out a mouthful of seawater as her head broke the surface. She was still yelling, shouting something at Reggie as he tried to help her.

"Get off… get off me," she shouted, fighting against the larger man. She swam over to Ben and smacked him across the face.

"Ouch," he said. He laughed, unable to help himself.

"Are you… *kidding* me?" Julie screamed. "Are you *joking?* What the *hell* was that? What in the world did you think —"

"Look," Reggie said, pointing.

Julie stopped screaming, and the three of them looked up at the cliff. Ben could see a few men standing along the edge, peering over the side.

"You think they'll try to make the jump?" Reggie asked.

"Not in a million years," Ben said. "I figured they'd feel like it's not worth the effort. I mean they shot at us, but still — I don't think anyone but Sharpe *actually* thinks we're a threat."

"Besides," Reggie said, nodding. "They're probably thinking they've got us covered."

Just then a massive light flicked on and the wide, thick beam of light shot down at them. It was an industrial-grade flashlight, and it was illuminating the ocean around them two feet into the water.

"They've got a clear view of us," Reggie continued. "And they know we can't just swim away. If we try to get to shore, they'll just hike down and grab us."

"Or shoot us," Ben said, his voice sounding more serious than he'd meant it.

"Ben," Julie said. "I'm still — I can't believe… I mean *what were you thinking?* What are we supposed to do now?"

The three of them were treading water in the bay, the dark, empty caves along the cliff barricaded behind sharp, jagged rocks. Even if Ben's plan had been to swim to shore, it would be a nearly impossible task. The surf would smack them against the rocks and the razor-sharp, barnacled surfaces finish the job.

It's a good thing that wasn't *my plan,* he thought.

He pricked his ears up, focusing on a sound in the distance.

"Hear that?"

"Hear *what?*" Reggie asked.

"Shut up and listen. Over there."

Ben pointed north, along the shoreline at the tip of the point of land, where it curved and headed back to the mainland. It was the sound of an engine, growing louder and more distinct every second.

"A boat?" Julie asked.

"Not just *any* boat," Ben said. "*Our* boat."

"What are you talking about?"

The boat was nearing their location, and Ben could now see that it was smaller than he'd hoped — Mrs. E hadn't told them what size they were going to get, so he'd expected it to be a small yacht, or at least a spacious ocean cruiser with a solid engine. Instead the craft seemed to be nothing but an 18-foot flat-topped fishing boat, with a simple inboard motor and captain's stand in the center of the hull.

But, as he had said, it was *their* boat. He could now depict the shape of the pilot herself — Mrs. E's massive frame, short hair, and wide grin was unmistakable — as she navigated the boat around the tip of the rocks and up alongside them. The light from the police, far above them, only made it easier for Mrs. E to find them.

"Hello, you all," she chirped down. "Need a ride?"

Julie whirled in the water and stared at Ben. "Ben, how...?"

"I sent her a text when we were pressed down. Told her where we were and sent a location just in case. I also told her we'd be at a lower elevation, and that we'd be wet."

"Good thing it finished sending before you made your little leap of faith, buddy," Reggie said.

Ben held up his waterlogged phone that he'd taken out of his pocket. It was off, and he knew it was unlikely it — or any of their devices — would be able to be turned back on. "Yeah," he said. "Good thing."

"I was already on my way to the boat dock," Mrs. E said. "I got Julie's text from earlier that you were all out having an adventure without me, so I woke up the owner of the boat and told him we would need the rental a bit sooner than expected."

"Well, I'm glad you did," Julie said, already making her way over to the retractable ladder at the back of the vessel. She pulled herself up and onto the back of the boat and then turned to help Reggie. When it was Ben's turn, he looked up at his fiancée and smiled.

She simply shook her head. "I vote we leave this guy in the water for a bit."

"Seconded," Reggie said.

Ben pulled himself up and in and then headed to the bow and pointed. "Over there," he said to Mrs. E. "They went to the island, and if we hurry we can get there in another few minutes."

She nodded and pulled out of the little circle of light they were floating in, and Ben heard the shouts of the police — and Agent Sharpe — from the clifftop. Their words were barely reaching him, but he could hear that they weren't happy, and they weren't about to give up the pursuit.

He sighed. *Out of the frying pan,* he thought.

Mrs. E jammed the throttle down and the tiny 9.8 horsepower Suzuki engine roared to life, aiming toward the Nea Kameni crater-topped volcano.

...and into the fire.

51

REGGIE

JUMPING OFF A CLIFF WASN'T SOMETHING REGGIE HAD PLANNED TO DO. HE had watched, horrified and amazed, as his best friend Ben, a man who was otherwise rather stoic and collected, lost his mind and ran off the edge of a cliff at the edge of the world.

The jump was a couple hundred feet straight down — nothing bad enough to cause any permanent damage, Reggie knew — but it was the breaking waves and foaming churn of the sea that worried him. A miscalculation could have sent Ben into the rocks.

But as it turned out, Ben was fine.

So Reggie had taken a deep breath, promised himself that he'd smack Ben across the face for making him do it, then jumped off into the sea.

Reggie had never practiced cliff diving as a sport, but he'd made more than a few hairy jumps in his time. He specifically remembered a time skiing in Russia with an old friend, and together they'd gotten into a bit of a bind in the bowls behind Dombay. He'd taken a route through a heavily forested area that ended with a steep 50-foot drop just beneath the ski lift, and his friend Latia had been forced to follow along his foolish route, both of them ending up waist-deep in fresh powder, unharmed but coursing with adrenaline.

And in another life, he'd trained executives and wealthy individuals in survival techniques at his compound home in Brazil, and for one special session, he'd hired an old Army paratrooper guide to give him — and his clients — the ride of their lives.

Jumping from a perfectly good airplane was now something Reggie could say he had done, though he had no desire to repeat it.

But jumping from a cliff, at night, while being chased by cops and Interpol agents was *not* something Reggie had ever done. The fall had been uneventful, though he had a bit of a shock at the temperature of the water when he'd hit. He'd resurfaced and smiled, laughing at the situation while simultaneously wondering what the hell sort of plan Ben had cooked up.

Julie, on the other hand, seemed to have been a bit more concerned with their predicament. After she hit the water and came up, spitting saltwater from her mouth and acting as if Ben had forced her to jump into a pool of molten lava, Reggie watched as the enraged woman smacked Ben and laid into him.

Ben was all smiles, however, and within a few minutes Reggie understood why: Mrs. E was racing toward them, locating them on Ben's phone's GPS before it became unusable and waterlogged.

Good work, friend, he thought. Reggie had given him a quick nod before climbing out of the ocean and into the boat.

But the fun wasn't over. Reggie could barely see in the dying light *another* boat — *Sarah's* boat. It had docked against a short, stubby protrusion from the flat rocks of Nea Kameni and was currently offloading its passengers. He saw the larger frames of the men who'd kidnapped her, as well as Sarah herself, bound and now blindfolded.

He felt his blood heating up, his entire body no longer remembering that it had been completely submerged in chilly ocean water not moments ago. He clenched his fists and stared at the dark, ominous island at the middle of the bay.

Ben leaned toward him, toweling off his hair with a rag he'd found underneath one of the seats. "We're going to get her back, brother," he said.

Reggie nodded, but his fists clenched harder, his knuckles white.

Where are they taking her? he wondered. *What do they* want *with her?*

He tried to piece it together. First her father, then Sarah herself. *What did they have in common?*

They were both scientists, academics. Well-respected in their larger academic communities, despite the fickle peers they kept. They both had a knack for problem-solving, a love of history and their ancient past, and a desire to understand more fully the true legacy of their ancestors. They both wanted to educate the rest of the world, only using their platforms and popularity for spreading the message of history: learn from your past, and you can learn about your future.

Reggie, as a history buff himself, completely understood their stance. He had grown to admire Sarah and her father over the time he and Sarah had dated, and he had often found himself daydreaming about a life spent as her husband, following her around the globe as she cracked cases and solved ancient riddles.

A present-day Indiana Jones, he thought. *'Diana' Jones, perhaps.* The thought usually made him smile — in the fantasy he'd play security, the strong-arm brawn to Sarah's unmatched wit, helping her solve ancient mysteries her anthropology background put in front of her by pushing around corrupt officials and overzealous locals.

But tonight the fantasy just left a deep pit in his stomach — he watched as Sarah was manhandled out of the boat and onto the dock, then up onto a narrow pathway cut into the side of the hill that sat at the base of the volcano. He felt rage, a feeling he rarely allowed himself to feel. That emotion, he'd reasoned long ago, was reserved for the worst of the worst — situations that required the use of force, and force that was unwaveringly and unquestionably extreme.

He did his best to push the emotion out of the rational side of his mind, but he failed. The rage built, and nothing Ben or Julie or Mrs. E could tell him would change that.

The last time he'd felt this angry he'd murdered a man with nothing but the tiny protrusion on the clasp of his watch.

And this time, he'd make sure he had more than a watch.

52

GRAHAM

We are trying to find the solution to an ancient problem.

Her abstract, vague response was still somehow smug, as if she had the answer all along.

"*What* problem?" Graham asked. "You people think that I'm going to be of help to you because you've threatened me, threatened my daughter. In truth, I may have obliged from the beginning if you'd have just *told* me what it is you're after." Graham felt his confidence growing, his desire to reach a conclusion stronger than his longing for safety. "You think that by threatening me you'll get me to comply with something, but the truth — and you *know* this — is that I'm clueless. I have *no idea* what you want from me. It's almost as if you think that by threatening violence I am going to suddenly remember..."

His voice drifted off.

"Yes?" Rachel asked. Her voice was small, inconsequential. Almost pleading. She was playing a role, and that role had suddenly changed. Her demeanor shifted completely, going from evil captor to something akin to a parent, patiently waiting for their child to figure something out for themselves. "What is it, Professor?"

Graham knew then that he'd been played. He had been trying to figure her out, as well as her two henchman, to determine what it was they were after. He was the captive, the prisoner, but *they* were the ones holding a ticking time bomb that threatened to detonate. *They* were the ones with the *real* deadline, and he'd assumed they would eventually grow desperate.

Risking his daughter was not something he had been prepared to do, but since it had happened, he had reasoned with himself that it was the only obvious escalation: they had few cards to play against him, and by bringing in his daughter they could simultaneously benefit from his duty as a father to want to protect his child as well as use her for her own vast amount of knowledge.

But he hadn't suspected that he had been playing into her whims the entire time. He hadn't suspected that all of this was a ruse, a decoy set up to make him believe the answer was something deeper, something far more *vast* than anything he could imagine.

The truth was that he knew *exactly,* in that moment, what it was she wanted. The answer she sought was right there — it was the reason he had run up against so much trouble with his last paper, the one that had mysteriously been 'unpublished' from the university's circulation. The paper that had been a point of contention between him and a few of the Ancient Histories scholars he was friends with.

"This is about the paper, isn't it?" he asked. "The one referencing *Timaeus* and *Critias*." He paused, trying to judge her reaction. "The one about *Atlantis*."

At this, she leaned forward. "What *about* Atlantis, Professor?"

"That Atlantis is not just some 'lost continent,'" he said. "That Atlantis is a *history* of a civilization, one that describes a people bent on domination, so much so that they chose to go up against the most powerful nation known to the world at the time."

"Greece," she said.

"Athens, specifically," he answered, feeling the lecturer within him begin to take over. "The Atlanteans thought they were powerful enough to defeat them. And they would have, if not for a cataclysmic event that stymied their ability to continue reinforcing their barrage against the Athenian strongholds."

He was now in his element, the pacing continuing but his demeanor changing to that of a professor ready to lecture on something he had spent his life studying, a professor so excited about his curriculum he couldn't help but portray that excitement through his monologue.

"They thought they could defeat the Grecian troops, and they could have — easily. But they planned a wave of attacks, over the course of many years, betting on the training programs and war academies they had established in their homeland to provide them with the young, fresh troops who would continue the onward progress."

Rachel was smiling now, but Graham could not have cared less. He was in full 'professor' mode, oblivious to his students.

"They would have beaten the Athenians, *soundly,* if not for an event that shook the foundations of their society."

"What event, Professor?" Rachel asked, softly.

He had practiced this delivery. He knew it top to bottom, had *rehearsed* it as if it was a speech he was going to give in front of the president. He knew the arguments forward and backward, knowing that the academic establishment would never accept his theory at face value. He would need to *prove* his point.

"The flood."

"What flood?" Rachel asked, her whisper growing more intense.

"*The* flood. The same one that shows up in nearly *every* origin story we have. Ancient civilizations gave us their histories, almost all of which have a common thread that involves a 'flood of epic proportions.'

"Noah's Ark?" Rachel prodded.

"Yes," he said. "The same flood. The Christian histories are merely retellings of the same worldwide catastrophe, but the epicenter of the event was the Mediterranean. The Aegean and Black Sea, to be exact. The Atlanteans lived on an island in the present-day Aegean Sea, and thanks to many millennia of dominance and isolation, were allowed to advance beyond the capabilities of their continental neighbors. Shipping and sailing, farming and agriculture. Their closest peers were the Athenians, and they would have prevailed against them. The Athenians even 'stayed the course of their mighty host,' to use Plato's own words. But then the flood..."

He stopped. *Why am I explaining all of this to her?*

"You know this already," he said.

She nodded. "I read the paper."

He frowned. "But it was taken down. The university must have —"

"*We* removed it, Professor. I had my IT department hack into your university's server and delete the article, then scour the web for any references of your paper, then reach out to the linking source and file a DMCA claim against it."

Graham knew exactly what she was referring to. The Digital Millennium Copyright Act of 1998 as well as the related regulations and rules regarding online privacy that had been passed in the following years had provided a security blanket for content creators, in that they had an easy way to protect their intellectual property assets. The problem was that many organizations, afraid of the litigious society they were a part of, tended to act first and ask questions later. A simple DMCA claim, even if falsified, would be met with a swift removal of offending content by the host without so much as a question.

For Rachel, it was probably quite simple for their computer whizzes to get into the university's servers and delete the original files, a follow-up DMCA claim sent to the leading search engines requesting removal of links and references to the article, would have made it nearly impossible for anyone to find it.

"Why?" Graham asked. "The information I compiled is freely available elsewhere, and —"

"But you *packaged* it all up for us, nicely presented in a way that would make it impossible to ignore. Truth be told, if your research ever reached the public, our plans would be set back, if not completely destroyed. We don't have the ability to prevent or control the academic scrutiny, nor the throngs of archeologists and anthropologists who would descend on this area."

"*This* area," Graham said. "Where exactly *is* 'this area?'"

She shook her head. "Sorry, Professor. I can't disclose that information to you. Not at this time." She swiveled and began to leave the room. Before she reached the threshold she turned back to face him. "But, I want to prove to you that we are, ultimately, on the same side. We have no interest in harming you or your daughter — we want your *help*. While I'm not just going to *give* you the answer, I won't deny you the attempt at an educated guess."

She made an expression somewhere between eagerness and intrigue.

He looked around the room, as if seeing it for the first time. "Atlantis?"

Surely not, he thought. In truth, he had no idea what a civilization like Atlantis would have 'looked' like. What architectural features they would use, or what characteristics would have defined their buildings, roads, temples, and homes. He was an archeologist, but the exact composition and stylistic elements of their culture were as foreign to him as they would be to anyone.

Still, looking around, he somehow sensed that this place *wasn't* Atlantis. It wasn't the island of Santorini, or anywhere close to the nearby sunken island of the Cyclades Plateau.

It felt wrong, somehow, like the stones this place had been formed from had been used not for their building properties, chosen specifically for the task, but because they were the only stones available. As if it had been constructed in haste. Even though it was a perfectly sound room, structurally coherent and satisfactorily reinforced, it didn't scream *sacred* or *important* to him. Instead, it seemed to have the feel of a staging area, an anteroom that belied the importance and the very presence of a larger, more grandiose chamber.

He stopped, suddenly realizing.

He knew of one civilization that had used this style of architecture, one civilization that had built their buildings and monuments from the stones found far away, but their homes and crypts and lesser structures from the stones found right beneath their feet.

Rachel watched him, studied him. She was questioning him, silently. Waiting for him to come to the conclusion he had been putting off since he'd gotten here.

It can't be true, he thought. *It's not possible.*

"I was right all along?" Professor Lindgren asked. "I was right in my paper, wasn't I? *That's* why you took it down."

She smiled, then nodded. "More right than you know."

"We're… in *Egypt?* Just like I predicted?"
She nodded once again.
"The Giza complex. Cairo."
"Yes, Professor."

53

BEN

THEY REACHED THE DOCK TEN MINUTES LATER, AND BEN HELPED REGGIE up and out of the boat. Reggie was in his 'lock and load' mode, a state Julie had named after she'd seen Reggie shift into a close-minded, narrow-focused mindset with one goal and one target in view. He wasn't able to think about anything else, and he was hardly capable of communicating while in that mode.

As intense as it was, it usually only lasted a minute — Reggie used the shift as a way to lock his target into view, analyze the options and possible routes to success, and prepare his mind and body for a serious and deadly attack. Ben and Julie had seen it firsthand, and they knew to stay out of his way and let the man smolder.

Ben focused on his own preparation. *What's the plan?* he asked himself. *What now?*

Julie was already on the dock, running up toward the beginning of the trail where the rocks met the wood planks of the short boardwalk. There was no one else around, but Ben moved cautiously anyway, careful not to alert anyone who may have been spying on the open bay behind him.

He walked next to Reggie, waiting for the man to speak, knowing that a word or two would mean he was finished with his moment and ready to engage. Ben looked at the hill in front of them, charting Julie's position at the base of the trail in his mind, and then seeing the distance from the bottom — where they were — to the top of the hill. The hill seemed to flatten off at the top, just before continuing up a steep incline to the base of the volcano, where it rose to the clouds far above his head.

At that time, Ben heard two things — from in front of him, and at the base of the volcano where the hill ended and the steep rise began, he heard a man shouting down toward them. He was frantic, running toward them while waving something in his hands.

An RPG.

Ben knew the weapon from video games, but he wasn't sure exactly what sort of 'rocket-propelled grenade' launcher the man was holding. All he knew — and all he *needed* to know — was that the weapon was coming closer to them, and that the man aiming it toward him had the high ground.

The second thing he heard was the rhythmic beating of a helicopter's rotor wash. It was flying in from behind them, just over the horizon and making a beeline for the top of the hill.

"Get down!" Reggie yelled.

It was too late, however. Ben was already moving toward Julie, who hadn't seen the man and his sickening weapon from her perch directly below him. The man lifted the RPG and fired, the screech of the ignited propellant causing immediate terror for Ben.

Shit.

He reached Julie just before the detonation. He had lost track of Reggie, but Julie was wide-eyed and scared, apparently unaware of what was about to transpire. The explosion knocked him off his feet, but since they were close to a tall stand of boulders, the majority of the pressure wave dispersed without causing damage.

He wrapped himself around Julie, his large body easily covering the majority of her exposed frame. The heat washed over him with a fury, the open areas of his body screaming in pain, but just as he thought the searing fire would consume him and his fiancée, it subsided. He fell back, breathing heavily, sweat covering his body.

"Wh — what was that?" Julie asked.

"You don't want to know," he answered, already looking for Reggie.

Reggie had run the opposite direction, opting instead for the boat, where Mrs. E was still idling near the dock.

The dock, however, could no longer be described as a dock. It was a mass of tangled wood and metal, charred posts cracked and sizzling, smaller pieces burning brightly against the dark water. Bits of smoldering ash fell from the sky, drifting down into the bay and landing on the surface of the water with a bright sizzle.

Worst of all, the dock was no longer a single stretch of artificial land. The structure had been completely sheared in half, a gaping hole now burnt into the center of the length of wood planks.

The hole was about fifteen feet in diameter, completely cutting Ben and Julie off from Reggie and Mrs. E in the idling boat, and Ben knew the boat wouldn't be able to push in toward them much farther without going aground on the sharp rocks at the base of the hill.

"What now?" Julie whispered.

Her fear bled into Ben. He looked down at her, suddenly realizing that their fun and games had come at a massive price. They were stranded, stuck on a pile of rocks in the middle of a *larger* pile of rocks in the middle of a sea, unarmed and without a means to defend themselves.

Reggie was shouting at him, and only then did Ben snap out of his funk. He shook his head, trying to clear his mind and focus on the next step rather than the devastation laying in front of him, and watched Reggie's mouth.

He couldn't hear anything, but he couldn't quite read Reggie's lips, either. *Something about 'boat.'*

Boat. Get — boat, as far as he could tell. *What the hell is he trying to —*

Julie was pulling his arm, nearly yanking him out of their hiding spot. His eyes widened, suddenly realizing what it was Reggie was trying to communicate.

Get to the boat!

He lunged forward, knowing Julie was going to be able to move faster than him and deciding she was better off alone for the moment. He forced his heavy legs into action, pumping and stretching them to their maximum force, aiming for the spot just beyond the gaping hole.

Just get to the water, he thought. There was no way they'd be able to jump from their side of the dock to the boat, but there was a chance they could make it to the water, and then swim the rest of the way to the boat.

At the very least, the water would protect them from the next RPG detonation.

Or so he thought.

Ben picked up speed, aiming toward the hole cut through the middle of the wooden dock, not bothering to worry about Julie or Reggie or Mrs. E or anything else in his life. He wanted to survive, and he wanted to get to that boat.

He heard a whistling sound. His mind fell into a slow-motion subconscious, his feet pounding slower and slower on the top of the planks. He could hear his breaths, feel his heart pulsing, heavier and heavier each step, knowing that he wasn't going to make it.

He heard the whistling grow in volume, feeling the hairs on the back of his neck standing up as they anticipated the impact.

He knew it was close. Too close.

He wasn't going to make it.

Julie was suddenly in his vision, taking the leap just before him.

Good, he thought. *So good. She's going to make it. She's going to be —*

A brilliant blast of light shook him and threw his legs out from under him. The world turned on its axis, his vision blurring and simultaneously shifting sideways.

54

BEN

EVERY SENSE AND NERVE IN BEN'S BODY FLARED UP AT ONCE. *HEAT, SMELL, fire, danger, run, hide, pain.*

He screamed, but still couldn't hear anything over the sound of the explosion. It felt as though he'd been placed inside a snow globe full of lava and fire, then shaken up and tossed down a staircase. His vision was screwy, his mind a blur.

Julie, he thought. *Get to Julie.*

But he couldn't see Julie. He couldn't see anything but orange and white and the smear of tears covering his eyes, trying to protect his vision from the flash. Then he felt her — bumped her, to be exact. She fell, and he fell with her, off the edge of the dock, or whatever hard surface he'd been running on, and then into the chilly water.

The water surged up around him as he was pushed under by his own weight. It felt refreshing, cool, and seemed the perfect antidote to the fiery hell that had just been rained down on him. Julie was still in front of him, and he could see her petite frame kicking and fighting against the heavy waves. He saw her resurface, but he kept his head down, focusing on getting as far away from the remnants of the RPG detonation as possible.

And, if possible, to stay hidden.

He didn't want their pursuer sending down any more of his death missiles. He knew sending an RPG down into the water hoping to hit a couple bobbing heads wasn't a great choice, considering their low accuracy and necessity for a hard surface for proper detonation. That said, he also didn't want to leave his fiancee's and his fate in the hands of a crazed grenade-launching madman. And if the madman happened to get lucky, he knew the top of a man's skull was a hard enough surface for an impact detonation.

He turned underwater and looked behind Julie, barely able to make out the darker shadow of the boat's hull against the lighter skyline above it. He kicked his legs and arms and shot forward, propelling himself toward the shadow.

Reggie was telling us to get to the boat, he realized. *He could see the gunman. He knew he was aiming down at us.*

But the man had fired, sending Ben and Julie crashing into the surf, safe but rattled.

That means he's reloading, Ben realized. *And I bet I know what his next target is...*

He kicked harder, hoping Julie had understood the message as well. They needed to get to the boat and get inside before the man finished reloading his weapon and sending down another grenade.

Ben knew for a fact that a boat was a *much* bigger target than a single human bobbing in the waves. They were waiting for him and Julie, but he knew it would be stupid for them to wait too long.

He broke the surface, taking a huge gulp of air, and immediately heard Reggie yelling. The boat's motor was idling noisily as well, the chugging sound of the engine nearly drowning out Reggie's voice.

"Get in the boat, Ben!" Reggie shouted. "What's taking so long?"

Reggie had a huge smile on his face, but Ben knew better than to think the man was in a good mood. To anyone else, that face meant joy, happiness, ease, nonchalance.

To Ben, it meant Reggie had his game face on.

He swam a quick breaststroke to the boat, pushed Julie in, and started up the ladder himself.

55

REGGIE

Reggie had barely finished hauling Ben and Julie up and onto the boat when he felt a surge of force and fell sideways. Mrs. E had thrown the engine into reverse, immediately pulling them ten feet straight back, deeper into the cove. Reggie grabbed the back of a chair and caught his balance, only to be thrown sideways again as Mrs. E slammed the boat back to a gentle forward throttle.

"Come on, E," he shouted. "You trying to throw me out?"

"Trying to beat him," she shouted in return, calling to him over her shoulder.

Trying to beat who? Reggie thought. Just as the words passed through his mind he followed Ben's and Julie's gaze up to the rocky pathway.

Shit.

The man had finished reloading, the giant tube on his shoulder now staring down at their tiny boat.

"Okay, team," he yelled. "Change of plans — again."

Ben and Julie didn't hesitate, and Reggie watched them jump off the port side of the boat, back toward the destroyed dock. Mrs. E was in motion as well, her large strides carrying her to the back of the boat in two easy steps.

"Get out," she said as she hustled past Reggie. "I need to look for —"

She didn't get a chance to finish the sentence, and Reggie didn't get a chance to start his own escape. The whistling shell sang in the air, louder and louder until it smashed into the bow of the hull, a direct hit on the narrow, v-shaped front. In the split second before impact, he closed his eyes and turned his back to the explosion.

The blast lifted him and carried him clear of the wreckage, the cool water of the Aegean quickly counteracting the searing heat of the fiery explosion. He landed facedown, stinging his chest and legs, but was otherwise unharmed.

He resurfaced and tread water, looking around. He had landed behind the boat about twenty feet, but he could see that the boat's front half was completely gone. Chunks of smoldering debris sizzled as the heated plastic and foam came into contact with the water. Smoke billowed from the back half of the boat's hull, a fuel line or oil leak slowly burning. He doubted the boat's engine would explode — the fuel tank had already been decimated — but he wasn't about to swim back over and check it out.

He turned to his left, noticing Ben and Julie standing on a jagged strip of wood that had once been a support post for the dock. They were leaning out toward the water, where a tall, thin silhouette of a woman swam toward their waiting hands.

Apparently she'd succeeded in grabbing whatever it was she'd gone back to retrieve, as she swam with one arm, the other arm clutching a tiny, briefcase-shaped object. A box with a handle, black and hard plastic. Julie grabbed the case from Mrs. E's hand while Ben pulled the woman out of the water. Reggie also saw that Mrs. E was holding her left arm — the one that had been dragging the case.

Reggie swam toward the dock as well, keeping an eye on the man still standing on the pathway. He wasn't sure if the man was trying to see how many of his enemies had survived his latest attack or if he was simply out of ammunition.

Reggie hoped it was the latter.

Still, the fact that the man wasn't moving was a bit unnerving. It meant he was confident, not at all fazed by the brutal explosions and carnage down below him.

And it meant that he was probably just waiting until all of them were standing together on the ground. He could have only one grenade left, and he wouldn't want to waste it on two of them, only taking out half the invading party.

What would my next move be? he found himself wondering. *If I were in that man's shoes, what would I do? What would I be thinking?*

He'd been trained long ago as a sniper, to observe the battlefield below him — or in this case, above him — and try to understand every player's motives, drives, tactics, and movements. It was like a game of chess, every move affecting every other move, but every move somewhat predictable.

I would wait until we were all together, Reggie thought. *Until I knew without a doubt that my last shot would count.*

The man had already wasted three grenades on them, and while those shots had done a fantastic job of shaking them up and scaring the daylights out of them, they hadn't achieved their ultimate goal: destruction of the enemy.

Reggie waded to the dock and pulled himself out. They were outgunned and outmatched, the enemy sitting on its perch — the literal high ground. The climb up to him wasn't impossible, but it wasn't fast, either. They couldn't exactly rush the man.

And if the beating rotors he could now hear from the top of the little volcanic island were any indicator, he wasn't alone, either. He had friends, and those friends were most likely armed as well.

As he exited the water he joined Ben, Julie, and Mrs. E at the edge of the cliff — right where Ben and Julie had been standing earlier — the only place on the ground out of range of the enemy's RPG. For now, at least, they were safe.

But Sarah's up there, he thought. *They're getting away, and there's not a damn thing I can do about it.*

"What's the plan?" Reggie asked, looking around at his wet, sopping team. "We don't have the high ground, we don't have any weapons, and —"

"Actually," Mrs. E said. "We have this."

He frowned, looking down at the black case Julie had handed her. He watched as she snapped it open, understanding that it was a waterproof box — the sort of dry storage container often found on boats and yachts to house anything that didn't agree with saltwater. Whatever was inside, therefore, would be totally dry and ready for use.

"It's not much," she continued. "But I have a plan."

He frowned again as she handed him a tiny pistol she took out of the dry storage box. *How the hell are we going to rush a guy with an RPG carrying a peashooter?*

He turned the gun over in his hands, realizing that its weight was off. Even for a snub-nosed weapon like this one, it still should have felt like a rock in his hands. But the longer he examined it, the more he noticed that everything about the tiny gun felt off — it wasn't even made of metal.

A streak of waning moonlight hit the weapon and it emerged from the shadow. Reggie saw that the pistol was actually made of hard, bright-orange plastic.

"Is that a flare gun?" Ben asked.

Mrs. E grinned, then nodded. "It is. I had a hunch there would be one on the boat, and I was right. We've got five rounds — all high-reflectivity, high-sight flares, orange-pink color."

"And you're thinking we're going to alert the authorities with it?" Reggie asked. "Let them know we're under attack and then just wait it out?"

"No," she said. "I am thinking it is our only chance at getting past that man with his rocket launcher. And it is our only chance at getting to Sarah."

56

REGGIE

The Orion Safety Alerter Coastal Signaling Kit was the full name of the cheap plastic flare gun, and Reggie turned it over again in his hands and tried to work out a plan.

He knew the flares were 12-gauge, and in his limited experience knew that despite the gun's lightweight, cheap construction, they were accurate up to about 500 yards. He'd seen them shot in training expeditions while serving in the US Army, and he'd fired one once or twice when he was younger.

Still, as a defensive weapon it was a last resort. The type of thing he preferred to use only if his hands and fists were already taken out of commission.

Worse, as an *offensive* weapon it seemed downright risky.

But it's all we've got. He knew Mrs. E was smart for finding and retrieving it, even though using it against the RPG-wielding man above them still felt like a suicide mission.

But we do have numbers...

"We've got numbers," Ben said, reading his mind. "We could rush him."

Reggie nodded. "This thing is accurate at close range. It'll at least leave a bruise, if not knock him on his ass."

Julie jumped in. "And if we stay close to the cliff, I don't think he'll be able to pick us off. He'd be firing almost straight down and it would still be a tricky shot."

"Right," Mrs. E said. "But he might be working his way down the path as we speak. If he gets to that switchback about 100 feet away, he will have an open shot."

Reggie nodded again, looking at his friends and teammates and analyzing their ad-hoc plan. *It's not much,* he thought. *But it's all we have.*

"Okay," he said, reaching into the open box in Mrs. E's hands and grabbing a few of the 12-gauge flare rounds. "Let's roll. Ben, Julie, you guys stay behind me. Mrs. E, you're rushing first. You're big, and plenty fast enough. He comes around that corner, you let him have it."

Mrs. E was already smiling, nodding along. "You got it. But I do not want to take him myself," she said. "Get a shot in if you can."

Reggie pocketed the other four rounds and held the gun lightly in his right hand. Accuracy with a small weapon like a pistol was far lower than a long-range weapon like a rifle. He was a dead shot with a pistol, but only in proper conditions — a range, his own trusted piece, no wind. Without those variables in place he was still far better than the average red-blooded gun-toting American, but tonight *none* of those variables were in place. It was dark, he would be firing mostly blind, using a cheap piece of plastic weaponry that had been manufactured by the thousands in some Chinese factory.

To top it off, he'd be firing into a man who was *very* interested in killing him and his three friends, and *very* equipped to do just that.

He didn't feel terribly confident about their odds of survival, but it didn't matter — Sarah was up there, getting forced into a helicopter. Once that happened, all bets were off. They might be able to take down a single enemy combatant with a flare gun, but he *seriously* doubted its effectiveness against a flying machine.

"Ready?" Mrs. E asked.

He nodded, tensing his finger around the trigger and feeling the spring-action pressure.

Mrs. E didn't wait for further instruction. She barreled ahead, running full-tilt up the narrow path cut against the mountainside. Reggie watched her for a few strides, then followed. He needed to time it right — too close to Mrs. E and a wrong step could send all of them plummeting to their deaths on the rocky spires below. Too far behind her and he wouldn't be of any use to her.

Mrs. E slowed, turning at the end of the switchback, then started up the opposite stretch of path. He watched Ben and Julie begin to round the turn as well as he continued behind Mrs. E.

Before Mrs. E reached the top of that stretch, the big man bounded down the turn and stopped. He was carrying the RPG loosely at his side while he ran, but quickly swung it up and onto his shoulder.

And then pointed it directly at Mrs. E.

"Get down!" Reggie yelled. Mrs. E didn't need any additional encouragement, and she was already curling into a roll. Reggie watched the man's aim shifting, following the large woman as she ducked. At the last second, he shifted again and brought the barrel of the RPG up.

Now aiming directly at Reggie.

Crap, he thought. He launched himself up and to the right, landing on a small protrusion with his right foot. He pushed upward, now standing on the protrusion but still in motion, his momentum carrying him forward. At the top of his swinging arc, he pushed off again with his right foot and was soon flying forward, headfirst, toward the man.

He sailed over Mrs. E, his speed overtaking her, just as the man fired his last rocket. It pushed through the air with a whitish tail of smoke trailing behind, directly into the space Reggie had been standing in less than a second before. As if in slow-motion, Reggie watched the missile as it passed next to his left side, inches below his nosediving body.

At the same time, he brought his arms up and forward, aiming the flare pistol at the man's head.

No, he thought, suddenly changing his mind. *Too small a target.*

Just like the man's rocket was a detonate-on-impact explosive device, the Orion 12-gauge flares were like simple fireworks: built-in propellant would carry the charge forward, eventually fizzling out in a fiery and bright flash of light. *Unless* its forward motion was stopped by something solid, at which point all of the explosives causing the forward motion would be compacted into a single ball of fire.

A human skull was certainly solid enough, but it was too small a target for accuracy, especially fired from a cheaply made piece of plastic while lunging through the air on the side of a cliff.

He shifted his aim to the right, flicking his wrist just before he fully depressed the trigger. The charge shot out and sailed to the right, its energy carrying it directly toward the space to the right of the man.

But it wasn't *empty* space — unlike the man's failed last shot, the flare wasn't heading for dead air. The man was standing near the cliff, and right to the side of his head a large section of boulder jutted out from the surrounding rock face. This was the area Reggie had aimed toward, and this was the spot the flare hit.

The impact was quiet, but the blast it created was massive. Orange and yellow streaks of light streamed every direction, and a sizzling ball of fire grew and bounced off the rock, right into the man's face.

He screamed, dropping his RPG tube, and fell to the ground. Blinded and scarred from the hot propellant, he scratched at his face as Reggie landed.

Right on top of the man.

He hit the man's lower half, knocking the wind out of both men, but Reggie rolled to his right and recovered. The man was coughing and still wiping his eyes, mostly unharmed but still in significant pain. He pulled himself up into a sitting position…

And that's when Mrs. E's boot caught him in the chin. He went out immediately, his head lolling backwards as he fell, down for the count.

"Nice shot," Mrs. E said.

"Nice kick," Reggie replied.

Ben and Julie caught up, and the four of them regrouped quickly as they took stock of the situation. Reggie took a deep breath, checked the man for a pulse, and stood up again.

"Can't stop here," he said. "Sarah's up there."

The helicopter above them roared to life, the beating of the rotors growing in intensity.

No, he thought. *Please don't tell me we're too late.*

He broke into a run, hurdling the man on the pathway and rounding the last switchback before the final ascent to the top of the mountain. He picked up speed as he neared the top, but couldn't see anything over the bushy edge until he was almost level with the mountaintop.

At that point all his fears were realized. The heli was hovering a few feet off the ground, and a man — the other one from the bar — was standing on one strut closing the door. He pulled the handle and swung the metal hatch closed, but Reggie caught a glimpse of the inside of the chopper.

Sarah.

Sarah was inside, her hands ziptied. She was blindfolded and her mouth was open, and it looked as though she was screaming something. He couldn't hear anything over the sound of the chopper.

The man slid across the strut to the passenger side door, opened it, and entered, closing the door behind him. *Apparently they don't want their other goon,* he thought. The unconscious man was still laying on the rocks somewhere down below.

Reggie picked up speed, trying to beat the clock. He was running full-tilt, but the helicopter was still a hundred yards off.

It began to rise, the angle of the blades shifting to provide more lift for the craft. It was already four feet off the ground and increasing speed, now moving closer to Reggie. He knew without needing to calculate that the aircraft would be traveling far too fast, and it would be far out of reach, by the time it passed over him.

She's gone.

The helicopter changed direction slightly, but then tipped its nose down and flew off over the Santorini bay, the dark waters below only slightly darker than the craft itself.

Reggie tried controlling his breathing, but the events of the last two hours were finally catching up to him. They'd lost, and now there was nothing else left to do.

He sat down on a rock just as Mrs. E, Ben, and Julie crested the rise and joined him. No one spoke, and Ben reached down and placed a hand on his shoulder.

It's over, he thought.

57

JULIE

"Now what?" Julie asked, breathing heavily as she slumped down, hands on her knees. She was exhausted, the events of the last few hours wasting the moments of rest she'd gotten when they'd first landed in Santorini.

She knew the others were, too. Ben was heaving, his larger frame obviously finding the climb and race up the pathway to the top of the Nea Kameni crater difficult. Reggie, too, seemed beat.

Beaten is a better word for it, she thought.

The only one among them who seemed to be completely fine was Mrs. E, who'd recovered from her kick and brief tussle with the gunman and was now standing with her hands on top of her head, waiting for the rest of them to decide on a course of action.

She was older than all of them, and almost old enough to be Julie's mother. But the woman they all only knew as 'Mrs. E' was a trained professional fighter, an expert in Krav Maga and other hand-to-hand combat, and generally in better shape than Julie would have thought possible.

She was the polar opposite of her husband. Mr. E liked to solve problems with his mind — he was brilliant, an investor and businessman, and he had singlehandedly grown his startup into one of the world's largest telecommunications companies *and* kept it under tight personal control.

The couple couldn't have been more different — Mrs. E was tall, thick in a muscular way, and extremely outgoing. Mr. E was essentially a recluse. Julie had never met the man in person. He hid behind television screens and always appeared gaunt, even sickly.

But his intelligence and careful planning had gotten them out of more than one sticky situation in the past. Julie wished they could call him now and give him an update.

Instead, they were alone on top a volcano, all of their phones trashed by the seawater and totally useless. They were tired, wet, and being pursued by Interpol and the local police, and now they had no leads as to the whereabouts of Sarah Lindgren.

"That helicopter was a Sikorsky S-92," Reggie said.

"So?" Ben asked.

"It's a long-range chopper, used for offshore oil rig deployments. Total range exceeds 600 miles."

Ben stared down at his friend. "...So?" he said again.

Reggie shrugged. "Well, if it was fueled up somewhere here on the island, that means Sarah could eventually end up 600 miles away from here."

Julie's heart sank. "Which means she can end up 600 miles in *any* direction."

Reggie looked up at her, then shook his head. "Not necessarily." He stood up slowly, then pointed southeast, toward the edge of the main island, where the thinner strip of Akrotiri lay at the southern edge of the bay. "The chopper went that way."

"Back to Santorini?" Ben asked. "Why would they go back there? They just came from there."

"I know," Reggie said. "They didn't. I'm almost positive. Think about it — a long-range chopper, fully fueled — it could haul all the way over the Aegean Sea *and* the Mediterranean. And they're heading that direction."

"What's after Santorini that way?" Ben asked. "Crete?"

"Close, but Crete's too far to the west. I think they're heading somewhere else entirely. And if I'm right, I think it could be a major clue about what this is all about."

Julie waited for Reggie to take a breath and continue.

"We're thinking about this all wrong, guys. They nabbed Sarah's old man first, because he knew something about Atlantis that they wanted covered up."

"Right."

"And they wanted it covered up badly enough they were willing to kidnap his *daughter*, too. Probably as leverage until they get whatever they think her father has. So we're dealing with an organization here, probably more than just a few people. They've got resources — enough that renting or buying a Sikorsky and some thugs with rocket-propelled grenade launchers isn't that big a deal to them. So we've got a twisted, angry billionaire situation *or* we've got a twisted, angry group of people who've got something to prove and enough resources to use to prove it. I think it makes more sense to assume it's not just one person doing all this."

"I'd agree with that," Julie said.

"And *whoever* we're dealing with has a thing for the past — their interest in Atlantis, kidnapping an archeologist, *and* an anthropologist. Whatever they want, it has something to do with ancient history, before Plato even wrote down his thoughts on the mystery civilization.

"Remember in his writings? He's basically telling us that he didn't come up with this stuff. He heard it from a guy who'd traveled."

Julie's eyes widened. "Solon."

"Exactly."

"And he traveled to *Egypt*."

Reggie smiled at her. "Right again. And there's plenty of evidence to suggest that Atlantis and the ancient Egyptians were somehow connected. They're relatively close to one another, if you think about it — not even an ocean apart."

"I'd bet not even 600 *miles* apart," Ben said.

"That's what I'm thinking, Reggie said. "I need a map to be sure, but I'd put a lot of money down on the bet that there's *nothing* in that direction for 600 miles until you hit Egypt. Specifically, Cairo. It's right on the Mediterranean, right at the mouth of the Nile."

Julie grinned. "That's got to be it, Reggie. It *has* to be. Sarah's going to Cairo."

"Well, that's all great," Ben said. "But how are *we* going to get to Cairo?"

"Right," Mrs. E said. "We cannot exactly float back to the mainland — the police and Interpol are looking for you."

"Looking for us."

Mrs. E turned and gave Ben a questioning look, then put her hands up. "They do not know who *I* am, remember?" she smiled. "I was just a passing boater who happened to pick you up. They were shooting at *you*, not me."

"Well fine," Reggie said. "We'll be sure to send you to make any public appearances on our behalf, then."

"Guys," Julie said. "Still not sure how we're supposed to get all the way to Egypt. We're on the middle of an island, *in the middle of another island*, in the middle of the Mediterranean Sea."

Before anyone could answer, Julie heard the sound of a boat speeding their way. It was closing in fast, obviously more powerful and sleeker in the water than the boat Mrs. E had piloted.

"Get away from the edge," Reggie said. "Probably the local police, coming to check out why there was a fireworks show out here."

"No," Julie said. "There's only one person on the boat. Can't be cops."

She looked down over the edge of the cliff as the others sidled in next to her. Sure enough a single silhouette was visible on the narrow vessel, a single driver with no passengers. And even in the dark, Julie could tell that it was small enough of a craft that there was no room to hide anyone anywhere on board.

"That's... weird," Ben said. "Maybe a local fisherman?"

"Heck of a boat for a late-night fisherman."

The boat was traveling faster than Julie had originally thought. It was up on plane, but the bow of the craft was still feet out of the water, the motor housing on the rear end deep beneath the surface. It was going to be less than a minute before their new visitor arrived.

"Should we go down and see what's up?" Ben asked.

"I think so," Julie said. "But Reggie, you still have that flare gun?"

58

BEN

THE TRIP DOWN THE EDGE OF THE VOLCANO WAS MUCH QUICKER THAN THE way up, mostly because they weren't worried about someone trying to blow them up. They jogged down the three switchbacks and landed on the gravely shore, the twisted and smoking remnants of the boat dock floating among the gashed and charred remains of the boat.

Looks like a battlefield scene, Ben thought. *Unreal.*

He was nearly dry, but his shirt was still heavy with dampness, and the effect in the cool night air was to make him feel almost cold. He stopped next to Julie, watching with interest as the man — curly-haired, young, and fit — jumped out of the boat.

"I know that kid," Reggie said quietly, standing on Ben's right.

"You *know* him?"

"I've definitely seen him before. No idea where, though."

The 'kid,' a young man in his early twenties, walked over, holding up a hand as a peace offering. Ben tried to examine his person, to see if he was carrying a weapon or otherwise hiding something. He'd had enough getting shot at for one night.

"Hey there," the man said. "Name's Alexander. Alexander Whipple." He stuck out a hand and Mrs. E — confident in her own abilities, should the kid try something stupid — shook it.

Reggie's mouth dropped. "Alex *Whipple*? You were in the field with... you know Sarah?"

Alex laughed. "Dr. Lindgren, yes. I'm one of her students. We were together in Michigan."

"We're a long way from Michigan, son," Reggie said.

Ben frowned. Reggie sounded almost patronizing, as if he was intimidated by the young man. Ben had to admit that Alex was rather handsome — attractive features, a healthy crop of dark hair, and he was almost as tall as Ben. He even still had the lean figure of youth.

Maybe Reggie's jealous, Ben thought, smiling. *This should be fun.*

Alex kept his calm composure. "Yeah, I know. Sorry to barge in on you like this, but — uh, where's Dr. Lindgren?"

Ben felt Reggie tense up next to him. *Calm down, buddy,* he thought. He knew Reggie was currently a tightly wound spring, but he hoped he could hold it together a bit longer. *No sense getting us into more trouble tonight.*

"Sarah's — not here," Julie said. "Why are *you* here?"

He held up his phone, which had a map and a dot on it. The blue dot was in the middle of the waters between Santorini and Nea Kameni. "This is Sarah's location, according to my phone. As of about thirty minutes ago."

Reggie bolted forward, stopped only by Ben's hold on his left arm.

"You're *tracking* her?" Reggie shouted.

"Whoa, no," Alex said. "I'm — this is just the app we use to keep track of each other. She had it on and running on her phone, but it lost signal on the way here."

Reggie was seething, but Ben knew it was more about Sarah's kidnapping than anything this kid was saying. Ben knew the feeling — someone the man loved was being threatened, and there wasn't a damn thing he could do about it. He'd be acting the same way if it were Julie in this situation — she had been, after all, and he was acting the *exact* same way.

"What do you know about Sarah?" Reggie asked, his voice still faltering. "Where is she?"

Alex seemed surprised by Reggie's intensity, and he backed up a few steps, now standing in a few inches of water. "I — I don't know, man. Like I said, I've been following a dot on a screen. I was flying back to Cairo to visit family, but something she said at her apartment had me shaken up. I mean, she was *really* weird about it. Like something big was going on.

"I thought she would have told me she was flying all the way to Greece, but no — nothing. So when I landed in Cairo and saw she was heading this direction, I took a flight in. It's only like sixty bucks for a one-way, and with the money she gave me I found a cheap —"

"Alex," Julie said, snapping her finger. "Focus. *Why* are you *here*?"

"Right," he said. "Sorry. I flew in and was on my way to the hotel, but her dot moved again and she ended up here." He paused. "Or... right in the middle of the ocean."

"She's alive, buddy," Julie said. "Don't worry. But someone took her."

"*Took* her?"

"Yeah."

"Who — why would they —"

"Alex, calm down," Ben said, stepping forward and grabbing the kid's shoulder. "Thanks for coming all the way out here. We're with a group that's been sent out to find her and get her back. We're on the case, and we're not going to stop until she's back."

He nodded. "O — okay. So…"

"So don't worry about us, and don't worry about her," Ben said. "Why don't you head back into town? We're staying at a hotel in the area, and we've got four rooms. You're welcome to one of them."

"But I wanted to come out here to make sure —"

Ben felt Reggie's hand on his shoulder as he spoke. "You know, kid," he said. "Before you go, we could use a ride."

59

REGGIE

Who is this guy? Reggie thought. *And why is he so concerned about Sarah?*

They were speeding back to the edge of the Akrotiri peninsula of Santorini, the southernmost tip of the circular island. The idea was that while the police would be searching for them, and their Interpol friend would certainly have his feelers out for their location, the CSO group might be able to sneak back onto the mainland for a few minutes while they waited for their ride.

Their ride, in this case, was a private jet that had been arranged by Mr. E. Now that they had a working cellphone, thanks to the young newcomer Alexander Whipple, the group was taking turns borrowing the phone and planning out their next course of action.

Thanks to the GSM-ready chip in the phone and Santorini's relatively small geographic footprint, cellular service on Alex's phone was strong and reliable. Reggie used it first, discovering that Cairo, Egypt was in fact just a little over 550 miles from their location, and it was in exactly the direction they'd thought. They'd determined that Cairo was as good a place as any to continue the search, and once they were on the ground they'd be able to further hone their search radius.

Mrs. E had then called her husband and filled him in, and he had arranged for a private Learjet co-op to lend him a transport for their team. The plane would be able to travel faster than the Sikorsky, so they might be able to make up some lost time in the air. They were to meet the pilot, a man who owned a private airstrip on the southern side of the island, in an hour. He assured them he would have the plane fueled up and ready for departure as soon as their Uber arrived onsite.

Akrotiri was miles away from the main Santorini metropolitan area, and plenty far away from where the local authorities had intercepted them. From there, the plane ride would be about five hours, after which they'd land in Cairo and drive to wherever it was they thought their next clue led.

The problem, Reggie knew, was that they didn't *have* the next clue. He hoped that the plane ride would allow them some time to relax, rest, and come up with a solid plan to track down Sarah. If there were lucky, they'd also find Sarah's father where they found her.

Finally, Alex called one of his professors back at his university, a man he claimed was a mentor and a well-respected geneticist. He had Mrs. E drive the boat while he sat in the stern bucket seat and conversed with the professor. Reggie wasn't sure what had him so excited, but Alex was animated, talking with his hands and nearly dropping the phone a few times.

What a nerd, Reggie thought. He tried to recall where he'd seen the kid. He was almost positive he'd never met him, but there must have been something…

That's it. He remembered a picture on one of Sarah's social media profiles, where she was standing in front of a massive cliff with a few of her students. Alex was one of the students, and he was standing close to his professor.

Very close to her.

Reggie shook the thought away. *I'm not the jealous type.*

Or am I?

He smiled, realizing that this kid, some twerp from Sarah's university, had nothing on him. He was military trained, chiseled, fit, and far more experienced — in every way — than the young twenty-something.

Still… Reggie couldn't shake the feeling that there was something else going on between his latest fling and her student.

They were almost at the northern beach of Akrotiri, and Mrs. E informed them all that they'd be docking within five minutes.

Reggie walked back to the rear end of the boat as they powered in toward the dark shoreline, confronting Alex.

"What was that all about?"

"Just talking to my genetics professor."

"About… genetics?"

Alex smiled. "Yes."

"Anything in particular? We're sort of under a bit of a crunch, so I find it odd you're chatting nonchalantly about some midterm assignment."

"It's not about an assignment," Alex said, his composure immediately darkening. "It's about something Dr. Lindgren and I were working on."

"You and Sarah were in the field together, yeah?" Reggie asked.

"We were. In Michigan. Trying to prove the existence of a nontraditional settlement route to the Americas."

"A non... you mean something besides the 'walked over the frozen ice bridge' route?"

"Exactly," Alex said. "The Berengia Passage is a proven route early settlers walked to reach the Americas. But Dr. Lindgren strongly believes that there was *another* route, one that potentially predated the Strait by millennia."

"By *millennia?*" Reggie asked.

"Maybe. I'm not sure her ideas have been well-received, but I came along as the geneticist, to provide a different anthropological perspective than what she might have been able to explore on her own."

"And?"

Alex's demeanor changed. Where he was at first dark, a bit taken off guard, and possibly angry, he was now lit with an exuberance and excitement Reggie hadn't seen in days. "*And* I just heard that my professor and mentor received my studies and hypothesis, and he feels it's worthy of a second look."

"You're excited because your professor told you your study wasn't complete junk? Man, you academic types are so fickle."

Alex frowned, but the excitement never left his face. "I'm *excited* because it further proves that Sarah's theory was correct. I think she was on to something, and now I've got even more proof to help her case."

Reggie chose to ignore the fact that Alex had slipped into an informal tone, using Sarah's first name. "And what exactly was this 'study' you did?"

"Well, I think it'll take a bit longer than two minutes to fully explain, but essentially I believe I have found *genetic* proof that there was a group of settlers that reached the eastern shores of the Americas *long* before the Vikings."

"Before the Native Americans too, you mean?"

"Well, I'm saying these settlers *were* the Native Americans. But they came to America *long* before the nomadic tribes from present-day Russia."

"They came from the Bering Straight *before* the people we knew about?"

Alex shook his head just as Mrs. E slowed the watercraft and aimed at the small wooden dock extending from the beach. "No," he said. "I'm saying they didn't come from the Bering Strait at all. They came from somewhere else entirely."

Reggie examined the kid, suddenly feeling — and mirroring — his excitement. Everything they'd learned tonight seemed to be falling into place, in a strange, crazy way. The puzzle was far from finished, but he felt as though they now had most of the pieces.

They started walking toward the front of the boat, where the port-side bench was acting as the stepping-off point to the dock. Ben and

Julie were already up, standing on the stair and preparing to hop across to the floating dock.

Mrs. E hovered and idled the engine, getting within a few inches. Alex started forward, but Reggie grabbed his arm.

He swung around, a bit of fear in his eyes.

"Hey, kid," Reggie said. "One more question. Do you have any idea *when* these guys came to America?"

Alex shrugged. "Sort of, but it's hard to tell for sure. Best guess I have, based on..." he stopped. "Well, like I said, it'll take a bit more time to explain everything, but..."

Reggie waited.

"Best I can tell, they came sometime between 11,000 and 10,000 years BCE."

60

BEN

THE FLIGHT WOULD BE A GOOD FIVE HOURS OF WELL-NEEDED RESPITE FOR Ben. Even though he hated flying, he had to admit that sitting in a luxury jetliner cabin, an entire row to himself, dry, and a stiff drink in hand was a decent way to travel.

They'd been given a change of clothes; one of the small perks of Mr. E's brilliant mind for detail was in thinking through some of those small items that often were forgotten. In this case, he'd had the flight crew purchase a small wardrobe of clothing at an outdoor store in town before preparing their plane. The sizes were a bit off, but Harvey Bennett wasn't about to complain about the way he looked.

He was dry, and he was comfortable. He had a mystery to solve, and Alex — young as he was — would be a good asset to have. His comment about the timing of the westward expansion of early humans was intriguing, and he was excited to hear more.

And best of all, he was holding a cold glass of whiskey. It was Irish, something from the Bushmills distillery, but he was far from picky and Reggie had informed him that it was a very quality selection.

"Ben," Julie said, suddenly standing above him in the wide aisle between the rows. "You up?"

He nodded. "I can't sleep on planes. The rest is good, though. We all need it."

"No joke," she said, twisting around and plopping down into the seat next to him. He couldn't help but notice her petite, tight figure as she bent around the chair. "I think Reggie's been working on something back there."

Reggie had taken up his position at the back of the plane, opting for silence and isolation instead of camaraderie and companionship with the others. Apparently he hadn't slept much, if at all, and when Ben popped up to look, he saw his friend's head down, his tongue poking out the side of his mouth. *Deep in thought.*

"Is he ready to explain what it is that's got him so worked up?"

"I think so. He told Mrs. E he figured something out, and she told me. Alex is already back there, bugging him to let him in on it."

They'd decided to bring Alex along, since he had been on his way to Cairo anyway to see family. He'd done them a huge favor rescuing them from the island, and the least they could do was offer the kid a free ride home.

Ben laughed, stretching. "That's pretty funny."

Julie smiled. "Yeah, I think our old pal's a bit jealous."

"A *bit*," Ben replied with a snicker. "Guy's so worked up about this Egypt issue he doesn't even realize he's got a major competitor in Alex."

Julie threw her head back and started to laugh, then stifled herself. "Stop it! He's just preoccupied." As if remembering why they were all there, and what was at stake, her temperament changed. "He's… just stressed, that's all. With Sarah gone now, he's not quite sure what to do. That's why he can't sleep."

Ben nodded. "Can't blame him. I'd be the same way."

Julie laughed again. "Right. You'd be destroying everything in sight. Cracking skulls and all that."

Ben looked up at her. "Well you know, you're worth it." He winked at her.

"Come on, Casanova," she said. "Let's go see what they've figured out."

They walked to the back of the plane and waited in the second-to-last row, both of them standing and leaning over the seat backs so they could see Reggie and Alex, sitting side-by-side now, looking down at Alex's phone's screen.

"You besties figure anything out yet?" Julie asked.

Reggie's face told Ben he wasn't exactly enthused by Julie's description of their relationship.

"We… know that Egypt is where we're supposed to be heading," Reggie said.

"Good. I'll tell the pilot to keep on going in the same direction," Ben said.

"We figured out that Cairo is where the Sikorsky is headed, because Alex's research shows that Egypt has a lot in common with the ancient Atlanteans."

"Wait…" Julie said. "What? *Egypt* and *Atlantis* are related?"

Alex winced, looking sidelong at Reggie. "Well, not exactly. I guess you'd have to assume that there *was* an ancient Atlantis first."

Reggie frowned. "You know what, kid? Let's just go ahead and assume there *was*. Got it? And that 'Atlantis,' or whatever it was, is now under the ocean on a massive island just northwest of Santorini."

Alex put his hands up in front of him. "Okay, okay. So — in that case, Egypt and Santor — *Atlantis* — *do* have a lot in common. They're geographically close, of course, but they could also have some similar history. If these 'Atlanteans' are the same group of people I've been studying, I think they taught the Egyptians just about everything they knew.

"If we believe Plato, the Atlanteans were around somewhere about 10,000 years *before* Plato wrote about them. At that point in time, Egypt was nothing but an idea, if that. Nomadic hunter-gatherers would have been the only people around. But at some point in Egypt's history, called the 'Predynastic Era,' we started to see civilization emerge. Pharaohs showed up, their version of kings, and the groups began to converge into a unified people."

"That's Egyptian History 101," Ben said. "Even I knew that."

"Right," Alex replied. "But what's interesting is that if you ask some people, they don't buy the idea that these nomadic tribes eventually coalesced into one larger group and taught themselves how to farm and build."

"They don't?"

"They don't," Alex said. "Because most scholars agree that civilizations develop slowly over time, domesticating animals so they no longer have to hunt, then farming land so they don't have to gather fruits and nuts, and learning to build sturdier structures the longer they stayed in one place.

"But their development into a powerhouse civilization happened remarkably fast. It's as if they woke up one day and suddenly knew how to farm, keep animals, build massive temples and structures, and generally be a civilized society all in a matter of centuries, as opposed to the millennia it usually takes."

"Wow," Mrs. E said. "So you are implying that the Atlanteans *taught* them?"

"Well, I'm implying that *someone* did. I don't know if Atlantis has anything to do with it or not, but my point — and my research — is that there was *someone* teaching their ways to the rest of the world, long before we thought that was possible." Alex cleared his through. "We *also* know that there are some interesting similarities between their genetic makeup."

"Really?" Mrs. E asked. "How can you know that?"

"Well, again, we can't know anything for sure. *But* we can find similar genetic compositions in the DNA of both strains of humanity. The Egyptians and this older, unknown race — going with Reggie's assumption, Atlantis."

"Strains of humanity?" Julie asked.

"Sorry — races. Every race is a bit different, of course, but we're all human. So we can use modern genetic testing to analyze similarities between these races, and then compare and contrast the results. We're pretty accurate with the results, but we're not exactly sure about *why* we're seeing those results. Meaning we don't know if a particular genetic trait was a mutation, a bloodline-related addition — someone married someone else from a slightly different race — or something else entirely.

"We *do* know, however, that there are groups of genetic material that exist only for certain racial profiles. We can then follow the historical proliferation of these groups, starting from their origination point — the earliest place in the earliest time we believe that group of genetic material appeared."

"That's fascinating," Ben said. "It's like a map with timestamps of where and when humans came from."

"Exactly," Alex said, smiling up at him. "It's not perfect, but it's pretty dang close. Anyway, we can map these different groups, and the races that eventually came out of them, and then get a better idea of how humans migrated — and propagated — across the globe during prehistoric times."

"Wait," Julie said. "*Prehistoric* times? I thought this was all for modern-day stuff? How do we *really* know where certain groups of humans were back then? I mean, if we're digging up bones and stuff, there's not a whole lot of difference between races of Homo sapiens, right? So how do we tell the difference?"

"That's what I'm studying. And my mentor is one of the premier experts in the field. Basically, we *do* study modern-day humans. We access the database of human mitochondrial DNA samples in repositories worldwide, then compare those results with our own data. And our own data shows that these 'groups,' called 'Haplogroups,' spread around the globe in statistically significant chunks. We can test a person now and see what Haplogroups are present in their DNA, then compare that to the map, showing the general route that combination of groups took to end up in their present location."

Ben nodded along. "That makes sense. So you're saying there's a group — a Haplogroup — for the Atlanteans, and that they ended up in… Egypt?"

"No," Alex said, glancing at Reggie. "Again, I'm not saying, or willing to admit, there's an 'Atlantis' at all. *But* there is a Haplogroup that seems to have originated more than 10,000 years BCE, and that they had the technological knowhow to build sailing vessels."

"Sailing vessels? These guys knew how to *sail?*"

"Sure," he said. "Polynesians did it long before we used to give them credit for. But what's more remarkable is that they did it over *far* greater distances. If they started in Santorini, where you guys think these people were from, getting to Egypt would have been nothing but a quick hop over a puddle to them. My research shows that they traveled all the way to the Americas, by way of island and continent chains, over the course of thousands of years.

"And my research proves that they were able to do it long before we even thought humans were capable of writing anything down."

61

JULIE

JULIE'S MOUTH FELL OPEN. "SO WE'VE GOT GOOD EVIDENCE THAT THERE were humans, *civilized* humans, traveling around the world, eventually settling in America?"

Alex nodded. "Best I can tell, yes. The Haplogroup X lineage is traceable all the way to American Indian tribes, mostly centered around the Great Lakes region. But what's interesting is that the X group of genes doesn't really have *any* noteworthy presence in the far-western United States, Northwest Territory, Alaska, or Asia."

"So they didn't come from the Bering Strait," Julie said.

Alex shook his head. "They couldn't have. It's impossible." He pulled out his phone, checked that it was connected to the in-plane WIFI network, then motioned for them all to lean in closer. "Here, look. I'll show you an image of the map I'm working on for my research."

He flicked around the screen and Julie saw a map of the world, certain countries and regions darkened by pencil-drawn splotches.

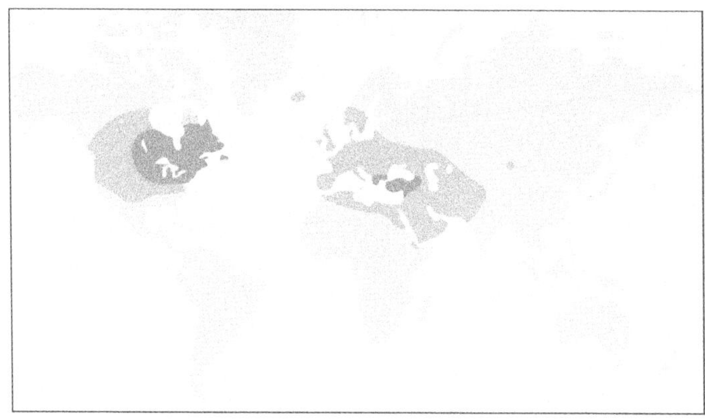

"These dark areas show the places where there's at least a small presence of our modern-day society's ancestral descent that test positive for the Haplogroup X group of genes, and the darkest areas are where the concentrations of Group X are highest.

"If the *first* settlers to the Americas came from Asia via the Bering Strait, there would be pockets of humans that can trace their lineage back to one of those regions that test positive for Haplogroup X. But there aren't. Instead, we've got pockets of humanity exhibiting Haplogroup X around the Great Lakes, New England, then up through Nova Scotia, Greenland, the UK, then down and around the Strait of Gibraltar.

"Following it back further, we've found the genes are strongly present on *both* sides of the Mediterranean, including Egypt. Best guess we've got is that the original location — or home — of these Haplogroup X'ers is somewhere in the present-day Aegean Sea."

Julie swallowed. "Alex, that's exactly where Santorini is."

He nodded, looking down. "I know. As crazy as it sounds, there might be something to your 'Atlantis' theory."

"I don't think it's just a theory anymore, kid," Reggie said. "If you give me your phone, I'll show you the research Sarah's old man was working on."

Alex obliged, and handed Reggie his phone. Reggie found a browser and opened a tab, where he loaded a map of the Aegean Sea. It took a moment to load, but eventually Julie could see that he'd loaded a map created by satellite imagery, showing a bit of the underwater contour of the ocean floor in the relatively shallow sea.

Reggie explained what Mrs. E had previously shown them, that Plato's description of an island on which the civilization he had called Atlantis *perfectly* matched the geographic features of the now-sunken island to the northwest of Santorini. Santorini itself, Reggie explained, was included in Plato's description — the 'ring within a ring' of the concentric volcanos.

Alex nodded along, his eyes growing wider the longer Reggie talked. Eventually he sat, silent, as he looked at everyone hovering around him.

"This... this is big," he said. "This is *very* big."

"We agree," Reggie said. "And you've given us another major piece of the puzzle. It seems like this civilization predates even the Ancient Egyptians, long since thought to be the first highly advanced civilization. But I'd bet that your ancestors in Egypt weren't as clever as they thought — I'd bet they were taught a lot of what they know by some visitors. Some *Atlantean* visitors."

"I think you're right," Alex said. "It's hard to argue with. My research basically proves that there was *some* advanced civilization floating around the globe, teaching people how to live and work and build cities, *long* before anyone thought that was possible — and I'm pretty convinced the epicenter of this civilization was somewhere right in the middle of the Aegean Sea. I used to think it was Crete — maybe the predecessors to the Minoan civilization, perhaps — but this... this changes my mind. And the *second* strongest concentration of Haplogroup X is in Egypt. Cairo, to be exact."

"Wait," Julie said. "What about remains? The bones of whoever these people were? Shouldn't we be able to find them and determine exactly how old they are?"

Alex nodded along, as if anticipating the question. "Of course. Well, consider that the vast majority of the civilization is now buried under soot and earth, and all of that is completely submerged underwater. So there's not much to find, really. Even with state-of-the-art submersible technology it would take a lot of luck to find a spot worth excavating, and even then it's a crapshoot — most of what we'd dig up would have to be carted away to clear the area. Underwater excavation is a timely, and *very* expensive process.

"Add to that the fact that bone decomposition is a matter of decalcification and dissolution, and since the hydroxyapatite and collagen are —"

"You're saying it's not possible," Reggie said.

"No, I'm just saying it's highly unlikely. Most of the human matter would have disintegrated. It would simply have ceased to exist after that amount of time, and —"

"But that's only 10,000 years," Ben said. "What about dinosaurs? We know *they* existed, and they were here long before 10,000 years ago."

Alex nodded. "Sure — you're talking about fossilization, usually through permineralization. The thing is, we believe fewer than ten percent of all animals that ever lived became fossils, and those usually happened through sedimentation, drying, and crystallization of the 'hard parts' of the animal. So if this civilization left *anything* behind, it wouldn't have been preserved underwater. Any fossilized remains we find will almost without a doubt be somewhere *besides* Santorini. Which is another reason to look elsewhere, and it's still unlikely that we'll find anything large enough to test."

"So we're going to Egypt, for sure," Ben said. "It's all too much of a coincidence. Both Sarah and her father were digging around in Atlantean history, which would eventually lead to Egypt. These guys — whoever took her — want something from them, and it's serious enough that they'll potentially kill to figure out what it is."

"But where in Egypt?" Julie asked. "It's not like we can just look for a black Sikorsky helicopter and say, 'there it is!'"

"Actually," Mrs. E said. "All of the air traffic in this region is heavily regulated. It is like flying anywhere near Washington, D.C."

"So someone's watching the skies for us?" Ben asked.

She nodded, smiled, then reached for the phone Reggie was still holding. "Yes, someone is surely watching. The question is whether or not my husband has access to those records."

"You think he might?"

"If it's a public flightpath, sure. If it's a government vehicle, he will only be able to see a redacted callsign for the craft. But with a bit of narrowing things down, as well as the fact that our target is traveling quite a bit slower than most commercial jets, he should be able to give us a few good options."

"That's fantastic," Ben said. "And if we're lucky, we'll be able to have our pilot do a flyover so we can see if one of them is our match."

Alex looked up at them. "So what should we do until then?"

Julie stretched. "I could use some shuteye, actually. Any more detective business?"

"Not at the moment," Ben said. "Julie's right. Let's all get some sleep if we can. We've got a couple hours or so before we start our descent, so do your best to rest."

With that, he turned and walked back up to his row of seats, his drink sweating in his hand.

62

SARAH

SARAH HAD BEEN BLINDFOLDED ALMOST IMMEDIATELY AFTER SHE'D BEEN shoved into the boat, feeling her skirt riding up her legs as she was forced into the deep seat. *Why did I think wearing a skirt was a good idea?* she thought.

One of the two men that had grabbed her, Ivan, had not joined them in the chopper, hanging back on the cliffs after their boat ride. She could only hope that the faint explosions she'd heard had been Reggie and the others fighting him off.

But she was still unable to do anything — the second, smaller man who'd kidnapped her had joined her in the back of the helicopter, keeping her hands zip tied the entire time. The pilot and copilot said nothing to her or her kidnapper during the flight.

That had been over six hours ago. Now, she was being shoved down a corridor in some facility somewhere, still blindfolded. After disembarking from the chopper she was led down a few flights of stairs, and she could feel the air turn to a cooler, more humid heaviness on her bare arms and legs. *We're underground,* she thought. For some reason the thought panicked her, and she tensed up, only earning a curt response and a shove from the man pushing her along.

She felt the ground beneath her feet, uneven and cobbled. Each bump and valley had been smoothed down over time, but felt like a single cold, hard piece of stone. The air was heavy, stuffy, as if the walls were slowly pressing in on her — and since she couldn't see anything, she had no idea if they were or not.

She was led down a few more hallways, all of them short, and all of them feeling narrow and low-ceilinged, judging by the sounds reverberating back to her as they walked along.

At the end of the next hallway her captor paused, holding her back.

He grumbled something indecipherable, and then she felt the blindfold lifting from her eyes.

Her eyes adjusted slowly in the dim light, but she could see that she was now standing in front of an open doorway set off the hallway. The interior of the room was dark, darker even than the hallway she'd just been led through, and it took her a moment to see clearly inside.

Something inside the room shifted, and Sarah jumped. Then, as the figure grew closer, she recognized the man.

"Dad?"

"S — Sarah?" the man responded.

She felt her throat catch. She stumbled forward, no longer being held back by the man who'd pushed her along into the dungeon. She embraced her father, feeling his warmth and noticing at the same time that he felt frail, nearly fragile.

How long has it been?

"Sarah," he said again. "You're here. You're really *here*."

She sniffed, then smiled. "I'm here, Dad. Are you okay?"

He was about to speak when she saw his eyes widen. She whirled around, seeing the door to the small chamber she and her father were now standing in swing closed. The man outside the room shut them in, and she heard the cold, metallic click of a lock turn on the outside of the door.

"Wh — where are we?" she asked. Her mind was racing already, working through the possibilities. They were six or seven hours away by helicopter flight from Santorini, so it was unlikely they could be anywhere outside the perimeter of the Mediterranean Sea. Of course, she had no idea which direction they'd been traveling — she'd been confused, scared, and angry as hell when they grabbed her, not to mention blindfolded. If they had been traveling north, or even northeast or northwest, that could put them somewhere in northern Europe, perhaps even as far away as France or Russia.

Might as well be anywhere, she thought.

Still, there was something about this place that was intimately familiar. The style of architecture — if she could even call it that — the feel of the place, it seemed like somewhere she'd been before. In all her years studying ancient history, she'd come to know the buildings, the infrastructures, the stylistic specialties of many of the most well-known ancient civilizations.

But this place, from the floors to the ceilings to the walls themselves, each chiseled out of smooth-cut stones, seemed to be a mishmash of *all* of them. It was a smorgasbord of design, a cornucopia of ancient traditions, as if a museum had tried — and failed — to capture and integrate the design characteristics of all known peoples into one, singular product.

"We're in Egypt, Sarah," her father said, his voice low and gravelly. "Cairo, actually."

"Cairo? As in *Giza?* The pyramids?"

He nodded. "We're underground, obviously," he said. "I confirmed our location with our host, a woman named Rachel Rascher. And yes, I'm okay, believe it or not. They have actually taken quite good care of me, considering."

Sarah's head spun. "Rachel... *Rascher?*"

Where had she heard that name?

"And we're underground... under *what*, exactly?" she looked around, spinning a complete circle as she examined as best she could the dimly lit room. She knew the Great Pyramid and its two smaller counterparts, which together with the tinier pyramids and the surrounding buildings made up the entire Giza Complex, was situated on a grandiose, massive, 5 kilometer-wide plateau of carved limestone. It was a solid foundation, and modern technology *still* couldn't produce as flat a surface as the one the Great Pyramid of Khufu sat on.

The foundation, a sprawling expanse of limestone that covered more than six football fields of space, had been shaped and carved with exacting detail: less than an inch of height difference from one side to the other. It was an absolute marvel of architectural prowess, a Wonder of the World for good reason, and something she and her colleagues had spent hours discussing during her undergraduate term.

But the point was that the foundation of the pyramid was literally rock-solid, and deep. The limestone mass of rock was not impenetrable by modern technology, but it would be impossible to excavate and construct anything beneath its surface that was more elaborate than a rough, round hole in the ground.

"My hypothesis is that we are standing beneath the surface of the Giza Complex, but not beneath one of the pyramids."

She frowned. "One of the ancient temples, then? Or —" she stopped, suddenly realizing. "The Great *Sphinx?*"

He nodded. "I believe so. The Sphinx, as you know, is still quite the enigma, even to egyptologists. Its age and reason for existence is at best a mystery, and its purpose is even more of an unknown."

"It's a sentinel," Sarah said, "built to stand guard over the Great Pyramid."

"Of course," her father said, smiling. "A sentinel, yes. But not to stand guard over the pyramids."

"No?"

He shook his head. "According to the Kolbrin, the ancient Egyptian texts that reference some of the same events found in the Old Testament, the men of Zaidor built the Sphinx, long before the pyramids were constructed."

"Zaidor?" Sarah asked.

"Some think it's the word Poseidior — the Men of Poseidon, in that case. They were great astronomers and came from their land which also had been recently destroyed. They came and built the 'Great Guardian,' or 'Rakima,' which we believe to be the Sphinx. Only later did Egyptologists ascribe the Sphinx to a protectorate role over the pyramids.

"But you must ask yourself *why?* Why would it need protecting? There are a thousand tons of rock separating the outside world from whatever tomb may have been inside the pyramid. Why build *another* structure in front of it?"

"And there was no tomb," Sarah said, recalling pieces of the discussions and lectures she had attended over the years. "There were never any remnants of a tomb found, nor were there any *records* of there being a tomb inside the Great Pyramid."

"I know, Sarah," Lindgren said. "Which means it is that much more unlikely that a race such as the Egyptians would have a need for a *secondary* protector. It would have been a colossal waste, protecting a finished pyramid that was to remain completely devoid of any life — or death — for millennia."

"So… what is the Sphinx for, then?"

His smile shifted into one that was almost mischievous. "My thoughts — and I've had ample time to think about it — are that the Sphinx *is* still a temple of protection. A warning to outsiders, and a reminder to its builders of the great secrets it is guarding."

"What kind of secrets?"

"*All* secrets, my dear," he said, the mischievous smiling. "The Sphinx is guarding *all* secrets. Everything its builders knew and discovered. Everything they wanted hidden for all time, for whatever reason. They wanted something that would warn outsiders that to enter its presence meant death, unless they were worthy of receiving its welcome call."

"Receiving its welcome — Dad," Sarah said. "You're being ridiculous. We're standing in a *jail cell* under a ton of rock, somewhere in Egypt, and you're working up a long-winded lecture to explain to me that the Sphinx is just another ancient temple?"

His smile faded, but only slightly. "First, I've had ample time to 'work up' a lecture, so you are hardly hearing a rough draft. Second, I'm *not* talking about 'just another ancient temple.' I'm telling you that I believe the Sphinx is the guard of the *greatest* treasure ever found in human history. I'm telling you that the Sphinx is guarding the treasure — and the story — *of* human history."

Sarah was unconvinced, but her father was no amateur. If he had reason to suspect they were at the cusp of something miraculous, she wanted to know the details.

"The Sphinx, my dear Sarah, is guarding the Hall of Records."

"The Hall of — wait, really?"

He smiled again, the mischievousness no longer present on his face. "Yes, Sarah. *The* Hall of Records, the same Hall of Records that has been mythologized for ages, undocumented and merely the subject of verbal lore. The Hall of Records that serves as the single, sole repository for the complete and condensed knowledge of the first of the Great Civilizations."

"The *first* of the Great Civilizations?" Sarah asked. "Dad, you're talking about —"

"Yes, Sarah," Professor Lindgren replied. "I'm referring to the Hall of Records that was built, filled, and protected by the race of Atlantis."

63

GRAHAM

PROFESSOR GRAHAM LINDGREN STOOD IN THE CELL, WATCHING HIS daughter's reaction. She was brilliant, far smarter than he could ever hope to be. Her entire life had been a series of surprises, from her discovery of her near-eidetic memory during her childhood years to her excellence in nearly every academic pursuit during her grade school years.

But during her last years of high school — the 'terrible teenage' years that he and Sarah's mother had long feared — Sarah's personality had blossomed and changed. Where she had once been studious, hard-working, and interested, she was now sarcastic, aloof, and arrogant. She used her intelligence to smart-off in class, earning plenty of detentions and the wrath of more than one high-school teacher.

She was still excelling academically, racking up numerous promises for scholarships by the time she was a junior, but Graham and her mother were beside themselves to figure out how to understand — and parent — their only daughter. They tried family retreats, counseling, and disciplinary actions, all to no avail.

Finally, and reaching the end of his patience, Graham tried sitting his daughter down for a heart-to-heart talk. One academic to another, he'd explained. He had asked her why she wasn't focusing on her studies, on getting into a great school and getting a solid education? After all, didn't she want to become a well-respected scholar like her old man?

She'd replied with a statement that made him at once more angry with and more proud of her than he'd ever been: *'I don't want to research the same crap everyone else is studying. There's more to this world hidden around it, and I want to find it.'*

Her career in the sciences, he'd determined, had begun.

It had been more than a decade since that talk, and the sarcastic, asinine girl was now a beautiful, intense, strong-willed young woman, and he couldn't have been more proud. She was everything he'd wanted in a daughter, and then some. She was on her way to surpassing his own achievements, and there was nothing more on this earth that a father could want.

But he had seen in her eyes the resentment. The momentary flash of grief that she'd shown when he'd explained his theory. She wasn't just incredulous, she was sad.

He knew she was upset that he had wasted the last few years of his life chasing something that was completely ridiculous. She wouldn't accept that his research had, in fact, led him — and her — to this very spot. She *couldn't* accept it. She had no reason to believe that some ancient legend, the fabric of which had been spun by Plato and then quilted into something new by countless historians, dreamers, and conspiracy theorists since.

There was an inherent dismissal of the perceived facts when it came to items such as this, Graham knew. He had been trained to discard hyperbole, to ignore the pressing concerns that capitulated toward a necessary truth.

In other words, as an historian, he had been cautioned and conditioned to be wary of all things that implied a *different* outcome than that which the 'resident authority' — in history's case, 'collected wisdom,' accepted.

"Ockham's Razor," he said, softly.

The door behind him clicked open.

Sarah swung around and Graham watched as Rachel Rascher herself walked through the door.

"Welcome, Dr. Lindgren," Rachel said. "My name is Rachel Rascher, and I am in charge of the Prehistories Division of the Ministry of Antiquities for the Egyptian Government. I'm glad you're finally here. It is my absolute pleasure to introduce you to the greatest-kept secret the world has ever known." She waved her arm up and around with a flourish.

"A dark, dank chamber?" Sarah asked. "We've got those back home, but you usually have to be dead to get inside one."

Rachel smiled, but Graham could see the burning desire to snuff out Sarah's sarcasm in her eyes. "Clever, but no. I'm referring to the *larger* compound — not this room."

"And what *is* this compound?" Sarah asked.

"Well, I believe your father was just starting to explain it," she replied. "Professor?"

Sarah turned to face her father. He felt his arms and shoulders sag, the weight of knowing what was in front of him finally beginning to wear him down. And not just the explanation of what this place was — that was the easy part.

He was worried about what it all *meant*, if it were true.

"I was just talking about Ockham's Razor," he said.

"And I am *equally* intrigued to know why Ockham's Razor is relevant to our situation, Professor?"

Graham looked at the two women, both watching him. One doubting him, the other mocking him.

"I — It's just..." for the first time in a long time, he was speechless. He hadn't prepared a lecture, written a lesson plan, or even read the chapter. There *was* no chapter. "It's just that I believe this whole discovery, Atlantis, the Hall of Records, it's all well explained by the concept of Ockham's Razor. 'The simplest answer is most likely the truth,' and all that."

"So the *simplest* answer is that Atlantis is *real*?" Sarah asked.

"Yes," he replied. "But before we even get into that, Ockham's Razor, as you know, isn't *exactly* what I just explained. That's the simplified version. Essentially, William of Ockham was *really* saying that he believed that we should not add additional layers of confusion, or opinions, on top of easily deciphered facts. We should not 'multiply entities' when calculating a solution."

"So Plato was right? Everything he wrote?"

Graham looked at his daughter. "No, of course not. Not if we are determining what is *fact* and what is *allegory*. But if we structure the problem that way, the confusion dissolves away. Any decent translation of Plato's own words can then be examined, and any reasonable, rational mind can determine that which Plato means to be part of his overall story and that which is historic fact.

"He is writing at once a *history* of his known world, as told to him by — at the time — credible sources, as well as telling a *story* — an allegorical device used for teaching purposes — of that same world. But with a reasonable approach, and an assumption that Plato is not trying to mislead us, his words are easy to understand."

Graham looked back at Rachel Rascher. She was nodding along, excitement growing on her face. "Yes, Graham," she said. "That is *exactly* right."

"So his documentation of Atlantis is just that — a documentation of its history, its existence, and its fall. Plato used its existence and subsequent destruction as a tool to explain the value in not becoming too prideful of a race. He used his dialogue to explain the truths he was wrestling with as a philosopher.

"But that doesn't mean that Atlantis *wasn't real* — it was absolutely a civilization of people, one that threatened and persecuted the ancient Athenians. Eventually they were destroyed by a cataclysmic event that swallowed them up 'in a day and a night' — a common phrase in Ancient Greek that meant 'an unknown and inexact amount of time.'"

He paused to take a breath, and only then noticed that Sarah was sitting on the mattress on the floor of the room. Rachel was standing by the door. Both women's faces were riveted on him, watching his every move.

"So the Atlanteans *were* absolutely real, Sarah," he said. "They existed, just as Plato described. They may not have been the fanciful, fantastic race of flying-car Jetsons our own history has created out of the myth, but they were real. So Ockham's Razor states that the simplest answer, after extracting the additional, hypothesized layers that have been mounded up on top of the original myth, is that Atlantis was, without a doubt, a real race of people.

"The Atlanteans were a race of people that existed long before history even *allows* them to exist. What we've considered possible for determining the age of ancient societies — Babylonians, Greeks, Egyptians, Mayans — it's all based on a physical world that exists *today*. But if you ask any cosmologist, or anyone knowledgeable in Earth Sciences, they will tell you that the best we can determine of what our world looked like 10,000 years ago is an educated guess. We simply *don't know*.

"So the ancient Atlanteans were 'advanced,' only in the regard that they were far more civilized than other peoples of that time — the nomadic hunter-gatherers that came to the Americas over the Bering Strait, the Pacific Islanders, the early African tribes. Those people coexisted — though they may not have known it at the time — with the Atlanteans. And Atlantis, as a race, was the predecessor to the Babylonians, the Sumerians, the Minoans, the Greeks — all of them — they were able to sail, and navigate the oceans using celestial waypoints.

"They rose to power through their civilization efforts, teaching their neighbors, including the ancient Athenians and Egyptians, how to farm, cultivate crops, study the skies above them, and build monuments and structures to gods they believed in.

"They may have been 'before their time' in the sense that they had achieved what no other known races before them had achieved — true civilization, a balanced and meritocratic society — but they were certainly not the elevated, magical race of alien beings our stories have turned them into. They had no flying cars, no magical spells, and they were certainly not a race of alien beings.

"They were, for lack of a better word, *normal*. And if we had another original text besides *Timaeus* and *Critias* that referenced Atlantis, we might have more 'simple answers.'"

He stopped at that, waiting to see the reactions on the womens' faces.

64

BEN

Ben's drink had long since stopped sweating, the ice now completely melted and the drink quickly warming to room temperature, but he himself *had* started sweating.

They had landed in Cairo and were taxiing down the runway and over the wide expanse of morning sun-heated light-gray tarmac, the waves of heat distorting the air a the ground. Ben shook his head, waking up abruptly, and groaned.

It feels like the middle of the night, he thought. *Why am I always* more *tired after I sleep on an airplane?*

He shook his head again, blinked away the remnants of sleep, and sat up in his chair.

The sun smacked down on the airport and surrounding buildings with an intensity he hadn't ever known. It was hard, abrasive, and dry. Even with the air conditioning on inside the plane, the air was still dry and still somehow stuffy. He sniffed, feeling the inside of his nose go dry as his body tried to adjust with the sudden change in humidity.

"You awake?" Julie asked.

"I am now," he said.

"Alex is telling us he can arrange a ride from here to the Giza Complex," she said. "From there, it's pretty much a tourist trip — and a tourist *trap*. It's going to be slammed, since school's out and the weather's nice."

"This is *nice* weather?" Ben asked, incredulously. He pulled himself up and stood in the center of the plane's fuselage, the only place that offered enough headroom for him to stand fully without cocking his head to the side.

He saw Reggie and Alex at the back of the plane, still deep in conversation, and he turned to Julie to find her smiling. "Looks like they're getting along," he said.

Julie rolled her eyes. "They haven't shut up, actually," she said. "I couldn't sleep back there. I moved up to the row right behind you." She pointed with her thumb to the row across the aisle from Ben's.

Ben raised his eyebrows. "You could have shared my row." As if she didn't know what he meant, he added, "if you know what I mean."

She rolled her eyes again. "Right. *That's* what I wanted. A little hanky-panky in an airplane, full of our friends."

He shrugged. "Just sayin'."

"Anyway," Julie said, changing the subject, "Alex has an idea. He thinks there's something about the Great Sphinx that's worth examining."

"The Sphinx?" Ben asked. "That's that weird cat-thing?"

"It's a *lion* with a Pharaoh's head, Ben," Julie said. "And yes. That's the one. It sits right next to the Great Pyramid of Giza, facing due east, guarding anyone who might try to sneak into the compound."

"Anyone sneaking in from the *east,* you mean," Ben said, snickering.

She sighed. "Just... come hear what Alex has to say."

The plane taxied to a stop at the small regional airport's terminal and pulled in to the gate. The pilot announced over the intercom that they had arrived, and where they might find their bags inside.

Ben wasn't sure if it was just the pilot's habit to explain the baggage claim at this terminal or if he was making fun of them for having nothing to their names — no bags, no clothes, no cellphones.

He followed Julie back to where Alex and Reggie sat side-by-side, deep in conversation. Mrs. E was perched on the seat in the row in front of them, leaning over and listening. Alex was consumed with his own monologue.

"...and then decided that the Sphinx — and likely the rest of the pyramids in the complex — was *far* older than we initially thought. Or, at least, older than most contemporary Egyptologists think."

"Is there data to back that up?" Reggie asked.

"It's empirical, but sure," Alex said. "There were a couple of researchers who were able to gain access to the Sphinx and run some tests and calculations. This was all, of course, expressly forbidden by the Egyptian government, and —"

"Wait," Ben said, "your country's government *doesn't* want people studying its ancient structures?"

Alex shook his head. "For the most part, no. They're scared, honestly. There are too many contradictory opinions about what the structures are, how they were created, and when they were built. Things that should be obvious, like the fact that most pyramids are tombs, are misleading. The Great Pyramid of Giza, for example, isn't a tomb at all. There was never anyone buried inside — no mummies, no sarcophagi, nothing. It's like it was built to be *just* a temple, but then it remained empty for eternity."

"And these guys who studied the Sphinx found what, exactly?"

"They claimed there was water damage around the base of the Sphinx, in the pit in which it sits."

"So," Ben said. "It rained? What does that prove?"

Alex smiled. "*Everything,* really. Ben, I'm not talking about a little bit of rain — the kind of water damage that's clearly apparent on the base of the Sphinx implies that it was subject to *a lot* of rainfall. *Hundreds* of *years* of rainfall, no less."

"So we're talking monsoon-level torrential rain?" Reggie asked.

"Yes, exactly," Alex said. "And that is simply impossible, given the Sphinx's age. There hasn't *been* a period of that much rainfall in the Nile River Valley since the Sphinx was built a few thousand years ago."

"Unless…" Julie said, leaning forward.

"Unless the Sphinx *wasn't* built a few thousand years ago," Reggie finished. "Unless it was built *far earlier.*"

Alex's smile grew. "Exactly. The last time there was significant rainfall that could have caused the scoring and horizontal erosion on the Sphinx's foundation was somewhere between five- and seven-thousand years ago. A handful of Egyptologists have been considering this alternative for many years, myself included. We believe that the Egypt we know was not born out of nothing; we believe that Egypt was influenced — greatly, perhaps — by a far older, far more advanced civilization. *This* civilization was the group who built the pyramids and the Sphinx."

"So your theory is that somehow this group that grabbed Sarah and her father are at the Sphinx?"

"Sort of," he said. "I don't think they're interested in the Sphinx itself, necessarily, but rather what's *underneath* it."

"Underneath it? I thought it was a solid mass of rock?" Ben said.

"It is," Alex said. "But there have been some theories and predictions that it's sitting on top a massive subterranean complex — a sort of 'secret tomb,' if you will."

"You believe these theories?"

Alex nodded. "There's already proof that there are cavities beneath the structure. In fact, a tomb was found beneath it, accessible via a narrow, vertical shaft at the rear of the Sphinx. Inside there was a decaying wooden coffin and some hieroglyphics on the walls."

"That's amazing," Julie said. "What happened to it?"

Alex laughed. "Tourism. In 1926, a Frenchman poured concrete down it, rendering the whole thing inaccessible, in order to 'clean up' for the upcoming tourism boom."

"You — you've got to be kidding me," Ben said. "That's desecration."

Alex shrugged. "Look, you don't have to tell me. Egypt has long since been under scrutiny for the way it's handled its ancient artifacts. And even if the government wasn't constantly screwing things up, there have been *countless* lootings, raids, and desecrations of the monuments since they were built. The capstone on the Great Pyramid, for example, and the white casing stones that used to be on every side of it — both long gone. Who knows how many priceless artifacts have been lost to time?"

Ben nodded. "Makes sense. So you're thinking that this tomb isn't the only one? That there might be a larger one somewhere?"

"I *know* there's one," he said. "The government's been hiding it, preventing anyone from accessing it. But believe me, it's down there."

"Have you seen it?" Mrs. E asked.

"No, unfortunately. They won't let anyone get close. But there are hundreds of eyewitness accounts of a 'large, tomb-like complex' sprinkled throughout history, even though the government denies it. To make it worse, the most famous account, and one that gets the most play is from a psychic. Even though he obviously heard it or read it from somewhere before, he passed it off as his own 'vision' and that's the account the Egyptian government references most often, because it's the easiest to discount."

"A *psychic?"*

"Yeah," Alex said. "Edgar Cayce. He 'predicted' that beneath the Great Sphinx was the Hall of Records, a huge collection of knowledge and wisdom from an ancient race that predated the Egyptians by thousands of years."

Ben flashed a glance at Julie. *That's too big a coincidence,* he thought. *That* has *to be what they're after.*

"Is there any reason to believe that the Hall of Records is the collected wisdom of the ancient Atlanteans?" Ben asked.

Alex looked up at him. "You know, it always sounded ridiculous. But I honestly believe there's *something* down there. I've *always* believed it. I love Egypt, and its history, but civilizations don't just 'wake up' one day and build giant pyramids using perfect mathematics. It's clear to me that Egypt *came* from somewhere. After listening to you guys, it sounds like it *has* to be the Atlanteans. There's just nothing else that makes sense."

Ben nodded. "That's what I'm thinking, too."

"Off to the Sphinx, then?" Reggie asked.

"You got it," Ben said. "Let's go get Sarah back."

65

GRAHAM

"Very good, Professor," Rachel said. "*Very* good. You are exactly right. Plato wrote about a very *real* race of people, one that was able to exist in relative isolation for over a millennium, allowing them to develop what would have been, at that time, a highly advanced civilization. They were able to exact complete control over their environment, farming and domesticating animals, working the land, fishing the sea and rivers, and becoming what no other society at that time was able to become — an isolated, safe, and advanced race of people. The most *pure* form of humanity that has ever existed."

Graham watched his daughter taking in all of the information. He hadn't spoken to her in months, but the look on her face suggested that she was in total disbelief. *She's thought about this already,* he thought. *She received my gift, and she's started thinking about it.*

He wasn't sure exactly what the artifact was that he'd found in Greenland — as an archeologist, he was usually wary of any objects that seemed too out-of-place in their environment, but at the same time it piqued his curiosity. Greenland was, for all intents and purposes, an archeological wasteland. Artifacts found there had often been left by passersby — no one in history had ever called the continent-sized island home for any significant length of time.

So finding something unique like that, something that was clearly an artifact from a time before history could remember, had an impact on Professor Lindgren.

And to find the piece in Greenland was simply fascinating.

He knew his daughter was trying to prove the theory that there had been visitors to the New World long before the nomadic tribes had traveled over the ice bridge of the frozen Bering Strait. He'd had similar suspicions during his career, but to date no hard evidence had turned up.

But when he'd found the artifact, he didn't even bother having it tested in his lab for authenticity or submitting it to peer review. He'd sent it to Sarah immediately, only pausing to open the artifact and examine the interior — and the stone that had been sealed inside.

And, best of all, if Sarah's research turned up anything of value, he had a strong feeling that it would coincide with his own research, the project he had been working on of late.

He knew his daughter was exceptionally intuitive, able to take seemingly unrelated pieces of a problem and put them together into a unified, understandable solution. He had given her the pieces — or at least *one* of the pieces — knowing that her own studies were slowly, eventually, leading her down the same path, and if he was right, he knew she would eventually understand what it was that he had been working on.

He hadn't anticipated being kidnapped, of course, but he had known that his most recent paper had caused a bit of an uproar in his academic circle. Further, it had been completely wiped from his university's servers, leaving no trace that it had ever been published.

When that had happened, Professor Graham Lindgren knew that he had stumbled upon something that *someone,* somewhere, wanted to keep hidden.

He had no idea it would lead to *this,* however.

"But that's… that's not enough," Sarah said, finally. "It's good — I believe you. *Both* of you. But it's not *enough.*"

"What do you mean?" Rachel asked, her head turned sideways a bit, inquisitively.

"I mean, I've been studying things like this my entire life — I'm an anthropologist, but my dad has been an archeologist all my life, and a great one at that. Trust me when I say I *grew up* around speculations like this, and even if he was crazy enough to believe this story — sorry, Dad — I can't believe *you* would be."

Rachel smiled. "I appreciate the vote of confidence."

"*Trust me,* lady. It wasn't meant as a compliment. I'm saying that you wouldn't have *wasted* how many countless thousands of dollars of resources building — or excavating — this place if there wasn't more to it.

"I can buy the idea that there *was* an ancient, advanced race of humans. The geography checks out — Santorini and the Cyclades Plateau are absolutely perfect for that — and the myths and legends all had to have come from *somewhere.* But even taking William of Ockham into account, extracting the layers of hyperbole and conjecture from the barebones analysis, Plato's stories in *Timaeus* and *Critias* alone aren't enough to corroborate an actual claim that *this place* —" she waved her hand around the shadowy, confined space — "was built by Atlanteans."

Rachel's smile grew, and Graham could see that she had not at all been fazed by Sarah's insult. "Yes, Sarah."

Sarah turned fully around, facing their captor head-on. His daughter wasn't quite a head taller than the shorter woman, but he knew if it came to it, Sarah wouldn't be at all troubled with taking Rachel down. He'd never *seen* his daughter fight, but he had a feeling there was a level of feistiness and dominance in his daughter he'd never been privy to. He had been married to her mother, after all.

Rachel Rascher continued. "You, also, are correct. What you and your father do not know, and what the rest of the world will be *dying* to find out, is that there was *another* book by Plato."

Graham felt his knees grow weak. *This is the type of discovery that careers are made on.* "Another... dialogue?" *That's not possible.*

He thought about it for a second, realizing then that not only was it *possible* there was another manuscript of Plato's, it was *likely*. While most of Plato's manuscripts that had been published and made widely available had been copied from the many fragments and completed versions, there were many pieces of his codices, tetralogies, and fragments of papyri that were at best incomplete. At worst, they were mere allusions to longer, intriguingly absent works from the great philosopher.

Remains of many of Plato's works, as well as copies of those works, were constantly being dug up, examined, translated, and sent to museums for restoration. Some of them were pieces of works that were well-known to Greek academia, while others were so indecipherable they might as well have been undiscovered works.

Why couldn't there be something more complete that is still undiscovered? he thought.

"Plato wrote a third piece to coincide with his words about Atlantis in *Timaeus* and *Critias*. In this dialogue, where he recounts an in-depth conversation with Solon, the man who had traveled to Egypt and heard about the ancient Atlanteans, Solon tells Plato where to find the Atlantean Hall of Records, the place where their entire mass of knowledge and wisdom is supposedly kept."

Sarah was clearly taken aback. "And you... you *have* this book?"

Rachel nodded without even pausing. "Yes, I do. My great-grandfather was part of an elite scientific community that was working to retrieve this knowledge, to exalt it for the rest of the world, proving once and for all the purity of his family's race, all the way back to the original —"

"Wait a minute," Sarah said, interrupting. "Your great-grandfather was a *Nazi*, wasn't he?"

Rachel's face twisted into a soured expression. "My great-grandfather was the *leader* of a fine group of men who worked their *entire lives* to find the solution to a problem —"

"He *killed* innocent people. Men, women, and children."

"He was not a part of the larger edict that led to the concentration camps, Sarah. He was merely trying to —"

Graham saw the change in Sarah first, likely before even Sarah noticed it. Her demeanor shifted, suddenly understanding what her goal was, and what her role here was to be. She rose, straightening her back and pushing out her chest as she stretched out to her full height, towering over both him and Rachel. Her nostrils flared once and her jaw set.

"*That's* what this is about," Sarah said. "You're some deranged Neo-Nazi, bent on world domination through some vague idea of proving that your 'race' is superior to the rest of us. You and the 'Aryan dream.' In that case, you and 'Hitler's Dream Team' can go f —"

Rachel held up a hand, and a man entered immediately through the open door. Unlike Rachel, this man was *clearly* not amused by Sarah's tirade. He stepped forward and grabbed Sarah's wrist, yanking it back behind her body and twisting it up behind her shoulder blade. She screamed in pain, and Graham rushed forward.

He ran toward his daughter, but Rachel stepped in front of him. She held up an arm and he fell headfirst into it, surprised and dazed by the sudden speed and strength of the tiny woman. He rolled sideways, just as Rachel smacked the foot of her palm down onto the back of his neck.

He faltered, then fell. Before he could get back up again, a second man, this one larger and even more sinister than the first, had rushed into the room and applied the heavy boot of his left foot onto Graham's head, pressing it into the hard stone floor.

"Professor," Rachel said. "I want to thank you for your cooperation thus far. It has truly been a pleasure getting to know you. But your daughter does not seem to share the same respect toward my goal as you do, and I am therefore going to have to make an example out of her."

Graham couldn't see her face, but her feet — black boots that matched the soldiers' — were standing right in front of his face. Her toes could have brushed his nose without much movement on her part.

He sensed a struggle, hearing shuffling and commotion somewhere just outside, in the hallway.

Sarah.

He was in the room with only the other soldier and Rachel herself. Once again his daughter had been taken from him.

Once again he had had everything he cared about ripped from him.

"You and your daughter are both very competent," Rachel said. "But we have no use for both of you. I want to know where the compound is that you retrieved from the artifact, and I want to know *now*."

"I – I don't –"

"Not here," Rachel said. Graham felt himself being pulled roughly to his feet. "There is one last trial planned before we reveal ourselves to the world, and I believe it will be one you won't want to miss, Professor."

66

BEN

The ride to the Giza complex was uneventful, made even duller by the massive amount of commuters on the road. Traffic was a nightmare, and what should have been a twenty minute drive from the airport was over twice that.

Ben held Julie's hand in the car, neither of them speaking. Alex and Reggie chatted in the backseat while Mrs. E drove, but Ben's mind was focusing on what their next move was. As the leader of the CSO, it was his duty and responsibility to protect his team. He knew Reggie and Mrs. E were more than capable of handling themselves, but he wouldn't be able to forgive himself if something happened to Julie and Alex.

When they arrived at Giza, Ben called a team huddle. "Listen," he said, before anyone opened a door. "We're enemies of the state here. We're not welcome, and this isn't the type of country to ask questions first. Besides that, if Sarah's captors have any sway with the local authorities, and my guess is that they do, we're already in over our heads. They're not going to just let us walk in and starting snooping around their ancient sites."

"What's the plan, boss?" Reggie asked.

"Well, that's sort of where I'm stuck," Ben said. "But there's something we used to do all the time back at the national parks. In order to test our systems and processes, as well as the overall satisfaction level of our service, we'd hire other rangers from other parks to come down and do a sort of 'vacation' stay at our park.

"They'd come in, dressed casually — not in uniform — and just ask about stuff. Our guest services departments and most of the rangers and other staff had no idea that they were a government employee, running an audit."

Reggie laughed. "So your plan is to just walk in to the visitor's center and say, 'hey there — we'd like to dig around your Sphinx, if that's okay?'"

Ben shrugged. "Yeah, sorta. There's no way the hourly staff at their centers knows our faces and names, right? I mean we're not really welcome here, but we're also not internationally known criminals."

"Actually, that might work," Alex said. "It at least can get us in the park without having to sneak in. It's worth a shot. And if it doesn't work, we can at least sneak in after, but this is a far better option than trying to just get around the guards."

"There are guards here?" Reggie asked.

"Oh yeah," Alex said. "Lots of them, too. The Ministry of Antiquities announced a few years ago that they were turning over the bulk of the management and maintenance duties, including security, to private contractors. And there have always been Army guys around. That, combined with the increase in encroachment from nearby buildings and golf courses, means higher — and better — security in general.

"Heck, in 1995, UNESCO removed the Great Pyramid from its list as a World Heritage site because of a proposed highway that was going to pass too close by. The highway was moved, UNESCO put it back on the list, and here we are. Now, with tourism at an all-time low because of terrorism threats and an unstable economy, there's a much higher amount of peddlers and scam artists working outside the complex, preying on the few tourists that are here."

"So, basically, we're going to be bombarded by street urchins or guard dogs," Reggie said. "And you're saying our best bet is to just walk in the front door and keep things above-board."

"Yes," Alex said. "There are fewer guns pointed at us that way, at least."

"Okay," Ben said. "So the key is to just act casual, as if we're just tourists. In a sense, we are. We're curious about the Sphinx and want to see it. Nothing more, nothing less. Once we're in we can try to gain access to one of the auxiliary buildings and snoop around. If Sarah's here, it shouldn't be impossible to find her."

Mrs. E nodded in the rearview mirror and opened her door, followed by Alex and then Julie. Ben slid out of the car, stretched, and suddenly wished he was back inside the vehicle, where it was cool and air-conditioned. *It's* hot *out here,* he thought. *Way too hot.*

He had no idea how people had ever decided to live here — his own cabin in Alaska got stuffy in the summertime, and this place was at least forty degrees hotter.

He sniffed, shuddered, then walked toward the main building sitting just in front of the most massive monument he'd ever seen.

The Great Pyramid of Giza rose 481 feet into the sky, towering above the two other massive structures that sat near it. The pyramid pierced the sky above it, breaking into the low clouds that had settled over the area. For centuries it had been the world's tallest building, until population growth and engineering prowess rose to the challenge.

My God, he thought. *I've never seen anything like it.* Ben had of course seen pictures of the pyramids, but to see it in person, in real life, was absolutely breathtaking. Like the Colosseum in Rome, it was hard to believe a structure like this could have been created by humans.

And humans that had no real technology, he thought. *No bulldozers, earthmovers, or even decent polycarbonate shovels.*

At that moment he knew the truth. "Alex," he said.

"Yeah?"

"You said there was a time when this place had a bunch of rainfall?"

"Yeah."

"It would have been a *lot* cooler then, I suspect."

"Definitely," Alex said. "The climate would be completely different. Almost tropical."

Ben nodded. "That's what I thought. These structures were *definitely* built way before the Egyptians claim."

"Why do you say that?" Julie asked.

Ben pulled the collar of his shirt open to try to get some air moving beneath it. "Because it's *hot*. Miserably hot. No way these guys would have built something like this in this heat."

Julie and Alex laughed. "*That's* your theory?" Alex asked. "Sounds scientific enough, I guess."

Ben grumbled under his breath and kept walking. They reached the front entrance, an underwhelming brownish building with a low and flat roof, with no windows. The building stood next to a long electric gate, and throngs of people were crowded on both sides of the gate, either waiting for their time to enter or waiting on more people in their parties.

Ben could also hear the commotion of the shouting hucksters, rattling off prices in English and Arabic, and he even heard the strains of one enterprising young man shouting in French as he held up his colorful Egyptian scarves at a band of women waiting nearby.

Ben caught sight of a sign written in Arabic and English: *ENTER THROUGH TICKET BUILDING.*

He walked toward the building, the rest of his group in tow, and saw two armed soldiers standing on either side of an open door. Ben tried not to scrutinize them and call attention to himself, but at the same time he wanted to know if the men were eyeing him as well. Unfortunately their eyes were concealed behind sport sunglasses, but they didn't budge when he walked by and stepped through the door into the dark, low room.

His eyes adjusted and he saw the ticket counter to the right. Alex took the lead and walked up to the counter. He spoke in Arabic with the man behind the counter for a moment, and then handed the man a credit card and a few bills from his wallet. The man smiled, swiped the card, and handed Alex enough wristbands for his entire group. The man handed Alex a receipt and stuffed the bills into his pocket.

Ben nodded in approval and accepted his wristband. "Work out a little deal with him?" he asked Alex.

Alex nodded. "Told him I was showing some American tourists around."

"That's… all it took?" Reggie asked, putting on his wristband.

Alex looked around, his eyes landing on Ben. "I also told him the big guy back here was 'special,' and that it would be great if we could get the child's rate for him."

Reggie and Mrs. E laughed hysterically and shuffled their way through the visitors toward the exit at the back of the building.

"What?" Ben asked. "You told them I was… Jules, do I look 'special?' What's that even mean?"

Julie grinned and grabbed Ben's arm, pulling him away from the counter and toward the door. "Shh," she said. "You don't want that guy to think we were pulling a fast one."

Ben rolled his eyes, but patted Alex's shoulder as the young man passed in front of him. "Glad you're here, buddy. Thanks."

Alex nodded, looking up at Ben. "You got it. Whatever it takes to find Sarah."

Ben took a deep breath, then plunged himself back out into the swirling heat. Reggie was suddenly right next to him, yanking his shirt and pulling him sideways.

"Hey —"

"Keep it down," Reggie said. "And stay in the shadow of the building."

"Why?" he asked, but he stepped to the side anyway.

The others were there too, huddled out of the way and mostly staying in the shade of the low building. Thanks to the building's location on the east side of the complex, the morning sun was casting a long, rectangular shadow on this side of the ticket office.

"Look," Reggie said, pointing.

Ben followed and saw a group of armed men standing nearby, surveying the crowds as they poured through the ticket office. Unlike the guards at the front door, however, these men were wearing the insignia of the Egyptian military.

And standing in the middle of the group was a man Ben immediately recognized.

Agent Sharpe.

67

BEN

"INTERPOL'S HERE?" BEN ASKED. "HOW —"

"They probably tracked the Sikorsky," Reggie said. "There's no way it would have had a solid manifest and flight plan submitted to the local authorities, so it would have been easy to track if they knew what they were looking for."

"And they were on the hill when it took off," Mrs. E added. "So they certainly would have known what to look for."

"This is bad," Ben said. "So much for walking in and pretending we're just tourists."

"We *are* just tourists," Reggie said. "Alex bought the tickets, remember? They won't know his name, so his credit card information won't be passed along to Interpol or the government here. We're still flying under the radar, we're just going to need to tread lightly from now on."

"You think they'll shoot at us?" Julie asked.

Reggie shook his head. "Even if they wanted to, it would cause a riot. It's too busy here." He looked toward the Sphinx, sitting almost due west from their location. Once we get away from the crowds, though, we'll be out in the open."

"They shot at us back in Santorini," Julie said. Ben heard the question in her voice.

"They were acting on a whim," Reggie said. "Sharpe isn't a rookie, but those cops back on the island probably don't get to see too much action. And he probably didn't give them the full story. For all they knew, we were international fugitives."

"Technically we *are* international fugitives," Ben said.

"Well, that doesn't mean we need to be shot at. Still, those guys aren't regular grunts. I think their insignia is the patch for the Mukhabarat."

"The muck-what?" Ben asked.

"The General Intelligence Directorate of Egypt. They're the country's CIA of sorts. Mainly focused on providing intelligence to the government, but also tasked with counter-terrorism operations."

"Counter *terrorism?*" Julie asked. "So we're terrorists now?"

Reggie shook his head. "We're not, but whatever's going on with the group that captured Sarah might be involved in something like that. But that *also* means they're going to be *really* picky about just letting us roam around here, too."

"Meaning we might get shot at," Julie said.

Ben saw the abrupt shifting of one of the Egyptian soldiers. He motioned in their direction, and Sharpe's gaze suddenly fell toward them. Ben locked eyes with the man.

Shit.

"Okay, they saw us," Ben said. "If we run, we're screwed. Whatever Sharpe told them about us, I don't think the Egyptian army is going to mess around with fugitives running around their historic landmarks."

"Yeah, probably not," Reggie said. "But the Sphinx is *right there.* Maybe we can ask them to escort us—"

The men started walking toward them just as Reggie cut himself off.

"Okay, this is *not good,*" Reggie said.

"What?" Ben asked.

"That guy next to Sharpe," he said, referring to the man marching alongside Agent Sharpe. The man was huge — nearly a head taller than Sharpe, and made of thick, solid muscle. "I recognize him."

"You *know* him?"

Reggie shook his head. "No, but I wouldn't mistake that face anywhere. That's one of the guys who took Sarah. He was in the bar, with his other goon, the one we left back at Nea Kameni."

The soldiers and Sharpe picked up their pace. They were still on the other side of the wide, expansive terrace from Ben and his group, and there were hundreds of tourists milling about between them. But Sharpe and the others were locked onto their position and would be through the crowds in fewer than ten seconds.

"Guys," Ben said. "We need to go. *Now.*"

No one spoke, but Reggie took point and darted to the left, aiming for the south edge of the square, where there were fewer people. Ben saw his goal — he was working to keep the throngs of people in the center of the square between them and the soldiers.

"Follow him," Ben said. "Go!"

Just as they all broke into a run, the soldiers and Sharpe started sprinting, pushing and jostling people out of their way as they aimed for Ben's position by the ticket building.

Ben followed the edge of the building toward the south, then cut right, following Reggie and the others. The quadrangle was narrower on this southern edge, and a low wall of ancient rock stood at the far west edge. *That's our goal,* Ben knew. Reggie was heading straight for it, and if they could just make it there, they'd be —

Crack!

The sound of gunfire rang out, but Ben didn't bother looking behind him. Screams immediately filled the air as well, and he knew the hunt was on.

And we're the prey, he thought.

Two more shots were fired, then the unmistakable sound of a three-burst round from one of the assault rifles the men were carrying. Ben didn't know how many people — if any — were between his back and the shooters, but he still didn't dare look back.

The screaming of the tourists in the square grew in intensity to a dull roar in the back of Ben's mind. It was there, but it wasn't the immediate focus. He was in a race for his life, and in a race to protect his friends' lives as well. Nothing else mattered.

Reggie had reached the wall and vaulted over it, then turned around to help Alex, Julie, and Mrs. E. Ben was panting in the heat, but he sped up and shot himself into the air. His foot struck the top edge of the wall just as Mrs. E slid over the wall.

He pushed, using the wall's top edge as a step, flipping his body sideways and rolling through the air over the line of rocks.

He landed in a heap on the other side, dust and sand flying up and into his eyes and face. He coughed, feeling a sharp protruding rock hammering and bruising into his back, but he didn't care.

We're alive.

He sat up. The low wall's top was only inches above the top of his head, and he knew this was far from a permanent hiding spot. The soldiers would be on them in seconds, and there was nothing but sand and emptiness between them and the Sphinx, looming in the distance.

"Gotta keep moving," Reggie said. "Let's follow the wall all the way down to the end. We'll have no cover then for a few hundred yards, but we can run flat-out and get to the Sphinx complex. It's set down into a moat of sorts, so if we get into the ditch we might be able to get some cover again."

"And then what?" Julie asked. "They're just going to hound us until we're out of breath. There's nowhere to go."

Reggie pointed to the northwest. "That's the Valley Temple Complex, right next to the Sphinx. It's a maze of stone. We get in there, we might have a chance to get behind them."

He looked at Ben, and Ben knew immediately what he was thinking. *We get behind them and we might be able to disarm them.*

Ben nodded, and Reggie took off, once again leading the way.

He heard a few smacks of bullets impacting the other side of the wall.

Once again under attack.

68

REGGIE

Reggie knew only a marginal amount about the Great Sphinx and its surrounding area. He knew the Great Pyramid, situated to the Sphinx's northwest, was the last remaining wonder of the world, and that it had stood in this area for countless thousands of years, the actual age of the structure a point of contention among Egyptologists.

But during the flight to Cairo and Giza, during the downtime between bouts of conversation with Alexander, Reggie had brushed up on some of the history of the place they were now running through.

The Valley Temple, as it was called, was a sprawling stone complex sitting just to the south of the Sphinx and its own temple, and it was thought to have been the temple built for the remembrance of the Pharaoh Khafre, an Egyptian king who had ruled over four thousand years ago.

The Valley Temple is roughly square, about 150 feet to a side, and made up of a few different 'chambers,' each hewn from limestone that had been cut and quarried from the area surrounding the Sphinx plateau. To Reggie, the top-down view of the complex looked like some sort of spacecraft, like a two-dimensional Starship Enterprise:

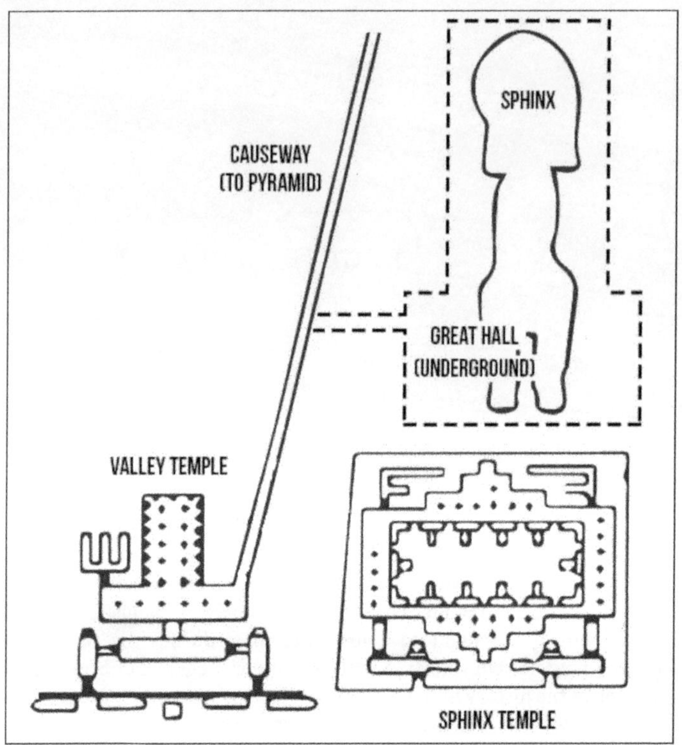

The temple had been completely covered in sand until the 1800s, so it had been preserved well and hidden from looters and thieves. The result was a temple complex that was miraculously well-kept, the walls and columns still standing erect, only the roof that used to cover them missing.

Egyptologists ascribed the temple's founding to the era of Khafre's reign due to finding a bust of the pharaoh upside-down in a pit inside the temple. The problem with using this simple associative method for dating the structure around it is, of course, that the bust would have been added to the temple at any point *after* it had been built — including thousands of years after.

That sort of age-by-ascription was common in Egypt, Reggie knew, and one of the main problems he had with the academic community. The Great Pyramid itself had suffered from similar aging methodology, and current efforts to properly date the massive pyramid were constantly under attack by Egyptological 'purists.'

The most telling reason Reggie had found to think that the Valley

Temple — and the Sphinx, its own Sphinx Temple, and the rest of the impressive structures that made up the Giza complex — was far older than the accepted wisdom claimed, was something he'd discovered while quickly skimming a report of the Sphinx and its surrounding buildings. The original 200-ton limestone blocks that formed the Valley Temple had been later encased with granite facing stones. But those granite stones had been perfectly shaped to fit the weathered, eroded facades of the limestone blocks they were intended to cover — meaning the limestone blocks had been around for a *very* long time.

He had been intrigued by the information, filing it away in case it was something that was necessary to their operation in Giza. Now they were running toward the low-ceilinged temple, unsure of what lay inside.

Reggie ran at the front of the line, knowing that he could count on Ben to keep up at the rear. The gunshots had subsided for now, but he knew it was only because the men chasing them were well-trained. They wouldn't waste ammunition by firing stray rounds. They would wait until their shots were clear.

He picked up his pace, nearly diving forward with every long stride, until he was at the entrance to the Valley Temple. A circle of Asian tourists stood nearby, startled and afraid, but they were moving away from the entrance slowly, keeping together and trying not to make eye contact. He was glad they were working their way toward the front gates, but still in disbelief that their pursuers had actually opened fire on them in the middle of the day, not caring at all about the innocent civilians and passersby.

It told him that the Mukhabarat weren't about to lose the opportunity to take them out. They were here to do a job, and that job involved making sure Reggie and his buddies were completely out of the game.

And he knew all too well how they intended to accomplish that mission.

All of it told him that they were no longer dealing with just the Interpol agent, Agent Sharpe, who had seemed decent and harmless enough. Now they were in the thick of the battle, chased by a group of people who would risk collateral damage and killing innocent bystanders to hide whatever it was they were trying to hide.

And to hide Sarah.

He surged forward, launching himself into the front door of the Valley Temple. He ducked instinctively, even though the ceiling was high enough to not pose a threat to the top of his head. He stopped for a brief moment, catching his breath and waiting for the rest of his team. In the brief respite, he took in the interior of the grand temple, seeing the pictures and descriptions he'd read coming to life before his eyes.

He wasn't sure if having information about the Valley Temple or the

Sphinx would help them stay ahead of their pursuers — and it certainly wouldn't help them not get shot — but it only reaffirmed his suspicions that there was something *very* strange and off-the-record about the entirety of the Giza Plateau.

69

JULIE

JULIE'S SIDES WERE SPLITTING WITH THE GROWING PAIN OF EXERTION. THEY were safe — for the moment — inside the Valley Temple, but Reggie had barely stopped to wait for her and the others before motioning them onward into the depths of the ancient structure.

He had researched the buildings that made up the plateau, and combined with his love of and knack for history as well as Alexander's firsthand knowledge as an ex-resident of Cairo, she felt they were in good hands.

Still, she wished those hands had *something* in them that could fire back at their pursuers. Reggie had told them that the men following them were with the Mukhabarat. The security force was in charge of anything the Egyptian government deemed worthy of their being in charge of; they had a near-carte blanche in dealing with local threats to the Cairo and Giza governments.

And Julie knew also that Agent Sharpe was not only out of his jurisdiction, he didn't *have* a jurisdiction. The fact he was here was surprising — Interpol wasn't a police force, but merely a communications firm that assisted national and local governments. He was probably feeling as overwhelmed with his involvement as Julie was with her own, but she knew there wasn't anything he could do or say to call off the Mukhabarat men. They were on a mission, and Julie and her team was the threat.

They would eliminate the threat, or they would fail.

And she didn't seem to think they were interested in failure.

She followed close behind Reggie, Mrs. E, Alex, and Ben just behind her. They twisted through the near-empty expanse of the Valley Temple. Most of the tourists had been scared off by the impending violence and gunshots, and were making their way to the eastern gates in droves. A few stragglers — either people unaware of what was taking place or choosing to remain ignorant — stayed behind, reading inscriptions and walking among the pillars of stone in the temple.

Julie hoped for their sake that the men following them wouldn't be careless enough to crack off shots as soon as they rushed inside.

Reggie turned right up ahead, then immediately left. Thanks to the lack of a roof covering their route, Julie could just barely see the top of the Sphinx's head in the distance, and she noticed that the winding path Reggie was taking through the column-laden temple was going to end up somewhere near the southeastern side of the Sphinx.

Just as Julie took the left turn, she saw Reggie step through a plastic sheet that was blocking a doorway at the northwestern corner of the Valley Temple. The doorway was narrow, hardly wide enough for a pair to fit through side-by-side, and a sign stood next to the door stating the purpose of the closed-off section in English and Arabic.

Causeway currently closed; no public access.

Reggie didn't stop to ponder the sign's meaning or ask the others for their opinion, he simply ran through the thin plastic sheet, tearing it from the weak painter's tape holding it to the stone walls. Julie followed behind him, finding herself running down an infinitely long tunnel. The 'causeway' was also roofless, and the bright sun illuminated the entire strip of stone pathway that ran the distance between the Valley Temple and its destination, somewhere near the front of one of the pyramids.

Julie didn't know what the causeway's original purpose was, but it was clear that it was now used for some sort of construction project. She hurdled paint cans, sawhorses, and other tools and supplies as she ran. More plastic sheets covered the stone walls, and scaffolding had been erected in a few places over the top of the causeway, allowing workers to pass overhead as necessary.

Reggie ran ahead, then stopped at an intersection with another passageway that branched off the causeway to the right.

"This shouldn't be here," he muttered, breathing heavily.

"What do you mean?" Julie asked.

"This causeway," he replied. "It's just a long and straight stone passageway, probably meant to bring water up to the pyramids. There weren't any offshoots, from what I remember."

"Maybe you missed it?" Julie said, just as the three stragglers behind her caught up, all of them panting.

"No," he said. "I mean, it's newer, too. Look." He pointed to the walls around the main causeway, then at the newer passageway. Julie had to admit the new branch looked to have been cut recently, the fresh corners and edges still sharp.

"You're right," Ben said. "So... do we take it?"

Reggie looked behind him, then nodded. "They're going to be right behind us, and there's no other exit from the Valley Temple besides this causeway. It's too long to run the length of it before they're on us, so we'll be sitting ducks. This fork is the only way to go. They're probably —"

Before he could finish, Julie heard the sound of heavy boots — many pairs of them — echoing louder through the causeway.

"They're almost here," Reggie said. "Come on."

Julie didn't hesitate. She followed Reggie into the perpendicular branch off the main causeway. It was covered, and thus darker. Reggie had slowed down, so as not to miss any dangerous ledges or obstacles, and Julie kept up.

70

BEN

The doorway that had been cut into the side of the causeway wall led to another hallway, this one a bit higher, but narrower, than the original Egyptian one. It was darker, too, owing to the fact that this hallway still had a roof — or at least the bedrock that the hallway had been cut out of hadn't been cut all the way to the surface. Sand and chips of rock piled along the sides of the hallway, and a light coating of dust picked up and filled the air as they walked inside.

Ben couldn't at first see exactly how far the hallway had been cut, but after a few seconds his eyes adjusted and he saw that the hallway ended only twenty or so feet ahead.

Unfortunately, the way it ended was in a thick, massive metal door, completely closing off access to whatever lay behind it.

"Not good," Reggie said.

"Definitely not good," Ben echoed.

Ben heard the footsteps behind them growing in volume, and he could see the shadows of the soldiers looming in the longer causeway.

"What is it?" Alex asked. "It's obviously modern."

"No idea," Reggie said. "Probably some sort of access corridor for maintenance or something."

"Whatever it is," Mrs. E said, "it is locked." She pulled on the handle again and the door didn't so much as budge. "We are stuck here."

Ben felt the adrenaline rush he had been on immediately leave him, and his heart sank as he looked at Julie. He moved in front of her, blocking her view of the main causeway. *And blocking their view of her.*

He wouldn't be much of a shield, but it was better than nothing.

"Should we rush the hallway?" Ben asked.

Reggie was standing next to him, both large men standing shoulder-to-shoulder in the smaller corridor, completely filling the space. "We don't really have a choice, I guess," Reggie said. "On my count."

Ben nodded, then sucked in a deep breath and let it out.

"One," Reggie said, his voice a whisper.

Ben watched the shadows bouncing toward them, growing larger and fainter as they neared their position. The heavy footfalls thundered down the causeway, and the cacophony of it all made it sound like there was an army bearing down on them.

"Two."

Ben knew they had less than three seconds before the soldiers and Sharpe reached their position. Three seconds to prepare whatever defense they had in mind — in this case, nothing more than hoping their surprise attack took them off guard. Three seconds to tell Julie —

"Three!"

Reggie lurched forward just as the first soldier rounded the corner. Reggie flew at the man with an unbelievable speed, his shoulders hunched but his head up, aiming the crown of his forehead toward the chin of the first man.

The *cracking* sound of the impact — bone on bone — reverberated even louder than the footfalls, and it took Ben a split second to realize it wasn't just the impact from Reggie's head-butt that had made the sound.

The *second* soldier in the line of the men running down the length of the causeway had reacted to Reggie's attack with a quick pull of his trigger. The assault rifle's retort sent the round sailing toward Reggie, landing in the thickest part of his upper thigh.

He screamed, falling sideways, just as the first soldier — the man whom Reggie had hit with his head — recovered and lifted his own rifle.

Ben stopped dead in his tracks. He had been running as well, but his speed was no match for Reggie's and his friend had taken off and raced in front, reaching the causeway and the first man in the line a second before Ben.

Now, Ben was standing at the intersection of the causeway and its smaller corridor, staring down the barrel of a Maadi MISR 7.62mm assault rifle.

He swallowed, then closed his eyes. Reggie groaned from his spot on the ground in the causeway, the blood on his leg beginning to pool around him.

This is it.

He heard a loud cracking sound and he held his breath. The sound was followed by a smaller, lighter squeak, and he dared a glance at the soldier.

The man wasn't looking at him.

Instead, the soldier had his eye on something over Ben's shoulder. Ben let out the breath, then turned around.

Behind Julie, Mrs. E, and Alex, the metal door at the end of the corridor was opening.

"Hold your fire!" a voice shouted.

Agent Sharpe.

Ben recognized the man's voice, and when he turned back around he saw the Interpol agent standing next to the man holding a gun in Ben's face.

"Wait! Don't shoot!" he said again. He pushed the man's rifle down, stepping up and into the smaller corridor.

The door behind Ben opened fully, and he heard someone shuffle out. He turned around, his back now to the gunman and Agent Sharpe. He saw a woman — short, a bit stout, but with a youthful face that was bright and cheerful. She stepped fully out the open door, and Ben could see that there was another man standing directly behind her.

And he, too, was holding a weapon.

"Welcome, Gareth," the woman said. "This must be your team. The *Civilian Special Operations,* I believe?"

Reggie didn't speak.

"I hope you are ready to learn what all this fuss has been about. Please, come in." She motioned for the five of them to follow her, but Reggie didn't budge.

"I'm not going anywhere," he said. "Until you tell me where Sarah is."

The woman smiled. "Of course," she said. "I'll tell you what — I'll make you an even better offer: come in and see what she's been helping us with. She's been helping her father figure out a crucial part of our research. They are both unharmed, and would be quite excited to see you."

Reggie frowned, then looked at Ben. Ben shrugged, just as he felt the barrel of a rifle press into the small of his back. Agent Sharpe was suddenly standing next to him.

"You can't get us out of this?" Ben asked Sharpe. "You know we're innocent."

Sharpe looked over at Ben.

"What?" Ben asked. "Can't you just make a call? Tell everyone here what's going on, and that we haven't done anything wrong?"

Sharpe examined his face, then with a heavy sigh, dropped his shoulders. He lifted his pistol slowly, then held it up to the back of Ben's head. "Sorry, Harvey. I — I can't."

Ben's mind was racing. *What the hell is happening?* He turned his gaze back to the smiling woman.

"Thank you, Agent Sharpe," she said. "Your work is greatly appreciated."

She knows him?

Then, as afterthought: *she's* working *with him?*

Ben felt his temper beginning to build. They thought they had all been *chased* here, when in fact they had simply been *corralled* here. They had been chased into a trap, and that trap had just closed.

"My team will follow all of you — Mr. Sharpe included — inside, and lock the door. I hope you understand that our security here is *mostly* to prevent tourists from wandering around in places they are not safe. This corridor —" she held up her hand at the rock-cut hallway — "is fresh, and although our engineers have assured me of its integrity, they are certainly no Aryan builders."

She turned around and began walking back inside, the man standing behind her stepping out of the way.

Mrs. E and Alex walked inside as well, followed by Julie.

I guess we really don't have a choice, Ben thought.

Reggie sighed, but he didn't fight. Ben knew the man wanted answers — but more than that, he wanted Sarah back.

71

BEN

Ben felt the growing anger in him fighting against the genuine curiosity he was feeling.

This place... it's amazing, he thought.

He wasn't an archeologist, and he'd never been much an historian. The closest claim to either of those titles was a distant niece he had who was working toward a successful career as an archeologist. Still, there was something about this place that told him they were treading into uncharted territory. The walls, the ceiling, the floors — all of it was cut from the same stone, and all of it had an earthy, empty, *dead* quality to it.

Like walking through a tomb, he thought.

He'd been in plenty of caves — mostly against his better judgement — and this place had the same feel as an underground cavern. The humidity was higher, but the temperature was thankfully lower than the sweltering desert outside. It wasn't perfect, but it was comfortable.

"This area is the antechamber for the Great Hall," the woman said, narrating their journey through the dimly lit hallways. Ben noticed that the lighting was supplied by mounted bulbs that hung from their chains, all the power running through extension cables and piles of cords. "The Great Hall, of course, is beneath the Great Sphinx itself. It has been lost to time, but that is mostly due to the work of Egyptians themselves, who have done a remarkable job erasing its existence from the global record. It has taken me nearly all of my career here to convince the government to allow my team and me to excavate and explore the Hall."

Julie picked up her pace and reached a spot just behind the woman. "What are you talking about?"

"There will be time for that," she said. "But we need to hurry, as the final trial is about to begin. I'll explain on the way."

The final what?

The woman continued talking as she led them down the corridors. "I have been in charge of the Ministry of Antiquities' Prehistory Division for four years now. My mission was to rejuvenate and protect the ancient history of the Egyptian people, but what that really means is that I'm in charge of ensuring a steady income stream from tourism.

"However, I was interested in not only *protecting* our great monuments and artifacts, but *expanding* them. My family knew of a long-hidden hall, filled with the recorded accounts of a great civilization, far more ancient than the Egyptians. They worked their entire lives to find the 'Great Hall of Records,' but ultimately failed. Their work, however, will not go undone. When I took the job, I used the information and knowledge I had collected over the years to find this place and begin the excavation. Eventually, I knew the Great Hall would reveal itself to me."

"We're in the Great Hall of Records?" Reggie asked.

She shook her head. "No — this is the antechamber, or chambers. We've converted it to our office space, and kept its true identity hidden from the government."

"Why?"

"Because the government isn't interested in the truth," she said, quickly. "The government is interested in money. And stability. And preserving the belief that *Egypt* is the first great civilization."

"You don't think they are?" Julie asked.

She smiled. "I do not. The ancient Egyptians were no more than a band of roving barbarians. Their 'kingdom' was nothing before my ancestors came. They taught the Egyptians how to farm, how to learn, how to navigate. They taught them how to be a *civilization*. Their architecture, belief systems, religion — all of it — was learned. What the Egyptians want to believe is a lie. A lie that's been fed to the rest of the world since the rediscovery of the Great Pyramids."

Ben could sense that they'd struck a nerve with the woman, and that she was either about to launch into an elaborate diatribe or just get angrier and shut down.

But he wanted her to talk, so egging her on was worth the risk.

"The Egyptians *built* the pyramids, though," Ben said. "So why would anyone believe that someone else —"

"The Egyptians *learned* to build the pyramids from someone," the woman snapped. "They didn't just wake up one morning and decide to start erecting the tallest building the world had ever known — or would know for centuries beyond. They were *taught*. Like everything else they're credited for, they *learned* it."

"From who?" Ben asked.

"From my ancestors."

"And who, exactly, are they?"

The woman stopped, now standing in the middle of a long hallway.

Ben could see offices set inside rock-cut rooms. Strings of single-bulb light fixtures hung in each room. Most of the offices were closed, large metal doors mounted over the original openings, but the chambers he could see into were sparse and undecorated, with only a computer and desk in the space.

"My ancestors are the original inhabitants of the Holy Land. They are the original proprietors of the Garden of Eden. They are the one, true race of pure humans, designed by God in God's image. They were the chosen people, meant to populate the earth and procure their place as the 'rightful ones.'"

Ben's eyes widened as she spoke. *She actually believes this crap?* "That's… that's the sort of stuff that got Hitler into some trouble," he said.

The woman glared at him. "My great-grandfather would agree."

Ben frowned.

"He was a brilliant scientist, hired by Hitler and his party to observe, study, and experiment with different strains of genetic material. Of course, at the time, genetics was a very new field —"

"I think they called it *eugenics*," Ben said, not trying to hide the disdain in his voice.

"Call it what you will," the woman continued. "My great-grandfather was part of one of the original teams that worked for Heinrich Himmler. He created many of the tests to study the effects of hypothermia and how to combat it."

"And how many people did he kill in those experiments?" Reggie asked.

The woman swung around to face him. "His research led us to much of the medical knowledge we have today."

"His research led to innocent men, women, and children being murdered for absolutely no —"

"Enough," she said. "The past is the past. I am interested in the *future*. My work here is nearly complete, but for one small piece."

Ben flicked his eyes down at her. "You mean you've found the *actual* Hall of Records?" he asked, looking around. "Not just this big, empty tomb?"

She nodded. "Of course. It is as real as the ground we are standing on."

"Then what's the problem?" Ben asked. "What's the missing piece?"

She looked back at him as her voice dropped a few decibels. "We don't… have a way to *open* it."

72

REGGIE

REGGIE WATCHED THE WOMAN WITH A GROWING SENSE OF UNEASE. HE WAS already angry — his leg hurt like hell and was beginning to bleed all over his pant leg — and Agent Sharpe, the Interpol guy, had apparently been double-crossing them the whole time.

Worse, he still had no idea where these whackjobs were keeping Sarah and her father, and time was running out. This woman, apparently some high-ranking German-born government official, was now wasting their time talking about Nazis and her ancestors.

On a normal day, Reggie would be at least intrigued by a discussion about World War II history; he would at least be willing to take the moral high ground and listen politely if he were ever in an argument with someone trying to clear the Nazis' bad name.

But today was *not* a normal day.

He watched Ben and Julie, then Mrs. E and the newcomer, the young guy named Alex. Alex was the only one among them who appeared scared, the fear on his face hard to miss. The others, however, were equally as afraid — he knew they were just better at hiding it.

Ben seemed to want to keep the woman talking; for what reason he did not know. Reggie was ready to move, to take action, but there was nothing they could do without earning himself another gunshot wound and putting Sarah in even more danger.

Come on, Ben, he thought, willing his friend to wrap it up. *Let's see what she's got planned.*

As if reading his mind, the woman turned and faced him, directly. "You're Gareth?" she asked.

He nodded, his face contorted in pain. "That's me," he said. "The one bleeding out."

She smiled as if he'd just told her he needed a Band-Aid. "We can get that wrapped up," she said, motioning toward one of the soldiers. The man left the room and returned a moment later with a roll of gauze he threw at Reggie.

The woman continued. "But first — I'm assuming you want to see Dr. Lindgren?"

He felt his heart speed up a few beats as he finished wrapping the gauze around his bleeding thigh. *Yes.* He nodded.

"She's waiting for us. The last trial is about to begin, and since it's rare we have an audience, I thought we could wait until we were all assembled."

Reggie frowned. *What is this 'trial' she's talking about?* It was the second time she'd mentioned it, and it was still unclear just *what* in the world they were working on down here.

"Right this way," she said.

Reggie limped forward a few steps but his leg was growing weaker and the pain stronger. Ben was suddenly at his side, and he helped him along. They rounded another corner and Reggie saw a long, dimly lit hallway standing in front of them. The woman led them down about halfway and then into a larger rectangular room.

A double set of folding tables, each eight feet long and three wide, had been set up side-by-side to form a larger, almost square table. Cheap plastic folding chairs had been placed around it.

"It's not much of a conference room," she said. "But we don't really have a lot of conferences."

Reggie also saw a bright orange extension cord trailing into the room, ending just underneath a television stand, on which was mounted a massive flatscreen TV. The television was on, but the screen was blank.

The woman nodded to one of the big men that had followed them in and he hustled over to the television, first rolling it out in front of the table and then pressing a few buttons on the back side of it. Reggie was deposited into a chair by Ben, who took a seat between him and Julie. He felt the slight relief of taking the weight off his injured leg, then the immediate searing of pain as his blood worked overtime to try to heal the wound. His brain did its part, releasing endorphins and adrenaline into his system to combat the effects of the pain.

But it wasn't helpful; Reggie knew that by masking the true damage, he'd be more apt to overdo it, injuring himself further. And if the gauze wasn't able to stop the bleeding soon, he'd bleed out in the basement of the Sphinx.

At least we're already in a tomb, he thought.

The man fiddled with the television a bit more, then an image appeared onscreen: a dark, empty room. It looked exactly the same as the room they were currently in, save for one curious feature.

Rather than a set of tables in the center, the room they were watching had a small stand, on top of which rested a bell-shaped object.

It looked like some sort of vase, made of ceramic or clay. Reggie could see that there was a smaller opening in the top, circular in shape.

Where have I seen that before?

The shape wasn't *exactly* like that of a bell; it was elongated and instead of its base being the widest section, the object tapered off again a bit, coming to a smaller circle on which the rest of the object sat.

He recalled what the woman had told them. *My ancestors... my family... history... Nazis...*

Nazis.

He sat upright, sucking in a breath as the pain lanced up his leg.

"What's wrong?" Julie asked. "Your leg?"

"No — I mean, yeah. Hurts like nothing else, but that's not what —" he turned to find the woman standing at the end of the table, still smiling.

"Are you ready for the trial?" she asked.

"What is that?" Reggie asked her.

"That room you are viewing is the room right at the end of the hallway. It's —"

"I'm not talking about the *room*, lady. What the hell is that thing in —"

She continued, completely oblivious to the outburst. "— And that wall on the opposite side is actually the *doorway*, we believe, to the Great Hall. Our scans show a massive, hollow space just beyond."

"What is the *bell* on top of that stand?" Reggie asked. "Is that *the* bell?"

"The bell?" Ben asked.

Mrs. E and Alex were seated across the table from them, with the soldiers and Agent Sharpe standing around it. Reggie tried to see a way out, but there was none. They were outmanned and outgunned. Even his trusty watch, which he'd used before in a pinch, wouldn't be of much use.

"*Die Glocke,*" Reggie said. "The Bell. A Nazi research project, said to be some sort of magical device."

"It's not magical at all," the woman said. "It's *science*."

Reggie continued. "People said it was all sort of things — they said it could levitate, that it could fly, that it used red mercury to function, that it was alien technology. It's never been proven, because it's never been found. But most people believe that it existed, and that it was some sort of weapon — part of a class of top-secret advanced weaponry the Nazis were researching called 'Wunderwaffe."

"Wonder Waffles?" Ben asked.

"Close," Reggie said. "'Miracle Weapons,' actually. The V-2 rockets are an example of the weapons to come from the program. Die Glocke, 'The Bell,' was said to have been one of them."

"It *is* real," the woman said. "But what you are looking at is a copy. The original is in a museum in Athens."

Julie coughed. "Wait — *what* museum?"

Reggie saw Agent Sharpe tense up. His face was a mask, but his eyes were hinting at something.

"The National Museum of Archeology in Athens."

"That's… that's where all those people…"

Reggie knew what she was talking about. He'd heard the news reports as well, read the articles. It was international news for a week, before the vicious cycle of information wars took over again. *137 dead. So many people...*

"That event was one of the last ones to use the synthetic compound we were working on," the woman explained. "It had its imperfections, but it was also quite enlightening. It allowed my team to further their research by a few weeks, and I believe we'll be able to create a perfect copy of the original compound and continue with our final event —"

"Wait," Reggie said, holding his temples. His head was pounding and his leg was throbbing, but he pressed on. "Hold on a second. Compound? What research? But what the hell are these 'trials' you keep mentioning? Is this what the Nazis were *really* doing with this… bell?"

She looked at him. "My great-grandfather was in charge of the *Die Glocke* project; he found the bells and put them to use for the Reich's research."

"The Nazis didn't create these?" Julie asked. "And there's more than one?"

"No, and yes. My ancestors — and his ancestors — were the ones who created the test. They created the technology. Their descendants tried to copy the compound that tests the purity levels, as they were the ones who were going to bring it around the world, to continue what the Ancients started."

On the television screen as the woman spoke, Reggie noticed movement. A door had opened somewhere offscreen, as the room brightened a bit. Two silhouettes appeared, their dark outlines rendering them unrecognizable.

Except...

Reggie leaned in closer. *Is that...*

He thought the person on the left looked thinner — smaller. And then when the person was pushed farther into the room, he knew.

Sarah.

He pushed his chair back, flying upwards and planting his good leg on the ground. "That's Sarah!" he shouted. "You son of a —"

He felt a crack, and immediately fell back into his chair. The soldier standing behind him had smashed the butt of his rifle into the back of his bad leg, cracking a bone somewhere inside. He groaned in agony but didn't fight back.

Ben, next to him, was seething. The big man was staring a hole through the television, his eyes fixed on the screen.

Reggie watched on. He could tell Sarah was fighting, struggling to get free. But the man who had pushed her inside had the advantage, and with a final shove he flung her across the room, almost to where the bell was sitting, and left.

He saw her scream out, but heard nothing.

"The trial is about to begin," the woman said. She pulled out a walkie-talkie from her pocket and started talking into it. "Bring in Professor Lindgren."

Reggie's eyes widened. For a moment he forgot about the pain he was in.

One of the soldiers standing behind him turned and opened the door. Two more men — scientists or employees by the looks of them — pushed in a gray-haired, tired-looking man. He was feeble, holding onto the mens' shoulders as they led him in, but he seemed otherwise healthy.

And the determination in his eyes told Reggie everything he needed to know.

This is Sarah's father.

The woman nodded at the man, then spoke again into her radio. "Dr. Shaw, we're ready in room 23."

Reggie heard a man confirm, then give a five-second warning. Reggie's eyes were glued to the television.

Five seconds, he thought. *I have five seconds to figure out what to do.*

He knew that meant he'd have to take out the soldiers, with an injured leg, with no weapons, then run down the hallway and get into the locked room.

In five seconds.

He let out a breath.

Ben squeezed his shoulder.

Mrs. E and Alex were staring at the television, their faces registering their shock.

He heard Julie sobbing quietly.

73

SARAH

THE SCARIEST MOMENT OF SARAH'S LIFE, UP TO THAT POINT, HAD BEEN many years prior. Once, when she was about eight years old, she and her mother and father had hiked to the top of a waterfall, where they had a picnic on a large, flat rock that overlooked the falls. The view and the setting was unbeatable, and Sarah remembered the scene vividly.

When they were ready to leave, Sarah stood up and prepared to hop across the rock's surface to the shore, but her foot slipped on a wet spot, and she fell backwards.

Over the edge of the waterfall.

Her mother had seen the entire thing happen and lunged forward, just barely grabbing Sarah's shirt as she fell over the side. Her mother fell to her stomach and stretched out, holding onto the shirt and reeling her daughter in carefully, slowly.

Sarah remembered the feeling of falling, then the feeling of knowing she was about to die.

She remembered that feeling even more vividly than the scene itself, and it haunted her to this day.

Today she was feeling that same feeling, but the panic had been replaced by confusion.

Why is this happening? What *is happening?*

She was locked in an empty room, nothing but some weird artifact standing silently nearby.

The bell-shaped object in the center of the room was electronic, apparently, as she could see a black cable snaking around the room and disappeared into a cabinet that stood in the corner. A hose, coiled nicely, sat next to it on the floor.

The bell suddenly whirred to life.

What the?

Sarah studied it for a moment. It looked familiar, but she couldn't place where she'd seen it. She walked a slow circle around it, noticing that it was gently heating up. She placed her hand out, feeling the radiant temperature building on the bell's surface.

Her face was heating up, too.

She wondered if the bell was giving off some sort of ultraviolet light, something that would cause sunburn. She rubbed her arms and hands. *Am I heating up?*

The bell's whirring sound rose in intensity and started to become an ear-piercing screech. She covered her ears, but was shocked to feel how hot they had become.

I need to turn this thing off, she thought.

She looked around, frantic. Her panic grew and her breathing became more labored. *It's like I'm breathing thinner and thinner air.*

She whirled around again, her eyes now displaying everything in a blurry, incoherent frame. *Something... I need something...*

Her brain was mush, and the heat was now radiating out from her. She stepped toward the door, then started banging.

"Help!" she shouted. "Please! Dad!"

She knew there would be no help. She was being punished. Or rather, her father was being punished — she was just the sacrificial rat in whatever experiment this was. Whatever their captors were looking for, they hadn't found it.

Her father hadn't been able to tell them what it was.

He hadn't even *known* what it was.

She knew that if he had, he would have told her — or he would have told *them*. He wouldn't have let it get this far, let them take his only daughter...

The cord.

She scrambled over to the corner of the room, aiming for the cabinet. Before she reached it, she fell. Her knees had grown weak and her vision was now dancing faster than the room was spinning. The bell's sound was blood-curdling, the noise blocking out even the rising pain in her face.

The pain.

She touched her face. It felt like it was about to melt, as if she'd been exposed to some sort of intense chemical radiation that was eating her alive.

She crawled over to the cord.

So close.

She yanked on it. *Please.* She pulled it by twisting her wrist backwards, then bending her arm into it to apply more pressure. She needed leverage, and she found it by grabbing her wrist with her other hand.

Nothing happened.

The cord didn't budge, and the cabinet it snaked into barely shook.

No...

She tried again. She pulled, harder this time, shaking the cable as she tried to roll over and put some weight on it. She was too weak to stand, but she knew she could put enough force into it to unplug it.

She felt it give a little, just a bit. *Yes. Please.*

She tugged again. *Turn. Off.* She tried willing the cord to unplug itself — prayed, even.

The heat in the room had grown to an insufferable level. She couldn't breathe, didn't want to. Her breaths were jagged, each one taking a bit of life from her chest. She began to wheeze, drool building on the side of her lip and caressing down over her cheek — it was far cooler than the air in the room, and almost soothing.

She rolled to her other side, her strength nearly gone. *One. More. Time.*

She yanked on the black cable, as hard as her arms could manage.

It didn't give.

She sobbed once, then closed her eyes and lay her head down on her shoulder.

74

GRAHAM

Dammit Sarah, Graham thought. *Get up.*

He was crying, the tears flowing freely down his face. No one seemed to care — no one even noticed. They were all, just like he was, fixated on the television screen that had been rolled into the front corner of the room.

He'd watched on in horror as his only daughter, his only family remaining on this planet, had been shoved into the room at the end of the hall. *Room 23.* It was the room that apparently served as the entrance to the Great Hall of Records, but Graham had been suspicious of this story from the beginning.

For one, Rachel Rascher had allowed him to examine the room himself, hoping that something inside might 'jumpstart a memory' about something that might help her. He'd sworn to her that he had no idea how to open the 'door,' if such a thing actually existed.

Rachel hadn't believed him since they'd brought him in — she had been dead-set on proving that Professor Lindgren was hiding something, that he knew of some way to open the Hall's entrance chamber.

He, of course, did not. He had never seen the place before in his life, and aside from a few references in mythological sources, he had never *heard* of the place.

She claimed it had been built by the ancient Atlanteans. That they had somehow traveled here and taught the Egyptians how to build, farm, and act like a civilized group of people.

All of that he could believe.

He could even believe that this woman, Rachel Rascher, was descended from that same race of people. Over the course of his career, he had seen more than enough evidence to believe that there had in fact been some sort of ancient race of humans, and that those humans had expanded their reach to all corners of the globe. He had *discovered* some of that evidence.

But what he *couldn't* believe — what he would not believe — was that this same woman would go to such lengths to prove her point. That she would terrify him and his daughter wasn't surprising.

That she was threatening to *kill* her for it was.

And now, watching the horror unfold on the screen, he had to come to grips with the reality.

Sarah is going to die.

My only daughter is going to die because of me.

He was still confused about how this was his fault, but he was past caring about that. This *was* his fault. He had failed to take care of her, and now he was paying the price no father ever in their wildest dreams thought they would have to pay.

Get up, Sarah.

Sarah didn't move. She was sprawled out on the floor of Room 23, her legs and arms spread-eagled over the rock.

Rachel began to talk, and Professor Lindgren tried to ignore her words. It didn't work.

"At this point, the compound is heated to a point where it turns into a vapor, nearly a gas. This is similar to one of the compounds the Nazis used in their concentration camps to gas their prisoners.

"Like us, the Nazi party was trying to understand how to replicate the compound that they found here. They failed, as we have, to create a perfect copy, ending up with the infamous compound, *Zyklon B*, used in gas chambers at the death camps. But we are far closer, and you are seeing the effects now."

She looked again at Agent Sharpe. "Unfortunately our trial in Athens revealed another set of chemical errors in the compound. We brought one subject back to our lab and administered a second dosage, but she was unable to survive that test."

Sharpe's jaw clenched, but he didn't move.

She lifted her hand to the screen as she continued, as if she were nothing more than a museum curator pointing out a new acquisition in their French Impressionists wing.

"Dr. Lindgren is slowly asphyxiating, her lungs contracting but not finding enough oxygen in the air. But unlike the *Zyklon B* gas and its alternatives, this compound has a *psychological* and *hallucinogenic* effect. Dr. Lindgren's brain is registering heat — it is not actually hotter in the room, however. Her face feels, to her, as though it is melting. The skin peeling off from the bone, and —"

"Stop," the man in front of Graham said. He was tall, but he was sitting awkwardly in the chair, holding his leg, which was bleeding and dripping all over the floor.

Rachel continued. "She will die of poisoning if she doesn't asphyxiate first. But most of our test subjects —" she looked around the room, her eyes landing on Graham and the man standing at attention in the opposite corner — "were able to withstand the lower oxygen levels for a significant amount of time, leading me and my team to believe we had in fact found a *pure* subject."

"You're testing her *purity*?" one of the women at the table blurted out.

"Yes," Rachel answered.

"By *killing* her."

"I admit, we are unsure exactly how the Ancients' compound actually works, but our best guess is that only by subjecting their bodies to extreme stress levels can the compound analyze their genetic composition. In a very literal sense, it's a stress test. The strongest survive, and the weak break."

"You're a monster," the woman said.

"I'm a scientist. And I am *very close* to understanding exactly how this process works. Dr. Lindgren is but one of many subjects we've studied, and — judging by her skin tone — she will, unfortunately, not pass."

Graham rushed forward, but the two men who'd carried him in had been replaced by a large, buff soldier. He restrained him without even flexing.

"You murderer!" Graham shouted.

Rachel turned to him and smiled. "There is still time, Professor. Tell me how to open the door and I'll let Sarah go." She turned back to the television for a moment and then addressed Graham again. "From what it looks like, Sarah has approximately one minute — maybe one and a half — to live."

He was still crying, but he forced the tears back and allowed his rage to work up into the front of his mind. "I — I'll kill you," he whispered. "I'll murder you. And everyone here."

"There's no need for unnecessary aggression, Professor," Rachel said. "Like I said, just tell me how to open —"

"You *can't* open it," he shouted. "It's not *real*. You believe a fairy tale — a myth. The Atlanteans, or whoever they really were, were just a *race* of people. Just like the Minoans, or the Babylonians. They were around back then, but they didn't… they didn't run around building fanciful pyramids and using bells to poison the 'unworthy' masses."

Rachel opened her mouth to speak, but the man sitting in front of Graham interrupted her.

"He's right," the man said. "You bought into a lie, lady. You're delusional, and you're going to have to pay for that."

He stood up, slowly, and the man sitting next to him stood as well, helping the injured man to his feet.

"That woman in there — she's…" the man faltered as he saw the image of Sarah, unmoving, on the floor. "She's *everything* to me."

He glanced at Graham. "And this guy — her father — he doesn't know how to open your stupid vault. Can't you see that? He wouldn't be lying to you. Not anymore. Look at her in there. You think *any* father could bear to see their kid inside that torture chamber and not come clean? You think —"

"My father was not pure," Rachel said.

The man's jaw dropped. "You — you tested your own *father?*"

She nodded. Graham thought he could see a flash of light in her eye. The sparkle of a tear, revealed by the single bulb that hung over the table. As quickly as it appeared, it sunk back into her eye.

"You're sick, lady."

Graham looked again at the television just as the woman sitting next to the injured man spoke. "She's getting up!"

Graham's heart began beating faster. *Maybe there's a chance...*

He was nearly certain they were out of time. She'd told them that Sarah had less than a minute left.

But she was moving. Sarah was rolling around, trying desperately to find her feet. She got to her knees and started shuffling toward the opposite wall, barely able to keep her balance. Finally she stood on shaking legs.

Come on, Sarah.

He wasn't sure what she was doing — what she was thinking. But she had it in her mind to stand up, and she was doing it. Graham saw the stubborn, beautiful, determined woman at that moment — her mother. She wasn't going to die lying down in a puddle of her own saliva. She was going to —

Sarah fell, lurching forward and smacking hard against the rock wall, face-first.

Graham's heart sank, and his head fell.

No.

Sarah lay crumpled against the wall, not really on the ground but not really standing, either. Her face and chest was smashed flat on the rock, her feet about a foot away from it. The rock wall had caught her fall, but it seemed the timer was up.

"Well, that was exciting," Rachel said. "Now, if we can —"

Her voice was interrupted by the sound of a deep, low rumble. It grew in volume until Graham felt the ground shaking beneath his feet. He felt the fear in the room as all eyes danced around to one another, no one having any answers.

For a moment they were all on the same team, a group of scared humans in an underground room that could be collapsing around them. They were the same then, each as confused as everyone else.

The rumbling grew again, but then became steady.

75

GRAHAM

"What is that?" Rachel yelled. "What's causing that? Is the demo team working today?"

One of the soldiers shrugged while another shook his head. "I don't think so, ma'am."

The rumbling continued, and Graham noticed dust falling from the cracks in the room where the ceiling met the walls. Small pieces of rock chipped off and became part of the swirling sandstorm falling onto their heads.

The two men and woman in the row of chairs in front of him started moving, too — the two men barreled toward Graham, narrowly missing him as they hit the soldier standing guard behind him. The woman jumped over the table and tackled Rachel.

Graham couldn't believe how fast they moved, and he wondered how injured the man had been, or if he had been faking it to conserve his strength.

The two men caught the guard by surprise and lifted him completely off his feet and smacked him — hard — into the closed metal door behind him. He groaned, but his head fell and they dropped him to the floor, knocked unconscious.

Two other soldiers and the man who had been standing at attention started toward the door as well, but Graham got in their way.

If my daughter's going to die today, then so am I, he thought.

He lifted his arms up and tried his best to emulate an NFL-quality stiffarm.

The man didn't so much as slow down, bringing his arms up and over his head in a stiff uppercut, blocking Graham's arm. The third man — the one wearing a suit instead of the soldiers' uniform — simply pushed Graham to the side as they passed.

He fell, but glanced over his head as he hit the ground. He hadn't stopped them, but he had slowed them down. He saw the two men who had been sitting at the table — one thinner, almost scrawny, one large and bear-like — turn and face the oncoming attackers.

One of the soldiers raised his gun and pointed it at the larger man, but the thin one lifted the subcompact assault rifle he'd taken from the soldier at his feet and fired twice, rapidly.

Graham covered his ears, but it was too late. Even though it was a tiny machine gun, it sounded as though a bomb had gone off in the enclosed space, and the hard walls didn't help.

The soldier slumped, then fell to the ground, dead. The second man was stunned, but recovered quickly. He fired a shot from his hip, but it hit the rock frame around the door. Graham was relieved to see that the two men had ducked outside just after they'd fired.

"Get them! Now!" Rachel yelled.

Two other soldiers that had been standing guard in the room ran out, while the odd man in the nicer dress and the last soldier in the room tried to peel the woman off of Rachel, who was now on the floor, wrestling.

Who are these people? Graham thought. They had snapped into action as if their entire attack had been planned.

Then he grew angry. *Why didn't they attack sooner? It's too late now. Sarah's going to be —*

He looked up at the television and frowned.

Where the wall had been a few moments ago, nothing but a black shadow loomed. Sarah was nearly lost in the dark, but he could see her slightly darker silhouette, kneeling in front of the black sheet.

She's alive.

"Sarah," he said. He still couldn't hear his own voice, or anything else, but he popped his ears and sat up. His knee had taken a good hit, but it was nothing. He stood, his eyes still glued to the TV.

"What's happening?" he asked, to no one in particular. "What is — what is that?"

Slowly, around the room, heads began to turn toward the television. Rachel sat up, the woman who had been attacking her apparently interested as well, as she was now standing and watching, too.

"It — it opened," Rachel said, her voice not hiding her awe. "She did it."

Graham wasn't sure what he was seeing, but slowly the room on the screen came back into view. The black sheet was, in fact, another chamber — now opened. The silhouette was of course his daughter, and the bell, on its tiny tower, was still standing in the middle of the room.

"She's alive," he said.

"She's alive," Rachel echoed. "She passed the test."

Graham's anger returned at the mention of the test. *She put Sarah through this. On purpose. I will kill this woman,* he thought. *I won't stop until she's gone.*

He clenched his fists and walked around the table toward Rachel.

"Hold it," one of the soldiers said, digging the end of his rifle into Graham's chest. "Not another step."

"Yes," Rachel said, "let's go see, shall we?"

She looked around the room, as if shocked to see what had transpired.

On the screen behind her, two more silhouettes — the two men who had taken down two of the soldiers — walked into Room 23. They stopped on either side of the bell, watching Sarah as she looked out into the black nothingness.

Graham took a deep breath. *My daughter's alive,* he thought. *She's fine. She opened the door. She's fine.*

He tried to repeat the mantra over and over again, but his heart was racing, beating out of his chest.

He led the way out of the room and started down the hall toward the room at the end. The door was open, and he could see the outline of the bell inside.

Beyond that, he could see his daughter standing at the edge of a deep sheet of darkness. *The Great Hall,* he thought. *It's real.*

As he neared the room, he saw the two men come into view as well, both staring awestruck at whatever it was they could see. He walked closer and saw Sarah holding her right hand up, clutching something on her chest.

She turned around and met his eyes as he stepped into the room. He saw her then, scared, the same little girl who had nearly died on a waterfall so many years ago. The same fear, the same questions.

But there was something else.

There was a look in her eyes told him that she was still putting pieces together. It wasn't just fear — it was intelligence. She'd figured something out. He looked at her hand, the hand that was clutching the —

The necklace.

He'd put the necklace in the tiny artifact before sending it to his daughter. The chain was his ex-wife's — Sarah's mother's — but the opal stone on it, the stone onto which he'd glued the tiny silver ring that linked to the necklace itself, was the thing he'd found inside the artifact.

When he'd finally opened the artifact, the stone had been in there, unpolished and rough. Opal, he'd thought. A common gemstone, and his daughter's birthstone.

She was clutching that necklace now, holding it tightly in her hand.

And there was a look in her eyes that told Graham that the necklace had something to do with how this monstrous rock wall had been opened.

It had *everything* to do with it.

76

SARAH

It worked.

Sarah watched the door — really nothing more than a massive slab of solid rock — open. She felt the cool, stale air come rushing into the room, mixing with the poisoned air of Room 23.

She took a deep breath, feeling the life come back to her. The air was old, but it was safe. She smiled, a tear falling over her cheek. She wiped it away, then stood watch at the edge of the enormous chasm that had opened in front of her very eyes.

She was holding the stone in her hand, the one her father had put inside the artifact.

Not opal, she thought. *This isn't opal at all.*

It looked like opal, with its whitish complexion, flakes of shining mineral sparkling out to the surface. She was familiar with her birthstone, and while this rock could have easily passed as opal, she knew now that it wasn't.

Reggie was there, behind her. She could sense him. She heard his breathing, knew it was him. Someone else was there, too, and farther away a third person was walking, entering the room. She didn't move.

"Sarah," a voice said, softly. "Sarah, are you okay?"

She turned around finally, facing her father. She wiped another tear from her eye and nodded, smiling, still holding the stone. "The — the necklace..."

"I know," he said. "It wasn't opal."

She laughed. "No, I guess it wasn't."

She noticed Reggie then for the first time, seeing his leg dripping blood onto the rock floor, and she rushed to him. He grabbed her, trying to hold her up but she felt his torso shaking from the pain.

"It's okay," he said. "We can — we'll have time later."

She nodded.

She turned back to the third man in the room, Ben. "Thanks, Ben," she said. "Thanks for helping me."

He seemed to be more surprised than anyone, with a look of genuine confusion on his face. "You got it, but… you know, we're not out of the woods yet."

Sarah looked over his shoulder and saw Rachel Rascher standing in the hallway just outside the door, three men holding dangerous-looking weapons standing around her.

"Hello, Sarah," Rachel said. "You passed the —"

Sarah ran toward Rachel, her fists clenched, but Ben caught her and held her. "Not now," he whispered. "They still have the upper hand."

Sarah saw the men up close, recognizing one of the brutes who had taken her from the hotel, and nodded. *Not now,* she agreed, *but their time will come.*

"I must say I am impressed," Rachel said, stepping into the room. "We thoroughly examined this room for weeks, as did my father and great-grandfather before me. We saw no cracks, no mechanism that would suggest —"

"Did you apply current to it?" Sarah asked.

Rachel frowned. "Electrical current? Of course not. Why would we?"

"The door is electrically charged," Sarah explained. "That's how it opened."

"I don't — I don't understand."

"I have to say, I'm as confused as she is," Ben said. "You're saying these people who built this place had *power?* Like real, electrical power?"

Sarah looked at Ben, but focused on the soldiers and some other people stepping through the door and into the room. Julie, followed by Mrs. E, followed by —

"Alex?"

Alexander walked toward her, then embraced her. "I'm sorry," he said. "I didn't know your father was…"

"It's okay," she said. "How did you find me?"

He held up his phone. "Your phone pinged an update with your location every ten minutes. Just like you have us do on a site."

She smiled. "I forgot to turn it off."

"Good thing, too." He paused. "And I'm glad you're okay. But yeah — how'd you open the door?"

She showed them her necklace. My father gave this to me. It was in the artifact he sent me."

Rachel shot a glance at her father, who sulked in the corner. "It's just a rock," he said. "You were looking for some sort of powder, or liquid. I figured this rock was added later, making it like a jewelry box or something."

"It's not just a rock, though," Sarah said. "It's not opal. It's *tourmaline.*"

"Tourma-what?" Ben asked.

"Tourmaline. A relatively common stone, found all over the place. But this strain — this coloring — it's pretty regional. Found in the Mediterranean, especially the islands."

Professor Lindgren smiled. "Not, I might add, in Greenland."

"And it opens secret doors?" Reggie asked.

"Yes," she said. "This one does. Tourmaline is actually electrically polarized, and works like a piezoelectric conductor. Apply a quick bit of pressure and you get a small amount of voltage."

"When you hit the wall..." her father said.

"Exactly," she said. "When I hit the wall, the stone was smacked against the wall, causing enough pressure to send a charge — albeit a small one — into it. Whatever system is in place is set to open whenever there's an electrical current active."

"You've got to be kidding me," Ben said. "The Egyptians built an *electronic sliding door?*"

"No," Rachel said. "The *Atlanteans* did. Furthermore, they never told anyone how to open it. That's why the Egyptians left it here, unopened. My ancestors came here, too, and were unable to gain access. This door to the Great Hall was left here as the final resting place of the collected wisdom of Atlantis and their civilization. Only to be opened by the pure."

Next to her, Ben pinched the bridge of his nose. "'By the pure,'" he said. "That means... all of the killings the Nazis were a part of — the massacre — it was to find these people they thought were 'pure?'"

Rachel nodded. "Yes. Furthermore, it was to cleanse the races that were decidedly *not* pure."

"But they were looking in the wrong place," Ben said. "'Purity' had nothing at all to do with *race*, did it?"

Rachel stared at him.

"It was about having the *key*. That's it. Just a tiny rock."

"How did you find out about all of this? Your great-grandfather was a Nazi, but how did he know? How did he find this place?"

Rachel didn't answer. Sarah watched the interrogation, interested. She was curious, but the feeling didn't supersede the anger she was feeling.

Agent Sharpe stepped closer to Ben. "Because of the *Book of Bones*," he said softly.

"What?" Sarah and Ben said in unison. *What is the* Book of Bones*?* she thought. Then, *Sharpe knew about it?*

"The Book of Bones," he said. "The lost book of Plato. A full account of the Atlantis civilization, including where they traveled and where they left their final fortune — the Great Hall of Records."

"And your great-grandfather had this book?"

"A version of it, yes," Rachel said. "The only full original we have was found by the Egyptian government and was wasting away in a museum until my team rediscovered it. But there are fragments of the scrolls still out there. One of these fragmented copies was in a chest that had been passed down through my family. My great-grandfather was only able to read a portion of the text, as it was decaying and written in an early Greek syntax."

"Greek?" Alex said. "Interesting."

"Why?" Ben asked. "Plato was Greek, right?"

He nodded, but didn't explain, apparently lost in thought.

"And this 'book' told your great-grandfather to test the different races of people for their purity, and then kill anyone not pure enough?"

Rachel glared at him.

"Sounds to me like your entire family was a bunch of murderous, racist nutjobs."

Rachel nodded, then turned to face the gaping wide opening of the Hall of Records. The interior was still pitch-black, and Sarah couldn't see farther than twenty feet into the massive space.

Sarah frowned, wondering what Rachel was doing, when she heard a sickening *smack.* She turned and noticed Ben falling to the floor, the butt of a rifle retreating back into the hands of one of the soldiers who'd snuck up behind him.

She heard the unmistakable sound of magazines clipping into the bottoms of rifles, and turned to see not just the three Mukhabarat soldiers who'd followed them in, but *three more* soldiers behind them, waiting outside the door, all of them pointing their weapons inside the room.

Sarah herself had two men aiming directly at her.

Status quo, she thought. *Rachel still has the upper hand.*

"It's time to go," Rachel said, still facing into the Hall. "Dr. Lindgren, would you and your father step this way, please? I want to keep you around in case there are any more doors that need opening or puzzles to solve."

Ben groaned from the floor, and Reggie's face was pale, contorted with pain. Alex, Mrs. E, and Julie were staring at her, but none were moving. Their arms were up, palms out, above their heads.

"And the rest of them?" Sarah asked.

"They are not necessary to the rest of our mission," Rachel said. "Kill them."

77

BEN

Ben's neck was throbbing where they'd smacked him with the rifle, but he hadn't been knocked out. He had, however, been sent to the floor, where he groaned and 'played dead' for a few seconds.

That's when he'd heard the woman give the order to kill them.

Ben had been in some sticky situations — figuratively, like the time in Antarctica when they'd been pressed into a corner by a contingent of Chinese forces, as well as literally, like when he'd been sticky, wet, muddy, and exhausted in the Amazon rainforest. He'd fought against ruthless criminals, been tied to a chair and beaten senseless, and hung from a rope off an Antarctic cliff.

But he wasn't going to die here today. He refused to watch these idiots kill Julie, his best friend, and innocent civilians. He refused to go down without a fight.

The problem was that his best friend, the man he'd trust to face down a grizzly, was nursing his own injury. He wouldn't be much help. Mrs. E and Julie, as well as the newcomer, Alex, were all too far away from the action to do any good.

And Sarah and her father were shellshocked, probably still too shaken up to offer support.

He sighed. *Sounds like it's up to me, then,* he thought.

He shifted around so that he was laying on his side. He noticed that the three soldiers that had been in Room 23 with them had been joined by three more equally large soldiers, each holding equally menacing weapons.

Six on one, he thought. *Not bad.*

Ben kicked his leg out as hard as he could at the soldier standing over him, aiming for the soft spot just under the man's knee. It buckled with a *crunch,* the knee blowing out backwards and sending the guy down. Ben kept moving, knowing that the outburst would cause the attention to move toward him.

Which is great for Julie, Mrs. E, and Alex, and really bad for me.

He yanked the rifle out of the man's hands as he flailed around, then rolled into the side of the room to dodge a kick from the second soldier.

Get to the door.

The door was the key to winning this fight, Ben knew. If he allowed the three new soldiers into the room, his advantage would quickly come to an end. He needed to get the door closed — and blocked.

"I got you," Reggie said. Ben turned to face his friend, unsure of what he meant. "The door, I mean," Reggie said.

Ben grinned, then nodded. He fired a burst of shots out the door, sending the soldiers there darting out of the way, then he slammed the door closed.

Reggie was already there, having limped over as Ben was fighting. He fell down in front of the closed door, pressing his back up against the metal panel. Two rounds pinged against the opposite side of the door, but they didn't push through.

Ben didn't wait to help Reggie get situated. He turned around and jumped sideways just as the third soldier opened fire. Julie rushed forward at that moment, taking advantage of having the man's back to her. She brought her hands, fingers laced together, crashing down on the side of the man's head. He wasn't wearing any protection over his skull and the knuckles of Julie's fists cracked against bone and caused him to stumble forward.

Ben sent two rounds into his bulletproof vest, and then one into his thigh. It was enough to send him wheeling backwards into the corner of the room, where he dropped his weapon and grabbed at his leg.

That's for Reggie, asshole, Ben thought.

They weren't out of the fight yet, however. Ben turned around to take stock of the situation and found that only Julie, Reggie, Agent Sharpe, and Sarah were still with him in the room.

Everyone else was gone.

The woman, two of the soldiers, Professor Lindgren, and Alex had disappeared.

78

BEN

The pounding on the door continued — either the soldiers were trying to get in or their bullets impacting the solid metal door. Reggie seemed to be asleep, but Ben knew better. The man was in pain, and he was clearly trying to focus all his attention on keeping the door closed. He had the heel of his foot dug into a tiny imperfection in the rock floor, and was using his strength and the solid stone floor as leverage against the soldiers.

"What happened?" Ben asked. "Where'd they go?"

He marched up to Agent Sharpe and began to clench his fist, ready to punch the man in the head.

"Stop!" Sharpe cried out, shrinking back. "Please, I didn't — I wasn't trying to play you."

"*Play* you?" Ben yelled. "You completely *duped* us. You didn't *follow* us here, you *led* us here!"

"I know — I'm sorry, like I said," he said. "I was forced to."

Ben stopped. His fist was still clenched, but he forced his chin up and relaxed his shoulders. "By who?"

"Her," Sharpe said, pointing into the abyss. "Rachel Rascher."

"Explain," Julie said, at Ben's side.

"She reached out to me a month ago. Told me she needed my professional opinion, and that her government would pay my consulting and travel fees — and they did. I came down here and found out that she was planning something. There was going to be some sort of 'test,' and she needed my support.

"She explained a bit about the test and I — of course — was appalled. I told her I wouldn't help her in any way."

"What did she want you to do?" Julie asked.

"She wanted me to help her cover her tracks. She was going to do something in Greece, and needed someone like me to make the paper trail work, to give her and her team an alibi."

"The bomb in Athens," Julie said. "That was her."

Sharpe nodded, holding in a breath for a few seconds. He let it out, and Ben could hear his voice beginning to shake.

"I didn't know exactly what they were planning, I promise. I agreed to help her because I didn't have a choice?"

"Seems to me you did," Ben said.

"No, that's just it — you don't understand. I had *no choice*. She told me it was a matter of life or death. But not for me. My sister. My only sibling."

"She was threatening your sister?"

He nodded again. "Yes. Jennifer Polanski."

"Polanski," Julie said. "Where do I know that name?"

Agent Sharpe sighed. "She's married to a guy by that name. A politician, and a real piece of work. He did a lot of work with the Greek government during their post-bankruptcy phase, and is sort of a local celebrity there now."

"Ah, right," Julie said. "And your sister is his wife."

"Was," Sharpe said. "They were both at the museum in Athens."

Ben looked down at the ground. "Shit. I'm sorry for your loss," he said.

Sharpe stared up at the ceiling, at the single tiny bulb that lit the room and part of the larger space beyond. "It's — it's okay. He didn't make it. She did, but was taken to a hospital, and then..." he stopped, catching his breath. "And then she was taken here."

"*Here*?" Ben asked. "Why? This isn't a medical —"

"I know," Sharpe said. "That was the threat. She told me to take care of the logistics, which I did, and that if she helped me achieve her final goal — gaining access to this hall — she would let my sister go."

"So you think your sister's here somewhere?" Julie asked.

"I do think that. I *have* to. She didn't make it, but her body is here somewhere. I have to find her." He took another deep breath, then straightened up to his full height. "Harvey — Ben — I'm sorry to have tricked you. I won't be able to forgive myself for that, but —"

"Don't worry about it," Ben said. "It's nothing."

"It's not nothing."

"Well it doesn't matter now. Your sister's in here somewhere, and I've got a team in that..." he looked out into the deep black nothingness of the huge hall. "Whatever *that* place is."

He reached out a hand, and Agent Sharpe clasped it. He looked at Julie, who nodded. *It's go time,* he could almost hear her saying. He turned back to Sharpe, who seemed to have found a second wind. "Help me make this right."

Sharpe nodded.

"And if you shoot me in the back, I'm going to be real pissed."

Sharpe smiled. "I don't have a weapon."

Ben chewed on the side of his mouth for a moment while he looked around the room.

When he saw what he was looking for, he spoke again.

"Know how to use one?"

79

JULIE

Room 23 was effectively locked — Julie and Ben had used the slack in the thick power cable as a rope, winding it around the door handle a few times until the cable was taut. The men outside the room were still trying to get in, and Julie knew it was only a matter of time before they were able to pry their way through the metal door.

That meant they had a head start, but not a large one. They needed to find the woman — Rachel Rascher — and the rest of their group. She'd disappeared into the massive hall with Alex, Mrs. E, Sarah, and her father in tow.

Julie was under no impression that the woman was going to let them live if she and her soldiers found them.

But Julie was certainly not going to let the woman get away once again.

Ben handed Julie and Agent Sharpe each a MISR rifle from one of the soldiers that had been taken down in the room. Julie was a better shot than he, and if they needed to take someone down from any distance, he'd rather have Julie's eye behind the sights.

He kept a pistol for himself, a Glock, a weapon he was familiar with. It broke down quickly and easily, and it was near impossible to break. Whatever mess they were about to jump into, a Glock would be as good a sidekick as any.

"Let's move," he said.

He and Sharpe split Reggie's weight between them and the group set off into the depths of the Hall of Records. Julie used the light from Sharpe's cellphone as a flashlight, working the lead slowly and carefully.

"Once we get around that corner up there, flick off the light," he said. "We don't want them to ambush us."

Julie nodded, then moved a few feet forward. "You think this 'advanced civilization' would have thought to add lights down here," she said.

"They did," Sharpe said. "That ridge cut through the rock to your right was probably a trench for some sort of flame."

"Too bad there's no Atlantean lighter fluid left in there," she said.

She made it to the end of the main space they'd walked through, and Julie noticed that the room seemed to be about the size of the Sphinx's base. *Makes sense,* she thought. *We're directly beneath it.*

It left them little to explore, however. A few pillars rose from the floor and connected to plainly decorated ceiling ornaments. The walls on all four sides were bare, smooth rock like the rooms in the preceding antechamber.

The only change in the rock-walled monotony was the turn Ben had pointed out. It happened to be the entrance to a stairwell, one that bent to the right and descended to another sublevel beneath the Sphinx.

"Looks like stairs," Sharpe said.

"It is," Julie answered. She turned off the light and gave the phone back to the Interpol agent, hoping that after her eyes had time to adjust she would be able to pick out something useful in the dark.

Unfortunately she was wrong.

"It's pitch black," Ben whispered. "I can't see a thing."

"Me neither," she said. "But we know where the stairs are. Maybe we can follow them down to the end and see if the other group has a light? That would at least let us sneak up on them."

At first she didn't hear a response, and then she realized that Ben must have shaken his head. "No," he said. "Too risky — if there's a stair missing or an edge somewhere, we could walk right off it. Grab the phone and put it in your pocket with the light on. That should at least illuminate the stairs directly in front of you."

She took the phone back from Agent Sharpe and turned on the flashlight, then stuffed the device in her pocket and wiggled it around a bit. Satisfied, she looked up.

The greenish glow emanating from her front pocket lit up just enough to see three or four stairs down at a time.

"That'll have to do," Ben said. "Ready?"

She nodded. "Ready as I'll ever be. Reggie?"

Reggie grunted from his perch hanging between the two men. "Yeah, I guess. I wouldn't have let you leave me behind, but I sure wish there was a set of crutches or something."

"Not comfortable?" Ben asked, shifting his grip on Reggie's torso.

"No," Reggie said. "It's not that. You smell worse than a decaying mummy."

"Well you'll have to get used to it, or I'll drop you down these stairs and let you crawl your way back out.

Let's roll."

Julie waited for Ben and Sharpe to get situated beneath Reggie's weight, then she turned back toward the stairwell. She lifted her foot and prepared to descend farther into the tomb.

She heard shouts and the sounds of heavy boots pounding the hard stone. Beams of light danced around the cavern.

"They got in," she said.

"Even more reason to get moving," Ben answered. "Let's get to the bottom of the stairs, then see about putting up some defense. Up here we're out in the open."

She nodded and steeled herself, then jumped down onto the first step.

80

SARAH

SARAH TRIED TO KEEP HER BREATHING STEADY, CONTROLLED. SHE TRIED TO calm her nerves, to ignore the rhythmic pounding of her heart.

She tried, but she failed.

She was terrified, and it didn't help that her father was gripping her hand, squeezing the blood out of it until both their fists were white.

She couldn't see his face, which she figured was a good thing. Seeing his face would mean seeing his fear, which would only amplify her own.

Her group had been corralled off from the larger group in Room 23 and split away. Two of the soldiers had pushed her and her father at gunpoint, as well as Alex and Mrs. E out into the large, cavernous space. The soldiers' flashlights illuminated the hall, revealing simple structural spires that held the roof up — the roof, she knew, that was the foundation of the Great Sphinx itself.

At the end of the empty hall, they'd found a staircase that led down to another subterranean level. Rachel Rascher had not even hesitated, throwing herself toward the stairs with a fury. She'd jumped the last two and ran into the next room, Sarah and her father close behind her.

Sarah didn't have a choice — she was safe for now, but only if she went along with whatever Rachel's plan was. The woman was crazed and delusional, but Sarah could also feel the excitement. She couldn't help it — as a scientist herself, Sarah was every bit as fascinated to discover what the Great Sphinx's lair had been keeping secret all these years.

So far, though, the answer was a resounding *nothing*. The 'Great Hall' was empty. The large hall that had opened with a touch of Sarah's necklace, the stairwell, and now the smaller room the stairs emptied into.

Rachel was spinning in a slow circle, pointing a flashlight at every corner and edge and flat wall in the space.

"It's... it's empty," she said. "There's nothing here."

The soldier whose flashlight she had commandeered stepped up to her as the rest of the group spilled out into the room. "Maybe there's another door, like the —"

"No," she said. "No, that's not possible. There's *one* entrance to the Hall of Records. The Book says so. It's clear that there is *one* entrance, and that entrance was in Room 23."

"What does that mean?"

"It means we're too late," she said, turning in one final circle before dropping the flashlight's beam to the ground. "We didn't get here in time. This place has been looted. It's gone."

"Gone?" Alex asked. "How do you know there ever *was* anything here? For all we know, this is just a crypt. A tomb, like the pyramids themselves."

"It's not a *crypt*," Rachel said. "You and the rest of the world have been brainwashed to believe that these people would build elaborate burial chambers for their kings and queens. Not so. The pyramids may have been *used* as tombs, but they weren't *built* to be tombs."

"What were they built for, then?" Mrs. E asked.

Rachel looked around the room, her eyes landing on the tall, broad-shouldered woman who'd addressed her. "They were built by my ancestors. They are a testament to their intelligence. An example of their power, and a warning to future civilizations."

Sarah frowned, then shook her head. "You're crazy. You sound like you're reciting some ritualistic chant. You actually *believe* that? That the pyramids here were built to *show off*? To scare people away?"

Rachel seethed. "I don't *believe* it. I *know* it. The *Book of Bones* — the lost book of Plato — says as much. This whole plateau was created to keep people out. The people who weren't pure."

Sarah groaned. "There you go again. *Pure* people? You've got to be kidding me. The bell that your Nazi friends used to 'test' people? It's a sham. Remember? I proved that — it's not a real test. The 'pure' people in the chamber were pure only because they had the key to get out."

She held up her necklace. "This. Tourmaline. It's a rock. Nothing more, nothing less. It didn't make me *pure,* but it opened the door. It's a magic trick, Rachel."

Rachel was rocking back and forth on her heels, shaking her head. "No," she said. "No, there has to be more. My life... my entire like I've been searching for this..."

"And you found it," Sarah said. "Congratulations. Now let's get out of here. For all we know that door up there closes after an hour, and we don't want to get —"

"No," Rachel said. "No, no. It's not... it's not *possible*. No one's been inside this space since it was sealed. It can't be —"

"Empty?"

Sarah turned to see who had spoken and saw Ben and Agent Sharpe holding Reggie between them. Julie was standing next to them, holding one of the soldiers' weapons.

The two soldiers that had accompanied them quickly pulled their weapons up, but Ben and Sharpe added their own guns to the mix and Julie spoke again.

"Keep them down," she said. "You try to shoot, you're dead. You move in a weird way that I don't like, you're dead."

Sarah felt the relief washing over her. She nodded to Julie, who returned the motion.

The two soldiers lowered their rifles, then stepped back to the sides of Rachel, protecting their boss.

Only then did Sarah notice the problem. *Oh no,* she thought. She looked up at Julie and the rest of the newcomers, but knew she didn't have time to warn them.

Rachel is holding the only flashlight.

The soldier that had been lighting the way had turned his light off a few minutes ago, leaving Rachel with the only flashlight in the room. It was the source of all the light — and it was the only way Julie's group was able to see.

Rachel knew this, too, and Sarah watched the woman slowing moving her finger over the button. She squeezed her eyes shut, hoping that by preparing her eyes for the oncoming darkness she would be able to see better. But that plan, Sarah also knew, depended on there being *any* light whatsoever.

She needed to do something else, and there weren't too many options to choose from. She looked around at the standoff, then made up her mind.

She was in motion by the time Rachel flicked off the light. Sarah figured they had two, maybe three seconds before the soldiers picked up their weapons again and fired into the space Ben and the others were standing in.

She was wrong — the soldiers had anticipated Rachel's move, and their guns immediately came to life. Sarah heard the deafening cracks of the rifles. Two, then three more shots. She hoped the other group had thought to dive out of the way, but she had other things to worry about at the moment.

She crouched a bit, pulling her chin down toward her chest, and hoped her aim was true — and that Rachel hadn't moved from where she'd been standing.

The room was pitch black, but Sarah pushed off the ground, trusting her position and hoping for the best, and flew as hard as she could into Rachel's side.

The woman let out a guttural sound, something like the sound of a bag of rice being popped open and spilled onto the ground, and buckled sideways. Sarah wrapped her arms around the woman's thick waist and the pair shot to the floor.

Rachel's head hit first, but the impact wasn't apparently enough to knock her out. Sarah was about to roll off the woman's body when she felt a solid — and painful — punch to her jaw.

Good aim, she thought. *Especially in the dark.*

But Sarah wasn't one to take a punch and ignore it. She knew exactly where the woman's head was, even in the dark. She pulled her fist back and launched it forward, waiting for the crushing hit to smash Rachel's face.

Unfortunately, Rachel had anticipated the counterattack and moved her head, allowing Sarah's clenched fist to land — hard — against the stone floor.

The cracking sound that rocketed up Sarah's entire arm was only outmatched by the *feeling* of the blow. Her hand immediately froze in place, her knuckles and wrist shocked from the impact, her brain answering the signals of immense pain by throwing every alarm it had.

She screamed in rage, wrestling around on the floor to try to get a better grip on Rachel, but the woman was gone. She felt around with her good hand, but couldn't find anything to hold onto. For a brief instant she felt the fear creeping back in, the confusion and chaos of the exploding world around her not justifying the sheer blackness of the space. More gunshots punctuated the air, and Sarah wondered if they were fired out of frustration or if someone could actually see something.

It was disorienting, and Sarah took a second to lay still on the floor, trying to get her bearings once again. She turned her head toward where she thought the staircase ended and saw a gentle greenish glow.

A light.

She watched it dance around for a moment before she realized: *it's a phone. In someone's pocket.*

She had no idea whose pocket the phone was in, so she wasn't about to try to attack it, but it at least lit up the space enough for her to see her immediate surroundings. Rachel was nowhere to be seen, but there were two soldiers standing nearby, each pointing their weapons the wrong direction — away from the light.

Two more shapes shifted around the blackness of the room's perimeter, and what looked like three more people jumped and dove across the center, but she couldn't make out what was what.

Another shot rang out and Sarah saw the room come into view. A wash of light had entered the space from the stairwell — another flashlight or two, both brighter than the one Rachel had been using. She heard the commotion of the new soldiers entering, the pounding footsteps on the stairs telling her they were more booted thugs, armed well and ready for a fight.

We're outnumbered again, she thought. *There has to be something I can —*

Suddenly her vision was blocked by a towering figure — nothing but a shadow, as the silhouette once again cast Sarah into darkness.

But she knew the figure — the short, thin shape of the petite woman, who hadn't seen her and nearly backed up right on top of her.

Sarah stood up quickly and rushed forward, grabbing the woman's arm and wrenching it behind her back, lifting up and pressing it between the woman's own shoulder blades, just like she'd learned from the personal defense class she'd audited at her campus, and just like the guard had done to her earlier.

Rachel screamed in pain, writhing and trying to break free, but Sarah worked her other arm — the one with the throbbing, inflamed hand — through Rachel's side and back up and around her arm, ending up with her wrist pressed against the back of Rachel's head. Rachel's right arm was straight up in the air, her left arm twisted behind her back, and while her feet and legs were kicking and thrashing around to try to get into a position to fight back, Sarah wasn't about to let her go.

She spread her legs a bit so the tops of her feet weren't in danger of being smashed by the woman's heels, and she yanked backwards with her upper body, both tightening her grip on Rachel and causing immense pain in her own hand.

Still, she held on.

"Stop!" Sarah yelled. "I've got your idiot boss, and I'm going to break her neck if you don't drop the weapons."

She didn't, of course, know how to break the neck of a chicken, much less that of a grown woman. She had a feeling it was a bit trickier than movies and television liked to imply, but she had the basic idea down — wrench the head sideways as hard and fast as possible, popping the spinal cord off of its track and hopefully leaving the victim in a very bad place.

Everyone in the room froze. The five soldiers — the two that had been with her group and the three new ones who were now guarding the only exit back up the stairs — all had their weapons trained on her.

That would have been a good thing, but the rest of her team — her father, Ben, Julie, Mrs. E, and Alex — were all standing between her and the soldiers, directly in the line of fire.

Except...

She flicked her eyes to the right, not wanting to draw attention to where she was focusing, and noticed that there was one more man in the room that she — and apparently everyone else — had failed to take into consideration.

Reggie had been dumped in the corner by Agent Sharpe and Ben when the shooting started, but he was now standing — or leaning — against the back wall near the doorway.

He slid sideways, slowly making his way behind the soldier closest to him. He had no weapon, but Sarah knew he wouldn't need one. He was angry, in pain, and running on pure adrenaline.

Not a good combo if you're on the other team.

81

REGGIE

Reggie was in a lot of pain, but his body was refusing to quit. He had pushed himself up carefully, slowly, trying to not draw attention to himself. He had then worked his way down the wall, using the stone surface as a crutch but moving slowly enough that the scratching sound of his clothes on the wall didn't raise an alarm.

Finally in position, he raised a fist, took a breath, and threw it down.

He crashed it as hard as he could onto the neck of the man not closest to him but in the middle of the line of soldiers blocking the door — the same men who'd tried to enter Room 23 earlier. They'd obviously succeeded, and had now come to find their boss and offer support.

But they weren't ready for a pissed-off ex-Army sniper, trained in hand-to-hand combat and temporarily ignoring significant injuries.

The blow took down the middle man, and the other two soldiers predictably looked over to see what had happened. Reggie, however, was already in motion.

He used the distraction to grab the man's rifle, then swung it up and fired at the soldier on the far side. The man who was now weaponless dove forward, more scared than upset, hoping to not get a bullet in his back.

Instead, he received a bullet to the skull. Reggie fired the single shot without so much as thinking about collateral damage, knowing that with the light of the downed man's flashlight illuminating the entire room and his experience with small-arms firepower, he was in no danger of injuring anyone else in the room.

The man fell, his head a bloody mess, right in front of where Sarah was holding Rachel hostage. He fired another shot at the soldier next to Sarah, but missed. The last soldier with a weapon fired back at Reggie, but he had launched himself from his good leg back into the corner, then fired back.

That shot missed as well, but suddenly Ben was towering over the soldier and brought his fist smashing down into the man's face, sending him wheeling backwards toward the wall. He hit the wall hard, no doubt seeing stars, but Ben wasn't done.

Reggie watched in awe and satisfaction as Ben plowed his fists into the man's torso, head, and stomach. Every hit seemed to grow stronger, and Reggie knew he was seeing what happened when Ben got worked up enough to pop.

The man's bloody, contorted face told Reggie that he was solidly out of the fight, but Ben didn't let up. He hit the man three times in the face, twice in the nose and once in the man's left eye. His head fell, and still Ben attacked.

The other soldier standing ran over to fend off the attack, but Agent Sharpe stopped him in his tracks with a quick retort from his own weapon, sending the man to the ground.

Ben carried on, the entire front half of his body covered with a slick of blood.

"Ben," Reggie said. "That's good."

Ben ignored him. Nothing but Ben's own fists were keeping the soldier upright.

"*Ben,*" Julie said. "Ben!"

Finally, Ben stopped. The man fell to the ground.

Dead.

Reggie heard the heavy breathing of his best friend, the dark crimson covering his face like a mask. He was rocking slowly, heels to toes, working himself down.

"You okay?" Reggie asked.

Ben shook his head.

"Me neither."

Reggie looked around the room. He looked at Sarah, still standing behind Rachel, the slightly taller woman totally and completely beaten. Her father, Professor Lindgren, was wide-eyed and gawking at Ben, and Agent Sharpe was inspecting the bodies of the fallen soldiers. Julie, Mrs. E, and Alex were —

He noticed Alex for the first time. The kid was hunched over, heaving, his back to the wall opposite Reggie.

"Kid — Alex," he said. "You okay?"

All eyes turned to Alex.

"Alex?" Sarah asked. She immediately let go of Rachel and rushed over to Alex's location.

Alexander's eyes were barely open, and there was a trickle of blood dripping from his mouth onto his lap.

Reggie ran over and pushed the young man's shoulders back, revealing a heavy stain of blood on his chest.

"No..." Sarah whispered.

"It's okay," Reggie said. "He's going to be —"

He stopped. There was no point in sugarcoating the truth. Sarah knew; they all knew.

Alex knew.

His eyes were screaming, the pain seemingly waiting just behind them to burst forth and come pouring out, but the kid held his composure. His breaths were jagged, and only interrupted by Ben's heavier and longer exhalations.

"Do you feel okay?" Reggie asked.

"I — I..." Alex tried to speak, but his eyes were growing more intense by the second. Everything in him was willing him to keep it together, to not let the pain win out.

But Reggie knew better. There was no 'winning' when it came to a gunshot wound like this. He'd seen lesser injuries take harder men. Alex was not going to live another minute.

"It's cold," the kid finally said. "So... cold."

Reggie nodded. "That's good. That's your body protecting you. You're going to be —" he stopped himself again. *No,* he thought. *No more lies.*

"You're almost done."

Alex looked up at Reggie, and Reggie felt the tears collecting at the corners of his eyes. *This isn't fair,* he thought. *He was just a kid.*

"I did good. Yeah?" Alex asked.

Reggie and Sarah nodded, and Reggie couldn't help but let two tears fall onto Alex's hands, which were clasped in front of him on his lap. For his part, the kid was stoic, watching the world close in on him with two wide, yet fearless, eyes.

"I never wanted... I didn't want —"

Reggie held up a hand. "It's okay. We know."

He looked at Sarah, but she wouldn't return his gaze. Her eyes were riveted on Alex. Her student. Her colleague.

She's never going to forgive herself, Reggie thought. *She's going to live forever thinking this was her fault.*

And he, more than anyone, knew exactly what that felt like.

82

BEN

Ben wasn't inexperienced when it came to fistfights. He had been in his fair share of scrapes, on both the losing and winning sides. He'd been beaten, tied to a chair and nearly killed, and run through a gauntlet of pain that he had never known he could survive.

So he hadn't gone into the fight ignorant. He knew his capabilities, his strengths, and his weak spots. He knew that if he could get a good, solid blow to the man's face he would then be able to follow it up with a few more shots to the man's sides, a strategy that had proved to be a winning one in the past.

What he *didn't* expect was to be as fast as he had been. Ben was a large man, strong and surefooted, but he hadn't spent a lot of time in the gym or working out.

That is, until he'd met Reggie.

Reggie had created a training program for him and Julie at their Alaska cabin and CSO headquarters, and Ben had followed it, begrudgingly but thoroughly.

He'd changed his diet, strengthened his core, and gotten faster on his feet. He hadn't really had a chance to *use* the new skills until now.

So he'd surprised himself by how quickly he'd rendered his opponent obsolete, but he'd further surprised himself by how taking out the opposition did nothing for his temper.

He hadn't been satisfied when he'd felt the man's nose give way, when he'd seen the eyes become bloodshot and puffy, when he'd felt the wheezing sigh of failure escape the man's lips.

He hadn't been *satisfied,* and he had been far from tired, so he'd kept fighting. Toward the end he was fighting nothing more than a punching bag, a floppy, heavy bag of flesh that was offering no more resistance than a water balloon.

Only when he'd heard Julie's voice did he stop.

And only then did he realize he was the last one fighting. There was no one else to take down, no one else to neutralize.

He took a few deep, heavy breaths, then walked over to the rest of the group. They were standing around Alex, who was hunched over on the floor, bleeding from a nasty-looking chest wound.

Ben watched Reggie's and Sarah's face, knowing that the prognosis for the young man was not good.

Reggie wasn't a medic, but he had field training and plenty of experience. That he wasn't doing anything to stop the bleeding or cover the wound was telling.

Ben turned to Rachel Rascher, the woman behind all of this, and started toward her.

She backed up, pressing her back to the wall, her hands in the air. "Stop," she said. "Wait, I —"

"You did this," Ben said. His voice was a mix of rage and pure adrenaline, low and groveling. "You caused all of this."

"I — I was only trying to —"

"You're a Nazi," he said. "But you didn't even have a government or a Nazi regime backing you up. You had to rely on a handful of insane scientists, convincing them of their *purity*. You lied to them, and you lied to yourself."

"No," she said. "I did *not* lie to myself."

"Then you *are* delusional. This 'world' you're trying to create, it's *never* going to exist. Don't you understand that now? You're not 'pure.' Your employees aren't, and neither are the poor souls who 'passed' your test."

She sniffed, the fire still in her eyes. "It's real," she said. "It *works*. The original compound — it kills people who are impure. It saves those who are not."

Sarah strode over. "It's genetics," she said. All eyes turned to her. "And very simple genetics, at that."

Ben and Rachel Rascher frowned.

"Sickle-cell anemia," she continued. "It's a disease that is nearly 100% unique to people of African descent. And Tay-Sachs disease mostly affects Eastern Europeans or Jewish people."

Ben nodded along, but addressed Rachel. "So your fancy magic pixie dust is just a poison that kills most of the people it comes into contact with, but there's a handful of people out there with a natural-born immunity."

Rachel sneered. "The *pure*, original race of —"

"No," Ben said. "Just no."

"It's a natural accident," Sarah said. "It's not a magical elixir that reads genetic code."

You just don't understand," Rachel said. "You *can't* understand. This place — all of it — it's real. You don't —"

Ben stepped closer to her. "I understand enough to see that what you're trying to do here is hopeless. You *failed*, Rascher. And you're going to answer for that failure."

She shook her head. "I won't."

"You will."

He stepped forward, fist raised.

"You wouldn't hit a —"

He brought his fist forward with a heavy *smack*, landing it just behind her left eye, in front of her ear. She fell forward, cracking the back of her head against the wall, then her face against the stone floor. Ben stepped back a single pace, allowing her to hit the ground without his feet offering her head any sort of eased landing.

"Pick her up," he said, to no one in particular. "We're getting out of here."

There was a mess to clean up, both literally and figuratively. The CSO had inadvertently stumbled upon one of the biggest coverups in history, and there was plenty of work to do to understand this place, its purpose, and its creators.

And there was plenty of time to do that.

For now, he had to get his team out of this dungeon before they found themselves locked in. They could clean up the mess later, when they'd all had time to debrief, decompress, and simply rest.

There would be time to understand what had taken place here, what Rachel Rascher and her team had been trying to accomplish.

There would be time for all of that. But right now, Ben's job was to get everyone to safety.

Reggie was limping with an arm around Sharpe's shoulder, while Julie and Mrs. E were carrying Alex's weight between them. Ben knew the kid wasn't going to make it, but he was glad to see the group's refusal to leave him behind.

Sarah was helping her father, who was clearly shaken up and barely able to walk.

Together, the group ascended the stairs to the main hallway, then walked through the pitch-black darkness toward the bright, open hole that led into Room 23.

83

BEN

THEY WALKED SLOWLY, AS THERE WERE TWO INJURED MEMBERS OF THE group, Rachel Rascher and Reggie, and one who hadn't made it, Alex.

Sarah was sobbing softly, and her father had his arm around her shoulder, but Ben knew which of them was supporting the other. Sarah had proven to be far more resilient than he'd initially thought, even after working with her — and *surviving* with her — in The Bahamas.

Julie and Mrs. E were out front, walking through the upper chamber. The small room at the bottom of the stairs as well as this massive chamber were both empty, completely devoid of anything that might give them a clue as to what had happened here.

Ben, however, wasn't thinking about the history of this hall.

"Alex asked Rachel if the book she had — the *Book of Bones* — was written in Greek," he said.

Reggie looked up at him, moving forward on an injured leg while supported by Agent Sharpe. "Yeah," he said. "What of it?"

"Well he asked that after Rachel was trying to explain herself. She was talking about why she thought the only people who could enter the place were 'pure.' Why did he think it was interesting that the text was in Greek? Plato was Greek, so of course he wrote it in Greek. Am I missing something?"

At first no one spoke, but then Professor Lindgren coughed, clearing his throat. "Yes," he said. "You are. He wasn't surprised about the fact that it was written in Greek — what surprised him was the *word* she used. 'Pure.'"

"Why?" Ben asked.

"Well, I think it has something to do with the Greek translation. I'm a little rusty on my Greek, but I think the word is *Katharos*. It means 'clean,' or 'free from any contaminating substances.'"

"That's..."

"The rock. Tourmaline," he said. "It's *pure,* like a diamond. Free from any contaminants. Plato wrote what Solon told him — literally a *pure substance,* one that generates a charge when pressure is applied to it. Any mineral or gemstone that's not pure like that probably won't work."

Ben thought about this for a moment, then nodded. "Fascinating."

"Yeah," Julie said. "Or unfortunate."

"What do you mean?" Mrs. E asked.

"I mean that an entire *generation* of people was wiped out — 50 or so *million* of them, including war victims and civilians — all because of a bad translation."

Ben nodded again. "Yeah, I guess when you put it that way it's pretty unfortunate." He paused, frowning. "Still, I think it's pretty crazy how all this was real."

"It's not, though," Sarah said. "There's nothing here."

Ben shrugged. "Just because there's nothing here now doesn't mean there was *never* anything here. Whoever built this place — the Sphinx, the pyramids, all of it — they did it for a reason."

Reggie shifted his weight on Sharpe's shoulder. "Yeah, and maybe that reason wasn't to hide a massive library of knowledge. Maybe this was all built as a *backup.* I mean, it's close to where the Atlanteans called home, right? Maybe they came here first, taught the ancient Egyptians what they needed to know to build their temples, farm, become civilized. They laid down roots, just in case they needed them. But they kept going, kept traveling."

"Right," Julie said. "Remember what Alex was talking about? Haplo... something?"

"Haplogroup X," Reggie said. "He said that was how he could trace the movements of ancient peoples with that genetic characteristic from their origin to their final destination."

Sarah whirled around. "Wait... Alex said he had a way to do that?"

Reggie looked at her, confused. "Yeah — that was what he was all worked up about when he found us. Well, that and you. He was pretty torn up about you."

Ben felt the tension in the room grow. Alex had given his life to Sarah's rescue.

"What did he say *exactly*?" Sarah asked. "Tell me everything."

84

JULIE

As Ben, Mrs. E, and Reggie filled Sarah in on what Alex had told them regarding the Haplogroup X research he'd been working on, Julie focused her attention on another issue.

They had found *something* here. It was an empty hall, but it was clear it had been built for some purpose. Ben had voiced the concern a minute ago, that at one time there *had* been something here. Someone, long ago, had spent the time and energy to cut this hall out of the limestone and fill it with something of great importance.

Julie stopped, two feet short of the door that separated the Hall of Records from Room 23.

Limestone.

She frowned, then looked down at the stone beneath her feet. She kicked it with her toe, feeling the hard, unforgiving surface pushing back against her.

Something about limestone...

"What's up, Jules?" Ben asked, noticing that she had stopped. The others were all inside Room 23 now, and Mrs. E and Sarah were working to clear the mess from the door. The soldiers had apparently blasted their way in, as the metal door now hung from only a single hinge, and most of the bottom half of the door lay in twisted shambles in the corner.

"I just thought of something..." she said. "I'm not sure what it means. If it means anything."

"What is it?"

"Limestone," she said, still looking down at her feet. "This place is all limestone, right?"

Professor Lindgren nodded. "From the Mokkatam Formation, which is what the entire Giza Plateau rests upon. There was a lagoon here, fifty or sixty million years ago, and the compressed pieces of coral from that lagoon became a perfect resting place for the layers of mud and sand that came later and formed into the stone."

"And the pyramids were covered with that, right?"

"Yes," Professor Lindgren said. "The Great Pyramid had a bright-white casing of limestone as well, none of which is remaining today."

"And we know exactly where the limestone came from? The limestone that was used for the casing stones?"

At this, Professor Lindgren seemed puzzled. "Well, it's a matter of debate. Though Egyptologists often point to certain spots around the plateau, it's believed that the limestone of that purity had to be carried in, from somewhere far away."

Ben's head snapped up, and he made eye contact with Julie. "Purity."

She smiled, then nodded. "Purity. Limestone of that *purity...*"

"...may not have been *limestone* at all," Professor Lindgren said.

"That's what I'm thinking," Julie said. "Sarah, that necklace of yours — your father said he found it inside the artifact he gave you?"

"Just the stone. Tourmaline. Not the chain."

"Which means it was probably put inside the artifact by whoever dropped it in Greenland."

"And based on Alex's Haplogroup X data, it seems as though Greenland was right along the route the ancient peoples took from the Mediterranean Sea."

Professor Lindgren and Sarah seemed excited now, growing animated. Julie felt the excitement as well. Sarah walked over to her father and held out the necklace. "The Atlanteans traveled from the Mediterranean Sea to the Americas, visiting Greenland along the way. They also built *this* place. That means this stone is from the Atlanteans, and its purity — the nearly colorless white of it — represents the key to their empire."

"And I'd bet a good chunk of change that it's only found in places like Santorini," Reggie added. "Formed by volcanic activity, hydrothermal vents, that sort of thing."

Julie's mind was still racing. "So the Atlanteans used Tourmaline as a calling card, in a sense, leaving it places they'd traveled. To point people home."

"But why dump a bunch of it here?" Ben asked. "If they were building some sort of monument like a pyramid, why spend all that time digging up Tourmaline to use it as 'casing stones?' Seems like they were busy enough, traveling around the world and everything."

"They cased the entire pyramid in Tourmaline, at a huge cost in labor, freight, manpower, and resources. It had to be for a reason. If they wanted something that just looked good, they could have used any of the stone from the plateau itself."

Julie looked at Sarah. "You said Tourmaline was *piezoelectric*?"

"Yeah," Sarah said. "Apply pressure, and it generates a small charge."

"And the pyramid was cased in thousands of tons of this stuff."

"That's a lot of pressure," Agent Sharpe said.

"Exactly," Julie said. "So what would happen in direct sunlight? Say the sun beats down on it, causing the stones to expand..."

"And thereby causing a massive amount of pressure!" Sarah said. "That's it! The pyramid wasn't a tomb, or a monument. It had a *purpose*."

"It was a *weapon*."

"The *ultimate* weapon," Julie said. "Think about it — the compound would have been stored inside the pyramid, and the piezoelectric qualities of the Tourmaline would charge it when it was under pressure — pressure caused by the expansion of those stones from the heat of the sunlight. Enough of that pressure and it would emit an electric charge, which would further heat the compound inside. It would be the bell, but on a huge scale."

Ben was nodding in agreement. "And the builders could have used mirrors or funnels of some sort to direct the charge from the heated compound out the openings in the pyramid."

"On an enemy."

"Right," Ben said. "It's the perfect defense mechanism. Anyone approaching too close would be zapped. And it wouldn't take a lot of zapping of the guys on the front lines for the rest of the army to freak out."

"So the Egyptians had an amazing weapon in their possession," Sarah said. "Built by the Atlanteans themselves. But they didn't use it — the casing was removed and shipped off for other projects over the centuries to follow."

"And we know they never accessed the Hall of Records under the Sphinx."

"So they probably never knew *how* to use the weapon," Sarah continued. "They went about their lives, building smaller — and less perfect — pyramids, carving the Sphinx's head into the shape of one of their Pharaohs, and altogether forgetting about their mysterious visitors from thousands of years earlier."

"Sounds like we've got it figured out, then," Ben said. He turned to Rachel Rascher. "Should we see about getting this criminal into a cell?"

Julie was about agree when she froze again. "No," she said. We've got something way bigger to worry about."

85

JULIE

"Bigger than dealing with a racist Nazi who tried to kill us all?"

Julie steeled herself. *How could I have not realized it sooner?* "Yeah. The terrorist attack in Athens," she said, her hands trembling. "It was a 'trial,' just like she said —" Julie pointed at the still-unconscious Rachel — "and one she used to justify her Nazi-esque racial cleansing."

"But didn't she say something about —"

"A *bigger* trial," Sarah finished. "She did mention that they were going to 'reveal themselves to the world.'"

"I wonder what that means?" Reggie asked. "Probably nothing good."

"*Definitely* nothing good," Julie said. "And I'd bet it's something even bigger than what happened in Athens."

"So it probably involves this bell thing," Ben said. "A bigger version of what happened in the museum."

"Then we need to find it," Julie said. "It's out there somewhere. A bell, like the one in here, and the one in the museum in Athens. It shouldn't be hard to find, right?"

Reggie shook his head. "It could be. It might not be a bell at all — the key to the weapon working was the stuff inside it. Whatever it was that the Atlanteans created and put inside, and then electrically charged it to heat it up."

"So we're looking for a powder. Or a liquid," Ben said. "And some way to plug it in."

"Right."

Ben nodded. "Well, that leaves just about everywhere."

"Let's at least get out of this dungeon and back into a country we know we can trust," Julie said.

Reggie smirked. "Yeah? And which country is that?"

"Fair enough," Julie said. She knew the CSO was on something called 'workable terms' with the government, but their charter was still strictly domestic. They were bound by their agreement to officially operate in the United States, with jurisdiction extending to foreign countries based on the stated mission.

The problem was that the 'stated mission' had to be approved by the board, which was made up of all the members of the CSO, Mr. and Mrs. E — the founding partners — and individual members of each branch of the US military.

While the CSO and Mr. and Mrs. E had more than quorum for voting rights, the military was still... the military. Voting against the US military was never a great long-term strategy, even if the contract clauses of plausible deniability and political immunity were brought up.

The fact remained that the CSO's operations in Egypt and Santorini were *not* officially sanctioned missions, approved by any vote — they were here, technically, on a rescue mission for one of their friends. That Mr. E had funded the expedition was not a fact that would have a strong defense in court, if it got there.

Julie looked at the woman at the side of the room, passed out. She was just starting to stir.

"She'll know," Julie said, point at Rachel. "This is all because of her. That woman knows where this 'final test' is."

"We can't interrogate her," Agent Sharpe said. "It's against —"

"We can, and we will," Reggie snapped. "*We're* the ones who are here, *we're* the ones who caught her."

"You have no authority here," he said. "*I* have no authority here. I came here for my sister, who's dead now. I have no backup, no team. Yet. But if we get back out, I can make some calls. We can't just —"

"Sharpe, you need to stand down," Ben said, stepping closer to the man. "You've been blocking us every step of the way, but now that we're here, I will not allow you to prevent my team from continuing its mission."

"Your *mission?* Listen to yourself, Harvey. You sound like you think you're some soldier. You're a *civilian.* Your help here is appreciated, truly, but now that we've apprehended Ms. Rascher, I intend to take her in to the proper authorities."

Julie shook her head and looked around at the stalemate. Sharpe was fuming, his eyes crystalline. He was likely trying to deal with a range of emotions at the moment: his sister was dead, there was a neo-Nazi party hidden beneath the Sphinx, and now a crack team of civilians was trying to take justice into their own hands.

She walked over to him. She wasn't sure if she wanted to comfort him or punch him in the face — she understood what he was feeling, but she also knew they needed to finish this here, now. Bringing Rachel in would only incite a sparring match between all the international organizations that thought they had jurisdiction. There would be years of court cases, waiting, legal maneuvering, and jail time, but if justice were ever served, it would be decades from now.

And whatever 'justice' looks like, it won't be enough, Julie thought.

She stood face-to-face with Sharpe, trying to come up with the proper words to explain her case. They needed to find out — *now* — what Rachel knew, and how to stop it. There was no other choice.

She put her hand on Sharpe's shoulder. "None of us fault you for being here," she said.

"What?" he asked.

"None of us blame you. We would have done the same thing. We would have done *anything* to get Sarah back, and her father. That's the story we'll tell, if we have to."

"What are you saying?"

"If it comes to it, you won't get in trouble for any of this. We'll make sure of it, however we can."

"Thank you, but I don't think —"

Before he could finish the sentence, Julie heard the sharp retort of an assault rifle. Her ears were ringing, but she turned to see what had happened.

Professor Lindgren, shaking, was holding one of the soldiers' weapons, aiming it at her.

Aiming *past* her.

She turned around to face the two people on that side of the room and saw that Rachel Rascher was awake, her eyes wide.

She was bleeding. A gunshot wound in the side of her chest was leaking blood. She choked, then coughed. She fell sideways, then back against the wall, where she slid to a sitting position on the floor.

"I — I told her..." Professor Lindgren started. "I told her I would. That's — that's what I told her."

Reggie and Ben ran over to Lindgren and disarmed him, then held his arms as they led him out of the room. Sarah followed, her face a combination of shock and disorientation.

Julie raced over to Rachel, who was now wheezing and coughing blood.

"The final test," she said. "Where is it?"

Rachel sneered.

"Where is it?" Julie asked again. "Tell me."

Rachel tried to laugh, but her mouth was filled with blood and bile. She spat, nearly hitting Julie.

Julie watched, knowing the woman was going to die here. Agent Sharpe was looking down at them, watching the conversation but not moving to help.

"It's over, Rachel," Julie said. "There's nothing left. Give us something."

Rachel's nostrils flared as she stared up at Julie. She had a hard time focusing, and her pupils were dilated.

Her mouth opened, then closed again, then finally two words fell out. "Two… months."

"Two months?" Julie asked.

Before she could confirm, Rachel's mouth turned up once more into a sneer, then her head fell sideways, dead.

Julie stood up, then walked out of the room.

Two months.

86

BEN

Professor Lindgren was shaken up, but still lucid. He knew what he'd done, and his eyes showed little remorse.

Ben sat next to him in the hallway, waiting for Julie to come out. He turned to the older man, about to speak, when the professor dropped his head and looked at Ben.

"I told her… I told her I would…"

Ben put his hand on the man's shoulder. "I know," he said. "I know. I understand. Okay?"

The man looked into Ben's eyes with a curiosity, a question.

Ben cleared his throat. "I mean I *can't* know exactly what… how you feel. I don't have a daughter. Or kids." Ben felt his cheeks flush a bit. *Am I embarrassed?* "I just mean that I've been in a situation that's life-or-death, more than once. It's not easy to make that call."

"Was it the right call?" Professor Lindgren asked, his voice shaking. "I — I killed her."

"You did," Ben said. "That's done. How you go on from it is what matters."

"But she —"

"She did things that are inexcusable," Ben said. "Maybe she didn't deserve to die because of it. Maybe she did."

He shrugged and looked back at the doorway into what obviously had been the woman's office. Julie and Reggie were still in there, now joined by Mrs. E. They were tearing through the drawers in the little side table, turning over what little furniture there was in the room, and Mrs. E was clicking around on her computer, trying to gauge whether it was worth salvaging the hard drives or destroying everything.

Ben hoped she'd decide to salvage; any evidence they found down here would be useful in the coming months — the forthcoming government debriefings, the political meanderings, and the eventual indictments of whomever might have been working with this woman.

Ben looked around the nearly empty antechambers. *And where* are *those employees and scientists?* he thought. *There were a few people here before; they're all gone now.*

He got the feeling that the employees, staffers, and scientists who had been working with Rachel Rascher had fled the scene shortly after the shots starting sailing through the air, unwilling to risk their lives for their boss's pet project.

Still, Ben wondered how many of them would turn up afterwards, intrigued by the discovery of the greatest archeological secret in modern history, hoping to cash in on the now-leaderless faction's findings.

Ben also wondered how many of them were already working their own networks, plying information and favors out of their friends and colleagues, working to continue the research in a new and safer environment, out of reach of the impending fallout. Ben likened this thought to lopping off one of the Hydra's heads — where one existed, two would sprout.

Where Rachel Rascher had implanted herself as the de facto head of a neo-Nazi regiment of scientists and then subsequently been removed, two or more new 'heads' would likely spring up, somewhere in the world.

Ben sighed and took in a deep breath. *It never ends,* he thought. Nazis had been defeated long ago he'd thought. And their modern counterparts were nothing but clueless pseudo-activists with underwhelming social skills, but now they had uncovered an entire network of capable, dedicated party members, operating in total secret for years.

That meant their work here was not finished. Or rather, their work *somewhere* was not finished. Whatever Julie and Reggie found inside the office, whatever Mrs. E found on the computer, everything was a clue that might lead them to the next place. Rascher had been planning something, and Ben doubted that plan would have died with its initiator. Whoever was still out there, working on the bell and its mysterious properties, would take the reigns and commence the final act of Rascher's play.

"You'll have to stop them," Professor Lindgren said.

Ben had nearly forgotten the man was still seated next to him. He nodded. "We will." Then he smiled. "And we *will*."

"I'll help," Lindgren said. "However I can."

Ben nodded again, slowly. "I know. And we might have to call in that favor, as well. For now, though, we all need a little rest. And you — I think you should go find your daughter."

Lindgren stood up, groaning against whatever ailments his body had concocted, then stuck out a hand toward Ben. Sarah was hunched in the corner of the office, looking around at the CSO team as they made their rounds. She wasn't speaking.

Ben grasped the man's hand and shook it. "Thanks for everything," he said.

Lindgren shook his head and scoffed. "You owe me nothing, especially not a thanks," he said. "On the contrary, you all saved my life — and my daughter's. There's nothing in the world I can do to repay you —"

Ben waved it off. "Stop," he said. "We'd have done it even if we didn't like you."

87

REGGIE

Reggie had been scouring the room for nearly an hour, which seemed to be a task that leaned at least forty-five minutes to the side of in vain. There was no furniture in the room save for a computer desk and a small end table against the wall.

Mrs. E had confirmed that the hard drives on the machine would prove valuable to their ongoing search and exploration into what exactly had transpired here, and in the side table — after breaking into it with the delicateness of an overzealous jackhammer — Julie had found a small leather-bound journal. Inside the cover was an inscription from a Sigmund Rascher, no doubt the relative Rachel Rascher had spoken of.

The rest of the journal was in German, and none of the group could speak or read the language, but Reggie noticed a few instances of Greek, and assumed the work was a commentary and copy of the piece Rachel had mentioned earlier.

"What'd you find?" Ben asked as Reggie stepped out of the office.

"Well," Reggie started, "if you don't include a crappy old desk and a computer that was modern in the early 2000's, nothing."

Reggie saw one side of his friend's lips press into his cheek. "Nothing?"

"...and a journal."

Reggie laughed as Ben's eyes shot open. "A journal?"

"We think it's Rachel's great-grandfather's journal," he said. "It's in German, with long passages in Greek. So far, it's looking promising that it's a commentary on Plato's lost work — the *Book of Bones*, the one that Rachel and Agent Sharpe were talking about. It's not the whole thing, but it's a start."

"Wait a minute," Ben said. "Where *is* Agent Sharpe?"

Reggie was walking stiffly, nursing his injured leg, but it appeared that the bleeding had stopped. As such, he hadn't needed Ben or Sharpe or anyone else to help him along.

"He went ahead, to make sure we'd have a clear exit," Reggie said.

Ben eyed him, but didn't respond.

"Anyway," Reggie continued, "it looks like the same journal they mentioned. Not the original *Book of Bones,* but more than we have otherwise."

"I see."

"Other than that, nothing. Mrs. E thinks Julie or her husband can figure out how to crack the security on the hard drives, but even then it's a long shot — they're encrypted with better-than state-of-the-art, which means… I have no idea. But it's probably along the lines of getting Nick Cage out Alcatraz."

Ben frowned. "You *do* know how that movie ended, right?"

Reggie shrugged. "Analogies aren't really my thing."

"Right. Anyway, we need to hightail it out of here before the Egyptian suits come in and ransack the place. We'll be held up here for weeks, at best, answering stupid questions."

"Got that right," Reggie said. He turned to the rest of the group and called them over. "Ready to get?"

Julie and Mrs. E came out of the office. Professor Lindgren walked out closely behind, his arm over his daughter's shoulder. Both seemed distraught but also eager to leave.

"Sharpe's up ahead," Reggie said. "We'll head out the same way we came in. No sense trying to clean up here — the Egyptians already have a mess on their hands. We need to get out and stateside before the media and other ambulance-chasers get here. I imagine there's a *lot* of money to be made in the soon-to-come legal proceedings."

He looked around for any objections and, finding none, turned on a heel and started toward the tunnel that led out of the antechamber and toward the causeway.

The route was simple, and even without much light was easy to follow. Reggie led the group in a single-file line, and when he reached the entrance of the Valley Temple, he waited for Ben to step up next to him.

"Need something?" Ben asked.

Reggie didn't respond. Instead, he looked across the dark room, where pillars stood, methodically and meticulously spaced throughout the hall, providing numerous natural cover for anyone trying to hide.

He watched the shadows cast by the massive pillars. *There's someone here,* he thought. *Someone's waiting for us.*

He was wrong.

Instead of *one* person waiting for them, there were *twenty.*

Reggie jumped back into the causeway when he saw movement from a thousand different directions.

"Someone's here," he whispered.

"Who?"

"I don't know," he answered. "But a *lot* of them. Twenty or more. All behind the pillars."

A voice called out. "Harvey. Gareth Red. Come on out. We have you surrounded."

Reggie looked over at Ben. Ben's face didn't match the surprise Reggie's displayed. Instead, it was a twisted mess of pure rage.

Ben sucked in a breath. "It's Agent Sharpe," he said. "He double-crossed us."

88

BEN

Ben wasn't sure what to think. He wasn't sure what to feel. He'd long been a man of few words, but of many emotions — many of them conflicting. He'd tried for as long as he'd been conscious of that fact to be as stoic as possible — to let his emotions show only in situations he was unable to control them. And he'd spent plenty of years trying to make sure there was *no* situation in which he'd lose control and let his emotions show.

But his practice of Stoicism hadn't prepared him for a situation in which he would be double-crossed by an Interpol officer, promised camaraderie and support from a seemingly innocent man, then stabbed in the back by the same man, suddenly aided by twenty other gun-wielding agents.

He felt the surge of adrenaline kicking in, the telltale sign of emotion-filled drive starting to take over his better senses.

Thankfully — though he didn't feel that at the time — his best friend was there to hold him back.

"Wait," Reggie said.

"No," Ben replied, his voice every bit as serious as Reggie's.

"*Wait,*" Reggie said again. "They've got guns."

"*We* have —"

"They *all* have guns," Reggie said. "And they *all* know how to use them."

"Doesn't matter," Ben said. "We need to rush them. If we can get to the inside of the —"

"And what about Lindgren?" Reggie asked. "And his daughter? *They're* supposed to hold a counteroffensive with us? Flanking the left side and moving forward toward the exit while maintaining their perimeter control?" Reggie sucked in a deep breath. "Hell, what about *me?* I'm almost dead here. I haven't been able to feel my leg for almost an hour, and if it wasn't for my heart rate coming back down, I'd already be on the ground."

Ben seethed next to Reggie. He knew he was right. He'd been in tougher situations before, and Ben always leaned on Reggie's professional military judgment in times like these. And if Reggie's gut — and injury — told him to throw in the towel on this one...

"Come on," Sharpe yelled, his French accented-voice reverberating through the hall. "Let's get this over with. I have twenty-three men with me from the Egyptian Mukhabarat, and we have a statement from the Ministry of Antiquities' Prehistory Division that we are to detain and question anyone involved with —"

Ben looked at Reggie. "A *statement?* Is that like an Interpol version of a mandate?"

Reggie shrugged. "Doesn't seem like it'd have much weight here, considering. But those guns do say otherwise."

"What's our move, then?"

Reggie thought a moment. "You know, it's been a long time since I've been outnumbered twenty-four to three."

"Sarah's got a rifle too."

"Okay, so twenty-four to *four*. Not sure I count, though, at the moment. So let's call it twenty-four to three."

Sharpe called out once again. "Last chance, Harvey. Let me see your hands. Step out slowly."

Reggie looked over at Ben, and he could see his friend pleading silently with him. *It's over, man.* He was trying to convey sadness, surprise, but Ben knew he was as upset as he was. He set his rifle down on the sandy floor of the temple, then stepped forward, into one of the beams of sunlight breaking through the stand of pillars.

"Okay, Sharpe," he yelled. "I put my gun down."

Ben and the others followed suit, each of them stepping out into the central corridor of the temple after adding their weapon to the growing pile. Each of them came out with their hands up, behind their heads.

Sharpe said something to one of the men next to him, and two of the soldiers stepped forward and grabbed Reggie, yanking him roughly behind one of the pillars. They pulled his hands behind his back and bound them using a zip tie, then led him away.

Ben received similar treatment from two more soldiers, and within minutes his entire team — including Professor Lindgren and Sarah — was bound and being led out of the temple. As he passed by Agent Sharpe, he sneered.

"What's this about, Sharpe?" Ben asked. "We trusted you."

Sharpe hung his head. "Sorry, Harvey. I know you did. But this was never just about my sister."

"She was never here?"

"Oh, she was," the man answered as he walked in step with Ben. "But she was killed shortly after the event in Athens. Rachel Rascher would never have let her live. I — I used to think I could save her, but..."

"So she murdered your sister. Rascher's dead now, too. There's nothing down there. So... what is it?"

"Look, Harvey," Sharpe said. "It's not that I'm on her side with it. They're all quacks, as far as I'm concerned. But —" he stopped and looked around, then lowered his voice. "This is something that's been going on for some time."

"I know," Ben said. "Rachel said her great-grandfather —"

"No," Sharpe said, shaking his head. "I don't mean her research. I'm talking about this investigation."

"The Egyptians?"

He nodded. "The Egyptians, the Greeks, heck — even the Germans and the Russians are interested in the research and science. No one but the Egyptian Ministry of Antiquities knows the entirety of what's been going on here, but there's *no possible way* they're going to let some civilians waltz in and take it out from under them."

"You mean there's no possible way *you're* going to let us take it," Ben said.

Agent Sharpe looked at him, his eyes cold and calculating. "I'm just doing my job, Ben."

"This is why you wanted us out of the picture back in Santorini, isn't it?"

"My task has always been to protect whatever it is here so that the Egyptian government — and other interested parties — can keep it under wraps."

"You were hired to help perpetuate a lie, Sharpe."

"I was *hired* to protect history." He stopped. "Bennett, listen to me. You were *always* playing with fire with this. I did the best I could to protect you and your team — calling off the police when they opened fire at you, and trying to keep these soldiers from blowing your brains out when you first landed in Cairo."

"Gee, thanks for your support, Sharpe."

"...and I could *easily* have let these goons take you out as soon as you left the causeway. You think the Egyptian government cares about a few civilians playing CIA agent in their country — *without* their own government's support?"

Ben turned to size up the man. Sharpe was thinner and shorter, but he had a fit physique. But even with Ben's hands bound behind his back, he knew he could take him out with a well-placed forehead shot to the man's nose.

"You're quite the hero, Sharpe. What would we do without you?"

"Enough of the bravado, Ben. We're not going to murder you. And if I can swing it, I think I can get you all out of a prison sentence, too."

"Again, what would we do without you?"

"But we're going to need the notebook."

Ben looked at him blankly. "What notebook?"

"Don't be a fool, Bennett. You're already in the thick of it. One phone call and you're out of here, a free man, with your team intact and alive." He paused, making sure Ben was following. "But if I *don't* make that call..."

Ben turned to Julie, who was carrying the small journal they'd found in Rascher's office. She'd tucked it into her back pocket, and the tail of her shirt covered it from view.

Julie shook her head. *No*.

Ben sighed. "Sharpe, I don't know what you're —"

Sharpe stepped forward abruptly and socked Ben in the nose. It was violent, and Ben felt his body faltering as stars swam around his vision.

"Harvey, do not make me ask you again."

"There's something happening, Sharpe," Ben said. "A lot of people are going to die."

"Rachel Rascher told you that?"

"You heard it yourself, Sharpe. What happened in Athens — that was only the setup. Something *else* was planned, and we've only got two months to figure it out."

Sharpe smirked. "A dying woman told you two words, and now you've got a plan to save the world? You're as delusional as she was."

Ben's nostrils flared and his jaw clenched as he regained his balance. He glared down at Sharpe. "You're an asshole, Sharpe. I knew it when I met you."

"First impressions are hard to break, Bennett."

"Sharpe..."

"Whatever you think is going to happen is something *actual* organizations, like Interpol, the United Nations, and any local governments involved can take care of. And I don't think I need to ask you again to *stay out of our way*."

Ben looked over at Julie again, then nodded. "Give it to him, Jules."

She was about to protest, but he shook his head. Finally, she retrieved the journal and stepped over to Sharpe. He grabbed it out of her hand, then flipped through a few of the pages to ensure it was genuine. Satisfied, he pocketed it and turned back to Ben.

"Thank you, Harvey, for your *continued* cooperation with this —"

Ben lunged forward and smashed the upper half of his forehead into Sharpe's nose. The downward motion wouldn't cause the bone to shoot up the naval cavity, which meant it also wouldn't kill Sharpe.

But it would hurt — a lot.

Sharpe fell, crumpling to the ground like a rag doll. He whimpered a bit as he fell, blood spewing from his nose and spilling out over his chin and neck. He tried to wipe it off with a wrist, but it just smeared around his face. He tried to stand up, but fell back to one knee.

A few of the soldiers stepped closer, but Ben could tell they weren't about to execute their prisoners here, in the middle of a sacred temple.

Sharpe groaned, then rolled into a sitting position on the dusty earth. He shot a finger at Ben, pointing while holding his nose. "Get — get them out of here," he said. Then, to Julie, he continued. "There's a plane waiting. A private airport. It's in my name, but they're expecting you. Talk to the man at the gate."

"Mind taking these off?" Julie asked, motioning over her shoulder at her wrists.

"When you get to the gate," Sharpe said, wheezing through the blood. "I don't want you getting any bright ideas about exploring any more ancient sites today."

Ben turned to leave, but Sharpe continued shouting after him. "And *do not* come back here. I will be lodging a formal complaint with the Egyptian authorities that will effectively block your access to this country. If you try to enter, you will —"

"Never did care much for the heat anyway, Sharpe," Ben said, still marching toward the exit.

The soldiers parted, either aware of what Agent Sharpe had said or unwilling to try to stop Ben. The others, including Reggie, followed along, their hands still bound behind their backs.

Back outside in the heat, Ben found that the entire plateau had been closed, and that barricades had been erected in front of many of the entrances to the ancient sites. Walkways were devoid of tourists, only security guards and Giza employees milling about, many of whom were engaged in conversations with one another.

The Mukhabarat soldiers from the temple followed them out, a few of them holding their weapons up and at the ready as the team proceeded. None of the remaining employees paid much attention to them, either due to the fact that they had already been informed of the plan or that they were hoping to stay out of the way of the armed soldiers.

It was clear that the park had been shut down after the soldiers had opened fire on the CSO team, and the place had been evacuated shortly thereafter.

As such, they had an easy walk to the front gates, and while they received a few interested glances from some of the guards, they made it to the gate without being harassed. There, Reggie showed them how to use the edge of a sharpened piece of metal welded to the gate itself to cut their bindings.

When they had finished freeing themselves, two men dressed in blue jumpsuits with some sort of government patch emblazoned on the chest met them at the gate. They appeared unarmed, but they approached the group of Americans cautiously. The man on the left spoke to them in staggered English.

"You are the ones looking for an airplane?" he asked.

Ben nodded. "An airplane would be great. And one with some whiskey on board would be *fantastic*."

EPILOGUE

"Ben, it's pointless," Julie said. "Sharpe isn't going to let us *near* the journal. And even if he did, we'd need to study it for *months* to decipher it."

Ben looked around the table, then cleared his throat and spoke. "We don't need the journal."

"But you said we would go after these guys — whoever's carrying out the rest of Rascher's wishes."

"We are," Ben said. "And we're going to stop them."

"We don't even know where to start," Reggie said. "And again — we don't have the journal."

Ben looked down at his notes, organized haphazardly on the iPad sitting on the table in front of him. The group was back in Alaska, joined by Professor Lindgren and his daughter Sarah. Mr. E was absent, unsurprisingly, but Mrs. E was sitting next to Julie, across from Ben. They all shared the small kitchen table Ben and Julie had moved into the living room, and after a massive dinner of Ben's chili, they were debriefing and planning their next move.

"I think I have an idea," Ben said.

"If you're going to say 'break into Interpol and steal the journal…'" Reggie said.

Ben eyed his friend.

"…then I'm in."

Ben laughed. "Well, no, not this time. But I *would* love to get in Sharpe's face again sometime."

"You mean smash the crap out of his face with your head again?" Reggie mocked.

Ben raised an eyebrow. "Only weapon I had at the time. At least I was ready to fight. You were over there, bleeding out, just waiting for me to rescue you."

Reggie chuckled. "My knight in shining armor," he said.

"So Sharpe's not involved in this?" Julie asked, refocusing the conversation.

"No, I don't think there's a way to get the journal from him. But I'm not sure we need it."

"How's that?"

"Well, Sarah said that Rachel told her and her father that she had a copy of Plato's lost work as well. The *Book of Bones,* right? If it's like Plato's other works, other fragments and pieces — even whole manuscripts — will show up over time."

"So… we wait? Until one of these manuscripts 'shows up?'"

"No — let me finish." He turned to Sarah's father. "Professor Lindgren, do you remember what you wrote in the letter to Sarah? The invocation?"

Professor Lindgren took a drink of the wine sitting in front of him, then set the glass on the table next to his empty bowl. "'*We are twice armed if we fight with faith.*'"

"Plato," Ben said. "It's how we figured out you were leading Sarah to something related to Atlantis."

"Right…"

"But do any of you remember the getaway car in Santorini? The one that picked up Sarah?"

There were blank stares around the table.

"It was registered to a *priest*. A clergyman from Santorini."

"Okay, so you think a priest was involved in Sarah's kidnapping," Professor Lindgren said.

"Not necessarily — I think Rachel had a benefactor that was able to fund much more than what the Egyptian government was able to provide. I think she'd worked out an arrangement with a group that's even *more* interested in Egypt's true history."

Julie put her hand over her mouth. "You're talking about the church?"

"The *Catholic* Church, yes," Ben said. "With a capital 'C.' The Vatican."

"What — what would they have to do with any of it?"

"It's obvious," Reggie said, suddenly sitting straighter in his chair. "The Church has always been on the Egyptian's side of history. That the pyramids were built within the last few thousand years, and that the great civilizations rose up *after* the Great Flood."

"But then why would the Church fund Rachel, since she was trying to prove that the Atlanteans *predated* everything the Church believes?"

"Look at the big picture," Ben said. "The Catholic Church, historically, hasn't been interested in the *truth* as much as it's been interested in *controlling* the information. Priests used to read from bibles translated to Latin, even though parishioners didn't speak or understand that language, because they wanted to *control* the information found within. Only relatively recently did they begin translating bibles to languages the people could understand.

"If they control the message, they can control the populace."

"So they are interested in keeping hidden whatever Rachel finds," Mrs. E said.

"I believe so," Ben said. "They couldn't get into the Egyptian temple themselves, but Rachel was in a perfect position to accept funding from them. Remember, she had a completely different plan — she didn't care if the Church got to control the information after she was done with it."

"I see," Sarah said. "So we need to figure out if the Church has something that can help us."

"Exactly. But we need to do it in a way that doesn't bring attention to us."

Reggie scoffed. "So we can't just pick up the phone and call the Pope."

"Probably not. But we *can* try to get into the Vatican Archives."

"We could try," Reggie said. "But it's not likely. None of us have *any* of the qualifications needed to even get in the front door, much less get into the Archives themselves. Not to mention that they don't officially exist."

"No," Ben answered. "But we know someone who might be able to help us."

Ben held up his phone and waited for it connect. By his calculations, the man on the other end was in a timezone only a few hours ahead of theirs, so he should have been available. Besides, Ben had sent him a text message a few hours earlier to ask his permission to call.

The video chat connected, and a round, dark-haired man's face appeared on the phone's screen.

'Harvey!' the man said. *'How are you?'*

"I'm good, Archie," Ben said. "It's been awhile."

Father Archibald Quinones was a Jesuit priest who had been introduced to them by Reggie, down in the Amazon. He had accompanied them on their harrowing adventure, and had then helped fund the fledgling CSO as a silent partner.

His vocation as a Jesuit gave him access to church resources only a handful of men — and even fewer women — shared. Ben wasn't sure of anything, but he had a feeling the older man could at least point them in the right direction.

Ben held the screen up to the rest of the group, taking the time to introduce Sarah and Graham Lindgren, then turning the phone back to face him.

'Well, Ben. Sounds like you've had quite the adventure of late.'

"I would agree with that statement," Ben said, smiling.

'And I suspect your adventure is not yet over,' Quinones said. *'I gather from what you told me you need to break into the Vatican Archives?'*

"Something like that, I guess."

'Well, I suppose we should talk.'

AFTERWORD

If you liked this book (or even if you hated it…) write a review or rate it. You might not think it makes a difference, but it does.

Besides *actual* currency (money), the currency of today's writing world is *reviews*. Reviews, good or bad, tell other people that an author is worth reading.

As an "indie" author, I need all the help I can get. I'm hoping that since you made it this far into my book, you have some sort of opinion on it.

Would you mind sharing that opinion? It only takes a second.

Nick Thacker

FACT OR FICTION?

I've been asked by readers to include a bit more information about my books — specifically whether or not certain elements are "fact" or "fiction." I thought that since this book was one of the most in-depth, and required the most research in order to see it through to completion, this book would be a perfect one to start with.

I love to read books that include many truths and interesting tidbits; after all, that's what makes them interesting books in the first place! However, fiction is fiction — it's not real. But a story is only as good as its elements of truth, whether its a believable character or a real place or an actual mystery of science. I've tried to weave a tapestry that is, overall, fictitious in nature, while at the same time using threads that are based on actual facts.

Some facts and truths are stretched, but most of them are real-life examples of why the real world is often stranger than fiction (Lord Byron). As Tom Clancy so eloquently said, "the difference between fiction and reality is that fiction has to make sense."

Spoiler Alert: Oh, and before we begin: if you haven't read *The Aryan Agenda,* read it first! There are spoilers below! You have been warned!

So here you go, dear reader: some of the biggest ideas and mysteries I wrote about in *The Aryan Agenda,* explained.

The Great Pyramid of Giza

Obviously the Sphinx and the Great Pyramid of Cheops are real, but what *are* they, exactly? Most Egyptologists claim that the pyramids were built as tombs for their kings (Pharaohs).

In the "Great Pyramid's" case (considered great because it is the largest of them all, and for nearly four-thousand years was the tallest man-made structure in the world), it's the supposed resting place for and shrine to Pharaoh Khufu, based on an inscription in an interior chamber naming the king.

The problem? As Sarah explained in *The Aryan Agenda,* no one's ever found any tombs or sarcophagi inside. Since looting and robberies are a consistent part of Giza's history, it is certainly possible that someone excavated the tomb long ago, leaving it bare.

But why? What would be the purpose of stealing the mummified remains of the king himself? As far as I can tell, there has never been an aftermarket for dead mummies. And if it truly *was* a tomb, it would no doubt have been finished.

That's right — the pyramid is considered *incomplete,* due to the existence of a horizontal shaft that leads nowhere, as well as a vertical well-like shaft that also ends in a stone plug (and has since been filled halfway with debris and detritus). So the "Great Pyramid," thought to be the most elaborate and massive dedication to a king that ever existed (and would ever exist, since this pyramid's size was never surpassed by any future rival kings), was never finished.

While I don't necessarily believe the Great Pyramid of Giza/Cheops/Khufu was a *weapon,* I certainly don't think it was ever meant to be a tomb, and I'm not sure it was even built by the Egyptians. Celestial mapping and mathematical analysis proves that the entire Giza complex including the three main pyramids are arranged in a way that perfectly reflects the constellation of Orion and his belt. Could there be a more *astronomical* reason for their existence?

The Great Sphinx

As for the Sphinx, it too refuses an obvious solution to the problem of its existence. First, when you observe the profile of the great cat, you realize that it looks quite a bit more like... a dog.

And while the Egyptians held cats in high regard, they weren't exactly worshippers of lions. They *did*, however, believe that "Anubis" watched over their dead. Anubis was a god that took the shape of a jackal, as jackals were often seen in cemeteries.

And if you've ever seen the Anubis Shrine, one of the pieces found in the tomb of King Tutankhamen, you'll probably notice something peculiar about it:

...It looks *exactly* like the Sphinx, but with a different head.

Many people are surprised when they meet the Sphinx in person, as they notice immediately that the proportions are way off. And since the Egyptians (or whomever helped them) are known for being quite particular with their proportions and measurements, the tiny shrunken-head-sized face on the top of the Sphinx's shoulders seems a bit out of place.

The truth is that a pharaoh, hoping to cast his legacy upon the never-aging stone monument, had the head "refinished" in his likeness.

But perhaps the original head wasn't a pharaoh's head in the first place? Perhaps our Great Sphinx was no pharaoh, or lion, or anything else but a shrine to the god of the dead?

In fact, Robert Temple has done some miraculous work in this area, and most of what I've taken for use in *The Aryan Agenda* comes from Temple's work. I'll refer you to him for any further discovery.

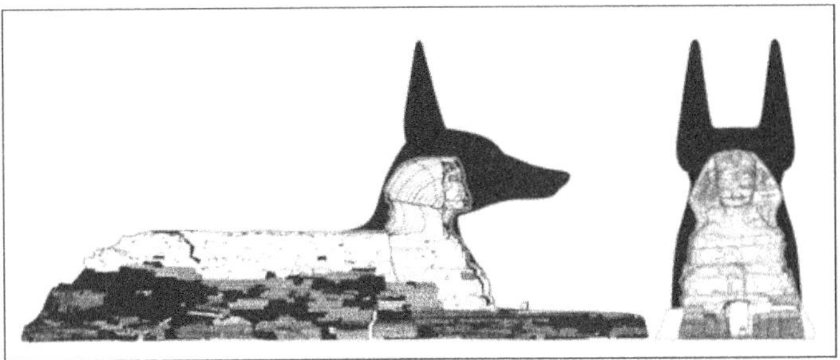

The Great Hall of Records

The Atlanteans supposedly kept their vast collection of knowledge and wisdom in a place called the *Hall of Records,* like an ancient Library of Alexandria.

How do we know this?

Well, a psychic told us.

Edgar Cayce, 1877-1945, one of the most renowned and well-known clairvoyants of the early twentieth century, able to talk with his (dead) grandfather and had plenty of "imaginary" friends, was dubbed the "Sleeping Prophet" due to his ability to self-hypnotize and "place his mind in contact with all time and space — the universal consciousness, also known as the super-conscious mind."

I'm not sure how much confidence I put in *one man's* psychic prediction, so I scraped around the annals of the web for more information.

I did find that Cayce *probably* didn't just come up with this theory on his own — there's a good chance that he'd heard or read about the theory from somewhere else.

But at the end of the day, there's just not enough to go on. In *The Aryan Agenda* (and later books, hint hint…), the *Hall of Records* is pure fiction. It's fun to have Ben and the CSO crew looking for buried treasure, but I'm not sure there's enough juice to make this fictitious account a real-life treasure hunt.

Tourmaline and Piezoelectric Effects

Once again the realm of science-with-flair, tourmaline *is*, in fact, piezoelectric. Piezoelectric properties are tapped in all sorts of technologies, like pickups in guitars.

And while tourmaline *is* capable of generating a little tiny charge, I hardly think it's enough to spark the switch that levers open a massive, ten-ton stone door.

But I grew up with Indiana Jones as a tour guide. He wasn't just an invention of Hollywood. In my mind, good fiction needs a good suspension of disbelief. Hopefully a tiny magic birthstone that can open doors doesn't require too much suspension!

Nazi Research and the Rascher Legacy

Sigmund Rascher was a real person, and his name has a deserving place in *The Aryan Agenda* as a WWII-era villain. Rascher, 1905-1945, was a German SS doctor who worked for Heinrich Himmler. He got his big break when Himmler took his side on the debate whether to use rats or humans in cancer research trials, and shortly thereafter Rascher set up shop testing on humans at a place called Dachau.

During his stint as a dungeon master, he led or participated in such experiments as testing how long a human body could survive submersion in extremely cold water and subject to high altitudes — how were they tested? Naturally, by throwing their prisoners outside for 14 hours while naked, or by holding them for three hours in a tank of ice water.

To make things worse (if they could possibly be worse), Rascher was found guilty of stealing a *baby*. While creating propaganda that claimed he could considerably extend the female childbearing age past 48 years (his wife's age at the time), he used pictures of his family, including their three children.

The problem was that Rascher didn't *have* three children... of his own. He was accused of purchasing or kidnapping the three children after his wife was found trying to steal their fourth child (so Rachel Rascher *isn't* a real-life descendent of Sigmund Rascher, because he tried to steal his children to further his career and reputation).

He was caught, by the way. Turns out he killed his lab partner and committed some sort of financial and scientific fraud. Himmler was pissed in only the way a Nazi can be pissed, and both Rascher and his baby-stealing wife were condemned to Buchenwald, then Dachau, where he was executed just before the camp was liberated in 1945.

Haplogroup X (mtDNA)...

When I was researching *The Aryan Agenda*, I was reading up on the history of genetics and gene sequencing. I waded through papers on Nazi-era eugenics, the grisly American side of the same sort of research, and plenty of other horrendous experiments and projects that history has done its best to forget.

While I got lots of ideas for future books from that stuff, I didn't feel like drowning *The Aryan Agenda* in dark, evil, top-secret experiments would make for light, easy reading. Instead, I focused on some of the *good* things that have come from continued genetic research and anthropological history.

One of the most fascinating elements of that research ended up in *The Aryan Agenda* with hardly any adjustments from me — and since I'm no geneticist, that's a good thing.

Haplogroups are, in fact, groups of mitochondrial DNA (mtDNA) that give us a record of the march of human progress over the millennia. By collating mtDNA data and mapping their existence around the globe, we can get a general picture of where (and when) people came from.

Haplogroup X is one of those groups of mtDNA, and the map that Alex uses to explain his research is accurate — the Haplogroup X group seems to have begun in the Mediterranean and Middle Eastern areas of the world, then small pockets show up on the chains of islands that include the present-day United Kingdom, Iceland, Greenland, and northeastern Canada. Finally, concentrations of the Haplogroup X genes appear around the Great Lakes region.

... And the Early American Settlers

More striking is the complete *lack* of existence of any Haplogroup X-wielding peoples that migrated over the Bering Strait. Since the Bering Strait migration is *supposed* to be the singular way early American Indian ancestors arrived in the Americas, it's easy enough to believe that the nomadic tribes of people started walking from somewhere in Russia and ended up somewhere in Canada — and eventually throughout the Americas. But there's a hitch: the Laurentide and Cordilleran ice sheets blocked any southern routes, covering Southern Alaska and the Yukon Territory. There was no way for human settlement to occur until these sheets melted and revealed an ice-free corridor. And those sheets melted around 13,000 years ago.

So we've got people stuck in present-day Canada until they were able to move south after 13,000 years ago. But excavations and archeological discoveries prove that humans were hanging out in Chile about *15,000* years ago, and feasting on mammoth in present-day Florida *14,500* years ago.

Where did they come from?

My theory? They sailed. Specifically, they sailed from the Mediterranean Sea up and around the northern islands, then ended up in eastern Canada and the United States. When did all this happen?

A study of the Haplogroup X movements show that there was some sort of massive migration taking place, spreading the genes around the world, about *21,000* years ago!

Santorini and the Cyclades Plateau

There is great appeal in placing Atlantis on a tiny island in the middle of the Aegean Sea. And when I began research for *The Aryan Agenda* and came across the theory of Santorini-as-Atlantis, I thought I was on to something spectacular. I even thought I had stumbled upon some long-lost research, and that I'd become one of the only members of a top-secret club of adventurers who knew the 'real truth.'

Imagine my surprise when, picking out a toy with my kids in Target, I came across a game called *Santorini* (*"...a strategy-based board game that's exhilarating and intellectually challenging! Play together and make family game night even more fun!"* — Amazon.com)

Seriously? My top-secret discovery was now so mainstream it was a mass-marketed kids game?

Oh, well. Time to put my experience as a *fiction* writer to the test: I began to dig up more and more information about Santorini and the surrounding area. History, archeology, oceanic water levels and crustal displacement theories. All of it.

So, while Santorini is still probably a wonderful place to visit (and probably a wonderful kid's game), I don't think there are going to be any Atlantean discoveries awaiting excavation there.

But there's a lot of area to search just north of Santorini: the Cyclades Islands are the last remains of what Plato refers to as 'a larger body' — the Cyclades Plateau, or Cyclades Island. It's a massive (continent-sized?) island that sunk beneath the waves 'in a day and a night' (a common expression in Ancient Greece meaning 'it happened quickly, at some point in the past'), leaving nothing but the tops of its mountain peaks poking above the surface, creating the many smaller islands that dot the region today.

Atlantis and Plato's Dialogues

I claim that Atlantis was real — I don't know if that's true or not, but it seems that in order to be part of the Fiction Writer's Club (stop Googling — it's not a real thing), we have to believe in Atlantis.

And while I was inspired by such seminal works as *Disney's Atlantis,* I didn't want to go the tried-and-true 'Atlantis is full of mermaids and has magical spells' route.

So I started digging. Thanks to the internet, I found out about a theory of Atlantis that made a lot of sense — namely, Christos Djonis' work on piecing together the exact details of Plato's description of Atlantis. It turns out that Plato *does* seem to be describing an actual place:

> *"...an island comprising mostly of mountains in the northern portions and along the shore, and encompassing a great plain of an oblong shape in the south extending in one direction three thousand stadia (about 555km 2), but across the center island it was two thousand stadia (about 370km 2). Fifty stadia (9km) from the coast was a mountain that was low on all sides...broke it off all round about... the central island itself was five stades in diameter (about 0.92km)." — Plato*
>
> — DJONIS, CHRISTOS. UCHRONIA?: ATLANTIS REVEALED: WHO WE ARE, WHERE DO WE COME FROM, ARE WE ALONE. PAGE PUBLISHING, INC., 2014.

Whether it's a mythical futuristic city full of flying cars and advanced humans is still up for debate, but I believe it was *at least* a civilization capable of great architecture, advanced shipbuilding and sailing, and a militaristic government that often threatened its neighbors (Crete, Athens, Egypt) with war.

I believe it existed right where the CSO team found it: on the Cyclades Plateau, now sunken beneath the waters of the Aegean Sea. Any excavations that could take place would have an enormous cost, if even possible.

So to me the myth is still a myth: a legendary island full of an advanced race of people who conquered, settled, and explored, long before history became a memory.

ALSO BY NICK THACKER

Mason Dixon Thrillers

Mark for Blood (Mason Dixon Thrillers, Book 1)

Death Mark (Mason Dixon Thrillers, Book 2)

Harvey Bennett Mysteries

The Enigma Strain (Harvey Bennett Thrillers, Book 1)

The Amazon Code (Harvey Bennett Thrillers, Book 2)

The Ice Chasm (Harvey Bennett Thrillers, Book 3)

The Jefferson Legacy (Harvey Bennett Thrillers, Book 4)

The Paradise Key (Harvey Bennett Thrillers, Book 5)

The Aryan Agenda (Harvey Bennett Thrillers, Book 6)

Harvey Bennett Thrillers - Books 1-3

Harvey Bennett Thrillers - Books 4-6

Jo Bennett Mysteries

Temple of the Snake (written with David Berens)

Harvey Bennett Prequels

The Icarus Effect (written with MP MacDougall)

The Severed Pines (written with Jim Heskett)

Gareth Red Thrillers

Seeing Red

Chasing Red (written with Kevin Ikenberry)

The Lucid

The Lucid: Episode One (written with Kevin Tumlinson)

The Lucid: Episode Two (written with Kevin Tumlinson)

The Lucid: Episode Three (written with Kevin Tumlinson

Standalone Thrillers

The Atlantis Stone

The Depths

The Atlantis Deception (A.G. Riddle's *The Origins Mystery* series)

Relics: A Post-Apocalyptic Technothriller

Killer Thrillers (3-Book Box Set)

Short Stories

I, Sergeant

Instinct

The Gray Picture of Dorian

Uncanny Divide

ABOUT THE AUTHOR

Nick Thacker is a thriller author from Texas who lives in Colorado and Hawaii, because Colorado has mountains, microbreweries, and fantastic weather, and Hawaii also has mountains, microbreweries, and fantastic weather. In his free time, he enjoys reading in a hammock on the beach, skiing, drinking whiskey, and hanging out with his beautiful wife, tortoise, two dogs, and two daughters.

In addition to his fiction work, Nick is the founder and lead of Sonata & Scribe, the only music studio focused on producing "soundtracks" for books and series. Find out more at SonataAndScribe.com.

For more information, visit Nick online:
www.nickthacker.com
nick@nickthacker.com

CPSIA information can be obtained
at www.ICGtesting.com
Printed in the USA
LVHW090447060419
613206LV00001BA/247/P